BLAME IT ON BOVARY

A Novel by
Elaine M. Wagner

Tremolo Books

This is a work of fiction. Names, characters, places, and incidents either are the product of the author's imagination or are used fictitiously. No reference to any person, living or dead, is intended or should be inferred.

Published by Tremolo Books LLC

2545 Concord Way

Mendota Heights, MN 55120

Visit us at Tremolobooks.com or Blameitonbovary.com

ISBN $13.97
ISBN 978-1-4675-8093-9

Kristin, this one's for you.

Sidonie and you are so alike,

beauty, charm and daring-do.

I had some wonderful help writing Sidonie's story.

My husband, Darrell Wagner, made me do it. His early death left me alone with my imagination and a word processor.

My editor, Jack Galloway, taught me how to do it. His inspiring prompts kept me growing. "Show, don't tell." "Say more." "Would it kill you to use a simile?"

My writing friends, the Scribes & Storytellers, helped me to get better at it. They laughed, cried, questioned and looked bored, as appropriate.

My children, Kristin and Douglas, always supported Mom as writer. They offered suggestions, lugged books to readings, and stored extra copies in the garage. Thanks, David. After all, it was my son-in-law's garage.

My granddaughter, Gabriella, promises to inspire more Sidonie stories. She is an adventuress in training.

Thanks and love to all of you!

Sidonie Adair's World

An unlikely heroine during the rise of artistic modernism

Women's literary history	Social and Cultural History
1909 – Eudora Welty born; *Three Lives* (Gertrude Stein); *The Romance of a Plain Man* (Ellen Glasgow)	1909 – Rise of the "Progressive" movement; first Model T Ford
1910 – *Twenty Years at Hull House* (Jane Addams)	1910 – NAACP founded; first long-distance flight from Albany to New York City
1911 – *Ethan Frome* (Edith Wharton)	1911 – First flight across the U.S. (68 landings over 49 days); Standard Oil and American Tobacco trusts dissolved
1912 – *Renasence and Other Poems* Edna St. Vincent Millay; *A Dome of Many-Coloured Glass* (Amy Lowell)	1912 – Massachusetts establishes first minimum wage for women and children
1913 – *O Pioneers!* (Willa Cather); *Virginia* (Ellen Glasgow)	1913 – Wilson Administration; Armory Show of modern art, a seminal modern art event.
1914 – *The Single Hound* (Emily Dickinson)	1914 Panama canal opened
1915 – *Song of the Lark* (Willa Cather) *Rivers to the Sea* (Sara Teasdale)	1915 – *Lusitania* sunk; Wilson "too proud to fight"
1916 – *Men, Women, and Ghosts* (Amy Lowell); *Life and Gabriella* Ellen Glasgow);	1916 – American punitive expedition in Mexico
1917 Carson McCullers born; *Love Songs* (Sara Teasdale)	1917 – Germans renew unrestricted submarine warfare; Prohibition amendment submitted to states; Georgia O'Keefe's first one-person show
1918 – *The Marne,* (Edith Wharton); *My Antonia* (Willa Cather)	1918 – "Fourteen Points; Wilson at peace conference; Battle of Argonne
1919 – *Age of Innocence* (Edith Wharton)	1919 - Treaty of Versailles (not signed by U.S.); 18th Amendment (prohibition of liquor)
1920 – *Miss Lulu Bett* (Zona Gale); *A Few Figs from Thistles* (Millay)	1920 – 19th Amendment (women suffrage); first commercial radio broadcasting; transcontinental airmail

Prologue
On The Horizon

They are a striking couple from this distance. When we're closer they become something beyond the stylized lines and graceful curves. The edges seem undone, as though events have left a slight tremolo in tissue and thought and movement. The ocean breeze again tosses her dark, thick hair across her face and into her mouth. For a moment she seems to reach to push it aside, but she becomes unsure, or uncaring. It's as if it wouldn't make any difference now. The simple sensation of hair touching skin is a comforting distraction, a feeling that somehow keeps her mind thankfully in the present. His face is on the wrong side of the sun. Shadow sculpts his cheek bones and you become aware of the hollows beneath his brows.

You find yourself wishing you could overhear as she looks up and he leans down. The pounding of surf overwhelms her words. The waves are coming fast. They should both run backwards to save their clothes. They should at least grasp hands to stop a fall. But on their own they struggle for footing. It's the oncoming surf that tumbles them into each other. It's the retreating surf that lets us hear them speak. At first they just laugh as they shake the sand from their feet and smooth the wet wrinkles from his trousers and her skirt. But then her face becomes as clouded as his.

"How long have we been here? It feels like it's been forever, but I'm still greedy for more. How much more do you think there is?" She takes his right hand and traces his lifeline. "Fate has been kind so far." She kisses his palm. "Your fingers have been even kinder." She spreads them open wide. She touches each one gently, tentatively, as if she's never before been introduced. And then she moves the whole hand to her breast where it looks very much at home. "Very kind indeed."

His left hand stays at his side. Those fingers drum his thigh. "Forever is a tricky word."

"You watch the horizon a lot." She follows his gaze.

"And I listen for rumors in the marketplace. You can never be sure."

"You worry so." She reaches again to brush aside the extravagant wave of hair that covers her cheek and her eye, and then instead arranges it so it hides the corner of her mouth as well. "But I do feel safe with you."

"I'm not so sure you should. A lot has happened. It may be hard to know when we're really safe."

"You think I don't know that?"

"I think sometimes you twist the meaning of words."

"And what's wrong with that? What counts is what a word means to me. At this moment, here with you, safe means satiated." She wraps her arms around his waist and rests her cheek on his chest.

He raises his arms, then stops just short of holding her. He's waiting for more.

"Replete." She gives it to him without guile, her face turned up. Her luxurious lashes do little to hide the openness in her eyes. Such generous lashes would ordinarily confuse and seduce, but there seems little of that here. Her eyes look directly into his. "My now is filled to the brim. The truth is I've lost faith in forever. So much so that I find I don't really need it. It's a crutch when you aren't making the most of this instant. This instant is what we have. Surely we've learned that much. I should have said I feel satiated with you, right here, right now."

6

"Then you have chosen well." He looks away first, again searching the horizon, this time through her tossing hair. "Still, I'm going to great lengths now to keep you safe, although I have never felt that way myself and for us it's just as well that I never do. Satiated. I have no quarrel with that."

Her face joins his in the shadow. Beneath its billows her hair hides their lips, and we can't see the kiss, but it lingers, and more words are exchanged. After the moment his eyes find the sand and follow it slowly out to sea. And then she moves slowly away from him, up the sandy beach toward the lighthouse. Of course he would follow, his footprints covering and obliterating hers before the surf makes both sets disappear.

Chapter 1

Blame it on Bovary

"Not to worry. I lost my innocence to a master. I was deflowered by Flaubert in the branches of an elm tree. More specifically, it was Flaubert's *Madame Bovary*. From there everything was a very natural progression. You won't be the first."

"Then why, little one, are you still wearing your pretty party dress under the covers?" He flips back the bedclothes. "You hop in my bed, yet you keep your clothes on. A woman of the world has more abandon."

"The first time was a blur. And, of course, I closed my eyes. Just as well. He was fumbling around so much it was distracting. The others were a blur for other reasons, lack of imagination being the most important." She strikes the three bells on her silver bracelet one by one. "I wanted to hear bells when he first touched me, bells when I first touched him, a cacophony of bells, when we were beyond touching."

"Obviously, you imagined more." He slips off her still ringing bracelet and lays it on the table next to the bed.

"I read Flaubert." She pulls the crocheted edge of the top sheet up and over her eyes and peeks through. She knows it is a nice frame for her eyes.

"And you think I will be less distracting and more imaginative? Perhaps because I am older than those many, many others, those legions that came before?" He pokes a finger through the lace and nips her nose.

"I choose you. It seems I'm actually becoming more aware of my choices." She opens wide the bed clothes and invites him inside. "I want expertise as well as imagination.

Your reputation is impeccable. And you are a writer. You create worlds. You can create mine."

He leans down and lets his index finger stroll down her cheek to her neck. It waits just behind her ear. "That's interesting. I thought I chose you. You were sitting in the corner, looking so forlorn, your chestnut lashes bruising your cheeks. You were looking down at your hands on your lap, as if you had never seen them before. Abused little fingers, with nails half bitten off." He kisses five of them. " Lucky for me you looked up as I passed."

"Luck had nothing to do with it. I chose the corner closest to you and your friends. You talked way too long about too many books. Appreciating, analyzing, dissecting. You do go on. Does anything ever actually happen in your little world? Happily for me, I like watching men carve things into bits and pieces. I don't understand it, but I like it. I know books better than I know men. It was also a good corner to escape my admirers. I sent one of them off to get me a glass of wine. I told the other I needed cake. Still another fetched me a napkin. I curled into the darkness of that over-stuffed chair and waited. Soon they would stop looking for me. Soon you would walk by. As soon as you did all I had to do was lift my head, toss back my hair, and look at you. I have been told I have beautiful eyes. One young gallant said they looked like chocolate cookies floating in a vat of cold fresh milk."

"Like the cookies his Mommie gives him before beddy-time, if he has been a very good little boy. It's true, with me you get expertise, imagination, and a lot better similes and metaphors. " He sits down on the edge of the bed and flirts with the yoke of her dress. "But as I said before, you also get old. Older anyway."

"You can erase the fumbles, the blurs, the not quites, the almost theres." She eases off his tie, widens the collar of his shirt, and reaches inside. "You can make it the first time."

9

"And you didn't fear the consequences with any of those fumblers? You are just a ingénue yourself." His words move him farther away than the edge of the bed. But he stays in the straddle. See how he touches the soft worn nub of the blanket. He's hoping it will steady his resolve, as if he any longer knows what he is resolved to do.

"I am eighteen years old, thank you very much. Have been for half a year now." When she laughs her shadow hair bounces on the pillow. "I grew up after my first real kiss. It was on the platform of a railway station. It was a kiss as long and tremulous as a train whistle. Smoke was coming from the chimney. Fog was rising from the tracks. Raindrops sprayed our cheeks. And then I felt the quake of the train braking over me, I felt as lost as if I was lying in the darkness between the rails as one boxcar after another thundered over. As he waved goodbye to me through the window, I was certain I was looking at the father of my child. I was wondering how I would go to Paris and study painting with a baby on my hip. For two weeks I took baths so hot that my bottom flamed a full fifteen minutes after I toweled off. "

"It doesn't work that way." He pushes the yoke back up.

"I know." She lays her hand on top of his and memorizes his knuckles.

"But you're not worried now."

"Fumbled balls can still go over the goal line. After all those bad plays I must be sterile."

"Heavens, enough experience to resort to a football metaphor." He smiles as he pulls his tie all the way off. "One of these young stalwarts must have been a quarterback."

"Boys' games! Mother calls you a man of the world and she doesn't see it as a good thing."

"And you think I care if you were to find yourself with child. You think I wouldn't abandon you to your disgrace?"

"You are a complicated man, but you don't like complications. I suspect you have learned how to keep them to a minimum."

"Then I should open the door and push you through it?" He leaves the bed. "Even your eyes perplex– downcast one minute, boring into mine the next. They are playing games with me like a - " The image is coming, he can feel it coming -

She jumps out of bed and presents her back to him. "Help me with the buttons. Mother always buys me party dresses with buttons on the back. She wants me to have time to think."

"That time may have passed." He stands behind her, letting slip the last little pearl. Her back is arching, her breasts are rising, and her hair is whipping across his face. He smells apricots, behind her ears and on her neck, apricots and mangoes, lilacs and lavender, the moon and the stars. Nonsense, he is thinking nonsense. She pulls away from him, but only long enough to face him, to finish him off with her eyes. Damn it, they are chocolate cookies, dark, dark chocolate. And they are wide open, melting into his. Chocolate melting! Good God! He has one-upped the boy's pathetic simile. Later, he'll think of something better, later.

Chapter 2
The Siren Call

Deep down in her heart, maybe even into her soul, Sidonie longs for a life lived somewhere or somehow beyond this time. One lived on her terms, even better, one with a similarly-motivated man. Her mother knows it, knows the feeling, knows the draw of a man from that particular breed. They move through the world so effortlessly and so confidently. Clare has known them, maybe even the one at hand. And now her charge is to steer her daughter around the rocks. Sidonie who is barely a woman, but by no means a child. Sidonie, who will have to see through the lecherous old ones and their younger counterparts all of whom have their own siren calls that need to be muffled.

Women hear the Sirens too. Homer would have you believe that only men are lured off course and all the monsters in the deep are female. Charybdis sucks under any boats that come her way. Scylla gobbles up sailors marooned on her shore or floating in her strait. Pretty faces, lovely voices, with the tails of sea serpents or the bodies of birds. Dog heads are attached here and there. Clare can't remember all the details, but she is sure she knows her *Odyssey* better than Sidonie. No matter. Sidonie takes her life lessons from more contemporary authors. Besides, the indirect approach works better with Clare's daughter. At least at first. Don't tell her why. Just tell her.

"Your hair is untidy, my child. Let me tuck in those curls tumbling over the collar of your dress. You will ruin your eyes if you let your hair cavort over your face."

"Yes, Mummie."

"If you pinch your cheeks too often you will get premature wrinkles. There's nothing pretty about pink wrinkles. Wrinkles in any color really."

"You, know best, Mum."

"This is the dress for you. The taffeta whispers so softly when you walk."

"But the collar scratches my neck, Mums, and the buttons on the back are impossible to reach."

"Mums" was cute but it was the beginning of the back talk and worse yet, the start of the secret smiles.

"Why are you reading that man's book anyway? God, he's just an old lecher. He's been preying on women for his whole sorry excuse of a career."

"He is not that old." A small smile, almost knowing.

"He is a born manipulator and Lothario." Sidonie is startled by the severity of the snap of Clare's head toward the corner of the room. So many lovely things in that little corner - a lamp from Tiffany, a vase from Moreno, and a few books, none of them his, of course, that have stood the test of time. Then there's the Spanish fan. God how Clare loves the dramatic flourish of an imported fan.

"Everyone is reading him. He speaks to the soul as well as the heart."

"More likely to the libido!"

"Mother!"

When Sidonie returns it is as though her mother hasn't moved. Sidonie comes in the door flushed, happy and two hours later than she should be from the signing party.

"I'm exhausted!" On hall table she tosses her new French hat, the one with the silly mink tufts on all three corners, and starts her dash upstairs. She is moving so fast that her mother can hear the rustle of a satin petticoat against tops of her shoes. Her ankles will be more than a glimpse as she takes those long, bold strides. But that is the least of it, Clare's afraid.

"That was a long autograph session, my darling. The lines must have been around the block." Clare pushes a novel between the cushion and arm of her chair.

"Some of us met and talked with the Mr. Elliot afterwards. You know those people that ask questions just to show off their perceptive literary analysis. They made the reading go way over time. I was the last to ask a question before it broke up."

Sidonie's open face is turned to her mother, but kidskin shoes are already tapping the third step. "I am so tired of listening to them pontificating. I will swoon if I don't have a nap before supper." Her eyes close dramatically. Clare is again aware Sidonie has taken to darkening those ridiculously long lashes in the way an actress might.

"What question was important enough to keep you waiting your turn?"

"Mr. Elliot, just who was the model for your enchanting heroine?" Sidonie's hand floats above the banister, ready for flight when her mother finally erupts. Clare isn't about to give her that satisfaction.

"Well, at least no one can accuse you of perceptive literary analysis."

"What's wrong with that question?" Sidonie gives up on the stairs. Her gloved hands are on her hips as she confronts her mother from the archway to the sitting room.

"It's a woman's question. It's an 'Am I anything like the woman you had in mind?' question. It's just as much a show-off question. It's worse. It's a look-at-me question. Please notice, poor, pathetic me."

"If you weren't my mother, and if I didn't love you so very, very much, I would say you were being vile." There it is again. Six months ago that chin would have broken free from the flute of her dove gray collar. The tilt would have been high enough to reveal a blue vein fighting its way to the surface of the sheer skin of her neck. There is none of that today, just that secret, knowing smile.

"If I weren't your mother I wouldn't care if you disgraced yourself in public."

"Is there any other place one can disgrace oneself? If you are all alone who is there to say you have committed an indiscretion? Is there an indiscretion if nobody sees it fall?" Sidonie relaxes a hip on the frame of the archway.

"Indiscretions have a way of seeing the light of day. Indiscretions reverberate, send ripples first, than crashing waves."

Sidonie runs across the room and kisses Clare's cheek. She would add a hug but the wing back chair and her mother's suddenly perfect posture bar the way. "How I would love to know how you learned about crashing waves. You don't even own a bathing costume. Perhaps it was something you gleaned in one of those evil books you wouldn't allow in the house, or maybe worse, maybe one of the dashing heroes splashed all over you and pulled you out and into the proverbial sea." Sidonie has the good sense to suppress it but Clare knows the smile is there, somewhere down deep, somewhere it can't be reached and slapped away.

"You're obviously too immature to go to Paris on your own. You can't even go to an educational book reading without calling unseemly attention to yourself. Imagine what you will do in front of a French audience, an amoral audience that would only smile knowingly at your hedonism. Your father will listen to me even if you won't."

There's a tender smile in Sidonie's second kiss. "You worry so, Mums." I think Father understands why I really must go to Paris if I'm to become the artist I can be.

God knows it's hard to know what he thinks most of the time though, maybe if he was here more than just to sleep, but then the money is nice isn't it, Mother dear?" The tender smile turns more wry.

Mums is left watching Sidonie sail up the stairs, her face in the wind, heading straight for a fate which will very clearly be of her own making. Clare watches her go. Of course, she worries. Of course she can see the gales ahead for this dear, strong-willed, passionate young woman. What to do with a child so out of place and time? There are choices coming and she is yet to understand the nature and impact of the consequences. It's not for lack of interest, but there's been no time, or experience. And even then experience can't be everything. If experience is, in deed, the fool's teacher, then what does that mean for Sidonie? Surely the details and stimulations of the moment can't be all that matter to her.

So yes, Clare will worry but she'll take comfort where she can. Don't we all? She was spared the question her daughter hasn't thought to ask.

"Who was he, Mummsie? Who were you swimming towards when you almost drowned? Whose song called you so perilously close to the rocks?

Chapter 3
Porcelain Ladies

For as long as Sidonie can remember she has loved her mother's parlor and longed to have it all to herself. Whenever Clare Adair is in the room she is in the spotlight. Wherever she sits is stage central. If she chooses the damask love seat, no one is foolish enough to sit next to her. Even if they happen to think of it, her fanned skirt makes them think again.

Everything in the room is perfect, serene, and timeless. Even the porcelain figurines on the mantel are forever caught in a graceful pose and a soft smile. Since childhood Sidonie has wanted to muss the hair of the faultless glass ladies, to pull off their gloves, take off their shoes and leave them barefoot. She always longed to see their tiny toes. Once, when she was old enough to know the consequences, but foolish enough not to care, she kidnapped one of them. She kidnapped the one that looked the most likely to welcome a change. She called her Arabella. She looked like an Arabella, like a child of the air.

The wind was tossing her full skirt. It was sending her petticoats into a lovely billow. Her picture hat was bending in the breeze. Sidonie would have liked Arabella more if one hand hadn't been holding onto the hat while the other held down the skirt. She would have liked to see Arabella toss her hat to the ground and let the wind play with her black curls. She would have liked Arabella to pick up her petticoats and run into the wind. It would have been lovely to see Arabella float on the wind like silk from a milkweed. Sidonie had a feeling that with a little encouragement her pretty captive might happily risk a chip.

Sidonie didn't keep Arabella captive long enough to really change her. Porcelain can't be remolded. The original paint held fast. And Sidonie took care not to avoid any chips. In the end, imagination can only do so much. Sidonie knew there was no changing Arabella. It was the world that needed changing anyway, not just a figurine.

Sidonie had sought after pretty things and lovely experiences as far back as she could remember. Now, back in her bedroom, she wonders how it really feels to be kidnapped. These days, she would consider it a rescue. She wonders what it would be liked to turn Marc's front room into her parlor. She would love to tear down his dusty old drapes and let the light come through his casement windows. She would put real flowers on the table next to his bed and rip off the wall paper covered with all those nasty cabbage roses. Of course, she would place her easel in the middle of the room, directly across from his desk. Maybe she would ask him to trade places, after all his writing paper requires less light than her canvases.

She hears herself sigh. She feels her bodice rise and fall. Sometimes her body knows things before she does. Marc's garret is not all that different from Clare's parlor. It has already been claimed. Sidonie looks around her bedroom and reminds herself. She already has her own place. Flaubert is on her end table. Her summer straw hat is propped on her bedpost. A bone china teacup is full of broken pieces of charcoal chalk. It's a big room, big enough for a writing table and an easel. It should be enough for Sidonie. But it no longer feels that way. She goes to her French doors, walks out on her balcony, and taking the combs out of her hair, lets it fall.

It would be grand if the wind would pick up and release some blossoms from the apple tree. That almost looks like a rain cloud. She loves to sleep to the sound of branches tossing and tapping against her window. Thunder and lightning come to her as a lullaby sung by a witch. Sidonie steps out of her shoes and wiggles her toes inside the silk of her stockings. Her stockings have never been damp or dirty. The worst they've known is a tear or a snag. Poor old things! They deserve better.

Chapter 4

A Cabbage Rose

"You must have been in love many times before me." Sidonie cues a compliment as she vaults over Marc Elliot's hip to the inner side of the bed. This way she won't fall off. The cabbage rose wallpaper smells musty and looks lumpy. While she waits for his usual measured response, she pushes her finger into the puffy rose closest to her. How many layers of wallpaper are dampening underneath?

"Had I met you when I was a young man you would have been the only one. I could have easily spent the rest of my life loving you." He smoothes down the back of her hair. Seems like the tangles are tickling his elegant nose.

"How many would you say, if you had to make an estimate?" There are ten cabbage roses in the bouquet, two short of a dozen.

"A gentleman does not keep count. And to estimate is insensitive."

"Was it all that many?" She pulls a strand of hair under her nose. A mustache could be fun.

"Why are you so interested in numbers, *ma petite*? Are you preparing for a quiz?" Now he piles her hair on the top of her neck, and takes a bite.

"Let's just suppose I was preparing for a quiz, one of those practical exercises at the back of an arithmetic book. You could help me with this one."

"I'm not interested in numbers. I already told you that." He bites a little harder.

"In the past twenty years Elliot loved twenty women in five countries only knowing three languages in which to say I love you. Of those twenty women just what

19

percentage heard the truth?" She closes her eyes, crosses her fingers and pretends to make a wish. She's not interested in numbers either. It's experience that counts. And she has already benefited from that. It's just fun to watch men dissemble.

"Would it surprise you to know I loved them all, at least for that special moment?"

"It would not surprise me. Disillusion, but not surprise. I expect deeper from you. Something far more insightful" She opens her eyes just wide enough to watch him from under her lashes.

"Men don't need to be in love to make love. Illusion is more important to women. I have to agree with women. Short of love, I go for that. With you I never have to pretend." He kisses the top of her head. It feels like a pat. "Most men don't worry about the distinction between real and pretend. For them it's good either way. Given time they forget which was which, who was who."

She can believe that. Some faces that once seemed so singular are now less distinctive, less distinct really. Was the chin that strong? Were the eyes blue or green? Still she protests, "I can't believe a person could go to bed with someone and forget them, love or not. It's so - " One wants to tell her, Sidonie, don't reveal too much, but she already knows. " – so intimate."

"Let's just say the image becomes less indistinct. Is this your circuitous way of telling me you are not in the mood?"

"No, this is my way of asking you why I feel the difference. You are here, but less here, farther away than you were a week ago." She wants him to wriggle out as poetically as possible. But she has this funny feeling.

He is into her hair again, pulling it away from an ear. "I couldn't be closer."

20

"I feel a wall, as if you have made love to someone else, between now and our last time together. I can almost smell her." He falls away, back into the pillow. His elbow jolts her shoulder as he puts his hands behind his head. She can feel him looking up at the ceiling. This response is too measured. She wishes she had her jingling bracelet now. She twirls her cameo ring instead. The feeling is no longer funny.

"It was a trick of the light from the window. We were just talking. Talking about you as a matter of fact. Her neck became part of the moon. I wanted to reach the moon. Every man does. It's what we're all after."

A cabbage rose is staring at her, more surprised than she is. Such a pretty speech, about someone else, someone who knows her well enough to talk about her. The stare is turning rude and Sidonie can't move away. Moving away will press her closer to Elliot, intrude on his lovely reverie. He is remembering a woman he is about to tell her he didn't love. It won't be any comfort. He might as well not bother. It must be Emily, Emily who just yesterday wanted her to meet this promising young painter.

"You understand. It was one of those moments you write about. It had nothing to do with who she was or who I am or my feeling for you. It doesn't count. It was a lovely illusion, a metaphor."

She could fade into the wallpaper or get her coat. She never liked cabbage roses all that much. Too big and too bossy. She scrapes her only long nail around the petal of the rude one. With time it will dry and fall off.

"Sidonie, don't be a child!"

She turns to respond, and then her eyes find a stained spot on the floor that seems almost to form the outline of a bird. It makes her smile. She lingers over a thought and then turns to go. The coat on her arm drags in the dust of the stairs. Lucky it is fur. Fur brushes off easily enough. By the time she reaches the door she is starting her own list of lovers. Marc Elliot, of course tops it. His lovely metaphors and the experience in his touch at each moment reveal the intensity of this man's unashamed love of women. Of course, she will love again. More than likely soon. The bittersweet smile returns as she realizes how quickly he will blur, but he could never completely fade away. How could she forget him? He was the one who betrayed her for one of those metaphors.

Time will tell who will forget whom. Metaphors that sound so fresh at first thought, become clichés when quoted once too often by too many people. Wait and see. A girl like Sidonie just might turn out to be an original.

Chapter 5
Playing Catch

Last night when Sidonie was in bed and sleep was just within reach, she tried to catch the moment between being *here* and being *there*. It rolled away, like a ring you slip off your finger, you put in a safe place, and then you forget just *where* that might be. Sleep came swiftly, awake left without a "by your leave." There was no time to fluff a pillow or pull a sheet to her cheek. Her legs lay where they fell, no time to tuck the right foot into the soft side of her left knee. Watching her lying there, breathing so gently, no one would have guessed she had even tried, except when her eyes opened for one last look at *here*.

This wasn't the first time, just the most recent. There was the Christmas she listened for bells. She closed her eyes the better to hear. The curtain of sleep fell between her and the sleigh of Father Christmas. She didn't hear the rustle of the crepe. These days, these nights, it was less a curtain and more a candlewick, drowning in its own melting wax. There wasn't even time for a flicker. A flicker would have been the *in-between-time* that somehow always got away.

She plays catch with sleep less and less these nights, lost in life's details. There is her new black hat with its chiffon ribbon. There are raised polka dots midst the chiffon, almost like the beauty marks a woman might fake at the corner of her eye or just above her upper lip. But Sidonie would never do that. Beautiful need never be pointed out. And someone is always looking, even if for a moment he looks away. And the memory will remain.

There was poem that came in the post the day before yesterday with his signature, then so dear. Her finger had run across the letters over and over again, smearing his big bold M, making her sorry she wasn't more careful. She would keep it, of course. Men have trophies. Why not women? Some night when she is lying in bed with another lover she may tell him about the poem written in her honor, the novel dedicated to her memory. "Poor besotted author!" They will laugh.

Who might that other lover be? Who could be more compelling than Marc? She already knows. He is that forbidden lover who turns up unbidden in those guilty dreams that should be nightmares, but feel so good. He is that dark figure who touches her shoulder and pulls her deeper into the dream, deeper into his hard, cold eyes. That's all she sees in his darkness, his eyes and the cruel straight line of his lips. He came to her dreams not long after Clare cautioned against the ones who take more than they give. Why had that idea intrigued her so, rather than repelled as it very well should? There were those little thrills here and there in private places when she dreamed of a stranger who excited her against her mother's better judgment. It sounded vaguely like Marc, but with Marc there was, in the end, nothing strong at the center. His will was too malleable if it even existed. Yes, he had hurt her heart very deeply, But it was unbroken, still beating and she still had choices.

Her dream-lover's will was stronger than hers without even trying, without charm or guile. He didn't need to lie. He never even implied a promise. He was even, measured, and suffered no pain. Who was to know if he actually cared or not. Still, he would change her, but he would be changed as well. Somehow she'd see to that, even if it meant they would both go up in flames.

Seemed the sleeping Sidonie wanted a love affair that would leave her transformed, not just saddened or disappointed. Somewhere deep inside she longed for a larger-than-life kind of love, something all consuming. Mother needn't worry. Dream-lover wasn't really real.

Real or not, she almost hoped he would come that night. Probably not, she thought. He wouldn't bother to compete with Marc. She would be unimportant to him until her disappointment with Marc wound itself down.

This night as she throws on her nightgown and braids her hair she doesn't know what to expect. Crawling in bed she lets her legs spread, instead of tuck. She deliberately places herself mid-leap between conscious and unconscious, prepared for an epic vault. Her nightgown is a cloud frozen around her hips. It will be simple, like playing statues. If you hold yourself very still, like your childhood companions once, the gods of sleep will be fooled into thinking you aren't really there. They will have no reason to tag you out or to push you from this place to the next. You will be in charge.

But the breeze from the window is moving, caressing, as gentle as a lover's fingertips. It soothes her cheeks, smoothes her lids, cools her thighs. It tempts her out of a game of statues and into a dream of Marc, a dream of his eyes, eyes that look as if they had seen everything, but see her as special, blue eyes she loved to send into a startled navy. She opens her own eyes for just a second, to slow down the slide and sees the dotted Swiss dress she'd dropped so carelessly to the floor. It will spend the night twisting itself into wrinkles, confusing its perfectly-patterned dots, sending them into an absolute tizzy. The dotted Swiss will be of no help catching in-between-dreams.

Through her closing lids she sees flashes of light. The flashes become freckles, the ones on her nose that her mother said would fade away. The freckles Marc said were charming. But the freckles did her in, didn't they? As she wonders how many there still are she is tipped into not really caring. Again sleep comes to her without a say-so.

All she ever wanted was to see it happen, to be aware, to unravel an every-night mystery. She didn't want to miss the mystery. She wanted to float in it and feel the dream creep from her toes up to her breasts, all the way to the bottom of her eyes. She didn't want to miss anything.

Of course she'll have to see Marc Elliot one more time.

*   *   *

Going up, the stairs are steeper. From this vantage she can see more clearly than she really wants to. Dust sticks in the crevices between the steps and the wall. She sees way too much because her feet insist on making a full stop on every step, one foot joining the other, before either can possibly move up. Watching her one might think she is waiting for the dream to catch up with her. Maybe this is a dream. She isn't really undoing her dramatic exit out of his life. She is just trying it out, seeing how it might feel, before she decides not to do it after all. She has to know it is a mistake. Someone, something will stop her.

His door is more imposing than she remembers. The dark wood demands permission to be entered. In the dark wood an image is emerging, a twisted face gnarled by the grain that is giving it substance. The face is offended. The mouth is turning down. The eyebrows are meeting. It is not pleased. Sidonie has a feeling it will always look displeased. It always was, always will be, and will always remain the same. Still, she isn't really frightened. If this demigod were all that powerful the paint on his doorknob would not be cracking. Perfectly good metal has been painted over, not once but twice. Brown as well as white paint is flaking off without her even turning it. The lion's head knocker dares her to touch with its mouth in an open roar. At least it isn't a cabbage rose. Lions are supposed to look vicious. A cabbage rose catches you unaware. The door is too dense to hear through. Still she tries. She stands very still. She holds her breath. But there's nothing. No noise seeps around the edges of the door, nor even at the bottom where a yellow light splinters across the threshold. He could be writing. A pen glides soundlessly across a writer's tablet. He could be in the bedroom with yet another door closed between them, all sounds muffled, from her ears anyway. Not hearing any voices doesn't mean he is alone.

She lays one finger on the lion's nose in a soft goodbye, but the knocker is loose enough to betray. It falls in a thunder against the wood. By the time he throws open the door she is on the next landing.

"Sidonie, Sidonie! My darling girl, you are going the wrong way!" He moves fast for an older man. His arms hold tight for a man who worshipped someone else's neck. "Sidonie, Sidonie!" He kisses her eyes shut. He kisses her mouth open. He sends her hat sailing over the banister so he can kiss her hair.

The chiffon bow catches on a nail and tears free. The felt circle becomes smaller and smaller as it floats down one flight, then two, then three, with no one caring where it might land or how dusty it might become.

The hat takes care of itself, landing safely on a clean rug on the threshold of an artist's first floor apartment. Not having a garret was his biggest disappointment. Finding a new beret will brighten his day.

Chapter 6

His Brand New Beret

Sidonie's ungloved hand feels the wood of the banister go from cool to warm to hot as she comes down the stairs from Marc Elliot's apartment. Sun light is streaming through the open door to 1 B. As she comes to the last step to the landing, the glare steals her sight away. With the toe of one slim boot she feels her way. She has dashed down three flights of stairs without measuring the distance. She is late. There will be questions. Mother always asks questions. Like where is her new hat? But now, suddenly, she has no idea where the floor is or if it is there at all.

His hand reaches out to catch her elbow. She knows it is a he before she sees him. She can smell his sweat. It smells like her hope chest, cedar mixed with old memories and the promise of new ones. In a moment she feels as if she were eight years old and about to do something she isn't sure she should, but is almost certain she will, maybe not now, but soon.

"Careful, careful, *Mademoiselle.* Mustn't step on my brand new beret."

Her feet planted, the sun out of her eyes, she sees him bend over to pick up her hat. It has no chiffon ribbon, but it is still her hat. He is as dark and slim as a shadow. After flopping it on his head, he turns one profile her way and then the other. He looks as young as she feels. His skin still has a bounce, doesn't quite square on his face. The bones of his cheeks have promise, but are hardly chiseled. His eyes are wise enough, if wisdom is knowing when to laugh. His eyes are green, bottle green, full of excitement, but not much mystery. He hasn't lived quite long enough for mystery. He is about to say something funny. At the corners his mouth is already laughing.

"Beau, non?"

"If it was truly your hat you'd know how to wear it." She fluffs the hat with one hand, while the other pulls the felt over his curiously jade eyes. Yes now they are jade and for some reason that has become curious. "There. That's much better."

"*La* mirror will decide." He pushes the door open with his hip as he uncovers his eyes, and looks openly back into hers. The look holds and his hand flourishes a welcome. "*Entrez, s'il vous plait.*"

"Don't let me get between *vous* and *la* mirror." Her laugh is for his unabashed vanity. Her French is to let him know he is not moving too fast for her. Hardly. She feels swift like a cat, a young cat, only just a moment ago a kitten. She has caught her first bird with a leap she didn't know she had in her. It feels as if she could do it again. No bird could fly too high. Now just to be sure she can keep him grounded she drops the lashes, but only briefly. This one will not require the full effect. Best to let him retain some balance.

"But you must come in. You must." He stomps his shoeless foot and blocks the way to the outside door. "You always rush by. *Vite, vite, depechez- vous.* I hear your little heels *vite, vite* by, sometimes up, sometimes down, more in the hurry going up than down. You have time then. I can tell by your footsteps."

She can smell the turpentine and the paint. She can see the easel. He is right. Every artist must have a beret.

"So this is modern art." She looks at the squares, angles, triangles and jagged lines on the canvases that line the floor. She sees only color, with no statement whatsoever, unless it might be, "Look at us. Bet you haven't seen anything like us before. You have no idea what statement we 're making, do you, *ma petite?*"

She hears his "Do you like them?" in the air, but, of course, he doesn't ask it. And, of course, she doesn't reply, "I'll bet I could do this in my sleep." But that doesn't mean they haven't heard each other. He for one doesn't want to spoil this moment with a discussion of art, even his own.

"My name is Jean-Paul Maurice."

"You have three first names?" She will not be impressed.

"Actually, I haven't decided on my name yet. It could be Maurice Jean-Paul. Or Paul Maurice-Jean. Or Paul-Jean Maurice. Which do you prefer? I have no idea what to do with the hyphen. But I know I want one."

"You don't look like a Maurice to me. Maurices are twenty years older."

"Older than what?"

"Older than me, silly boy. Who else matters?"

"Who indeed." He pulls a drop cloth off a chair. "Come sit awhile and help me decide."

"About your name or about the hat. It's mine, you know." She ignores the chair. There is too much to see in the room. And she likes to move around, loves to flit, flit and flutter, bird-like with never a worry about any nearby cats. She likes this young man who can't decide.

"I need your guidance with everything. You are my muse. I knew it the moment you came out of the darkness and into the sun."

"Well, first of all you are not French. Your accent is atrocious."

"But I must be French. Only French artists are taken seriously these days."

"What about Van Gogh?"

"Ah, but you see, he died penniless. But I like him. His art was not a photograph. It was a mirror of his poor tormented soul. I like tormented souls, don't you?"

"Yes, I guess I do. So much more interesting than people who think they have it all figured out."

"But you have some of it figured out. I can see by the tilt of your chin. And the way you walk. You walked into my studio with long strides. You stand in the middle of my room with your hands on your hips and appraise my floor, my ceiling, my walls like a battlefield commander. You dismiss my paintings. They are not worthy adversaries. No, no, I agree. I am just trying out different ideas right now. Boxes intrigued me for the last six months, until I saw your face. Now I ache to be Rembrandt."

"Well, when Rembrandt, not Braque is in command of your paint brush I will let you paint me. I don't want to be a box."

"Come. Stand over here. The sun loves your face. But I have a feeling it's your shadows I'm going to love. They will tell me not only how you look now, but also how you will look twenty years from now. No, no! Don't look that way. Trust me, I know these things. You will like how you look twenty, even thirty years from now. You have skin that will resist time, and those cheekbones, oh dear God."

She considers him again. A compliment or an aesthetic assessment? "I will not be painted as an old woman. Not yet. And a rose is way too predicable and sometimes nasty. Later when it is time. Now I want to see me as a young man sees me, this very moment. This moment is not to be lost in an affair with tomorrow. Draw me first."

31

"What?"

"In pencil. I have to know you can draw. I have to know I will not be cubed. "

"Please sit." He pulls out the chair again.

It has dried paint on the seat - orange, blue, yellow and white. The drop cloth was a little too late. A fingertip tells her it all dried awhile ago.

"Not now. I wasn't thinking now."

"Please!" He entreats "It won't take long. My fingers already know what they want to say. And see, my pencil is freshly sharpened. Please. "

Watching them is like watching children at play, two children who have just met on the playground, but who already know they will meet here again and again, sifting sand between their fingers, making roads, turning corners. He already knows he will be pleased with this drawing and that she will be pleased as well. He has caught her eye in profile, magnified it just a little bigger than it is, as if to make up for the limit of his black lead. He needs paint to catch the sepia brown of her lashes and brow, the two, no three shades darker brown of her eye, that one eye that is looking at him, memorizing the planes of his face.

"You are an artist, too?" He's thinking conversation might make her stay longer.

"I dabble."

"I doubt if you dabble at anything." Turn your head just a little. I don't want to miss the sharp turn just above your cheeks. Don't tilt your chin up. I will get your neck when I paint you from the side. But do laugh, whenever you want to. You're giving me a crooked smile. I love that. Symmetrical is boring."

"Symmetrical is pleasing."

"Only if you are an apple or an orange or a cube!" he laughs triumphantly. "So many smiles to draw. This will all be such fun."

Fun is the best word he has thrown at her. Simple, only three letters, an Anglo-Saxon root word. She doubts that Marc would find it distinguished enough to use. He is always looking for the best word, that word that tells everyone he is a man of exquisite taste. He would consider, but dismiss *entertaining*. Not enough feeling. *Amusing* would be good if used by a character who was enjoying the moment but felt superior to all the other people enjoying it, floating just above the crowd, looking down. *Enjoy!* That was the word she would choose. A moment with joy wrapped up inside. Like this moment. They are going to be great friends, no matter what else happens between them. And, of course, something will.

You have to expect something will happen, that things will change, that you will change. Young cats know that, especially, the ones that live under someone else's porch. But if they are very clever little cats, well, maybe not so much clever as intuitive, they will never doubt there will be another warm spot and another careless bird. And still another change. Cats don't prepare themselves for that. They just know. They don't move on till they have to.

She was right to see Marc again.

"What's your real name, Maurice-Paul-Jean?"

"Terrence. Paul Terrence, actually. Paul Terrence McCorkle. It's awful. Look at your face. You know it is awful. I can't draw your smile that way. It's laughing at me."

"No, no, I was just thinking it has possibilities. Paul Terrence is enough. And I will call you Terry as if we are that close, I know you so well, that I can use your middle name and turn it into the familiar. It will be my special name for you."

"Terry. I like that."

"You will have to put your new name on all your canvases, repaint it over the others."

"There are no signatures on my canvases. I told you. I had yet to decide. And now I think I will throw them all away and paint only you."

Her laugh warms him as it sends him into despair. There will be no way to put the sound of her laughter on the tip of a pencil, or even a paintbrush. But he will try. He has to try.

It will be fun watching him try.

"Come back tomorrow!" He crumbles up her half-finished portrait and throws it in the corner.

"But, but -"

"I must do you in charcoal. I must buy a new stick."

"I don't know if I can come tomorrow."

"Ah, but you must. Just as now you must go home. Go, Go! *Vite*! *Vite*!"

He closes the door behind her and rescues her picture from the dusty corner.

"Brilliant!" He congratulates himself. He found the perfect way to bring her back to him soon, very soon. Every time they see each other they will get closer. He is certain of that. He puts the sketch paper back on his easel and slowly and carefully works out the wrinkles. Then he runs to the window to see if she is still in sight and maybe even looking back. She's at the base of the front stoop, reaching down to pet that damn orange cat that sneaks in whenever he opens the door too wide. She's scratching its scrawny little chin. She's petting its arching back. She's saying something to it, her lips softly curved.

Maybe he needs a house pet after all.

Chapter 7
White Lace Curtains

You can see the three of them through the white lace of the cafe window, their dark heads bending over what should have been the menu. Sidonie bounces in the chair between Marc and Terry. She steadies herself on their shoulders with white-gloved hands. On the checkered tablecloth is a sheet of art paper. Across the paper, one long black line curves in and out in the profile of a woman's face. Even looking at it upside down you can see the woman dismissing someone with the muted back-handed gesture of an elegant hand. Her chin is pointed up. Her eyes are fixed on some distant point. Whomever she is rejecting has just walked off the edge of the page. The only color is the ruby dinner ring on her little finger.

The light from the window, though dimmed by the lace, plays tricks with the red paint. It puts sparkle into the jewel, over and beyond Sidonie's fledgling abilities. Looks like the sun has faith in her art, almost as much as she has in her eyes. She had convinced Terry that she was an artist like him. It shouldn't matter if Marc felt that way too.

"Tell her I was right, Marc. Tell her she should forget studying in France with Monet and stay here in New York, with us. It will be cross-pollination. She will be our muse. We will be hers. She will feed our art, we will feed her stomach, and with our combined talents we will launch an American Renaissance!"

"If I know Sidonie, and, trust me, Paul, I do, she'll want an advance on that commission. And as for France, dear boy, you really should try to at least glance at the Times now and then. Some ungodly number of French troops were killed in a so-called thrust to the east of Paris. The papers are saying it approached thirty thousand. Do you realize there were German soldiers actually celebrating the beginning of the war? So no more talk about this creature studying in France, or anywhere else on that continent. Besides, we'll get no musing out of her before breakfast. Darling girl, I recommend anything with eggs. Lila buys them fresh every day. They are still chirping as they sizzle. And then we can consider an altogether more civilized use of the term "thrust".

Sidonie smiles and tilts her head while Paul waits for the blush that never materializes.

"Trust me, *ma petite,* the French toast is m*agnifique!* Kissed with powdered sugar, in the warm hug of maple syrup. *Wunderbar!"*

"Don't listen to him, Sidonie! You'll miss the delicate taste of a gently turned yolk, wrapped up in all that - - - gook."

"You surprise me, Marc. I never took you for a poultry purist. And gook?" There is no way he can contain his delight. "You can't do better than gook?"

"The secret, my dear Paul, is to know when and how much to embellish."

"The trick, Most Esteemed Marc, is to know when you have reached perfection and stop right then and there."

"Gentlemen, gentlemen! Neither of you is perfection. Though when you turn a phrase from prose into poetry, Marc, I feel like a child learning her ABC's. And when you pull light out of a shadow, Terry, I feel as if I've gone through life wearing a blindfold. But, trust me, My Darling Dears, I know what my stomach craves without a tutorial. At this moment it is a French pastry, with too much raspberry filing to eat with a pair of white kid gloves. The secret to my stomach is excess. I love it when my fourth sugar lump spills coffee into my saucer. I am in heaven drinking a glass of orange juice with so much froth I have to lick it off my upper lip."

"I'll lick it off for you." Terry leans in as if he already had permission.

"Me first! I *knew* you first!" Marc pushes Terry back into his chair.

"Yes, Marc. You knew me first. But Terry was the first to tell me I could draw. I can't wait to hear what you think. Look! Tell me what you see. Do you agree? Do I have a gift for abstraction?"

"Sidonie, my love, nothing about you is abstract. You are the sun, lighting the world with your presence. You pitch that world into darkness when you sleep the night away. You are so here, so not here. You cannot be ignored either way. You are so very, very tangible."

"Come now, Marc. Admit it. Even the face of the sun is clouded from time to time. And those moments of allusiveness, being here, but only just, make us appreciate the return of its warmth, add to its mystery. Sidonie is layered in mystery, covered with veils. It is the secret of her charm and of her art. She is the mistress of that one small telling detail."

"The question, My Dear Gentlemen, is whether or not your Sidonie can draw. And if she can draw, can she do it well enough to spend her life learning to do it better? I have wondered, hoped, prayed that was true. My teachers have been encouraging. Terry sees it as a certainty. He says I only need to adjust my perspective. Say more with less. What do you think, Marc?"

"Terry? Where does Terry come from? Why does Sidonie keep calling you that, Paul? I thought you were auditioning Sebastian, Demetrius or Octavio."

"That was last month. This month I was seriously considering going *Francaise,* until the Sainte Sidonie baptized me Paul Terrence and gifted me with her own personal diminutive. You may call me Terrence."

38

Rolling the sketch back into a funnel is tricky with gloves. Tying the string around it is even trickier. If their debate wasn't so mutually fascinating the men might have noticed her false starts, might have seen her pick her purse off the floor. They certainly wouldn't have missed her pretty pout.

"I'd call you a pretentious fool, if I could figure out what you are pretending to be."

"I would call you a has-been if you had ever arrived."

They feel the jolt and the accompanying chill when she pushes her chair away from the table. Marc recovers first. He puts his hand on her sleeve, looks deeply into her eyes and says what he knows she has been waiting to hear. "Of course, you have talent, a well-spring of talent. You can do anything you choose to do. You are a marvel! You amaze and delight me!"

"Too much, too late. I'm off. I leave you and Terry to sort it all out. Who has the most faith in my talent? We'll have to see. As for me I think my morning will be better spent shopping for a new hat. I'll want a black straw with a white ribbon. A white velvet ribbon, I think. Wide around the band with long slim tails trailing down my back. The wind will send them dancing. Just for fun a rich widower will reach out and tug one. I will turn and smile. He will have no choice but to buy me the Louvre. He will dedicate a wing to my scribbles. If you hang in the Louvre your fame is assured. *Mona Lisa* should begin making room." She is standing now and looking at the door.

"Sidonie, please, please don't go! Marc is about to make a full apology. Aren't you, Marc?"

She turns back but only to advance her tale. "There will be croissants for breakfast and scones for tea. With clotted cream. I love clotted cream. On the bed table will be a tin of white chocolates in the shape of rabbits. Lingering in my mouth will always be a faint sweet aftertaste. Widowers can be so grateful."

"Paul, excuse me, Terry, is right. I was only being playful. You must know how much you're admired. I don't say more because I don't want to spoil you. Like a delicate flower, you require judicious watering."

They are up out of their chairs now; wood scrapes against wood. Terry's chair nearly topples over. "Sidonie!" they cry in unison, the first time they've worked as a team.

"Not to worry." At the door she smiles back at them. "You will not be alone for long. Lila is coming this way. I can hear the cackle."

What they hear are bells, the three silver bells fastened to the top of the door. Sidonie's slam crashes the bells into each other. Marc and Terry are left staring at each other.

"She'll be back."

"She has to come back."

"What will I do if she doesn't come back?"

"It's all your fault!"

"Idiot!"

"Buffoon!"

Marc and Terry are left to spend the next hour as they have countless hours at this very table considering from every possible angle every detail and all the minutiae of their relationship with their mutual muse. They return to the plans they are preparing for a salon and exhibition showcasing their work and introducing Sidonie to their circle.

Before leaving, Terry plunges into the foam that tops his glass of orange juice. "I only wish I could thank her." A foam flower blossoms on his nose. His nose is not all that offended. It has never been that grand a nose.

"What?"

"The froth! I've never enjoyed juice more!"

"You're talking orange juice?" Marc takes Terry's napkin and makes him neat.

"Well, it could be an analogy, but then you would know more about that then I do."

Chapter 8
The Back of Beyond

Terry's portrait of Sidonie caught the lights in the dark spill of hair and the depth of the bewildering eyes. But Marc was right, the bare shoulders and cleft of breasts upset Claire Adair even more than it did him. He must have known she would do something about it, especially when she saw his name on the poster advertising the show.

Sides of Sid

In

The

Writings of Marc Elliot

The Art of Paul Terrence

And in her own Self Portrait

Opening – August 20, 7-9

Lila's Back Door

Knock First

Of course Clare recognized her daughter's images on the poster. She'd watched those features change from infancy to young adulthood. Divided in thirds, the right panel of the poster showed Sidonie squared, the bad dream of some demented modern artist. There was enough about the features to make Clare look to the opposite panel. There her daughter was in a more familiar pose, teasing the world in general and her mother in particular. The middle panel was Sidonie exposed. An impressionistic mist clouded the bare tops of her breasts. But the mist wasn't high enough to cover the faded scar on her right shoulder. Cousin Adrienne pushed her down the stairs when their five-year-old self-interests happen to collide. Something about hair ribbons. Or was it an ivory comb?

And so it is that our Sidonie finds herself on a yellow streetcar stopping at what looks to her like the intersection of No Where and Not Just Yet. There are a few trees, some buttercups and a dog chasing a rabbit. A street sign begs to differ. These dusty paths do have names. Rudolph has just met Groveland, which holds some significance for the conductor. He is dinging a bell and yelling. "End of the line!" And, indeed, it seems to be. Still, Sidonie has already decided. This will be the beginning of a new adventure. As she starts gathering up her packages and purse, one of her gloves falls under the braided straw seat.

Through the blur of the dirty streetcar window she can see the man awaiting their arrival. He is smiling pleasantly enough and his dappled horse stands perfectly still. Looks like this is routine for both of them. The occasional spark on the overhead wires is no longer a jolt to their nervous systems. And, at the moment, there are no horseless carriages snorting behind. Too many ruts for a leisurely Sunday drive, Sidonie supposes, although, the muddy streets by the railroad station didn't seem that much better. This particular Midwest City had no sense of style that she could discern in the short time she was hustled in and out. But, she is willing to give it another chance, the very next trip downtown.

The man is wearing coveralls with lots of pockets. She's seen them in catalogs, never in real life. She loves pockets. She loves firsts. And these coveralls looks like some dutiful wife starched and ironed them. His straw hat is in his hand as he reaches for her elbow. Of course she is the first to jump down from the steel grate steps. The two other girls are still looking out the windows. She has this landing all to herself.

"Good afternoon, ladies. Sister Saint Dominique sent me to escort you to your new home." He doffs his cap and raises his voice so the other two girls can hear him above their excited giggles.

Sidonie is not looking for a new home or a pair of giggling friends, for that matter. She is still thinking of her two favorite, and altogether more urbane, co-conspirators. An all girl's college at the back of beyond was nowhere in their game plan.

"How far is it?" One of the girls asks.

"Not far. Soon as I load your luggage we'll be off."

Sidonie remembers her two forlorn accomplices waving from the doorway of their brownstone. Marc tipped his hat and Terry waved a salute. That was, she guesses, the reason she is no longer angry and not terribly worried. Her parents had been beastly enough. But she has no doubt that that her men will wait for her. You see, she has come to understand she's not that easy to forget. And she laughs to herself, everyone goes to Paris, France, but no one goes to St. Paul, Minnesota. This could be a lark. She will make it a lark. You have to learn to keep yourself happy when life takes you somewhere you hadn't intended to go. It's the best revenge against the inevitable.

She's been expecting a big black iron fence around the campus with the name of the college twisted into its arch. She's prepared to have it read, "Abandon all hope." She's looking forward to the drama. But there's not even a little sign, only a funny gray rock. A girl sits on its lumpy surface and reads a book. Looks like one of her fellow passengers will fit in nicely, the one who has done little else but read Bronte since they left the station.

At the rock the carriage driver pulls the horse into a left turn, careening into a private road that someone has sprinkled with white crushed rock. Good thing! The rock makes it easier to negotiate out of a big furrow. Other wagon wheels dug in nice and deep a time or two before. The white road is leading up to a three-story brick building at the top of the hill. Even from here the bricks look too red, the mortar white enough to still be wet.

"Here she is, Kildare Hall, the first building on the blueprint for St. Brigid's College. It's named after the sainted woman's hometown. The good sisters shrewdly chose her for the patron saint of the college. She's not only a scholar, but as Irish as Archbishop Ireland. There's no finer women's college on either side of the Mississippi thanks to his support. They'll be many buildings to follow. The nuns have the archbishop wound around their little fingers." It seems the driver has become a tour guide, and quite the fanciful one at that. The whole scene is becoming difficult to take seriously. But this is her new situation, and serious it is.

The train ride from New York had offered much to see. Big towns became small towns. She waved at a woman at a pump and a man at a plow. She watched a boy throw a jack-knife at a log. She felt like one of those stallions running along the side until a fence post makes him pull up short, still scraping the ground with his hoofs. He really would have kept on running if there was nothing in his way. But when Sidonie is excited she adds her own electricity to the air. Sit close and be wide-awake right along with her. Marc would choose to say, "bolted awake" if he had been lucky enough to ride that train.

Whenever the whistle blew it seemed to say, "Jump the fence, little filly. You can do it. It's not that high a fence. Come on, Sid. Mustn't be afraid of a little barbed wire."

These days she thinks of herself as Sid. As she renamed Terry, he had renamed her. He and Marc showed her a new side of herself, if only for a moment. She liked it very much. Being Sidonie felt nice enough, feminine, a little exotic, privileged. There was more strength in Sid, less compromise, a clear focus. Short but definitely not sweet. Being transplanted to *behind the forever* was not going to stop the sea change, the train change. Minnesota was far away from her parents - liberty, sovereignty, free will, choice. Honor thy father and thy mother still applied but it was easier at a distance.

Still, she had this sense she should at least look as wistful as the other passengers. She still had sand in her hair from being dumped out of the sandbox where she had been making castles with two of her favorite friends. They were good at the game, had built more castles than she had. Still they were more than happy to share the sand and they had some excellent ideas about building a moat, coaxing the sea inside, and finding a twig for an ant to cross over. She loved them both. But yes, they would keep. She knew they would be there when she was free to join them again. And they would know even more, be more famous and she would have one experience on them, being somewhere they had never even thought of being.

Still, she did miss them. There was Marc's hand on her breast, Terry's laugh in her ear. A part of her screamed out for them, but that part had to be muffled, at least for now. She had been too flagrant in her defiance. She had tempted the fates by being too happy, too public. She would know better next time. She hated seeing that shock on her father's face, hated even more, the stricken look on her mother's. There was a difference. Father's shock was like lightning striking a lone tree and bouncing away after the quick burn. But with mother the strike seemed deeper. Sid tried to figure out the difference, the reason her mother's hurt lingered. It was more than a mother seeing her daughter as herself one generation removed, and feeling tainted by her daughter's disgrace. But Clare Adair was in no mood to have that mother-daughter chat. Well, neither was she. She hated hurting Mums, but she was not about to make a promise she couldn't keep. It would only make things worse, and she hated worse.

"Not exactly the Sorbonne, is it?" A voice nudges her back into the wagon and on to the white stone road leading up the hill. It is the girl Sidonie had immediately identified as worthy of note. She had seen her sigh over a letter, fold it carefully, put it into her beaded bag and snap the clasp shut. Sidonie knows another romantic when she sees one, a real romantic, not one who lets a book do it for her.

"So I've noticed!" Sidonie agrees readily enough. She had seen a picture of the Sorbonne in French Class. She had dreamed about studying with the masters there. She had pictured the colors of her artist aprons, poppy red on Monday, Wednesday and Friday, and sea foam blue on Tuesday and Thursday. She knows it well enough

46

and this isn't even close. But it may have to do, for the news from France of soldiers digging trenches to protect Paris left her wondering if the Sorbonne would even be standing by the time she could get there.

"Still we are making history. This college was opened only 10 years ago. Mother says it will be the Vassar of the Midwest."

"Mothers don't know everything."

"Then you don't want to be here either?" Romantic-girl moves closer to her, across the worn leather seat. Her blond hair looks naturally curly. Sidonie likes the way it curls over one ear and leaves the other free. But she's not quite ready to confide. Not just yet. Friendships that start slowly last longest. She prefers a preface, believing that first exchange of names can tell a lot.

"I am Sidonie. Sidonie Adair. But I prefer to be called Sid."

"And I will call you Sid. It's delightful. Almost like I have a secret boyfriend. But don't count on Sid from the nuns. They prefer Christian names. I know. I've spent years being taught by this order. I went to St. Martha's Academy before this. After the sisters built Kildare Hall, they sent for the boarders and graduates from both sides of the Mississippi, St. Jerome's Academy in St. Paul and St. Martha's in Minneapolis."

"And what's your Christian name?"

"That's the problem. It's not Christian. Mother's not a Bible Reader. She called me Circe after some Greek or Roman goddess."

"Greek. It's from Homer."

"Either way. I would rather be an Amelia or even a Hazel, the color of my eyes."
Circe widens her eyes. "Rather unusual, don't you think?"

"My name's Amy." The girl with the book looks up and out of it. She blinks a little as if she is just coming out of a mound of heather.

Sidonie rewards her with a smile. She can't believe that *Wuthering Heights* is as intriguing as someplace else, when you first arrive, and everything is brand new. Still she knows a fan when she sees one, a bit of lace starched and framed, the better to hide behind when you are surrounded by people you don't know. Marc would be proud of her. That almost sounds like a figure of speech. And she's proud of herself for thinking kinder of Amy, almost sympathetic. "You're one of the lucky ones, Amy. Seems your mother must have been spared a course in classic literature. She named you a nice Anglo-Saxon name. Or is it French? No matter. My Mums was always making cryptic comments about sea monsters and water spouts and fates worse than death, although, I'm not sure where she came up with Sidonie."

Circe nods. "Yes, Amy, you're fortunate indeed. My mother used my classical name to inspire me. She always referred to Circe as the patron saint of domesticity. I was, she kept telling me, fated to be a goddess of the home. I would have preferred a less predictable fate. Circe, she also pointed out, was renowned as a healer. And I'm not really interested in nursing."

"Your mother should have read a few more stanzas." Sidonie couldn't help herself from adding. "Circe did her best healing in the bathtub and Odysseus was only one of the many men she bathed in her healing waters."

"Oh my!" Amy starts fiddling with her bookmark, pulling it up and down, finally losing her place.

Sidonie wonders how quickly she can send Amy's nose back in the land of lost, but relatively pure, love. For her own good, of course. Amy's obviously backward for her age, not quite ready. Sidonie decides to shock her back in. "Hermes was yet another."

"That explains it!" Circe bounces above the rocking seat. "That's why Sister Mary Mark never gave me anything above a C in religion. She did not approve of me or my patron saint."

"Is that one of your nun friends, Circe?" Sidonie inclines her head towards the sister dancing down the long front stairs, her black veil flying behind her. A good twenty steps, set off with pillars, like a miniature Parthenon. You can't fault the sisters for trying. Given time their building might age into importance. Sidonie is picturing a lovely whirl of white as graduates dance down the stairs, waving their diplomas at their parents, tossing roses at the beau, a cascade of red roses, the stems unraveling from white flowing crepe.

"That's Sister Raphael, the registrar. She's very nice and not all that old. She treats all of us as potential nuns or better yet, benefactors of the college. Her plan is to finish us off nicely, so we marry well, and endow the college."

"I've been thinking of being a nun." Amy looks at them both for approval, her eyes too pale a green, washed out by her freckles and paprika hair.

"Of course you have, dear. And I will be a benefactress." Circe pats her on the head, but her hand comes to rest on Sidonie's arm. "Sid, would you like to room with me? I happen to know there is an unassigned bed in my room and since we are the last to arrive it might be a natural thing to happen – unless you have someone else in mind."

"You are exactly what I had in mind." A girl with a love letter is eons ahead of a girl with her head in the pages of a romance novel.

She and Circe will whisper together in the darkness of their dorm room. She can see their heads together on the pillow looking up at the moon as it reflects on the ceiling. They will both agree that someday they will see their lovers again, someday very soon. And, of course, Terry, too.

Chapter 9
Forbidden Fruit

"I can't believe she's gone." Terry stands by the window watching the moon slip behind a cloud. Shadows deepen the stark planes of his face. He looks very much the black Irishman, only ten years of living later.

"I can't believe she went without a whimper!" Marc hooks his homburg on the doorknob, the only surface in the studio without dust. For this part Marc appears the English gentleman, completely out of his orderly element.

"It's your fault!" Terry spins around. Paint sprays from the brush he had been holding when Marc burst through the door with his news. "You made it easier for her to go. You gave her a reason to go. She would never have left us for a convent school if she weren't looking for a way out."

"You give me too much power. Sidonie is very mature for a young woman. She understands these things. She had already forgiven me the long white neck in the moon light." Marc smiles slowly, remembering, then frowns. "I can't believe she actually told you."

"I can't believe Sid wasn't enough for you."

"It's for the best."

Terry takes another spin. "For the best?" He puts down the brush and gives up pretending to paint.

"The longer these things last, the harder they are to end."

"I can't believe you would ever want it to end."

Marc rests his hand on Terry's shoulder, pretending to care. "No, you wouldn't. She is your first love."

"I only wish." Terry shrugs him off. "Maybe, someday, if she stayed. We are alike, you know. We play at life, but never with people."

"We'll talk again when you know more about the subject."

"If we are talking about love, I hardly think it is within the realm of your particular expertise." Terry walks back to his latest canvas. He has only gotten as far as the eyes. He always gets stuck on the eyes, more lost in them really. Maybe that's all he will do. He likes the way they float across nothingness. He is destined to paint them over and over again, on the face of every woman who poses for a portrait.

"Oh, I loved once. Once was enough. Too complicated. Still I am glad I felt it. One has to if one is going to write about it." He curls his fingers over and looks at his short, neatly filed nails. He isn't sure why. Perhaps it helps him believe that he is still in control, no matter what the complications.

"Yes, that's how you would think. Love for art's sake. What a fool you are! If you can think rationally about it and condense it into a paragraph of well-chosen prose, you have missed the awe."

"Only if you are a poor writer. And I am a very good one."

"Not a good lover, I would say."

Marc tries not to smirk. "It really bothers you, doesn't it?"

"It bothers me that you should be the first."

"Someday, if you are very lucky, you may profit from that experience. If a girl's first taste of the forbidden fruit is juicy, she will always want more."

"Bastard!" Terry throws a cloth over the canvas, as if to protect it from his rage. His eyebrows slash into an angry line.

"The truth is I could never be a permanent fixture in her life. It would almost be incestuous."

"So now you are going to tell me a lovely little story. Everything is a story with you. I suppose reality isn't good enough for your heightened sense of drama."

"Sidonie's mother was *my* first love. Clare Adair. Such a lovely sound! It should be spelled Clair Adair."

"What a lovely flight of fancy! Tell me another."

"It happened. Believe me, it happened." Marc goes to the window to do his own musing. The moon erases the puffiness of his eyes. It concentrates instead on the pulse beating on the far ends of his hard jaw line. Or is he simply gnashing his teeth? Hard to tell. Perhaps it's both.

Terry turns his back on Marc and the moon. At this moment both are beyond him, confound him. "I've only just met Sid's mother, admittedly, not in the best circumstances. But it was obvious. She is a woman of strong character."

"How do you suppose she got that way?" Marc walks back to his hat, puts it on his head, and smoothes the brim. "I'll make you wait for that chapter. It is called building suspense. Would you believe it? I was the one with no experience and she was my forbidden fruit?"

The apartment door closes between them. Terry does the expected. He sits down hard on a hard chair and puts his face in his hands.

Elliot should run out the front door and head for the opera. He is already late. Instead he sits down on a dusty step, pulls his hat off his head, and very, very slowly twirls it round and round.

Chapter 10
White Gloves

Marc doesn't go to the opera after all. He tells himself he doesn't want to come in late. It would be an affront to Carmen and she would suffer enough abuse in the course of the evening. In truth he is afraid Clare will be there, Clare not looking at him, Clare pulling her white gloves up to her elbows, Clare adjusting an earring, Clare still beautiful, still unattainable after all these years, Clare hating him for Sidonie.

He goes back up the dusty stairs to his apartment, takes off his evening clothes, and puts on his smoking jacket. He is, after all, a man of the world. He is no longer the boy who stood just inside the door, with his hand on the knob, with the still, small hope that Clare will call him back. He lights a cigarette to avow his manhood one more time, then goes to his desk to write a new ending. He will feel his way back to that moment and turn it around. He trades the pen for the cigarette and before the cigarette burns itself out, he is in a Victorian hotel room twenty years ago relaxed at the foot of an expansive brass bed.

*   *   *

He sees her hand on the back of his. He hears her say, "Darling boy, look. You can barely see it, but there it is. The veins in your hands are more deeply imbedded than mine are. The hands of a woman betray her first. Why do you think we wear gloves? To hide the betrayal."

"Love runs deeper than veins." He kisses her hand and thinks it is as beautiful as any he will ever hold. He runs his lips down the long tapering fingers. He can imagine them curling gently around a bird or holding firm to a man's heart.

"I love the way you talk. When you talk I forget the years between us. Yes, you will be a writer. I see many of your books on the shelves of my library. Maybe I will even be in one of them, but please don't tell the world I was married at the time. Disguise me a little. Say our families were at war. Say you were rich and I was poor. Find some other reason why we didn't work. Don't let the world know I was old enough to know better."

"The world doesn't matter. It's how we feel. Feelings don't lie. Feelings are a law to themselves. Feelings are pure, compelling, can't be denied."

"I will never deny our feelings. I am only saying they have run their course."

"Not mine."

"Not just yet, but soon. I'm not about to wait for that." She walks away, sits at her mirror, and doesn't turn her head to its most flattering angle as he has so often seen her do. She loves her long neck. She often adorns it with choker, pearls, diamonds. Not tonight. Tonight it's completely bare, as if her neck is waiting to be stroked, longing to be stroked, by any hand but his. A long white neck is destined to be his undoing.

Marc crumbles the piece of paper and throws it at the wall, even though he hasn't written one word while he allowed himself the luxury of this detailed reverie. The onionskin bounces off the white, stained damask and joins the more recent discards huddling under his desk.

Although he always left the roll top up you can see he feels good slamming it shut. And you know as well as he does that he has to see Sidonie again.

Chapter 11
Art for Art's Sake

Sister Rose Aurelia doesn't hear her coming. Sister is using the pointed end of a paintbrush to itch that part of her forehead trapped beneath her starched linen coronet. Curled on the stool in front of her easel, eyes closed, a smiling O on her lips, Sister Rose looks like a big black and white Angora. Any moment she will wet her paw, wipe her nose and swipe her ears or so Sidonie thinks as she slips back into the hallway, out of the sunlight and into the cool shadows of the 3rd floor landing.

She should have known better. Art classes over for the day, Sister is enjoying her solitude. She has pushed aside the Japanese screen that defines her personal work space and is enjoying the light from all the windows along both sides of the corner art room. Autumn sunlight brings a kinder warmth, more treasured because it will not last the month.

Sidonie tiptoes back to the top of stairs and presses down hard on the wooden plank of the top step. It doesn't take much to make the boards squeak. They are squeaky new. And if that isn't enough warning, she announces her arrival with a bright clear voice.

"Sister Rose, Sister Rose! The light is perfect. You must go down to the woods and paint the sun glowing through the trees. It won't be long before sunset. The day lilies look like melting wax."

"I'd love to child, but I have portress duties in ten minutes time. One of the sisters is ill. I do have a moment to talk about your sketch for extra credit. It shows promise. Much promise." Before Sidonie sees it coming Sister is off the stool and rapping the knuckles of her pupil's left hand. "Of course, it can't be displayed where anyone can see it."

"Ouch!" Sidonie rubs her hand with dramatic emphasis. The paint brush serves many purposes, it seems. "What a way to treat your favorite pupil. Don't expect a box of chocolates any time soon."

Back at her desk Sister Rose eases her most promising student's charcoal from the bottom of a brown leather folder. She hesitates just a fraction of a second before turning it right side up.

"You like it? He was the perfect model. If only we could have him pose nude for the class."

"Scandalous, scandalous child!" Sister holds the picture farther away from the crucifix hanging just below the starched white *guimpe* covering her chest. "You make me feel like I ought to go to confession, but I wouldn't want to send Archbishop Ireland into a fit of apoplexy! He has so many hopes for educating young women to the fullest extent of what he likes to call their 'intellectual equipment'."

"Sounds a little stuffy to me." Sidonie takes her picture away from Sister and looks at it fresh. It has been two days since she placed it in Sister's folder. She's thinking her David would be pleased, if she ever showed it to him, which, of course, she won't.

"And his Excellency always stresses that the transformation must occur under the protective hand of the Church."

"We both know an artist's hand works best when it is light as well as deft."

"Humph!"

"Don't tell me you never sketched a nude when you studied in Rome."

"I wasn't a nun then. There are higher standards for nuns."

"I would think there would be more generous standards for artists."

"I would have thought so too at your age. Well, maybe higher or more generous are not the issues, but focus. Or less focus as might be appropriate. A nice blur could be considered artistic." Sister stops looking over Sidonie's shoulder and not because it's a near occasion of sin. She's past that foolishness. Of course, there is also scandal, as if there were any way to scandalize Sidonie. "In those days when I was drawing a life subject I was looking at bone structure, skin texture, light and shadows across the face."

"Surely not the first time."

"No, not the first time." Sister turns away to hide her laugh, but shaking shoulders betray her. Sister is an imposing woman even without the heavy habit. There is a lot to shake.

Sidonie throws her arms around that ample back. The nun freezes and pulls away to face her. "It's because you were not raised Catholic. There doesn't seem to be any way to impress you with the distance that must be maintained between the religious and the laity. But by now you should know students don't embrace their teachers."

"I can't help it. I love you. I feel safe with you. Perhaps because you love me back, pagan and all."

"Yes, you are a pagan. Completely uncivilized! That makes you a terrible student, but a wonderful artist. Now let's talk of shading. You have the body right, but you have forgotten that it exists in a world with light and shadows. There is a sun out there shining on this man ,"

"Would I be back in your good graces if I added a few shadows, like here, and, of course, there?"

As Sidonie starts to point, Sister starts to looks away. Nonsense, she tells herself, who's the adult here, who's the teacher?! "Think of it as mystery. Every piece of art should have mystery."

"You mean leave something to the imagination, the wicked imagination?"

"Stop trying to shock me. I know it's fun for you, but I think you and I have more important things to share. Besides bringing the outside world into the picture with lights and planes, try to imagine what this young man might be thinking about."

"Finding a towel?"

"Sidonie, do you want our private lessons to continue?"

"Of course, I do. I'm sorry. I miss laughing with a kindred spirit."

"You miss your mother?"

"Kin we are. Laugh we don't, not together, not lately."

"Who do you miss, child? A sister, brother? Girl friends? You and Circe are as thick as thieves."

"She doesn't draw, she doesn't write. She sews buttons on her clothes and does her homework just because it is assigned. She can write love letters. I'll give her that. And she is always up for an adventure. But she doesn't smear pollen on her fingers and touch it to her nose. She never looks for a liverwort in one of its hiding places, under a leaf or behind a tree root."

"And you have friends back home who do that?"

"I have friends who define their day by what they create, not what they do."

"Then you are blessed my child. But for now your place is here. For now you must find your pleasure in your own solitary artistic pursuits."

"Of course, I find pleasure there. It's my fate. I'm meant to create. "

"You're telling me, Sidonie, that you have a calling?"

"Not exactly. Nobody on high had to tell me. I just know."

"Little Miss Independent!"

"And that's bad?"

"Knowing what you were meant for is a good thing, making up your own mind is a strength. I suppose it's too much to ask that you believe that The Supreme Being is directing your decisions, someone more personal than Fate"

"I don't hear voices if that's what you mean. But then I don't exactly believe that Fate makes decisions for me. Fate is just an expression. I guess I meant being an artist is part of who I am."

"I won't argue there. But here's what you need to accept, acknowledge. Once you know what you are meant to do, once you choose, you must make it happen with the choices you make thereafter."

"You mean choose models that won't get me expelled from school."

"Something like that, but bigger than that and sometimes smaller."

"Like what?"

"You don't really want me to get that specific, do you?"

"You're right. That would take the fun out of it and take it out of my hands."

"And heart. I have a lot of faith in your heart." And your soul, Sister thought to herself, although she wasn't quite sure why she was all that sure.

Sidonie moves toward Sister Rose. "I'm so glad I have you."

"But not to hug. Not till graduation day. Then it is permitted. I'll do something better. I'll give you a chance to share your art with others of like mind. I'm thinking of an art show in the spring. I have no doubt you will have a few pieces to contribute by then."

"Oh yes, yes, I would, I will. Could we take our easels into the woods tomorrow? Wouldn't it be wonderful to have a wall of flowers to last us till spring? There are still some perennials out there. And I can do a tulip and a crocus from memory. Oh, I can hardly wait. Thank you, thank you!"

"Now I really must go. I will see you at Vespers. Don't forget Vespers. And don't forget your chapel veil. In the library there is a box of them for the ill prepared or the non-Catholic to use. Not putting one on only makes you stand out."

"That's me. I love to stand out. But for you I will wear the black lace, bow my head, and pray for humble obedience."

"Try praying for something more attainable, like a passing grade in algebra. Sister Theresa is worried about you."

Sidonie is already squeaking the third step. "Geometry! I'm looking forward to geometry. I'm told there is art in geometry! Spaces, planes, squares, rectangles! I can hardly wait!"

Sister runs a hand across her habit, looking for a spot of paint or chalk dust. God forgive her, she hadn't asked Sidonie who had inspired her extra credit project. Of course, no one had posed. It was probably a Greek statue. Sister Marie Pierre had that mounted picture file for her world history classes. That tall case was full of file boxes with thousands of images. Among all those palaces, cathedrals or temples there must have been a Greek or a Roman nude. Michelangelo! It might have been a Michelangelo. His work was in the Vatican. Maybe his David inspired her. The fellow did look a little like David. But David had fig leaves, didn't he? No, if memory served he didn't.

College president Sister Saint Dominique watches her with interest. It seems that the old nun walks lighter these days, moves faster, and there is this secrecy in her smile. It appears to be a happy secret. God must be working some wonder in the life of her friend. Grace. They call it Sanctifying Grace. She shouldn't be surprised to see God at work in the life of a sister in Christ.

But then miracles are supposed to surprise us. Or what's a heaven for?

While the Sisters and the better-behaved members of the student body are at Vespers, Sidonie peeks into the refectory to see if the work on the light fixtures has been completed. Unfortunately, it seems to have been. The screws are all back in place, a flick of the switch reveals light all around the room, and there is not trace of plaster dust on the floor.

He'd been standing on the third rung from the top of the ladder when she first saw him. Dust sprinkled the long, hard, tan muscles of his arms as they reached for the ceiling. It was like powdered sugar that ornaments the golden fissures of a pound cake. There was sugar on his wheaten hair and thick eyelashes. His eyes looked bluer under their frosting. As his lean fingers plucked the bits of broken ceiling around the fixture he made more dust.

She asked him if he needed someone to hold the ladder. Startled, he sent a spray of the sugar on her head. They were united in fairy dust. She smiled the worry off his face. She was fine. Her hair easily shook out. He couldn't help but notice how thick her hair was, how thick were her own lashes. It could have been the beginning of a lovely intrigue if Sister Dulcima hadn't walked in with a pitcher of lemonade for the workman. But the encounter did inspire the sketch that Sister Aurelia couldn't help but admire. And there were more of those sketches, hidden under her mattress.

Tonight she'd share them with Circe.

She also had a sketch of Marc. She hopes he isn't another interlude. She'd expected more than letters. He is a writer after all. She'd expected he'd come to see her. She doesn't want to forget Marc. Not just yet. She'd like to crawl inside him, the way he crawls inside of her. She has this feeling she can do that. Crawl inside his very being, make herself part of him, indispensable to him, at least for this moment. She isn't concerned with his soul. Souls are forever. It's too early in her life for forever. Nothing is forever. But the moment and its lasting memory, that counts.

Chapter 12

A Lovely Light

It's Sister Rose Aurelia's favorite time of day. The last bell has sounded. The last afternoon class is dismissed. You can count on the students to head for anywhere else but this classroom floor. No one will be in the girl's bathroom. She steps in for a little quiet time. The chapel is a destination for many after the last student is tucked in her room or the library. Rose feels safe going in, although why she is going in she doesn't quite know until she stands in front of the long mirror over the sink.

At first she sees herself as she is now – a face pinched between white starch. A pin with a round black head is working its way out of the top of her veil. She should be used to that face. For decades she's pretended it doesn't matter. But she isn't used to it. She has never gotten used to being another penguin in a sea of penguins.

Then, suddenly her face breaks free, as if it feels just as disappointed, irritated, and angry as she is starting to feel. It has to get away. It leaves her shoulders and becomes smaller and smaller, lighter and lighter - light enough to float to the top of the glass, and then to blow toward the sides like a bubble on a breeze. But it isn't a bubble. It isn't round and ready to burst. It's a lovely oval with resilient skin, yet every bit as soft as a bubble, as if there is a cloud cushion underneath. And the cloud is pushing dew out into her pores and over her cheeks, onto the tip of her nose, her tiny nose. Her crushed crepe hand reaches out and touches the glowing moist tip.

Rain comes from clouds. Dew probably does too. It makes delightful sense. It makes even more delicious nonsense. She loves seeing her bones re-assert themselves. She can see her cheekbones re-form and her neck re-define. And, of course, there is a smile. Her face is pleased with itself. But then suddenly the smile takes its leave and there's a furrow between her brows. Even that is a treat. There is only one furrow and it is only there when she frowns. See! It went away.

Not only her face is young. The spot where she is standing is brand new territory, as if she hadn't started the journey decades ago. Her name was Alice then and this was the last time the dismissal bell would ring for her. It was early and she was about to matriculate out of high school and into the novitiate. She was about to become someone special, a bride of Christ. Only very special young women were called by God to walk this path. God had intended this for her from the moment He thought of her. He would give her hints, send her graces, and hope that she saw the signs. Signs, now that's a laugh. What if the signs were nothing but vanities of misplaced adoration. Or idolatry. What if the signs were nothing but omens for naïve, insecure adolescents? Come follow me. How about if I follow myself? How about if I allow myself to feel pretty without shame? How about if you follow yourself and I'll follow myself? I'll follow myself to Paris and the company of some handsome young libertine? How would I be lesser for that experience?

Looking in the mirror she remembered pretty. Well, the beginning of pretty, had she piled her strawberry blond hair on the top of her head, pinched her cheeks, and opened her eyes wide enough to show the green. A green shirt waist, that's what brought this on. Aunt Glo gave it to her for Easter - Aunt Glo who had once played on the legitimate stage. Aunt Glo who married again after Uncle Frank died, Aunt Glo who darkened her eyebrows with coal, Aunt Glo who was the only one to ask if this was something she really wanted, Aunt Glo who offered to pay her tuition to art school, Aunt Glo who promised she'd come back to see her favorite niece make her final vows, Aunt Glo who probably hoped she would know better by then, Aunt Glo who outlived another husband and married yet again. And then, after all that, ended her earthly life by looping a window sash around the top of the bathroom door and then around her neck.

There's a watercolor above the towel rack. Thank God it isn't one of her own. Thirty years of chastity, poverty and obedience has not eradicated pride, pride in her art. It isn't such a bad sin, she tells herself. Her art is God's gift. She knows that. He could have given it to anyone. It just happened to be her. And she's supposed to tend it, make it grow, and share it with as many others as possible, but not in a bathroom, hanging on a single nail above a soiled towel, and not a rose. She never painted a rose. Everyone paints a rose. Of course, if she found one that said something to her that it had never said to anyone else, well then, maybe she might.

The College is still young. Not many girls have stood in front of this long mirror and pinched their cheeks and run off to class or to the library or to chapel, bless their wicked little hearts. A few might stand here on their graduation day, and try to look past the reflection. They may wonder who will look back at them ten years from now, who they will be. No, they won't. Young girls never look that far ahead. They can't picture getting that old. It took such a long time to go from seven to seventeen. The summers were longer when they were little, long walks around the block in a new pair of Sunday shoes, lazy hopscotch afternoons. They had to grow three shoe sizes before they could wear their mother's dancing slippers. She can remember stepping into her mother's shoes with her own button-tops still on her feet. There was still plenty of room at the toe. Her white buttons were always a little gray. Mother always told her to wash her hands first. Now there is always a little paint under her fingernails. She likes them that way. She curls them under when she reaches for and kisses the archbishop's ring.

She pushes the small, black pin back in, just far enough to secure the veil without breaking the skin. She's not a hair-shirt kind of nun. She has never doubted that she was a good nun. She and God have this understanding. She does her best. And He applauds her on, especially when she reaches for what is out of reach . She has a feeling God sees Sidonie in the same light, the same lovely light as Sister does.

How gratifying a looking glass is at Sidonie's age. But the child, bless her, wants more from life than compliments on her beauty. Sidonie's next assignment just may earn her the accolades she desires. She will draw one of Sister's favorite subjects, the oldest oak on the college grounds. She must draw it first in charcoal, to get the feel of the composition, to grab hold of the strength of the trunk. Her fingers will float down the branches as they brush the tops of the fading leaves and cascade onto the ground.

Sidonie must then work from the inside out, like Sister Rose's God when He added the first people to His garden. He created the bones first. Then He added the muscles and tendons. Only then was He ready to smooth them over with soft, supple skin. He brush-stroked chestnut brown into the eyes, just a moment before He brought Eve to life, the moment before He dabbed in the lovely light.

Chapter 13
Sweet Surprise

The window hasn't been open since late last fall. A spring breeze is gathering up dust from the inside of the sill. The last remnants of winter are floating through the air in tiny brown swirls. To Sidonie each swirl looks like a tiny tornado, nothing to be afraid of, unless you live in a tiny town. But Sidonie has never felt small. Any other student, on the stool outside the President's Office, might feel as if she were sitting on the tip of a twister, in a camisole and petticoat, with nothing whatsoever on her feet. But Sidonie has a feeling she is being called in for a commendation or at the very least a congratulation. Sister Saint Dominique must have seen some of her growing body of work. Growing body of work! What a nice sound! Sister Rose Aurelia has been particularly pleased with her watercolor willows, one weeping in the morning mist, one weeping in the glow of the afternoon sun.

One last little storm lands on her shoe. She lets it stay. She always lets sweet surprises stay. Should a butterfly land on her shoulder she would be still, as still as she possibly could be. It's lovely watching the wings fold and unfold ever so slowly, yellow, black, maroon, maroon, yellow and black. This little tornado likes her. It's swaying from side to side, but it's still holding on.

She's never seen a real tornado, but she imagines what it must be like, and she sees herself waiting, till the very last moment, to run for cover. She sees the funnel gathering up speed, growing darker and darker, twisting into a pinprick of power when it touches the earth. Sidonie's no more afraid of power than of drama.

The President of this college is as dramatic as she is powerful. When she lights a candle in chapel it is like no one has ever done it before. She flies up the altar steps like a young girl running to her lover. She lights the wick like a sorceress about to cast a spell. She waits just a fraction of a moment for the fire to cast shadows on her face, on her audacious cheekbones, on her cavernous eyes, too deep to guess the color.

And when she speaks everyone listens. Sidonie needs to memorize every word of this meeting, if she isn't too busy planning Sister/President's portrait.

If you thought of Sister Saint Dominique as the wind, she would be spring, crisp, chill, occasionally, damp, but on the right side of summer. Sidonie has hopes of coaxing her from early April into late May. Once Sister knows Sidonie they will be the best of friends. She can tell. Every time they pass each other in the hallway or along the aisle of the chapel Sister tries to look stern. But Sidonie caught a smile once, just a little quirk, at the corners of her mouth, but it was there like a sliver of the moon, ready to slip out from behind a cloud. When Sister Rose speaks she looks Sidonie in the eyes as if she bears watching

"Miss Adair?" The registrar taps her pencil on the mahogany desk. "Miss Adair!"

"Yes, please?" *Please* always seems to surprise and disarm. Sidonie uses it on the nuns judiciously.

"Sister Saint Dominique will see you now."

Too late she remembers her little tornado. Her shoe has sent it into a scatter across the room and into a dark corner. It seems she will enter the President's Office all on her own. The registrar is opening the door. The windows are bigger in this room. There are two on the east wall behind the desk and two more on the north. Sister's also enjoying the breeze from an open window. But there are no dust balls anywhere in sight.

"Good afternoon, Sister."

"Sit down, Miss Adair."

At least this is a comfortable chair, with arms and a spindle back. Her feet touch. Mother taught her long ago how to sit demurely with her legs close together and her hands folded in her lap. Sister Saint Dominique will appreciate Mother's manners. There's something especially neat about this nun. In a world of neat nuns, all white starch and black gabardine, she looks like someone irons her hose and maybe even powders her nose.

"Thank you, Sister."

"Tell me, Child, just why did you choose our college?" Sister Saint Dominique comes out from behind her desk. She brings her question right straight across the room to Sidonie. It's a short walk, but Sister walks it tall and with purpose. She looks like an exclamation point about to punctuate a very important statement. It would be easy to sketch Sister Saint Dominique. She is one long, straight line. Sometimes the line curves like the neck of a swan. Sometimes it sways like a reed on the wind. Right now it is gracefully inclined towards her student. The line is very interested in her answer. Sidonie doesn't want to disappoint.

"I've heard it's the Vassar of the Midwest."

"And you think that's a good thing?"

"Well, of course. Vassar is a fine school."

"Then why didn't you go there, might I ask?" The eyebrows are dark. There must be dark hair under that veil. And her skin is dark, olive. Up close, she looks Spanish, a Spanish nun, a Spanish question mark. Sidonie decides a half-truth might serve her best.

"Everyone goes to Vassar. It's no longer all that special."

71

"And you think you are special?"

The conversation seems to be getting ahead of Sidonie. Sister Saint Dominique's expression is no help, no smile, no frown, eyes averted as if she didn't really care. But her head is tilted like a wolf listening for sounds in a thicket.

"I'd like to be."

"Yes, I suppose you would." The eyes are open now, only slits, but wide enough. "Unfortunately, my dear, wishing doesn't make it so. But here, in this place we deal with reality. The fact is, outside of art and the American novel you are just one of many students. I believe you are working at this, but so are many others."

Sidonie is standing up before she realizes it. My God, what an awful thing to say! She's just about to give words to that thought when Sister points a finger to the chair.

"Sit!"

Suddenly to Sidonie the back of the chair looks less like spindles and more like bars.

"I said sit down, Miss Adair. We're having this conversation because you are one of the few girls in your year not on the Dean's List."

"The Dean's List?"

"The list of students who have had grades good enough to write home about, students who will make their parents proud."

Sidonie can feel a tornado whipping up inside of her. The wind is blowing hot and cold. Not doing her mother proud? Sidonie's not being blown away, but she's definitely being scalded and frozen at one and the same time. The words can't help but explode from her mouth. "Then in my own way, I'm quite extraordinary, aren't I? I mean, if everyone one else is on the Dean's List why in the world would I want to be?"

The President goes about the business of preventing a smile from forming and considers Sidonie for a brief moment. "Ah, at least you have enough spirit to risk a demerit or two or three. Let's see if you have spirit enough to fight your own natural tendency to idle your way through life."

"Idle? I have enough canvases, watercolors and charcoals for my own show."

"Then you better plan on throwing one for yourself when and if you graduate. Because until your grades improve you will not be participating in any outside activities."

"Outside activities? Art is my primary activity."

"Exactly. We grow well-rounded young women here. We take pride in women who take pride in all their gifts. We graduate intelligent, talented and spiritual women who are dedicated to all their educational goals and who persevere to the end."

"Watch me." It's a whisper, but Sidonie's eyes are very loud.

"I will. And I will also listen. But believe me, this is the last time I will hear an insolent word out of you."

Sidonie hears "Off with your head!" She's standing at the foot of a throne and the queen is far from pleased.

"Make no mistake, Miss Adair, I am only indulging you this time because, obviously, your schooling has only prepared you for cotillions and coming out parties. I have forgiven you much because Sister Rose Aurelia has such high hopes for you." The President reflects just for a moment on Sister Rose Aurelia, the great unchallenged art teacher, who gets excited when she finds someone who can mix red and yellow and make orange. "Saint Brigid's College usually attracts students with a more academic, even scientific, frame of mind and definitely with more discipline."

It's the nude in the fairy dust. Somehow Sister Saint Dominique saw one of the sketches of David. Sidonie shouldn't have shared them with Circe. Circe was delighted that she had a friend with so much anatomical knowledge. She might have pulled them out from under the bed where they were hiding under the lining of the sewing basket and showed them to someone else. She wouldn't have told Sidonie. She would have sworn the other girl to secrecy. But if Sister Saint Dominique somehow saw the David wouldn't she be acting more scandalized?

Sidonie couldn't think of any other crime of consequence. Little infractions -like wearing her pajamas under her academic gown at early morning convocation, wetting her lips during confession to that sweet young priest - she had chronicled all of those in letters to Terry knowing how he would laugh. Perhaps someone had intercepted one of those letters. Or maybe there was one from Marc writing of his undying love. She certainly didn't receive one like that. She certainly deserved one like that. She certainly expected him to write one like that.

She should say something in her own defense, but defense against what, which crime? This couldn't really be about academics.

"Cat got your tongue, Miss Adair. That's just fine. Silence brings wisdom. I suggest you spend one study hour a week in chapel, in silent meditation. And you will be taking one less art class this semester. I have enrolled you in World Literature. You need to read the Divine Comedy. You need to visit the Inferno; you need to experience the circle where the sinners are tossed about for all eternity by a wind that, like they themselves, has no direction. They have passion, but nothing important to put that

74

passion behind, nothing that drives them to greatness, that makes them extraordinary, *special*, to use your words."

Sidonie has just been relegated to the fires of Hell. It sounds like her first guess was the right one. It must be the nude in fairy dust. She can hardly make it any worse. Might as well pretend she doesn't care. "So this is to be my penance? Ashes to ashes, dust to dust?"

More like "Dust bin to dust bin if you are not very, very careful!" Sister Saint Dominique smiles, goes to the window, and opens it wider still. It's the smile of a woman who likes to feel the wind in her face and the rain and maybe even a major snow fall. She's the kind of woman that should like Sidonie. "Go, Miss Adair. You are dismissed. For now."

The door closes between them. Sidonie can't see Sister Saint Dominique wipe her fingertips on the underside of her long sleeves. She doesn't hear her now least-favorite nun laugh into her wimple.

Sister positions herself behind her big mahogany desk, knowing, as always, she is just where she should be in the world. Her work makes a difference.

Out loud she says, "That one will be fine. But God help us should she decide to become a nun."

Chapter 14

Deja Vu

The white tent is going up right on the grass behind Kildare Hall. Sidonie watches from her dorm window. She is late for class but this is better than the circus. She has never liked clowns. Clowns are so insistent that she laugh when they want her to laugh. Clowns try too hard. Actors on the other hand seem more interested in telling a story. They are compelled to tell a story, as much to themselves as to the audience. Sidonie understands that compulsion. She loves getting lost in a story whether she makes it up or someone else does. And this is going to be a good one, told by Shakespeare, the master of all storytellers. She has seen *Hamlet, Macbeth* and a few others with her mother. She has always wanted to see *Romeo and Juliet*. But *Othello* might be even better. The star-crossed lovers are older, should be wilier, and bloody murders result, not just quiet, sad little suicides.

The sisters have been preparing their students for this performance for the last month. They've all read the play as well as reviewed what little is known about *the Bard. The Bard* seems like a pretentious appellation for someone who could just as accurately be called the Bawd. Sidonie has read some of the comedies on her own and she has the gift for getting past the stylized writing and reading between the laugh lines. It's bawdy all right, so bawdy that fairies fly down from the tree tops to roll in the dung. But in Shakespeare dung is moist and sweet and doesn't cling, especially not to lacy fairy wings.

The middle pole secured, the stakes are being driven. As the wind shifts one canvas flap hits a girl in the face. Startled, she falls to the ground. A young man with ridiculously blond hair walks over, bows, kisses her hand, helps her up, and smacks her on her bottom. Delicious! She's smacking him back. Those still holding on to the poles or pounding the stakes take a moment to laugh with them. Now the girl curtsies. She's very pretty. She curtsies very well indeed. Of course, these workers must also be the actors like the gypsy actors in the books she's read. Sidonie can see their covered wagons rumbling down the back roads, packed with a stage, a stage curtain and trunks full of satin dresses, velvet jackets, and hats with long red plumes. Between performances the lady gypsies tell fortunes in front of a campfire while the men practice swallowing swords. Delightful!

"Sidonie!" Circe calls from the doorway. "We've got to go."

"Just one more minute."

"And risk being told we can't see the play?"

Sidonie hadn't thought of that. "Off we go!"

*   *   *

It's warm under the tent, but not stifling, just cozy. The early summer, late spring breeze teases once more at the flaps. To Sidonie it sounds like clapping and she finds herself agreeing. The play is exhilarating and now it's almost over. She intends to clap and clap and clap for an encore, like at the opera. Bravo! She wants to see more and it's just as important that Sister Saint Dominique forget those few embarrassing bursts of nervous laughter. Ann, Peg and Margaret Mary couldn't contain themselves as one character after another fell dead across the stage. She and Circe knew better, even when one actor tripped and fell while his rapier was still plunging through the air. You can miss the magic if you look too close. Sidonie never wonders where the magician hides the rabbit or the ace of spades or the long silk yellow scarf, especially, if he is wearing a pair of handsomely molded tights and long tall shiny black boots.

She recognized Cassio right away as the young man with the bow, the kiss and the smack. Dressed all in green his blond hair looks almost white. Against that background his darkened brows and eyelashes are as pretty as any girl's. And she loves the way his character slips in and out of the plot, manipulated by evil forces, as

77

much a marionette as Othello. It seems to Sidonie that Cassio's charms are his downfall. And the beauteous Desdemona is too trusting. She walks right into her own destruction. Sidonie longs to rewrite Shakespeare and put rapiers and daggers in the appropriate hands.

After the performance the students run back to the parlors to talk with the actors about the production. Sidonie wants to do that, but she lags behind, waiting till everyone is out of sight, before walking across the abandoned stage. With the actors gone it is just a platform, a dingy platform at that, with scratches and smudges from all those long tall shiny black boots. Doesn't matter. She's having it all to herself. She stands in the middle, closes her eyes, and twirls around and round before planting her feet. She pretends them into boots, sliding in, feeling them reach up to her thighs. The flaps of the tent are clapping for her.

"Methinks not, dear Othello. Methinks I'd rather go to a nunnery than marry you. You always look so angry. You never look me directly in the face. You are always shouting to the audience. And you have the best lines. Males always get the best lines. Is this a dagger before me? I think I'll stick it in you before you stick it in me."

"Bravo, Bravo, Desdemona. Isn't that what I've been trying to tell you all through this bloody play! Well, maybe I wasn't. But someone should have."

Sidonie opens her eyes to see Cassio bowing to her this time. Unfortunately, he is no longer wearing tights or boots. "Oh, it's a lovely play. And you are a lovely Cassio, so deliciously duped. But wouldn't it be fun to change the ending every now and then? Haven't you ever wanted to?"

"Yes, of course. But I'm more interested in playing another part on another day. I'd suggest you think about being a playwright, but you do have stage presence." He kisses her hand on the top, "Your ladyship." Then turns it over and kisses the underneath.

An ordinary schoolgirl would be lost for words, would miss a beat in the conversation, and would savor the moment just a little too long. "Yes, I do like the feeling." His eyes look a little too triumphant. "Being on stage," she clarifies. "In the right costume." Sidonie looks around the edges of the tent, hoping some prop has yet to be put away.

Cassio goes to a scratched and dented trunk, pulls out a jeweled turban and puts it on her head. "I thought Othello should wear this, but he prefers his black wig." Cassio tucks her hair under the gold and black satin. "There! How does it make you feel?"

"Like a gypsy. I want a pair of gold earrings."

"I see gypsy. I see dancing girl. I see knife-wielding murderess. By God, you really are an actress. Look at your flashing eyes. Suddenly you look taller. And your hands are clenching and unclenching. I know an actress when I see one. I am not just a humble actor. I am director of this troupe, as well as its set designer, not to mention, head of costuming." He takes her hand again and holds it to his heart. "I know whereof I speak. All you need is skilled direction and gentle coaxing, I mean, coaching by a skilled professional. That would be me, Edwardo Garzero, at your service. But I must know. To whom am I speaking?"

"Miss Adair," Sister Saint Dominique has not raised her voice, but it is loud enough to break the fourth wall. "Don't you have somewhere else to be?"

*   *   *

The grass is still lumpy from the melting snow of April past. Two Aprils have actually past, and without a showing of any art from her hand. The toes of Sidonie's shoes are dampening as she makes her way back to her dorm room. She wants to look back to see what is happening between the two in the tent. But she just might turn to salt.

79

Besides its fun stamping on all these hopeful little weeds. Dandelions are replacing the last peeling clumps of purple crocus and the tulips with only one or two red petals holding on to their lonely stems. A new season is about to begin, a fresh start for summer, but to Sidonie it all feels a little too familiar. Summer comes around every year and winter never misses its turn. It is all so inevitable, as inevitable as that last scene. It feels as if she has played it before and knows the lines all too well.

Her mother is standing in the wings. Like Sister Saint Dominique she speaks in a stage whisper that reaches to the last row of the balcony and beyond. Like Sister, Mother Clare is costumed in her own religious habit – perfection – white gloves, starched lace collar, beaded purse and all.

"Sidonie Alana Adair! I always knew you would disgrace us, but I never imagined two men fighting for the right to dishonor you. Silly them, when all they have to do is wait their turn."

Terry is pulling his pencil out of Sidonie's hand, "Enough! You can draw well enough. You just need to draw less and say more. I will teach you how." Terry isn't kneeling, but he is hovering, reaching over her shoulder as if he would take her hand and move it for her, painting boxes, circles and an occasional triangle. His name entwines with hers on the lower right hand corner of the canvas.

And then there is Marc, looking deeply into her eyes, saying what he knows she has been waiting to hear. "Of course, you have talent, a wellspring of talent. You can do anything you choose to do. You are a marvel! You amaze and delight me!" His long finger is touching her cheek; running down her throat, making its way to her shoulder, playing with the strap on her evening gown. She never wore an evening gown with Marc. But when she thinks of him she thinks of a long black dress, flowing softly over her hips, and one strand of white pearls falling into the deep V of what is supposed to be a neckline. It got lost along the way, straying way too far for its own good.

It's strange. She steps on another dandelion. She amazes and delights men. She steps on still another. She appalls women. She walks around one still perfect tulip. While inside she always feels the same.

Mother would say, "Men will tell you anything to get everything."

Marc would say – What would Marc say? Not much, unless he was pressed into it. "You are a marvel!" Too much, too late.

And now this young man in tights says she's an actress. A wise young woman would stamp down another weed and do what is right for her and her alone. A wise young woman would never run off and join the circus or a gypsy caravan. But a wise young woman would miss one adventure after another.

Sidonie really thought she was an artist. Seeing something appear on a blank piece of white paper made her feel like a magician, no, more like a mischievous leprechaun turning the world upside down with his magic touch. With a swish she could sprinkle moonbeams across the sun. With a swirl she could splash snow on a rainbow. With a smile, she could make a man stand on his hands for her or kneel at her feet and tell her she had the gift. But when she believed him she passed on the wand and started somersaulting for him. She let all the Cassios and Othellos in her life turn her world upside down and topsy-turvy. And she suspects she might have even met an Iago someday and be intrigued.

It would have been so lovely to really be an artist, but she knows she's an actress. No one has to tell her that. She has been acting all of her life. She simply didn't value it till now. And now is the time to set her own stage. If she's going to be banished yet again she must be the one to choose the place and time. There's certainly no reason to come back. The past two years have brought little encouragement for her work, except for the always kind words from dear Sister Rose Aurelia. And Sister Rosie may want an art protégé desperately enough to make one up.

Sidonie has this feeling Sister Saint Dominique is about to suggest another school for the coming year. Could be on the east coast or the west coast or anywhere else than her beloved College of St. Brigid. Sister hates somersaults. They show much, too much petticoat.

Sidonie will pack only the prettiest of her dresses. Well, maybe a school dress to wear putting up the tent. She will leave her pretty watercolors, her pretentious oils, and her pathetic pencil sketches under her bed. Some silly schoolgirl will be impressed. Her little works will have a moment of admiration, a little show in a college dormitory.

Perhaps she'll roll up one of her sketches, one that rolls easily, doesn't take up too much space and pack it in her trunk. Of course, she will choose one of the Davids. She'll slip other Davids into a Bible, a hymnal or a daily missal. Maybe she'll leave a David in the trunk of a tree. Before it's too late a postulant may discover what she is about to vow away forever and have time for serious contemplation.

Chapter 15

"Mind the tangles!"

The footlights are blinding. When they are lit and the house lights are dimmed, Sidonie can't see the audience. She and the actors are in a world of their own. A dark, delicious red sunset shines through tall Corinthian columns. She can feel the warmth, touch the glow, and she truly believes she can walk down the canvas stairs and ride on that topiary pony in the garden below. Othello, Desdemona, and Cassio fly back and forth across the stage. They talk into each other's eyes with earnest passion. They turn their backs in anger, confusion, or just to temporize. They pause and look into the darkness, waiting for their next line. Past her they enter and exit, as she stands in the wings holding their next prop. They act as if she doesn't exist, although they depend on her to turn on the footlights illuminating their painted faces, to cue the violins that add nuance to their dramatic scenes, and to pull the curtains up and down, down and up, till it's time for their final bows.

As she watches she says the lines with them, particularly those of Desdemona, Emilia and Bianca. She dreams of stepping in and replacing those wives of Othello and Iago or even the lesser role of the courtesan. She has a feeling she would be a natural as a courtesan. She particularly likes the dangling emerald necklace and tinkling brass of the bracelets.

But the only woman whose credits are listed in the program is Jane Delehanty, who plays Desdemona. She's the one the others call Delehaughty behind her back. She's the one who insists on having her long auburn tresses brushed at the end of each performance, and now, of course, by the newest member of the troop.

Dame Jane pulls the brush out of Sidonie's hand and demonstrates, "Gently, smoothly, long strokes from the scalp to the ends with so few hairs left in the brush only I will know you've been there." She is still wearing Desdemona's cloudy amethyst rings, if not her air of deference and trust.

"Sorry. My mother always said it was important to stir up the blood in the scalp."

"You're mother never had her hair curled for two performances, five times a week. Try again and mind the tangles."

Sidonie doesn't answer. She doesn't want to talk tangles or mothers. Every performance, she watches the people taking their seats, hoping her mother will not be one of them. But no member of the audience is in gloves and plumes, with lips curled in scorn like a mother swan not particularly pleased with her duckling. This one is just a little too ugly.

"I notice you in the wings, Sidonie. Every performance you mouth our lines. Watch the ear, dear. These earrings are very long. Don't get caught on one. My ears are very tender. They look like perfect little pink shells, but shells don't bleed. Edwardo, Cassio to you, calls them half moons."

"I want to learn how to act. It's my dream." Sidonie sends a smile through the cracked mirror, which just may not survive another tour. Surely a fellow actress can understand. She had the dream first.

Delehaughty laughs back into the glass, avoiding the distortion by staying just right of the crack. "Your dream is my nightmare. Confess! You are hoping I will fall deathly ill and you will take my part." She puts her hand on her head and affects a swoon. "Where there's death, there's hope."

"I wish you and all the actors the best of health."

"You're not a good enough actress to deliver that line. And I'm afraid there would have to be a serious epidemic for you to play Desdemona, since Emilia understudies her, and Bianca understudies Emilia. But, I must warn you, even Bianca could be a stretch for a girl from a convent school."

"Well, I am learning just by being here. I am thankful for the opportunity."

"Ah, there was a little more truth in that delivery, perhaps because you truly believe it, now, anyway. Soon you will get impatient and want more and you will have to remember how you felt the first time you said, I am learning just by being here. I am thankful for the opportunity." Jane's imitation of Sidonie's voice patterns are not kind, too high, too affected, insipid really. And it doesn't help when she folds her hands in reverential prayer and dramatically closes her eyes.

Sidonie sees herself wince in the constantly watchful looking glass.

"It will be your challenge, my dear Sidonie, to pull those emotions back up to the surface. Unselfish gratitude. Unbounded enthusiasm. Tricky emotions. May take some dredging."

Sidonie keeps her silence, but fails to mind a tangle.

"Ouch! Thank you just the same, but I think I can take it from here." The Leading Lady laughs, knowing she has hit her intended target.

Sidonie steps back, knowing she has gone too far.

Always aware of her audience, Never-Plain-Jane dramatically brushes her long sunset hair down one shoulder and then the other. "You could do worse, Sidonie, than take tips from me. I have not only acted longer; I have life experience. I've more memories, more emotions from which to draw."

"Oh, I've had my share of memories, good and bad." Sidonie searches the mirror for more than the reflection of two women with competing reveries. The future is in there somewhere, if backwards and maybe even upside down.

"I can see you have. I see a man on your face. I see lost love! Excellent! Use it. But not just the sorrow. Remember when he first looked at you, really saw you and stood very, very still. You can see his eyes, can't you, the intensity, the focus. You are the center of his stage. You stand taller. You feel more beautiful, leading lady beautiful. You can't help leaning towards him, losing your balance, caught between unsure and unglued. His hands reach for your shoulders, then your waist. They linger before making their next move. You hear a little groan and it's your own. Edwardo! There you are! Come in and rub my back. It's full of knots."

"Your wish is my command, your Royal Haughtiness!" Edwardo twirls her chair around and kneels at her feet. He is still in his tights.

Sidonie moves aside as Cassio lays his hands on Desdemona's shoulders and back. His approach is gingerly at first, then harder and deeper, just rough enough, just tender enough to make her close her eyes and throw back her head. Shakespeare never wrote a happy ending for these two characters, but it was probably there, just waiting to happen, if she had somehow survived *Act V*.

He's letting his hair darken, probably skipping those lemon rinses she's heard about, staying out of the sun. Sidonie's not sure she likes it as well. It had been such a nice contrast to her own. Black on white, white on black. Pity. Her hair is almost black. Dark brown can be darker still in the right light.

"That will be all, Sidonie, except, remember what I said. You will command the stage and have fluidity in your movements if you keep in mind that first encounter and how your senses and your ego reacted to the ultimate audience. Imagine tango, duplicate the steps, and you'll recapture the passion. Passion is the key." She reaches over her shoulder and covers his hand with hers, but lightly, not to interrupt what has become a hard knead.

"What foolishness are you telling Sidonie." Edwardo kisses the top of his Jane's head. "I'm her coach. She can't serve two masters."

"Stay on your own mark, my love. This dialog is between women. I know, I know. In a pinch you can play one, but be one? I think not. I'll see you, Sidonie, half an hour before tomorrow's performance. Don't be late this time. Get the tickets and programs to the box office a little earlier. And tonight brush your own hair one hundred times as all our mothers tell us to do. Feel each firm, gentle stroke. Luxuriate. Pamper. Think of your head as a small kitten who can barely see, who can easily tumble, who has yet to learn to trust. And remember, I deserve no worse, probably better, definitely better. Kiss me, Edwardo, tell me I am the best leading lady you ever had."

"You are Desdemona. You are Ophelia. You are my Juliet."

"Don't mess my hair. Sidonie just untangled it."

"I will if I want to."

"Then you'll just have to brush it again . . . and again . . . and again."

Sidonie walks gratefully into the muffling sounds of a summer night. Crickets are her friends. She tries not to wonder what the frogs are croaking about. Someday she will have her own mirror and it will have a frame of gilded forget-me-nots. And before it she will blacken her lashes and redden her cheeks. She can see clusters of diamonds twinkling in the night of her hair, dark curls cascading past her neck and down her back, waiting to be lifted and kissed by a very blond leading man.

Chapter 16

Open Wounds

"I am no strumpet, but of life as honest as you that thus abuse me."

Of all Bianca's lines this is Sidonie's favorite. And not because it's her last and the one that gets her off stage in time to miss the massacre of *Act V, Scene 2.* when Desdemona will be smothered in her bridal bed and Othello will saturate the silk sheets with his self-inflicted wounds.

As a matter of fact, Sidonie would love to play a death scene. But this is almost as good. Bianca makes her final exit with her own open wounds. She's angry, disappointed, disillusioned, a woman used by many and valued by none. No one will expect a first-time understudy to do her justice. Won't they be surprised?

Sidonie is rehearsing in a hollow tree where the rest of the cast can't see her right leg pumping her red slipper into the bark dust. She hates when her leg betrays her. The first time was in Miss Loftus' class. She was standing in front of the teacher's desk reading her report on the Egyptian pharaohs and there was no way to stop her paper from shaking up, down and sideways.

Since that incident in Ancient History Sidonie has learned to make the quiver stop by planting her full weight on the balls of her feet. But this is the first time she's read a speech in a squirrel's larder. It's harder to plant on an uneven surface and then there are these cracked nutshells. Ouch! Besides, to Sidonie it only seems right to stand on tiptoe and reach for the starry, starry night while emoting *The Bard.*

"I am NO strumpet, but of life as honest as you that thus abuse me."

She is considering putting dramatic emphasis on *No.* The third word just may be the most important in that sentence. Bianca is standing up for herself. *No, no, no!*

Sidonie could deliver the line with her legs spread far apart as if under her dress she were wearing tall black boots. The ruffled skirt would fall in an arresting arc. Then with her hands on her hips she could shake her head ever so vehemently.

On the other hand, *strumpet* is an explosive word, perhaps the very word she should be shouting to the rafters. She can feel the Shakespearean spittle just thinking about it.

Then again *strumpet* is a hurtful word, a whore word. Perhaps poor Bianca would say it in a whisper, with a crack in her voice and her head hanging low.

"I am no strumpet!"

"Sweet Bianca!" "My most fair Bianca". In *Act III, Scene 4*, Cassio has nicer names for his courtesan. He pretty pleads, "Pardon me, Bianca." and gives her a handkerchief to dry her eyes.

It would be a lovely gesture if the handkerchief hadn't been Desdemona's, and before that Othello's, and before that Othello's mother's. Generations are affronted as Cassio tries to quiet his *strumpet*. Yes, this is another good scene for Bianca. She's feeling lots of things, none of them good and all of them dramatic. She's hurt by Cassio's inattention. She's suspicious of his protestations of love. And she's jealous of the woman who had slept in that room before her, wept and left her handkerchief behind. Sidonie understands these feelings. She loves the *strumpet* sentence best of all, too small to be called a monologue, but too powerful to be just one mere dialog exchange.

StrumPET!

Strummmmmpet!

So many intriguing variations!

89

I really am a natural born actress. I am so good I can do Shakespeare backward and forwards. My own internal compass has led me to this place on the map of my life. I can feel my life changing and my hand is at the helm. And it feels joyous! No, I am NOT a strumpet! I am a TRUMPET. And I'm soloing in the overture to Le Ballet Sidonie. Or is it La Ballet Sidonie? No matter. There is a red velvet curtain going up.

*   *   *

The footlights make Sidonie shine, but as always they blind her to the audience, except for that woman in white flicking a fan fourth row center. Why a fan? A cool breeze has been sending the flaps into a nice soft rumble since the performance began. Why all white? Is she trying to pull focus from the actors? Why now, when Sidonie has stopped expecting her? Sid strangles on the *no*, and bristles on the *strumpet*, the flick being as dismissive as any blow Bianca or Sidonie has ever suffered.

Sidonie's right leg wants to shake again. She pounds her slipper into the wood floor. It's a resounding thud. A man in the front row drops his cane. His wife's program falls from her lap. It's a good thud. It's an appropriate thud. It's a thud taking a stand. Bianca is not about to take *strumpet* lightly.

As the curtain falls, Sidonie smiles into the darkness and sends a silent *no thanks*. "Without your inspiration, Mums, I might have missed the perfect scene stealer."

*   *   *

Clare is not surprised that her daughter looks happy on stage. She saw Sidonie smile when she climbed the stairs to the stage that first rehearsal of that first recital of her first ballet class. Sidonie reminded Clare of a duckling hitting the surface of a sun-glistening pond and feeling her webbed feet paddle as if they always knew they could. Sidonie didn't need a mother swan to poke her from the safety of the grassy bank.

90

But this pond will never do. The water is murky and the fish are bottom dwellers. There are theaters with more *cachet*. French drama is very fashionable these days. And you needn't even go to France to perform in them. The war has sent European actors, directors and set designers scrambling to the safety of the States. And thanks to finishing school, Sidonie can *parlez-vous francais* with the best of them. Armed with impeccable pronunciation, she can fake what she doesn't remember. Acting is just memorizing after all, memorizing and pretending. Sidonie's a natural pretender. And she wants this so much, maybe even more than unsuitable men. In all likelihood a man had something to do with her running off and joining this gypsy caravan, but the joy she was having before she noticed her mother in the audience, is palpable and a very useful bargaining chip.

Find out what Sidonie really wants and make her work for it. That was the answer to controlling the incorrigible child. It will serve to quell the rebellious young woman. The question is: can she really act on a professional level? That last line had some fire.

Clare watches the wings for Sidonie's next appearance. Othello never seems to leave the stage, nor that villain Iago. And poor pathetic Cassio parades around looking tragically ineffectual. That was probably the last of Bianca. Desdemona is now the woman front and center. And she has Clare's attention as well as that of the rest of the audience.

Desdemona's plight rings a not too distant bell in Clare's psyche. Every word rebounds in her head like an echo gone awry. Othello's too dense to hear them the first time through. It's as if there were a loud wind howling behind his dark brow. His brain must be built of bricks in a wall so high, so thick that no other thoughts can climb over or go through. The only hope for Desdemona is her own resolve, her own will, to fight back or escape. Clare longs to tell her just how to do it. From what she remembers this play could do with a rewrite. The only Shakespearean play she hates more is *The Taming of the Shrew* which pits a man's will against a woman and celebrates his victory.

"Yet I fear you," Desdemona is saying to an angry, accusing husband, "for you're fatal then when your eyes roll so. Why I should fear I know not."

All women have something to fear from their husbands because all women are hiding something, holding something back. Even dense Othello knows that. Desdemona is not going to convince him of her innocence by feigning ignorance.

"That death's unnatural that kills for loving. Some bloody passion shakes your very frame. There are portents, but yet I hope, I hope, they do not point on me."

Please, please don't point at me! Clare wants to tell Desdemona to stop her whining, not ask for mercy and be righteously indignant.

"Oh banish me, my lord, but kill me not!"

She's handing over to him all the power on a silver platter, worse yet, a lace handkerchief. Has she never heard of scratching or hitting back or even running away?

"Kill me to-morrow; let me live to-night."

Oh please, don't grovel! Now Clare wants to strangle Desdemona herself.

"But half an hour."

Pitiful, pathetic!

"But while I say one prayer!"

A complete waste of precious time. God is a man too, and too often unforgiving. Desdemona shouldn't pray to either of them. Better she kick them both in the tights.

"O Lord, Lord, Lord!" Desdemona screams through the pillow, ineffectual to the very end. No one is going to hear her cries; they are just as muffled as the voices of all women who consign their fates to men.

Clare has to force herself to stay seated through the Lodovico's last line. She wants to run from the theater and kick a tree.

"This heavy act with heavy heart relate."

Suddenly Clare feels heavy, too heavy to rise for the much too generous standing ovation. These people feel they are in the presence of greatness. But then greatness is in the eye of the beholder and these poor provincials have seen precious little of that. Sidonie is one of the last called out for a bow. Clare almost regrets spoiling this moment for Sidonie. The red in her cheeks is not a rush of triumph. The eyes are too nervous, searching the audience for what she still hopes she won't find.

Clare is already rehearsing what she will say when she corners her daughter in the dressing room.

"Don't fret my child. You will have your theater if you really want it that badly, anything to distract you till you are old enough to know men will smother you, given half the chance. But you will have your acting career on my terms, a woman who knows life better than Shakespeare ever did." No, that's too honest. Try again.

"Sidonie, how delightful. You show real promise. Let me help you. Your father will buy you acting lessons. You must fully develop your talents. And when you complete your lessons I will give you a coming out party to launch you into society." Something like that, any way.

Desdemona is past saving. In every performance from here till forever she will scream through a pillow. But Sidonie, with Clare's help, will survive her *Act 5*.

Chapter 17
Votre Sidonie

Dear Mums:

You'd never believe how deluxe are my accommodations! The magnificence of my draperies is equaled only by the view from my window. Modesty and good breeding are the only things that keep me from pushing the panels aside and leaving the casements open morning, noon and night! Ah, the scents that float on the breeze from the courtyard below!

I should have written my praises in French. Magnifique! Charmant! I could have called the window la fenetre (with that cute little roof over the second e.) After all those years of anguished French lessons, I finally find myself thinking in French, instead of doing a mental translation before opening my mouth in the prescribed pucker. I suspect by the time I come home my speech will be punctuated with pardon mois, s'il vous plaits (another roof over the i) and tres (accent going down over the e) biens. I will have to do a linguistic somersault to revert to my mother tongue. I credit this advancement to Montreal, my fellow students, and Professeur DuBois.

Le Professeur firmly believes the French have a nose for the right word.

However, our first class assignment was to read an English playwright who was worthy of our attention – if only because of his International reputation. William Shakespeare, of course! I suppose it is easier for Du Bois to figure out if some of us can act if we start out emoting in our native tongue. Once that is accomplished he will move on to his personal favorites.

I can't believe how provincial I was before leaving the states. Here they laugh if you refer to Shakespeare as the Bard. So pretentious! So Anglo!

There is also much talk of the war here. The papers are full of it. The Canadians are most proud of their troops, But the lives being lost, some say by the millions. Somehow it seems closer here than at home. What is the talk there? What do you think America will do?

In any event, thank you so much, dearest mother, for this opportunity to grow and stretch in a cosmopolitan environment.

Je t'aime!
Votre Sidonie

P.S. I really haven't forgotten the names of my l'accents - aigu, grave and circonflexe. I was only teasing. I know you will pardonnez (hyphen) moi! I so love to tease you, Mumsy! Love again, Sid.

Chapter 18
Your Sid

Mon Cher Terry,

I slept with my first bed bug night before last. Actually, it turned out to be a family of bed bugs. Well, a few of them are orphans now. I was able to kill the bigger ones with the heel of my satin slipper. They moved the slowest, probably because they were gorged with my precious blood.

My plan is to send them all scattering before my next week's rent is due. If I am not successful I will have to seek different, more expensive lodgings. *Mums doesn't know I'm not staying at the respectable boarding house she picked out for me. But for now I kind of like living Bohemian and using my monthly allotment on more important things, like taxi rides into town or ribbons for my hair. It's Greenwich Village a la onions sautéing in garlic.* My bedroom window is just above the Dutch door of the kitchen. My clothes are permeated with those pungent cloves.

It's pointless to wear perfume, unless it's French. I suspect that's why they have developed such potent scents, to counteract the garlic oozing in and out of every pore and follicle in their gourmet-fed bodies.

Do I sound like an American snob? That would be a good trick. The French have taken that to greater artistic heights than I could ever begin to achieve. Don't mistake me. I have always liked that about the French. No false modesty there! Who can blame them for liking the view looking down their well-bred noses? But somehow the arrogance suffers in the Canadian translation. Something like the nouveau riche unintentionally making mockery of themselves by being too new and too rich.

And I also have to admit the curtains in my room may be a little too dingy. Dingy is a word with dirt wrapped up inside of it. The "g" brings to mind grime. The "d" stands for dull gray. My curtains are so besmirched that it's hard to tell their original color, let alone their original material. Cotton would have once been crisp. There would be wrinkles to indicate cotton. Chiffon would have once been flowing, but these poor panels are too leaden to do anything but fall hard. How I do go on! Next I'll be telling you about the chips in the porcelain washbowl and the paint peeling off the iron bed and the land lady in scruffy pink slippers who puts my rent in the pocket of her ragout-stained apron. And I did just say I like living Bohemian. Well, I do! I really do!!

I'm pleased to report that I absolutely adore my acting professeur (French spelling? One "s" or is it two?) who is as arrogant as he isn't French and as brash as he is American. What a weird sentence I just wrote. Trying to think in two languages makes my mind a muddle. And when you throw in Shakespearean prose meter all clarity is lost!

Don't you dare share this letter with Marc. I don't need any of his barbed criticisms. And besides, the more I see moonlight and swans with long white necks the more I want to hoist him on his own petard.

There I go, sprinkling more and more French into my thought processes. I am making my mother proud – at least with my French. Regaining her favor in other areas is a more formidable task. Altogether too many and too recent falls from grace! The most I can do is cloud the issue
and keep her guessing.

Quelle enfant I am, still rebelling against Mums, still trying to keep my silly little secrets! With you I never have to dissemble. And you certainly wouldn't

98

bother to correct my French. Should it be Qeul'enfant? If you don't care, neither do
I!

I love and miss you, mon ami! I command you to love and miss
Your Sid

P.S. When you answer this letter, as of course you must, and soon, please draw
some pictures in the margins. I suggest my eyes or one of my ears or better yet
my mouth. I want to be sure you remember me and that I am still your favorite
model. Adorez-moi? I should certainly hope so!

Chapter 19
Sincerely Yours

Dear Marc, dear, dear Marc,

So you "can't imagine why" I have written "everyone one else" but you" nice chatty letters." I can imagine lots of reasons, the first and most obvious being you are the writer. Can't you imagine how intimidating it must be for me to compete on your playing field? You have the way with words. You can make them thrill or chill with only a few whisks of your pen. And I have heard you say out loud a few short sentences that changed a life or at least the direction it was taking.

Yes, I have lots I could write about, especially people I have met. But they only serve to make me feel more the provincial. There's my professor, the most important man in my life right now, since he will ultimately decide if I have talent worth nurturing. Everything about him is quick. When he first walked into the classroom he took a quick look around. His eyes moved from one corner of the room to the other, up and down the aisles, into the eyes of each of his new pupils. He held a baton in his hand that he was either waving at an invisible orchestra or punctuating his snap judgments of each and every one of us. The sharpest stabs into the air seemed to say, "With you I am not particularly pleased." On the other hand, I've come to learn that a slowly raised eyebrow means just the opposite.

He called on me first. "Name, city, previous experience and why I should bother with you at all." It was my fault really. I chose the last row, the third seat from the window, right where the sun would spotlight my hair at that time of the day. I answered in French because I knew he wasn't expecting it from a below-the- border barbarian. It earned me the first of many raised eyebrows.

Later he would confide that he was American too. His last name was not really Monsieur Du Bois, but Mr. Woods. The Powers-that-be thought it looked better on the brochures. He was okay with the translation as long as they let him teach Shakespeare in English. Fortunately, everyone, even the French, respect Shakespeare. And, if we were very good students, he would let us run through his own plays. Like you he is a writer. It seems I'm destined to meet and try to charm writers, the one field in which I have no talent whatsoever. Still, he lets me call him Woody, of course, only when we are alone.

You MUST tell me how I caught your attention and kept it for as long as I did. Think of it as furthering my career! You owe me that.

Most sincerely, Sidonie

      *   *   *

To Whom It May Concern:

Have you ever written a letter to someone knowing you really shouldn't? Have you ever told them exactly how you felt knowing they wouldn't understand? You probably didn't care, knowing you were never going to send it anyway. Well, Marc, this is the letter I'm not sending to you.

Last month I wrote and told you exactly what I wanted you to hear. It was written and posted with malice of forethought. I was trying to touch you, to hurt you, to somehow penetrate your duplicity. And you probably saw right through it. No matter. This letter is written for me, to release what demands to be released, and believe it or not, it's not all about you. I've tried kicking a tree but my slippers are not thick enough.

I could write to Terry. He would understand or at least sympathize. Very likely he would make light of it, try to jolly me out of the doldrums, help me climb up a few landings and look down with that distance we call perspective. I'm not sure why I'm not looking for perspective. I only know that you are part of why I feel so empty right now. I guess I'm just going back to the first of my disappointments. You. There are more.

Just what do you suppose is a doldrum? Some kind of dungeon? I picture it as the crypt of the Cathedral of Dejection, Depression and Despair. The great wooden doors only open for the pilgrim without hope, with no illusions, with dreams left behind in the dust of the roads that brought her here, on her knees, head bowed, spirit broken.

But back to those other disappointments .It seems I am not a great actress, not even good. And I actually thought I was a natural! I perform well enough off stage, one on one, especially with other non-actors, most especially if they are male. *If I could charm with my less literary conversation how much more could I do with the words of a master! Especially if they come with stage directions!!* It seems I can't delve deeply enough into the author's words to make them my own.

Oh, I can do a credible love scene if the audience is satisfied with a lovely profile, eager lips, lush lashes, and an arched white neck. I am all that. But there is something missing when I am scripted. Maybe it's because I'm not able to forget for a single moment that I'm Sidonie playing someone else. I don't want to be someone else. I love being Sidonie.

It's not a bad thing to want to be exactly who you are. They call it "To thine own self be true." I think "they" is Shakespeare. But I'm down on Shakespeare right now. So I'm not about to give him credit of any kind. Being true to thine own self might even work for me theatrically if someone wrote a play about Sidonie Adair. I suppose I could find some young fledgling playwright and charm him into writing about me exclusively. But it would be a short career for both of us unless he never tired of writing about me, and audiences never wearied of seeing me take my bows. But inside I'd know I'm simply not an actress - one of several things I'm simply not. Let's list a few.

To put it simply I'm not the actress who will make audiences think they are hearing for the very first time by a fresh new character "A rose by any other name would smell as sweet".

I am also not the painter who will create a tear so real it rolls down the canvas and spills onto the museum floor. Sorry, Sister Rose.

And I was not the woman who could make you forget all other women. Sorry, I had to accuse one more time.

Yes, of course. I understand. White neck, moonlight, how could you not. My neck is fairly white, and long enough, but somehow not enough. Oh well. But I did love you, Marc, the way you walked into a room and sent it into a hush, the way everyone leaned your way and listened for that clever comment or cutting remark, the way you forgot them all when you looked up and saw me.

I loved you up close when no one could see or feel you but me and the cabbage roses in your wallpaper.

But I hated your generous mouth the night it couldn't choose words carefully enough not to hurt.

And I can't understand why you never followed me to The Back of Beyond. So many times I looked down that rutted little road to Kildare Hall and pictured you standing up in the open carriage and waving hello with your homburg.

I still love you, Marc. A woman, has to love her first, or the moment will be remembered as less than it was. And it was a lovely moment, the moment I slipped from wondering to wonder. I can even remember the in between. I can especially remember the in between.

If I don't send this letter I will have no where to put these feelings, to wash away the ones that hurt. I will have to find a waterfall and stand at its foot. I <u>will</u> have to watch the rush, the gush, the surge, the cascade from top to bottom, the plunge into the darkness below. My disappointments will plummet with the water. My pain will crash against the rocks, break into little droplets and disappear into the river. Below the surface my droplets will fuse with other uncaring, unknowing droplets and together they will stream into other rivers, picking up momentum as they lessen their hold on me. In the ocean they will collide with a whale that will suck them up and then spray them out into the drying rays of the sun.

But it's winter and the falls of Minnehaha are one big frozen cascade, like the biggest ice sculpture in the St. Paul Winter Carnival, if only the falls weren't in Minneapolis. The two cities enjoy a delightful rivalry. If you ever had come to visit me in Minnesota I would have explained. We would have laughed about it. No, it's Terry who would *have laughed.*

Is your heart frozen like the falls, Marc? Or am I the only one frozen out?

Questions, questions, questions! You get no answers if you don't send a letter. But this is the kind of a letter that would blister my cheeks reading it even a few years hence. My God, I'm embarrassed already. I said "hence." Only Shakespeare says "hence" any more. Did I tell you I don't like Shakespeare so much anymore? I may not be the greatest actress but I have a nose for false prose and melodrama. And you do too. You _too_ would be embarrassed, Marc, receiving this letter.

Once you found me delightful in my innocence. You touched me as if I were a gardenia, you know, the kind that turns brown at the edges with too much fingering. You touched me gently, with regret, knowing that the beginning was already the end.

It feels good knowing I will never send this letter. I can be as excessive as I want to be. I don't want to be excessive just to be excessive. Although, in general, I believe the secret to an exciting life is excess, too much whipped cream, too much chocolate, lots and lots of delicious regrets.

I just want to say what I feel in the strongest words I can think of. I want to gush like a waterfall, to pound the rocks like it is their fault, and to have no one say in a voice dripping with sarcasm, "Poor little wretch! How tragic for you!" Tragic is an excessive word. Thinking tragic will not wash away these feelings; but then again it can't hurt.

I can hear you say, "Time washes away everything. Time heals all." Yes, you might use that cliché. You are not above clichés, at least according to Terry. In case you didn't know, he is not your biggest fan. You never sounded like a cliché to me, but then I never listen closely enough to word choices. I'm always too caught up in the feelings the words inspired. My feelings are ever eager to be called to the surface, too eager, maybe not so eager anymore. You were never a cliché to me, even if you weren't the first to except when you used a swan as a simile for a woman's neck bending in the moonlight.

Still I'm not going to wait for time. Time is a man. Father Time they call him. Father Time and Mother Nature. Well, it's not in my nature to wait. I had hoped this letter would help me to move out from under these disappointments or at least to strike back at them, to smash them into manageable bits and pieces. Maybe if I were a better writer. Damn, one more thing I'm not. What am I then? Who am I? Who is this person I like so much and know so little about? These are questions you, of course, can't answer, even if you were to actually open this pretty envelope with its lovely watermarks. But then neither can I, not just yet.

Love,

Sidonie

P. S. I'm not really "Your Sidonie". I could have been yours forever if you picked your words more wisely - or simply kept your mouth shut - or better yet - saved the moonlight for me and me alone. But then who would that Sidonie be? How would she have turned out? I'm starting to ramble. I'm being redundant. I need editing, but never from you, no longer, not any more.

P.P.S. That last line sounds decisive. I like decisive – Never - No longer - Not anymore. Those words make the letter worth keeping and re-reading, from time to time. Better not seal the envelope. I'll just tuck it in, put it to bed and wake it up later. Or not. I get to decide. I could even mail it and wonder how you would look when you opened it and if you would read it to the end, to this last sad little period. It feels like there should be a string of periods, like tiny teardrops, even though I am not about to shed a single tear for you. All right, one last indulgence . . . .

P.S. Not sending this means the next time I see you I can say, "Marc, so nice to see you. You must take me to dine." And I can pretend you have left no marks.

106

Chapter 20
Blame it on Shakespeare

"Clare!" The voice catches her in the middle of a frustrated sigh. She had been fretting about Sidonie who has yet to join the line of debutantes waiting to descend the stairs to the ballroom. That voice, that breath on her ear ends thoughts of her daughter way before the exhale.

She moves a little forward and steadies her hands on the marble balustrade of the garden terrace where she has fled to cool her anger and frustration. There is an imperative in that voice, a heat in that breath. It isn't that his voice is so loud or insinuatingly low. He doesn't have to raise or lower it. After all this time, the voice simply has it, the power to make her pause, ache, long, and move away, but only so far. Her breath is coming too fast.

"Marc." She turns around to show she isn't afraid to. "I didn't know you came to cotillions. Of course, you heard Sidonie would be at this one. She's late, probably nervously primping. With practice the socializing gets easier. But the dancing is more challenging as time goes by." She flicks open her fan and pretends fast footwork has put the flush in her cheeks.

"Come!" He crooks a finger and leads her down the stairs to a little white pavilion. From the open doors of the ballroom, the music follows them across the dampening grass. "We have never danced." He smiles over his shoulder.

"We were never in public."

"We aren't now. This is a nice dark little corner of a very bright world. I like dark corners."

She should be insulted, but she isn't. She should pull away, before he reaches for her, as she knows he will. The shadows work their mystery on his face, adding elegance to his nose, and deepening his lips. But it's the yearning in his eyes that roots her. It's a feeling she recognizes all too well. These eyes have looked for her on the balconies of opera houses, in a passing carriage, on the arm of her husband. They have been looking across years, across lovers, even past her daughter, beyond her daughter. Clare knows. She has looked too, for so long. She expected it to one day be over, to wane and fade, like so many other of life's pleasures.

It doesn't matter who moves first. This is not surrender. This just is. They move together as if the same warm wind was coming at them from opposite poles. Because of them the wind becomes warmer, becomes a swirl of impatient lips, trembling hands, suddenly bare shoulders, and a fallen fan.

He only pulls away to look at her face and laugh with delight. "Clare." But it's when he kisses her hands, her gently-aging hands, the tops, the knuckles, the inside of her wrists, that she knows she is lost.

*   *   *

Sidonie looks around at the other young women waiting dutifully in line. For her part, Sidonie has never been good at waiting, particularly for an odd performance like this. She pulls at her hair and realizes one of her white gloves is missing, probably dropped while she was wandering around the garden putting off the inevitable. The glove itself is of no consequence. She has so many gloves and they are interchangeable. Her mother taught her that trick. Always purchase the exact same kind and you will never be at a loss. If she didn't need it for the promenade down the stairs she would simply go gloveless, unashamed of any nakedness. The wayward glove may be hiding in the bower of white roses next to this little white pavilion. There's also a wind at her back. It seems eager to help her glide through the overreaching ferns. Or so she thinks. Actually, it's a mischievous wind, maybe even a little malicious. And the moon is in

108

league. Its light is bright enough to illuminate that dark corner and that long white neck.

"Marc!" Sidonie chokes on his name because there is no way she can say "Mother!" This woman with her eyes closed, her lips seeking, her hands grasping, is not at this moment anyone's mother.

They break apart slowly, as if denying this intrusion is actually happening. Their hands still want to stay on each other's shoulders, waist, wherever. Sidonie stands very still. She will punish them with her presence, with their sudden realization. When the passion is completely flushed away they will see who is watching them. She will stay still till the moment one of them can start a sentence. It's harder for her mother. Her lips are wet with his kiss. Marc takes a tentative step towards Sidonie. She shakes her head and walks slowly backwards. She's memorizing this moment and these two people. She will never forget, but she wants to get the details exactly right. Clare is wearing her anniversary pearls. Marc needs a haircut. The little white pavilion has some peeling paint on the bottom step.

By the time Clare manages a strangled, "Sidonie!" her daughter is being welcomed by a willow branch into the darkness at the far reaches of the garden.

Marc regains his voice. "Sidonie, please come back!"

But then what would either of them say?

*   *   *

Every time Sidonie sways, every way she moves, candlelight dances across the folds of her pale blue taffeta gown. And she sways often, trying to look like she can actually hear the violins over the bits and pieces of silly conversation assailing her from the across the ball room, pretending she not only hears the violins but is enjoying their too timid refrain. Her pain requires more than a plaintiff violin. The piercing high note of a flute might be closer to the intensity. And it would take a trumpet, no four trumpets, to herald the Sidonie she feels herself becoming. Two women directly in front of her have just embraced and congratulated each other on their married daughters. Now they are starting on their successful husbands.

"Any day now Gerald will go back to his bicycle. When his car runs out of gas he will have no idea how to fill it up again. And he's terrified of blowing a tire."

"That's what a chauffeur is for, my dear."

"Yes, quite. I'll have to remind him of that. But he will drive around alone. Says he likes to think. I think he's just practicing. I let him go alone. Last time the wind took my brand new chapeau."

Sidonie pulls her beaded cloche down over her ears as if it could possibly shut out the pointless chatter. A Juliet cap should be galling, considering her aborted theatrical career. But its seed pearls are brightening the dark night of her hair. And, more important, they are goading her on. Do you really want to be one of Shakespeare's stock heroines? Are you that willing to drink poison, stab yourself, be strangled or suffocated just because your leading man dies, or falls in and out of love with you? Is Lady Macbeth's duplicity going to determine your "to be or not to be?"

Two men with big cigars puff dirty smoke through her rhetorical questions.

"Isn't it terrible about the war in Europe?"

"Not as terrible as it might be. After all it's over there, not here. And Wilson has kept us out of it,"

"You wouldn't feel that way if you had to cut your grand tour short, like we did. All of a sudden all the French men were in uniform and the casinos were closed. Every good restaurant was shuttered down. The cafes that were open only served potatoes and fish. My wife had the vapors. My daughter did nothing but cry. And I never had a chance to win back my losses. We got out of there on the first liner we could book."

She waves the smoke and their provincial opinions aside. Neither one of them has mentioned the real costs of the war, people's lives ending, civilizations crashing down. No concern is being expressed for the treasures of the Louvre as the German army plunders France. She's always dreamed of going to Paris and living in a garret and meeting Monet. And now none of that is possible. Will any art be left when the war finally ends? And what of the poor dear French people? She knows from reading Bovary that they are men and women of great sensitivity and real passion. They must be suffering so.

Clare Adair is across the room, in resplendent gold, set off beautifully by the red velvet drapes on the French doors. She has straightened her dress, patted her hair into place, and wiped her mouth. Anyone seeing her would guess she is wishing and willing her daughter a successful coming out. They would expect her to be mentally repeating the advice given over and over during the fittings.

"Stand up straight. No, not in the ballet position. But do move your hands and your head as if you were dancer. Ever so slightly incline your head to the man being presented, but don't offer your hand. You are a debutante not a courtesan." Imagine, courtesan coming from Clare Adair's lips.

Sidonie has played a courtesan, but Shakespeare provided the dialog and he never made small talk. If she's going to get through tonight she must make small talk. Small words, small ideas! Still, under lowered lashes, looking up, the little words can take on deep meaning. Before she disappointed the Bard with her interpretation of Bianca, she said whatever came into her head. I was deflowered by Flaubert in the branches of an elm tree. No, that wouldn't work here.

Her cousin Elizabeth doesn't seem to be at a loss. If only Sidonie was standing next to her. Elizabeth just said something, just a few words and the young man in front of her is already bobbing his head in appreciation and straightening his cravat, obviously hoping she approves of him. He's talking longer than his turn. Now he's writing his name on her dance card. Looks like twice. Elizabeth has been asked for her little book and its little pencil over and over again. The young men all walk away in a glow. And it isn't as if she is wearing a sparkling dress. In white ruffles cousin almost looks washed out. The pink of the sash should be closer to her face. And yet her prospective partners will light up.

Sidonie might do better standing next to this charming relative who knows nothing about the tempest whirling under Sidonie's pretty taffeta blue bodice. Elizabeth won't notice the clenching and unclenching of her cousin's hands. She is too occupied with the gentleman next in line and the one behind him. With her help Sidonie might be able to pretend what's happening in this particular room in the next dreary hours is more important than what happened less than a half an hour before in a little white pavilion in a bower of white roses.

Now one of Elizabeth's *beaux* is in front of Sidonie. He looks expectant. "Good evening, Miss Adair. I am so happy to make your acquaintance at long last."

Should she say, *Charmed, I'm sure?* No, that sounds too affected. Should she say, *Then why didn't you talk to me first, before Elizabeth, Constance and Marion?* No, that would be *gauche.* She is tempted to say, *Did you enjoy the cake?* There is still a bit of frosting on his upper lip. He is looking back over his shoulder at Elizabeth as he absently says the next polite sentence in his script. "You must save me a dance."

She slips the ribboned dance book off her wrist and watches him politely write himself into the fifth slot. She knows what he's thinking as he walks away. *Only five?* She was late in line after all! No matter. Five are five too many, she's beginning to think, five opportunities to play a game that no woman can really win. He moved a little too quickly. Etiquette dictates that no woman should be left standing alone until the next man is moving her way. Sidonie seizes the momentary lull to rush over to Elizabeth and insinuate herself into a new place in line.

"Sidonie! I've been longing to talk to you all evening. We have both stood here long enough to fill our dance cards. I want to know if you have any different strategies for making the reception row more fun. Let's go and admire the champagne fountain. Mustn't drink, till the official toasts. We'll just walk around it, like so, clap our hands in delight, admire, and then slowly move back towards the French doors and slip out into the garden. I will be close, but not conspicuously so, behind you. Mustn't frighten the mothers with a mass exodus."

Yes! She was right to run to Elizabeth. She will feed Sidonie the right banter to maintain this little farce. Tonight it would be nice to be scripted. Blame it on Shakespeare. But no, not in the garden! Sidonie puts a finger to her lips to indicate she is more than ready to conspire, but points instead to the doors that lead to the library.

"Genius! Pure genius!" Elizabeth concurs. "Absolutely no one will be reading tonight. We'll meet there in five minutes time."

They are completely alone as they pull together two tall library chairs.

"Sidonie, Sidonie, Sidonie!" Elizabeth cups both of her cousin's hands. "I so admire you! And tonight you are in your element. The Debutante Ball is your chance to show off your dark brown eyes and your curly lashes. And then you cleverly crown your lovely hair with that Juliet cap! You are pure confection."

Sidonie slips off the cap and offers it to Elizabeth who runs to the mirror over the fireplace and tries it on. Elizabeth primps. "Now I look like that piece of confection. I'm under the glass of a candy counter waiting to be put into a crisp white bag, then carried home and devoured with a *cafe latté*. We are all that you know. We don't get to choose. That's what it's all about. All we can do is watch and look for someone we would like to choose if we could and make them think they will die if they can't have our white chocolate skin and our gumdrop-red lips."

Sidonie has to smile. She's played that game before. She has risen to that occasion, when inspired by a handsome prince. The problem is when kissed once too often by two many princesses he turned back into an ugly frog. She joins Elizabeth at the mirror and adjusts the cap to its best angle. Sidonie can't help noticing that without the distraction of the nest of pearls she is all eyes, deeper and darker set than usual. There are smudges under her lower lids that are not makeup gone astray. But, thankfully, no tears, not even the smallest vapor.

"It's better on you!" Elizabeth returns the cap to Sidonie's head. "I guess I'll keep relying on charming conversation." Elizabeth smiles at Sidonie's reflection in the glass. "Before any social event I make a list of eight subjects to talk about, like travel or the opera. It's even better if you include a topic a man might like, say, horses or better yet, horseless carriages. Begin a conversation around any topic and I guarantee you, he will be so grateful you started the flow, that empty facts or figures, meaningless opinions will gush out of his mouth. Then all you have to do is nod yes, laugh and admire his wit. Meanwhile you look him over, he looks you over and before you know it you're on to the next one."

Sidonie has already overheard the horseless carriage conversation. It only ends in negatives. Everything ends in negatives in these conversations. *Bad idea. Never last. I'll lose my hat.* Still she nods and encourages Elizabeth to go on.

114

"Let me show you how it goes." Elizabeth takes up position in an imaginary reception line. "I say,

What a lovely watch! Is it Swiss?

He answers, Elizabeth lowers her voice,

As a matter of fact, I got in Geneva.

Oh, you've been to Geneva?

My family always summers there.

Oh, were you there this summer?

No, not this summer, the continent is too unsettled.

Explain "unsettled" to me. I simply don't understand politics."

It's not politics that Sidonie would be asking about. It's the Louvre. Monet. Rembrandt. All those works of art, all those lovely works of art in danger of destruction!

"Did you notice, Sidonie, how I gave the fellow every opportunity to instruct me, to exhibit his superior knowledge of the world? Did you hear me hold my breath waiting for his answers? You must have seen my eyes turn misty and how I lightly touched his arm. Believe me it works"

Sidonie nods again. She's having enough trouble staying in her own character tonight. She really can't see herself pretending interest in any war except the one going on right now inside her.

"And there are endless variations, even with the simple watch motif. Try asking, *How many jewels are in your watch?* That gives him a chance to brag about how expensive his watch really is. Follow up with *What watch company do you consider the best?* Then he can show off his expertise."

There is a round of applause coming from the ballroom. Sidonie is guessing the orchestra must be about to start the next dance set. Elizabeth seems to agree. "We better get back in and try out our conversational gambits on our dance partners. But you haven't shared any of your strategies."

Sidonie's thinking that going back into the ballroom will keep her end of the bargain she's made with Mumsy. In the garden she had promised herself never to call her mother anything but Clare. But in this farce she is playing with Elizabeth, Mumsy is more in character and more ironic. She is beginning to appreciate irony. If Sidonie quit acting, Clare would pay for acting lessons, followed by a coming out at a debutante ball, instead of on the stage. Looking back, it makes no sense at all, unless you are devious. And make no mistake, Clare is devious. Sidonie pauses at the doors to the ballroom, tilts her head and puts a finger on her pretty chin. She's thinking of Saint Brigid's. She's thinking The Back of Beyond. She's thinking Montreal. She's thinking of being moved on a chess board far away from Marc when their love was white hot. She's thinking Clare is a player and a pretty skilled one. She's thinking checkmate. She's thinking apples falling not so very far from the tree. She waves Elizabeth to go ahead of her out the now half open doors. But Elizabeth foils her by looking back just as Sidonie slides her dress off her shoulders.

"What are you doing," Elizabeth gasps. "You're going to tear it."

Sidonie laughs as she caps a bust of George Washington with her Juliet and shakes her dark hair free of all polite restraints. She pinches her cheeks, licks her lips and really smudges her eye makeup. It's a dramatic effect. Elizabeth understands that. After all is said and done, a picture is worth a thousand words. Those dark features against that white skin say it all - that and the tactile intensity beneath her hooded eyes. Sidonie lifts the edge of her skirt to the opening bars of the next Strauss. She sweeps through the doors, seemingly all hips and hair. Almost casually she has rearranged all the emotion and feeling in the ballroom. Every head turns. A hand goes to a woman's mouth. A knife cuts through a man's heart. Suspicion and regret linger in the charged air. And Sidonie, the dutiful daughter, really comes out. More Irony. Delicious irony. No one, not even Clare, can resist the glow of wicked joy.

Lucifer was one of the most beautiful of the angels. He was named for the glowing light of his being. She can't remember exactly but she knows the root of Lucifer is the same as luminous. She feels luminous, white hot. But surely it will not last the night. The feeling, though, is powerfully wicked, and who's to say it can't burn beyond tonight?

Chapter 21
Just Shy of Tears

Sidonie had never been to California. She had never even thought of coming here. No Monets or Braques to seek out. No Shakespearean tradition to follow. And a lot of other places would put even more distance between Marc, Clare and the girl Sidonie used to be. She is in California for one reason only. No one would possibly think to look for her here. There is talk now that President Wilson may finally take The United Sates into the war that rages still in Europe, and that young American men may be forced to enter the armed forces, and she worries about what may become of Terry if that happens. But what can she do in this enchanting landscape a continent away?

This is one of the most beautiful valleys in Southern California. She is surrounded by the five miles of rising and falling mountains and foothills. The Chumash Indians considered it sacred, named it Ojai after the moon, and held peace talks close to the sky. She's here because of a brochure advertising a free lecture on a Sunday afternoon when she has nothing to do. Actually, it's a week of free lectures by an East Indian man who promises peace. She's not really looking for peace, just an excuse to be somewhere else. These days she always wants to be somewhere else.

Sidonie appears peaceful enough as she lies on a soft slope and witnesses her first Pink Moment, that moment when evening begins its fall over the valley. The closest mountains and hills are deep purple. The ones farther away lighten into lavender. The sky is a linear rainbow of darker to lighter pink stretching up to that Ojai moon. Her mind is too scattered for pretty pink contemplation. She's still unnerved by the one thousand people who gathered here early this morning. They were all too eager to be told what to think and how to feel by someone they hardly knew and had no reason to trust. But then his name did embrace the lunar name of this sacred place. And the brochure explained that Amalendu truly means "pure as the moon". Nicely put, if true.

Whatever the realities, at midnight they will gather again, this time around a great bonfire lit by their new-found savior. As firelight recasts their faces they will chant the words they were told to chant. This is your mantra. It doesn't matter if you had something else in mind. This is your word. By the end of a week of long lectures Amalendu has promised to reveal the meaning of life and how each and every one of them can make their own lives meaningful. How nice and simple for them! Simple as God is simple, simple as Sidonie is not.

After this morning's experience she did consider dusting off the back of her black skirt and returning to Los Angeles and her little rented room. But the man of peace had thrown down a challenge she could not resist. Before she leaves she has to wipe that sickening serenity off his too handsome face. To her it is less serenity than complacency, the complacency of a man who has yet to be tested. Mary Magdalene might have felt that way when she first met Jesus. There must have been a time when she considered being his first temptation. That might be fun, she probably thought, and now Sidonie has to agree. Sometime this week, maybe tonight, she will find a moment to draw out, draw near, and play the Magdalene.

It's an easy enough game to play. In her relatively short life Sidonie has played several of its variations. She's feigned ignorance to get a man to look into her questioning eyes and see how beautiful they are. She's even faked a tiny cry, lost her balance, and pretended to need a strong arm so he'd discover her soft shoulders and petite waist. She's been known to make a fellow feel as strong as Hannibal and as wise as Solomon.

Amalendu is more of a mystery. A moat surrounds him, a moat dug deep by the twin shovels of mystical belief and personal magnetism. Those who peek over the edge do it at their own peril. It's much too easy to lose footing, fall down and drown in his being. Sidonie knows she can swim to the other side. Her strokes are powered by pain so strong it has come to feel like pleasure. She's buoyant with revenge so satisfying it's as close to ecstasy as she has ever come. Still, she feels his magic.

Voltage dances on his thick black hair parted just right of center, falling back in two asymmetrical waves behind his well-engineered ears. Magic nestles in the cushions of his lush lips. His nose has no angles, falling in a long smooth line and making only the smallest curve down over neat nostrils. But it's his eyes that make her want to get inside his head and see what he sees. He's always looking up and beyond and finding the view just shy of tears. His dark eyes seem full of moisture, glistening black, then brown, every once and again streaked with silver. She can see no pupils, unless they are contained in those strange circles within circles that suggest depth of being. Real tears would be glorious, especially if they were for her, even better if he is really as deep as he appears to be.

Before she works her magic all he'll want of her is another handmaiden. He'll expect her to break the surface of his lake like a raindrop and be visible for only an instant before disappearing into his still-as-glass surface. But when she bids him *adieu*, as of course she will, he himself will be pulled under. And then what will he find in the depth of his being? Neither peace nor serenity, she sincerely hopes.

She's finished loving men who can never love her intensely enough or long enough to really know her and touch her where it matters. She wants to feel life for herself, not filtered through someone else, how he sees her or admires her, how much he wants to draw near. Forget how much Terry loves her curls spraying across his face and tickling his nose. She's going to savor the wind in her own hair. Let Marc walk closer to the street so a passing car or a prancing horse won't splash the girl or woman beside him. Sidonie will paddle through her own puddles. And she's not about to wait for this holy man to ask her to come and follow him. He will be told, convinced, and swayed, before left bewildered and bereft.

*   *   *

She sits under the farthest tree with just enough of the midnight moon to light her face, with just enough tension in her body, to let Amalendu notice her attentiveness. Still, she asks no questions. She nods no nods. Ever so often she moves to a tree with less light so he will not see her when he takes a second or third look. Although she is farther and farther away she can tell by the lift of his head and the squaring of his shoulders that he has happily found her yet again. As the crowd disperses he finds her at the crest of her favorite slope looking at the stars. Her back expresses no particular interest in him whatsoever.

"Miss Adair? I'm told your name is Sydney Adair. I'm told this is your first visit to one of my camps. And that you came all the way from New York. Should I be flattered?"

"Sidonie. Three syllables, not two." She corrects before turning. He's asking about her personally as if he doesn't know or care that she is heiress. His people would have found out about that. Truth to tell she's probably disinherited by now.

"Sidonie!" He pauses over each syllable, as if he has just made it his own lyric mantra. "Charming! I understand you are an artist, Sidonie." Music again. His voice is lyrical. "I take it some level of success has allowed you the freedom to travel to California?"

"Oh I just do sketches, just humble sketches. I have a certain, what would you say, leverage, I guess, that motivates my family to underwrite my travel." She could have looked down and feigned modesty, but it's more fun looking him straight in the eye while she cavalierly dismisses her little talent. She wants him to know that being Sidonie is quite enough.

"Sketches, like haiku, can be snippets of insight just waiting for further reflection. Think, my child. Is that what your sketches are really about?" The circles within the circles are trying to suck her in.

"Snippets, yes. Insightful? You'll have to tell me." Now she's holding his eyes with hers. He hasn't heard about her theatrical experimentation. Just as well.

121

"We must know our own worth. We must never err on the side of false modesty."

"Modesty is not usually the side where I err." Sidonie takes one step forward, not waiting for permission to move into his radius.

He doesn't step back. "You're right, of course. Modesty is a worthless virtue. There is really nothing to be proud or modest about, is there. We are all only channels, channels for snippets, channels for earth-shaking ideas. We receive. We pass on. That's the plan. If you don't pass on you turn into a clay cup, a cup in danger of being dropped and broken with the wonder splashing down on barren ground."

"I never thought of it that way."

"That's why I'm here. That's the message I am channeling. We all serve the Purpose. The Purpose opens us, urges us, and enlightens us while passing through."

His brown hands are arresting, first folded together like a prayer and then opening in a benediction. Are there benedictions in his religion? She bends her head as if he is the Host raised above her congregation of one, as if she is unworthy to look at that golden circle. The chant of the choir is floating upward on a cloud of incense. He can feel it. She has him believing in benedictions. He wants to bless her hair. He wants to see her eyes again. Still she can't resist an irreverent question, even if risks the mood she is so carefully establishing.

"What about the cup people?"

"They simply don't count. Some are destined not to count. You want to count, don't you, Sidonie?"

She smiles more to herself than to him. I do believe. *Clap. I do believe. Clap, clap. And there are fairies in my garden and stars that grant all my wishes.* "Of course!"

"I know you want to count. I can hear it in your voice. The voice is where truth lies. The voice never changes as time goes by, except to deepen, to come more slowly, to express ideas with greater deliberation. Eyes can betray much more easily, especially when they are young and beautiful." He looks away and finally steps back. "Forgive me. I need the darkness of my room. I need to pull the draperies and withdraw behind them. Tomorrow morning many will want more from me than I now have to give. I need to fill up and to clear away, not an easy thing to do even in this beautiful setting, especially in this beautiful setting."

She looks at the trees, at the mountains and the hills, at the moon as if she doesn't know she is the most important part of that setting.

"Beauty is a puzzle within a conundrum." He steps still farther away. "It delights the senses, touches the soul, but distracts, confounds, and seduces."

"Of course, you must gather your strength." She whispers as if he were already in his bed, under silken sheets. "I will stay awhile and meditate under the open sky. You have opened so many doors, suggested so many possibilities. I am already changing, and it is just a little frightening." Now she lowers her eyes and offers her lashes.

He knots his hands together. Is that a tremble? He inclines his head. Is he hiding a smile? Softly he walks away and leaves her to her stars. She doesn't look over her shoulder to see if he is looking over his. She doesn't have to.

If he were Marc he'd be blowing a kiss. If she were the Sidonie she used to be she'd catch it with her right hand and touch it to her lips. Old habits are hard to break, but not impossible. Sometimes they can be usefully redeployed. She's experienced romance often enough. She's enjoyed its spontaneity, its unpredictability. But a calculated romance might be even more interesting, especially when she is the one moving the beads of the abacus. Sidonie waits until Amalendu's disciples circle and pull him inside before skipping her way to bed.

A man slips out of the shadow of a carved tribute to one of Ojai's earliest settlers. With his black hair, dusky skin and dark clothes, part of the statue's shadow still clings to him. He's been crouched behind the hand-carved American Indian woman long enough and closely enough to know her story as well as that of the couple framed in the light of the moon. Behind the drape of her robe there has been time to admire the proud lift of her head and the graceful bend of her elbow. She's been balancing a water vessel long enough to darken her oak to an ebony hue. Caught for all time in the performance of what must have been a daily chore, she radiates the beauty and dignity that comes from within, for no one else's benefit, except, of course, the master carver's, and now, years later, that of the shadow man. Although, it seems to him that posterity is the last thing on her mind. Her eyes are fixed and looking only as far as a companion tree.

He's become quite fond of her bare feet. They have to be dusty on the bottom. A practical woman, she'd made no attempt to hide her naked toes under her robe. The folds are tucked up and over the cord at her waist, so she can move freely through water and across the land. He likes his long-ago lady better than the female who was just basked in the magnificence of this holier than holy man. So much less artifice!

Amalendu's woman has a more deliberate way of dressing. Her black gown could be a nun's if a nun pulled her rosary belt tight enough to show off a slim midriff and tiny waist. Her black boots have no buttons or bows, but display clearly enough a fine arch and a trim ankle. And she knows exactly what she's doing standing with her legs that far apart. No one stands that close to a man unless she knows him well or wants to.

Still, the man left her alone beneath a darkening wood. "Sorry, Amalendu , that might have been your last chance."

He doesn't really feel sorry. Empathy is one of those useless emotions that get in the way of living the unfettered life. They frequently foul up things that need to be done. And speculating about someone's right to live is just as fruitless, pointless, really. Justice and honor only exists in the mind of someone in the need of a proper rationale. On occasion retribution can make some sense. It keeps things balanced and in order. But when all is said and done, remuneration is all that really counts.

To him this is just another job. But that doesn't mean it shouldn't be done with care and thought. Surveillance is step one in the process. How good is protection at special events? When and where can distractions be expected, distractions that would momentarily relax precautions or just make a person look the wrong way? He's learned one thing tonight. Amalendu does not insist that all women keep their distance. And this particular woman is not about to walk ten paces behind anyone.

Shadow-man tips his hat to his barefoot accomplice before losing himself in the forest of the night. It is one of those foolish gestures he permits himself when he feels anticipation in his step and an itch in the fingers of his right hand. He used to feel this every time. No matter. A professional doesn't count on adrenaline. As always the job is a process. And the true professional trusts the process. That trust will lead you to the right time and place. Here is too open, few places to hide, and longer distances to run. The time and place will come.

Chapter 22
Curious Companions

Sidonie insists on wining and dining him before he speaks to "the new crop of believers." New York is her town and she knows where to get the most American of salads, The Waldorf. Amalendu never before had apples in his salad or walnuts, for that matter.

Crop of believers is an oddly rural expression for a sophisticated New York woman, but then Sidonie is full of contradictions. He and she are curious companions. She is so worldly and he likes to think of himself as above and beyond. Still she seems sincere in her exploration of his faith, as fascinated by the messenger as the message. He has to wonder if it's the fascination of a cat for a mouse. But at this moment he is less concerned then content. The buns are warm, the honey sweet, and the light from the crystal chandelier is flashing through the cut glass bowl. Golden shards are criss-crossing the linen tablecloth between them. Sidonie looks lovely in pure white silk. He's never seen her in anything but black or white. There are no colored jewels on her ears, at her throat or around her wrists. She wears no rings. She just is.

He congratulates the white-gloved steward on the wine. Says it has true clarity. He has no idea what that means, but he has a knack for parroting phrases that impress an American audience. Precious little wine was served at his father's table. And there was never a tablecloth. He drinks lightly of what flows so plentifully in the Western World. Man looked to for wisdom must never stagger. Almost sounds like Confucius if Confucius had a sense of humor. Wise men may joke, never holy men.

He smoothes his napkin over his lap like she did when first sitting down. It's already smooth, but it never hurts to appear fastidious. He takes pride in his long fingers and keeps his nails freshly buffed. Holy men must always have clean hands, hands always worthy to touch the sacred. And when their hands are raised or waved the lightest of light cologne must flavor the air. He prefers fruity scents, suggesting harvest, plenty and renewal. Flowers are only temporary and merely ornamental. Flowers suit Sidonie. Today her perfume is white. Her hair is full of gardenia. The top of her dark head is just the right height to brush his nose.

Sidonie's telling him about the specialty of the house. Chateaubriand is prepared for two and served on a single platter. The man cuts it delicately thin. The woman feeds him with her fork. Between bites they toast or kiss. How does he like his steak?

Still on the cow Amalendu replies, softening it with a half smile. He must not embarrass her.

Sidonie smiles an *of course* before turning to the waiter. She'll have the filet mignon, medium rare. Seems she isn't that easily embarrassed. And a dish of asparagus with no sauce. She closes her menu, folds her hands on her lap and waits for him to decide. She's interested in his choice but not about to make it her own.

He likes when she asserts herself. Curious companions, indeed. So that's what Chateaubriand is. He'd wondered. His experience with French is limited. He will have to remedy that before Europe. She will come in handy in Europe. Right now he's not sure what to order from this confounded menu, but with the waiter hovering he is not about to ask her.

She loved the pasta the last time she was here. Has he anything against tomatoes? She has a way of lightening things, sweetening her audacity with a playful poke.

A tomato sauce is fine, he responds in kind. A tomato is a blameless fruit. Mushrooms are a contemplative sort of plant. And green peppers cleanse the soul, more than yellow, less than red.

She takes a cherry tomato from the antipasto plate, pops it in her mouth and closes her eyes as she bites down. A little juice flows out on her upper lip. She laughs again as she blamelessly tongues it off.

He has a feeling he wouldn't even be offended if it were steak juice. Nothing about this woman offends him. Nothing whatsoever. She brings delicacy to everything. She is a touch of fog, a glimpse of mist, the blur of a ballet dancer. She even listens delicately. He wishes this table wasn't between them. She always moves in close when he speaks as if she doesn't want to miss a word. He finds himself speaking even lower just to hear the swish of her petticoats, to smell the top of her head. She is delightfully undisciplined. It is wrong to play games with her. He will have to meditate on the why, why he does it, why remembering it gives him so much pleasure, why he has yet to sleep with her, although she seems willing enough. It shouldn't be a woman's idea. She should just acquiesce. The pasta sauce drips to the right of the Wedgwood cup, a cup so very proper, so very English, so very Western World. With one finger he pushes his saucer an inch over.

More coffee she asks? They have trifle here. Mother used to have an English chef and they had it every Sunday. Of course, she got the dish without the sweet sherry. But the layers of custard, fruit, sponge cake and whipped cream (Sidonie closes her eyes at the memory) were intoxicating enough!

No, please, he doesn't want any dessert. The pasta was heavy enough. He mustn't let the blood rush from his head to his stomach. Tonight his message must pass through him clear as the air, brisk as the wind, as cool as a fresh fallen snow, as pure as a virgin's breast.

She's not afraid to meet his eyes. She'd probably answer the question if he asked. But it doesn't really matter. Are the Seven Wonders of the World less wonderful the second time around? A holy man always looks for the wonder, never looks away when he finds it. Sometimes it's the top of a mountain, sometimes in a cloud of hair.

Just as often the wonder is reflected in his own eyes. He likes to look deliberately and directly into the eyes of a follower, so intensely that they are the first to look away. They imagine even more meaning in his gaze. And perhaps there is. He is only an instrument after all, a vessel, like a cut glass honey bowl sending golden shards across a linen table cloth.

Every night, each morning he meditates for more meaning and deepening understanding. And there are those times when comprehension enters and exits in words he never intended to say. Sometimes the meaning flees when the eyes keep looking for more, when they dare to search, when the only recourse is for him to look away. Now with Sidonie across the table he finds it's impossible to look anywhere else. So brown, so luminous.

Yes, a cup of coffee would be a lovely ending to this gracious meal. No cream and no sugar, thank you. Nothing must dilute the deep brown. He stirs the brown into rich waves. One wave nearly clears the cup. He lays the spoon across the saucer where it can cause no further harm to the linen. The linen is ivory, not white. At first he thought it was white. Ivory is almost nicer, more sunny, more warm.

*   *   *

No matter what the time of night, the stage lights of New York are never dimmed, but Amalendu remembers that burned out bulb over the back entrance to the auditorium. This is not the moment to be alone in a dark corner with the fair Sidonie, even with a chauffeur and body guard on duty. All too discreet, they will step out of the car, turn their backs to the car windows, and secure the streets. So instead he directs the driver to the front entrance where a crowd is already forming. Mustn't disappoint them he explains. He will see her later. He runs a finger down her cheek. She will want to freshen up for the lecture, won't she? He wants to straighten the yoke of her dress for her, but, of course, he doesn't.

At that more private door a man watches in frustration. He's just to the left of the naked bulb he's been unscrewing for the past two nights. Damn! This would have been the logical entrance for a personage with less vanity and more caution. He puts the gun back under his coat. There's something familiar about that woman. Could she have followed all the way from California? More likely there's one in every temple. He turns and heads for the bright anonymity of Broadway. It might be better to do this in Paris anyway. He has friends on the police force and places to hide in the French countryside. The war has everyone's attention focused on the Western Front.

That will make it easier for someone in his line of work to go about his business. And, of course he'll want to celebrate with a glass of real champagne. Besides, he wouldn't want his bosses to think this was too easy. Now where's that cigarette case? Good thing the light bulb is out. The silver would glow and betray.

Chapter 23

The Scheme of Things

Amalendu has looked at her, off and on all through tonight's lecture, almost as if he is checking her reaction, almost as though he's seeking her approval. Has she chosen that scarlet sari just for him? He's already taken her hand and led her from one cloud to the next. Soon he will want to fit her tiny piece of the puzzle next to his in that big scheme of things just over the horizon.

She's learned the art of not being seen, but always being felt and without hiding behind a veil. The trick is stillness. Gestures are small with hands close to the body, near the breasts, just a little away from the hips. Fingers move slowly as if caressing a kitten or savoring a rose or pulling lace off of a shoulder. There's never a full smile, only a tease at the corner. But the eyes, the eyes are always watching, understanding and memorizing, should this moment suddenly end.

Before he knows it Sidonie will be his touchstone.

A man at the back of the room has a question. The volume of his voice implies confidence. "Master," he begins, his salutation telling everyone he is about to ask something of great moment. The audience goes respectful with him. Two hundred chairs scrape forward across the wooden floor boards. The sudden surge reminds her of a lovely day on Cape Cod.

She was carrying the picnic basket back to the carriage, when the wind tore the scarf off her head. As she ran back across the sand to capture the illusive bit of silk, a flock of gulls swooped down. Wings flapped and shrieks were frantic. Each bird wanted that tiny crumb of golden sponge cake bouncing across the sand. They didn't hear the rumble of the waves foaming on the beach. They didn't feel the sun baking the feathers on their back. All they could see was the crumb. All they could think about was its taste. Not to be left behind she too leans forward. It's a small move as all enticing gestures must be. It's a small move because her body must not think her mind has lost control. She balances herself by holding on to the underside of the cane chair. A small smile to herself. Her whole body understands, feet as well as hands. Once her feet loved the twirl, to feel life whirl around her, to let the people in her life send her on a merry dance, to let fate blow them all merrily round and round. Now she prefers the circle, to encircle the people in her life, to circumvent their plans for her, to make them pirouette to her music. She is the wind. Fate is being buffeted. Life is being redirected, misdirected if she feels like it.

"Master," he repeats himself in what Sidonie recognizes as dramatic emphasis, "do you, like Jesus Christ, expect your followers to leave their homes and families to come and follow you?"

It's not the deferential question Sidonie expected. It sounds more like a challenge. But then she sees the two women, the young one clinging to the arm of the questioner, the old one hanging on his every word. Amalendu has to see them too.

He pauses, puts prayerful fingers to his lips and half smiles. "Different souls have different callings at different times. Look into your life now. Who are you at this moment? How far have you come? What people live with and through you? How have they benefited from your past experience? How will they benefit from your growing wisdom? Will they support your search for truth? Some will want to come with you. Some will fall away. Some you will have to leave behind. But remember we begin our journeys from where we are in the time and space from which we are called. There is something worthy about who we are and where we are or we wouldn't have been chosen. Build on, shore up, before you wash away."

The man at the back of the room has no response. Does he have permission to walk away or doesn't he? No matter, his question gives Sidonie hers. She stands up, holds onto the chair in front of her and pulls the air in her diaphragm up and out. "Do artists have a special call?" Her voice projects well, her question is clearly stated, and

Amalendu is surprised, surprised enough to annoy. She adds even more substance. "Do their works reflect the Ultimate Truth? If not, should they?"

Amalendu recovers quickly. A frown was just about to mar the clear skin of his forehead. He never frowns in public. To his people he is Serenity itself with his smooth black hair, gently formed features, long, lean hands and melodious voice. His message soothes his people, sending them into the depths of meditation without uttering a mantra. That's why they come, for the calm, for the peace, for a sky with no clouds, no sound of thunder, never a streak of lightening.

Then why does he look to her for these occasional lightening strikes, for these few moments when he can feel her inner turmoil? There's a storm inside her, a whirlpool that cuts deep down into her soul. It's his calling to calm storms and to still whirlpools, never to be pulled in. But resisting is part of the pull, the delightful ying and yang of having Sidonie close by. She stands there with her dark eyes focused only on him. Her breasts, her waist, her hips defy the sari that for generations has protected men from women. He wants no protection. If he let himself, he knows, he would enjoy being swept away. Someday he will have to calm her, but not just yet.

Sidonie can feel his eyes on her body, can feel his mind confusing his temptation with hers, can feel his heat even as she feels her own. Yes, she feels the attraction. He is a beautiful man and a deep thinker. It's an intoxicating combination. A beautiful man, a discerning man finds her intriguing. She's already played a lovely game of words with an author. There's an artist who loves to paint her. But this is something new, a spiritual man who is reaching out for her spirit as well as her body. Yes, she can feel that too and it's not that easy to dismiss, to move past, and go on unchanged to yet another man. This is more than a game.

"Lovely. You have answered your own question, Miss Adair. Their works, if well done, can not help but reflect. A better word than reflect is channel. When you are connected, truly connected to the Cosmos you are like a honey bowl reflecting golden shards across a linen table cloth, but only with the inspiration of the chandelier."

Lovely. He said lovely. She would have preferred brilliant. Lovely is a word for a woman, a pat on a pretty head. But she is lovely and so is he, body and mind. Why fight that? Together they are discovering each other, what fits, what needs tempering. Quiet. He's still talking. She doesn't always understand him the first time through. Lyrics are lost in the melody of his voice. Rachmaninoff comes to mind when he plays those deep, dark variations. Or maybe she is too intent on what she is going to say next or not going to say next.

"An artist channels when she loses herself in her creation, when she is no longer holding the paintbrush, when it is moving on it's own, when the strokes are unexpected, undirected by her conscious thought. An author channels when he is totally surprised by the next line in his poetry, the unexpected rhythm or rhyme. The potter channels when the vase comes off the wheel with curves not anticipated. All true works of art have already been created by the Universal Consciousness. Humans are merely conduits."

Being "merely conduit" isn't an idea that appeals to Sidonie. She doesn't have to agree with everything. She smiles, says thank you and gives up the floor to the others.

*   *   *

"Pull over here," Amalendu directs the driver.

It's a park. It seems they are not going directly back to the hotel. The night is chilly. She wishes she'd worn a warmer, less diaphanous scarf. Gossamer glows but throws no heat. . .

"Come." He says it again. And then, "Wear this." He carefully unwraps the silk scarf from its place at her neck and after a long pause places a shawl over her shoulders. Sidonie watches his eyes linger at her neck, and her head tilts just slightly. She allows him the moment. Cashmere. She knows cashmere. "I need air, open and fresh air. Do you mind?"

"No, it's a lovely night." And a lovely shawl, some might say. She fingers the weave, looks down at the color. In the moonlight it looks dove gray. It could be blue or even green, fairy colors that change with a passing cloud. She hasn't worn color for awhile now, even the muted ones. Colors try too hard to please. Black and white say this is me, just as I am, with no apologies. Still, tonight the scarlet revealed the luxury of her real aesthetic sensibilities.

He leads her through the trees, to the top of a hill, where the lights of the houses below make her feel too safe, too closely held. At least the homes are at a distance. The space between them and her makes her feel free and unfettered. To be held, to be free, there is a part of her that wants them both. Still.

His hand is on her shoulder, smoothing the cashmere. "Am I wrong? I sense that you are a born seeker. I sense that you have searched before and will search again. I find myself wanting to give you something to carry with you on your journey."

"I can think of no better compass." She gives his hand an approving pat. She can't resist adding, "A truly lovely lecture, truly lovely. Thank you for allowing me to watch and learn."

His head shakes once, ever so slightly, only noticeable if you are watching. Sidonie knows he is shaking off "lovely." He doesn't like it either.

Amalendu is getting more and more confused about what role Sidonie Adair will play in that plan. She knows he is. She adds to the confusion by steering the subject around an adjacent corner. It's too soon, too easy for commitment.

"I love your books." She looks up at him. I've learned so much from them. And I will learn more as I re-read. But I'm not an intellectual. I tell you that, not because I think you don't know, but to let you know that I know who I am. I learn by feeling my way. I learn through the people I touch and who touch me. Sometimes the lessons come from rash judgments, mistakes, mishaps, and sorry messes." It's a confession, one intended to intrigue, rather than seeks absolution. He must know who she really is to fall really hard, for it to count.

"Yes." Amalendu concedes. "Mistakes are a way of learning, a very human way, but it's the long way around, don't you see? My way is a short cut, a celestial shortcut."

She sees a bench. She wants him to sit down next to her, close enough to smell her perfume. But the stone looks cold. He snaps his finger and the driver comes out of nowhere and warms the surface with a blanket. The other man, the one who rode in the front seat passenger side, stands at a close distance, his hands straight at his sides. Amalendu waves them both away as he doubles the blanket over. More cashmere. They are sitting in a nest of cashmere. When Amalendu hears an automobile door shut he turns to her waiting eyes.

"Tell me your story," She moistens her lips. "How did you find the way to your world?" She's heard journalists question where he was born, his father's occupation, his higher education. All are looking for the fact that will reveal his Achilles' heel, the chink in his armor, the skeleton in his closet. He's ready enough with those answers. But none have posed it quite this way. And none of them were pretty young girls looking up adoringly. Pretty young girls are often satisfied with a fairy tale. Not Sidonie. She takes his hand. It's presumptuous. It's irreverent. But it's all he needs.

"I had a twin brother. We were identical twins in everything but temperament. He was always a little faster than me. He always reached a little farther. I was comfortable with that because his hand would always reach back for mine and pull me up with him. When he died, I realized he had gone too far to take me with him, just yet, anyway. He was uncovering the mysteries of this life and the next while I stood there wondering why the spikes on his climbing boots hadn't held fast."

"I always wonder how fate decides these things," she continues. "Are we meant to learn by losing someone? Do we become stronger standing alone? It doesn't seem quite fair to the one who dies just to teach us a lesson. But then maybe fate arranges those things to dovetail. The twin lost has completed his mission. The twin left is boosted up a rung in his unfinished climb."

"You think about these things, Sidonie? At your young age I would not have expected it. But then you must have lost someone significant to you in death."

"No one close, unless -" She pauses and pulls the shawl close. "- unless you count the death of dreams."

"And what dreams died for you?"

Now she has him intrigued. She laughs with a measured modicum of sadness. Her arm is this close to touching his. She leans away and lets him feel a breeze come between them. "My old dreams are unimportant. I want to know more about you." She wonders, but does not add - "And what you think of me. Just now, you started to miss me, didn't you?"

She gets up and walks towards the automobile. He's left to follow. Moonlight reveals how smoothly silk can mold the curve of a hip. A cloud passes over the moon and adds tease to temptation.

Clouds are like wishful thinking, only a wisp, little more than a prayer, but how well they protect us from reality's relentless glare if we let them, if we trust them, if we dare to dream another dream. With luck the wind will reunite her and her cloud. Right now she must walk fast and be his cloud, just a little out of reach. He must begin to realize that this will not be his decision after all, and maybe it never was.

The bodyguard expects the footsteps coming from the park bench. His focus is directed at an automobile coming slowly over the next hill. There's not much traffic in a park at this time of the night, especially one person traffic. This one person has just parked and is lighting a cigarette. Happy to have his charges safely inside the automobile, the guard jumps in, slams the door, and points at the road ahead.

"We just may have company."

Chapter 24

An Auspicious Moon

She's looking out the window from the back seat passenger side of Amalendu 's long black automobile. It's another day, another lecture, another ballroom at another fine hotel. But it's Paris where nothing ever becomes every day, especially along the Champs - a different landscape, momentous buildings, women dressed in the latest of styles.

It's late 1917, and the Americans have joined the war, and the numbers of dead young men seem incomprehensible. But the effect on Paris comes mostly by mail. Everyone knows or is family to one of the casualties. But still Paris life goes on, people come and go, they look busy, they somehow look unbothered. The men look dark, and the women seem casually, offhandedly stylish. And Sidonie herself has become exotic. She's chosen to wear a sari today that is a rainbow of colors, and dangling, tinkling gold bracelets. She likes the sound, the feel and the way it all draws his eyes. She smiles, but only to herself.

Most of her life Sidonie dreamed of living in the capital of the western art world and of the garret where she would paint with oils and cook with real French garlic. Montreal was close, but so North American. She imagined the delightful way that garlic would fuse with mauve and fuschia. But here she is breathing instead the incense imbedded in the pores of a holy man from India. She wanted exotic and she is getting it, folded into, around and over her like the shawl he told her to keep. She pulls it closer around her shoulders. It wants to fall off. It really doesn't belong, but it is part of the image she has assumed to please him. Sharing his clothing links her with his culture, imbeds in her soul his deep beliefs. Or so he thinks. For now she'll let him. For now it amuses her to be in costume, to wear the sari, the dangling rope beads, and the slave girl bracelets. All she needs to complete the package is a long bath in a pool of myrrh. She'll never cover her hair. She twirls a lock out of the carefully constructed upsweep of her hair. A tug turns it into an errant curl. Errant feels good.

The women strolling the Champs are in their own costumes. It's called French couture. The certainty that they are in fashion adds assurance to their steps and condescension to their glances. Given a chance to walk past those tall towers, through those grand arches, down those winding promenades, she would be just as *nonchalant.* Her dress is exotic enough to be next season's trend. She is a natural *Parisienne.*

She pronounces French well enough, when she speaks slowly. And speaking slowly means people watch you longer. Longer works for Sidonie. It's a harmless game. And the universe will lose nothing if she plays Emma Bovary for just a moment here and there, now and then.

She welcomes being someone else, somewhere else, and the country can't be too foreign. Here in France her mother would be *ma mere*, her father *mon pere.* They would be an entirely different set of parents. That is, if she ever talked to either one of them again. She has nothing to say to *Mere.* And *Pere* needs an explanation she is not going to be the one to give him.

She can pull off Bovary if she puckers her lips, talks through her nose, and bats her lashes.

Amalendu is laughing at her. There is delight in his low laugh. With her nose pressed against the glass she is a child seeing the world for the first time. He likes the child in her. He generally prefers his women unsophisticated and uncomplicated. Not to disappoint him, she feigns a giggle as she rubs a pretend smudge off his otherwise pristine car windows. "Sorry," she says. Then with a toss of her hair she complicates, adds sophistication, and lets him know she's not sorry at all. She knows he likes her that way too.

Paris for the man in the shadows is more business than pleasure. At the moment he is taking practice aim through the branches of a potted tree.

There are two, one on each side of the darkened entrance to *L'Hotel Paris*. They are pathetic trees, not really real. Real trees grow tall out of an uncaring earth. The sun can nurture or burn them out. It all depends on the rain. Is it constant or occasional? Real trees survive whichever way the wind blows. His is a pampered tree - trimmed into the artificial symmetry the French love so much. It's just full enough to hide a slim, dark man in a green overcoat, collar up. He quietly spits a leaf out of his mouth. The aftertaste is fresh, almost like mint. He mouths another, on purpose this time. Headlights brighten the sidewalk. Better early than late. No. It's the wrong car. He spits again.

Amalendu is pointing through the windshield at a temple. It seems they have one in Paris. That is probably where he is speaking again. He smiles and nods. He feels comfortable communicating with her *sans* words. She is moving up in the ranks of his followers from faithful to intimate. You're intimate with someone when you talk with a look, a gesture, the smallest touch. *Disciple* is a few more sunsets away. She loves sunsets. But they are hard to see in a city of tall buildings, unless you are on the top of one or gazing down stream on the river wending its way through. So far there has been little chance of walking up or down her favorite place. Face it. She wants to sightsee. She will always be connected to this world, to the earth, to plaster, to cement, to marble. She is not interested in meditating into the blank space of her mind. Her mind is never blank. She doesn't want it blank. Amalendu says she must choose a mantra. Saying it will clarify, focus. These days she prefers some things blurred. If she must have a mantra, M-u-m-s - - - M-u-m-s - - - M-u-m-s - - - comes to mind. The letters have a calming sound. Babies say the letter "M" first and then come to associate it with a loving, protective mother.

Clare laughed when she found her baby girl hiding in the back of the closet, with every necklace from the jewel box wound around her little neck. A few years later they both laughed at Papa when he came back from work carrying a brown cane with his black suit. They laughed at those who bet on the horse with the best track record rather than the prettiest name. They laughed even harder when Blue Hyacinth came in first. Pretty memories. Too bad her last image of Mums blocks out the rest, Mums with her eyes closed. Mums with her mouth open. Mums with white, bare shoulders. Mums's definitely not the word. A mantra's not supposed to make you laugh. And there's no irony in mantras. And Sidonie doesn't want her mother to be even a hum in her life.

It's more than growing up and away and after a time coming back again. Most mothers and daughters are in tandem all through life. One is up at one stage, one is down at another, the see-saw may even level off at some point. But this will no longer be true of her and Clare. Not after Marc jumped on Clare's side and sent Sidonie soaring off into space. She came down hard, but not hard enough to run back for comfort. It seemed only logical to keep running forward.

No, it wasn't really logical. She was propelled forward, compelled onward. Logic never had a place in her life and it never will. No matter who or what takes her off course she will never ask for directions or look back. She's come to realize that she will always find within herself, the urge, the intuition, the certainty.

Oh good! They're here. She recognizes their hotel with its potted trees. She's going to scoot over Amalendu, jump out first and wrestle the door away from the man running toward the car. She will be the one to hold the door open for Amalendu. With her eyes cast down she will bow, just a little, in the lovely deferential way of his part of the world. He will see what she wants him to see, how far she has come in her reverence for him. He will shake his head at her lack of decorum, but his eyes will be committing her to memory. He too knows that this is never going to last and for that very reason it is all the more delicious.

*   *   *

If the All Hallowed One follows his pattern he will exit the automobile first. Like royalty no one can sit before he reclines, no one can leave before he takes his. There have been other assassinations of holier men in places less open than this one. This prophet should know better. But then, they all trip up on their own holiness. They see their reputation as a shield. Their bond with their God is their armor. Heaven assured, they never think of death. This one has only one body guard and a driver. The driver will probably open the door. He waits for the front door of the automobile to open. The gun is cool in his hand, cool, as he is eager. *Ready* might be a better word. He hasn't been eager for a long time.

The doorman is certainly eager as he runs from under the canopy. He trips twice on his way to welcome the arrivals. He is coming alone. Seems none of the other hotel staff feels the need to protect their illustrious guest. An auspicious moon, a caressing breeze, a lapse in imagination deludes them all. The doorman has reached the back door of the automobile. He is positioning himself behind the door to make himself unobtrusive, as all good doormen must do. He is also making himself less vulnerable when the door opens wide. That's fine. Only an amateur sprays an innocent bystander. And the man with the gun is not an amateur. He must make that opportune shot before the driver and body guard stop looking up and down the street.

He always takes the surest shot. It doesn't really matter that he can hit a fly on the bark of a tree or the stem of a brain under a fall of hair. And in this case there is poetic justice in stopping this particular heart in mid-beat. A man's mind may take a false turn. He may think something is right when it is not. Reason is fallible. False reasoning can be forgiven. But a man's heart is true to his best or worst instincts. And

143

this man is true to the Devil or so it is said. Not that the gunman cares. He's playing judge and jury only to amuse himself. The inevitability of it all is getting boring. Not good, never good to be bored.

With both hands he steadies the gun. He finds bearing down works best.

The back seat passenger door bursts open and lights the surprise on the doorman's face. It also reveals in the dramatic sweep of a long robe. The brightly plumed pheasant is taking flight. A branch must have cracked. A stone must have broken the surface of a pond. Something made his prey move with less than usual serenity and lower to the ground. The hunter is forced to fire with no time to aim, just close enough to stall the bird in mid-flight. The second, surer shot will be the clean one as the bird flutters in panic or goes into a slow, rolling fall.

A soft green shawl falls off small shoulders. The smoke from the barrel turns the green into mist-grey, makes the small shoulders smaller still. A lace petticoat pulls up and over patent leather slippers as molasses brown curls break free all over the sidewalk. Two bracelets chime against each other before they clunk into silence against the cobblestones. There's still a smile on her face and light in her eyes as if she thinks she stumbled, as if she about to make a joke of the exuberance that sent her bounding out of the car off cue. It will be a joke at her own expense. She looks like that kind of girl. Her hand knows better. It's moving towards the blood coming out of her upper body. He hopes it's her shoulder or her arm. He hopes he has only clipped her wing. Maybe she will fly again. He doesn't know why he should care. She just cost him a kill. Still, there is something about this bird that holds his eye, something lush, almost tropical. Pretty, indeed, and yes, he's seen her before.

*   *   *

This red is too bright. These days she likes pastels better than primary colors. But it does seem her palate is constantly shifting. If she could really paint she'd probably be

144

an impressionist. Nice soft colors. Muted shades. Blurred lines. Like now. Every thing is wavy as if she were underwater. She could break the surface if only her arms would flutter or her feet would kick. Black is nice too, all encompassing. It devours other colors.

*   *   *

The automobile pulls away from the curb, as of course, it would. The driver must first and foremost protect his charge. The body guard has jumped into the backseat instead of the front. The gun fits nicely into the base of the potted tree. Time to execute Plan B - deflect the blame.

"Get an ambulance before this woman bleeds to death!" He yells at the doorman who is still cowering behind a car door that is no longer there. But then he probably doesn't understand English. The thwarted assassin tries again, *"Le docteur! Le docteur!"*

His handkerchief is bloodying from what has turned out to be chest wound . Too bad for her, but not bad for a hurried shot.

She's figured it out now. She's pressing her hand to her breast. "Amalendu?" She winces, feeling the pain for the first time. Sometimes it works that way. This can't be true! It's not really happening! That's what they all keep telling themselves. Just hold on to that thought, pretty one. "Amalendu?"

*   *   *

Amal . . .Amal. . . Amal. . . That would make an even better mantra. Why did it take her so long to think of it? Amal would love it. Where is he? For better or worse, he is supposed to be in charge. If his God is not on duty, his retinue of followers should be keeping them safe. Who is this man bending over her? He's not part of that retinue.

145

But he has a lovely arch in his dark brows, even when he scowls, even when he yells. Why does he keep yelling? "Le docteur! Le docteur!"

"Je suis un docteur." A gentleman pushes through the crowd in response. The gunman gets up and steps away. An engine is rumbling. The black automobile is back at the curb. The body guard leaps out, scoops up the girl and yells something Hindi to the driver. Probably something like, "Get us the hell out of here!" She's still looking at him. Her eyes are focused on him. Her mouth is about to say "Why?" If she lives she will remember him.

If he only he still had his gun. And there is Amalendu, big as life in the back seat, with the window all the way down. There would have been enough bullets for both of them.

Plan C – clear out.

*   *   *

Where is she? Where is her shawl? It's still on the sidewalk. It's blowing away. And she is floating, up and away, farther and farther away from the man with the dark scowl and the loud yell.

Chapter 25
Only Just

Two men come from opposite sides of a dark street. They both skirt the lamppost and choose the second bench on the path leading into the park. The older man sits down, lights a cigarette, and speaks his mind.

"Bit of a blunder, my friend – a cross continental blunder. You could have killed him in California or New York. Why France? I know, I know. You have more contacts in France, but that's no - "

"You know what they say in France?" The younger man stands still, his only gesture a slight shrug.

"The French say way too much for my taste. And with too many frills." Older man takes a deep draw on his cigarette. His hand is weathered but steady, like a seasoned sea captain steering through a storm.

"The French say very simply, '*C'est la vie.*' " The younger man's words are light, but his voice holds just as much purpose. He's been through his own storms and not in the safety of the captain's bridge.

"But, this was supposed to be about death, not life. Righteous Wrath was quite definite."

His salute is crisp. "You are absolutely correct, Sir. And no one hates to disappoint a client more than *moi.*" He kicks a rock into a bed of flowers with a kidskin boot. A white rose loses two petals.

"Mustn't forget the Organization that sold your services. It's just as disappointed. Satisfaction is guaranteed. Paris getting to you? Too much night life? Not enough?

You're beginning to sound too *blasé* for our occupation. As a matter of fact you look too *blasé* for our occupation. Just coming from the symphony or a fancy dress ball? Mighty delicate shoes!"

"The secret to our success has always been appearing to be what you are not and, just as often, appearing where you are not expected. And these shoes move as quietly as a ballet slipper. Besides, I have an idea that may please our vengeful little league even more, if they stop being angry long enough to think it through. The Organization should also like it."

"I'm listening. But only just." He buries his cigarette into the ground beneath his riding boot. He hasn't been riding for five years, but he, too, knows the value of suggesting things are other than they are.

"Righteous Wrath doesn't really want to kill this guy."

"They don't?"

"They want to render him powerless."

"The dead have no power whatsoever."

"And there you and they would be wrong. The dead have tremendous power. In the memories of their followers they become more handsome, more articulate, ever so much more wise, and in this case, hallowed, saintly, and even godly."

"A martyr. Of course. But they are willing to risk that. They think they can find a saint more to their liking."

"That's only because they haven't heard my plan."

"And that would be?"

"Take the holy out of a holy man and what do you have left?" The younger man continues his small war with the roses. He picks up the wounded one and finishes it off. The leather of his shoe is soft but his foot is merciless.

"An ordinary man."

"Exactly."

"And how would you propose to do this?" The smoker lights his second. He's tired of pretending he doesn't need to suck to the nub. And he is losing patience with this conversation.

"With an apple, of course, an apple from a forbidden tree."

"And how do you propose to find this apple? The experts are still arguing about the location of the Garden of Eden."

"Oh, Amalendu has already found the apple. He may even have taken a bite. Only his God is not interested in Bible stories. Neither are his followers. But I have a feeling that eating this particular apple breaks some very important commandments in their belief system."

"This all sounds very intriguing. But to sell your hypothesis I need facts, like what kind of apple, if it's still in the tree or on the ground, and how we can prove he ate it before he throws away the core." He blows smoke into his young friend's dark eyes.

"We can if there is a snake in the garden." Young friend takes the cigarette out of the mouth of his elder and borrows a puff.

"Enough with the flora and fauna. Pretty soon you'll be talking about step-mothers and poisoned apples." He wipes off the wet end of the cigarette on the cuff of his coat.

"She's an American debutante and Amalendu is her coming out party. She's pretty, empty, and disposable. Yet she was not disposed of. When I shot her by mistake her not-very-wise man came back to rescue her, risked his life to come back for her. I know few men, especially those of his cultural persuasion, who would do the same. He wants this apple. *Sorry*. He just risked death to save her. He might even risk his reputation to enjoy her fruit. *Forgive me*. I just have to follow this analogy to its conclusion. A snake weaving around his ankle could trip him into an indiscretion."

"Perhaps your snake-like mind is twisting a little too much."

"You don't follow me?"

"Yes, of course, but will they?"

"Intrigue. That sort live for it. Plotting, conspiring, laying traps, oh, they will love it."

"And so apparently do you, my friend. I've never known you to waste time, energy or bullets on subplots."

"Choose the weapon. Find the mark. Shoot the mark. Dispose of the weapon. This job is turning out to be a little more challenging. I'm simply rising to that occasion." He fishes in his vest pocket for his cigarette case. He snaps it open and then shut. Only a few flecks of tobacco remain inside.

"Maybe you should quit. And I don't mean smoking. Maybe the jobs are getting a little too challenging. Maybe you are the one complicating them."

"Maybe we just need to be more creative. We might attract a more demanding clientele, even more money, the satisfaction of a challenging job done well."

"Satisfy yourself with the money you're being paid. It's substantial enough. That's what I do."

"Admit it. This plan is better than the original - with no possible risk of canonization or, for that matter, resurrection. "

"The fact is you didn't kill him. The mission was not accomplished. And he has been warned. Righteous Wrath really liked the idea of a dead Amalendu . At this point they may really like the idea of a dead you. Before they agree on a different route, they'll need to be convinced. Check and recheck your facts and all those assumptions that are dangling between and under the lines. A very messy hypothesis, it seems to me."

"I know exactly where she is. I can figure out how long it will take her to recuperate. And I can imagine how eager he will be to have her by his side once again."

"You said she was pretty, empty and disposable. He may have forgotten her already."

"Trust me."

"God, I hate those words. They have gotten me in more trouble."

"Not with me."

Senior partner in crime stands up, flips their shared cigarette and disappears into the darkness of the park. His backward wave is a resigned go-ahead. He's not really resigned. He simply sees no point in arguing. Righteous Wrath may or may not buy the new plan. The Organization may or may not choose the same man to make the revision. Till now his associate has done the job assigned with ruthless efficiency, deadly calm, and no second guesses. This second guess will be passed on, but it will rise and fall on its own merits. Life's too short to risk defending a risk-taker.

Junior partner sits down and stretches his legs. They don't feel all that junior. One day he will retire, one day when it's all a bloody bore, one day when a pretty, empty, disposable girl offers no mystery whatsoever. Perhaps her mystery is only her novelty. Young, naive, waiting to be touched! Maybe the mystery is in the man, risking everything to touch youth and *naiveté*. *Naiveté*! Damn, he has been in France too long. The moon's at his back as he walks into the street and wonders how untouched she really is.

He has this hunch, but you don't talk hunches with your contacts, even when he is your captain and an associate of long standing. You don't let anyone know how often you think that way, feel your way, and that it has always worked for you, although sometimes *only just. Only just* is where the fun comes in.

Chapter 26

Slipping Away

She can't see the scarf any more. She's stopped reaching for it. She just may be wrapped in it. There's something tight around her chest, but it isn't a soft adornment. It's rough, more like gauze. It's a bandage. Of course, it's a bandage. She'd open her eyes to verify that but floating in darkness still feels good.

She can hear people around her. They're whispering. It's almost like a prayer. They're probably praying for her to wake up and ask those predictable questions, "Where am I? What's happened to me?" She's always hated predictable questions, and being predictable is even worse. Besides, she's more interested in the answer to a question they can't answer. Just where was she in those slippery slivers of time wedged between fleeting moments of consciousness? She's close enough to the last sliver to pull it out, peer and poke at it. But it keeps slipping away. It's like waking from a dream, pleasant or unpleasant, doesn't matter which, and trying to fall back asleep long enough to find out how it will all end. She must hurry. But that wretched scarf is just about to skitter around a corner.

"Her hand. It moved. It's on her chest now." Aalendu is hovering over her. Seems he is still a part of the waking world, so apparently no one shot him in the chest. And it was most certainly a bullet. There was no knife handle sticking out of her chest. Something had to cause that blood and now this ache. So the bullet part is becoming clear. She was shot, she fell, she didn't die and now Amalendu is at her bedside. "Sidonie, please stay awake!"

But someone else had hovered, back there, before this bed and these bandages, before the slivers, someone with dark brows that arched, and looked so very annoyed. His eyes didn't want to meet hers. They were looking to this side and then the other, on the lookout it seemed. When he spoke it was loud, a command, with no inflection, and no trace of concern. Still she felt lost when he moved away. She knew him didn't she?

But from where and when, another dream? It was too quick, he was too eager to go. It felt like escape. He wanted no part of her. How did she know all that? The eyes under the arched brow were familiar. But who was he? She wouldn't care now, except she knew his ice all too well. It had clinked against hers. His had more layers. His had thawed and frozen over many more times. If she melted just a little, she might add another layer. It might be safer. She wouldn't be left behind, alone on the pavement. But no, she would not be melted down and frozen over. Not even to be safe.

"Water!" She calls out for water that is running free.

Amalendu lets go of her hand. Funny she didn't even realize he was holding it. It seems his touch had not risen to the level of awareness. Something had happened to her, somewhere between those moments of wakefulness. Something had shifted within the slivers.

"You are safe now, Sidonie." He's back at her bedside. "I will never let anything hurt you again."

As if he had the power. No, the Magdalene Game has played itself out. It was played before, lost and won before, by people who really cared, who died with the caring. What does she care about? Slivers of time? Layers of ice? Living? Yes, living. The drink is not cold. She lets the tepid water run down her chin and into the nook in her neck. She moves her lips together just enough to catch the few drops she'll need before sinking back into her pillow and letting go.

"She's slipping away. Do something!" He calls out to someone, probably the doctor or a nurse who is checking her pulse rate. She needs to get out of here fast. She'll concentrate on the black brows, the voice without inflection. There's distraction in a puzzle, abstraction in a mystery, relief in thinking of someone who never had, and never will have any control over her, except for the one instance he knelt beside her and pretended to care. There was no thaw left in him. Somehow she just knows.

154

It's nine o'clock. Visiting hours are almost over, especially for a holy man with an entourage. Thanks to an assassination attempt, he is surrounded by armed guards. Shadow man looks for a darker place to slide back into. He spies a space between buildings with its own spider web. No one has dallied here for some time, except perhaps a snake crawling low to the ground. He waits till the room lights go out and the halls are dimmed. Then ready or not, here he comes. He has to see for himself if she is well enough, pretty enough to suit his purposes, if she will need to be forced or will she quite naturally entangle herself in his silken threads.

She looked beautiful soaked in blood, but then blood is his favorite color.

Chapter 27
The Company She Keeps

He's been watching for awhile now and he is still interested. It can be boring, especially if the subject looks over his shoulder, ducks into a dark corner, and sends up the inevitable prayer, "Please don't let that man be following me." It hardly seems worth tossing your cigarette, grinding it under your heel and putting the damn fool out of his misery right then and there.

But a girl you've already wounded opens her hospital window and points her face into a spray of cold rain. Your eyes focus and you straighten up. You are not going to be bored. It's like the first time you unbuttoned a girl's dress or you took your father's rifle into the woods. Something's going to happened. If there were a cigarette in your mouth, by now it would be dangling.

He has to ask himself why in Hell isn't she more afraid? She pulls up the shade several times a day. Sometimes she lets the sun fall on her face. Inevitably someone in white pulls her away and covers the window again. He would understand if she stood at the edge of the window and sneaked a peek around. She must know the man with the gun could be hiding in the bushes or behind a tree. She should at least wonder. She certainly should be wary. Most people in her circumstances wouldn't be taking any chances at all.

Maybe she's just an insipid romantic. But, Jesus, she doesn't look insipid. Her hair is romancing her forehead and cheeks, falling here, than there in the wind and rain. But what is it with the way she closes one big brown eye when eating a chocolate or smelling a rose? Is she a child? Is she a woman? Is she a crazy mix? Really shouldn't make a difference. Really should just be an interesting footnote in a little more challenging than usual commission. She's supposed to be a woman of deep religious conviction. But she's never worn a veil since he first saw her with Amalendu. Yes,

156

that was her in Ojai and again in New York. How devout a follower could she be after the night the protective arm of Amalendu's God reached out only so far? Is she really that devoted to a cause greater than herself? Not much, he'd wager. He's never seen her modestly looking down, her hands making that little temple. Her head is held high, whether she's thinking or feeling. She gazes at the corner of the room or the edge of some cloud, often with her hair covering just one eye. The effect is diverting. For God's sake. From the expression on her face, the way her lips part and moisten, she's thinking of a man rather than a god.

She looks like someone who might see a man like him in the street and take time to consider him. He wouldn't penny her for her thoughts. He'd give her no chance to convert him. But he certainly wouldn't mind getting in close. Of course, she could just as easily look away. She could dismiss him without a second thought. He's dealt with ice princesses before. You can usually melt them with an intense glance or words so low their meaning can only be guessed. This one could keep walking, her gaze on that cloud, her thoughts on that man. He'd dismiss her first. That's what he'd do. He'd give her one quick glance, then look down at his pocket watch, then across the street at the pretty girl lifting her skirt over the curb. A woman who notices being noticed can't help take a second look. She's almost his then. Almost can be the best moment of all. Almost has never let him down. Then again this one could still walk away, her thoughts her own, her hair over that one eye.

She's less predictable than any woman he has ever met before. Of course, he's come to know her more than most. For two weeks now, he's watched her from behind a half-closed door or while walking down the hospital corridor in a white starched jacket. Tomorrow he'll wear a visor cap and set a vase of white carnations beside the bed of a comatose patient or one too sleepy to ask, "Who in the hell are you? And why are you visiting me when the woman next door sits on the edge of her bed, no sheet covering her toes, her ankles, her calves and her thighs." Today he is too far away to see those thighs. He is across the street, squinting through the afternoon sun at her window, second floor, third from the corner. And he's about to be rewarded.

157

There is movement at the window for the second time today, another cold day. Yet here she goes again. Her long, lovely legs are unsteady, unsteady enough that she has to hold on to the sill to fight a sudden gust. She's enjoying the struggle, eyes closed, lips slightly parted, dark hair blowing back from her face. He's past enjoying the wind. He dresses light on the job. He wouldn't want a wool coat to catch on a branch or a heavy boot to announce his presence. And gloves take the sensitivity out of a trigger finger. But there she stands in hospital cotton, with no detectable shiver. Is she that cool a customer or simply focused on what she wants at this very moment? He knows that feeling. He knows how it feels to be caught up in the doing, all the how that goes into it is just so much smoke and mirrors. There is a resolve in this young woman, and focus, if only she were more careful of the company she keeps. But careful does not seem to define her. Not careful of windows, she will be careless of places she goes. She's been in one room far too long. She'll move fast when she makes her break.

It's really not so hard to hit a moving target. You just can't be sure which way the body will fall. Sometimes that makes a difference. More often he just wants to know enough to control what will happen next. It works best to slip away in the opposite direction. The fall, the roll, the sudden stop hypnotizes the occasional witness. She would look lovely rolling down a hill, skirts pulling up, that look of wonder on her face, lost in the momentum before the pain comes through. Was that a wince? He actually for one moment felt the bullet intended for her. Probably just a reminder that he only kills on commission. Sidonie Adair is not actually on anyone's hit list. If he has to kill her, of course he can. Of course he can. But why do something for nothing?

He himself never rolled down a hill. Not even as a boy, at least not on purpose. He didn't like being dizzy, being out of control. He didn't slide for that same reason. Sleds can't be steered all that well. And, as his father always reminded him, it is better to keep both feet planted firmly on the ground. And so he had no personal experience with the kind of joy, enchantment or delight that sends children plummeting down a hill on their own volition.

Open that window farther and she just might pitch out. He can see the temptation on her face, anticipation of release with its accompanying joy, enchantment and delight. But he can't feel joy or imagine enchantment or remember ever being delighted. He's had his feet on the ground much too long. Oh, he can shoot well enough from a crouch if he has to, but he likes to plan things with the odds on his side. He rarely has the occasion to use those words in a sentence – *joy, enchantment, delight* – let alone feel them. Release, maybe.

There's release in a clean shot and a fast get-away. Once you sink to the ground, lean your head back against a brick building, and hear only your own labored breathing you feel that first flash of relief. But not until there are no footsteps behind you and no shouting from down the alley do you congratulate yourself on a job well done and another capture avoided.

Fear of capture comes from the pit of your stomach. Fear of failure is imbedded in your brain. These feelings he understands. The fear that comes from the heart, making you hold on fast to someone you love, has never been part of his makeup. There's no one he is afraid to lose. He can walk away from anyone, even if she has lovely long legs, a sense of joy and is not afraid of him. Of course he can.

He's having too much time to think. Introspection is the devil's workshop. You start seeing targets as human. You wonder about them. They become persons with plans for tomorrow. You know this is not the day they would choose to further your scheme. They'd jump out of a five-story building or race across a flashing railroad crossing if they knew you were coming for them. They'd kill you if they had a knife, a gun and knew how to use it. You move before the scream has left their open mouths. Never raise a crowd. Sidonie draws a crowd without even screaming. Just as well to use her existence to kill a man's reputation. That was and is Plan B.

159

Right on cue the nurse pulls her inside, closing the window and drawing down the drapes. The sun has fun with windows, especially closed ones. He can still remember what it did to the windows across the bay from his father's house. Every sunset his sister told him how much she longed to play in that house on the other side of the lake. It had golden windows. "Just imagine how lovely the little girl's bedroom must be!" As her big brother he looked forward to explaining the grass-is-always-greener theory. She would protest, then cry and he would feel superior. He only had to wait for the right moment. He knew he'd find it, if he were patient. Like when he pulled the dime out from under his pillow just as she searched in vain under hers. "Lucky for me," he had laughed, "The fairy can't tell the difference between a boy or girl tooth."

Little girls pucker up their faces just before they cry. They have no trouble feeling.

He waited longer to discredit Father Christmas. He needed another Christmas of feigned belief to get that ball and bat. He knew he could hit it high and out of the park. That he could anticipate. You flex a muscle. You strengthen a muscle. You have a talent. You excel. And his parents expected nothing less. He was their child after all. Everything came easy to them. Only later would their world turn to ashes. And so it would for him, easy, then ashes, but not just yet.

Women were a surprise. His lovely mother had told him so many times, "No one likes a scowl. It's like a cloud covering the sun." His successful father phrased it this way. "A man of few words is a man with fewer friends."

But the more he scowled, the less he said, the older he got, the more women seemed to see in him, imagine in him. They just never imagined he would tire of listening to them so soon or that the brightness of their smiles would eventually push him around a corner or into the mist. They would be left wondering if he had been real or if they had only imagined him.

Illusive is good, in his line of work. He'd like to sit down on that bench. But people on benches are noticed. They invite conversation. At the corner there's a newsstand. Maybe that's the place to loiter till she comes back to the window. Pulling up the collar of his gray coat, he goes for that short walk, all the while wondering why he doesn't just leave for the day. There is no real reason to watch her open a window yet again. The plan isn't to shoot her through one. And she isn't going to be getting out of the hospital for a while yet.

He's got a cigarette here somewhere. He pulls his hand out of the last empty pocket. He should quit reaching for something to occupy his hands, for someone to engage his mind. Every day life has become every day. Thoughts of her, interesting as she may be, can't really change that, not for long anyway.

This isn't like him. But it's true - he's always been a little out of step where women are concerned or in fact anyone is concerned. Most of the time he likes being different. His parents recognized his limitations early on, but didn't seem to mind them all that much. They were just as emotionally contained. What emotion they had they spent on each other. They fed him, clothed him, and educated him. They were not about to be bored getting to know him better. They knew he was odd, but then to them odd was better than boring. If his truth was always in reverse, like the image in a mirror, it was only a source of mild amusement to them. He'd learn soon enough. They couldn't be bothered talking to him about the puzzles he'd worked out for himself, like the difference between precious and fragile.

Life is not precious. It is just fragile. Life ebbs out of a body quickly, like air out of a child's balloon. One minute it is puffed up, bursting with its own sense of color and plumpness. The next minute it is a soggy piece of rubber stuck on a branch or caught on a bar over the gutter, not knowing what it is or why it is in shards. It has only a dim memory of being bright yellow, and that memory is slipping away. Why do parents buy children balloons that will burst and break their hearts?

He doubts if anything is really precious if precious is defined as being of lasting importance. Nothing lasts. Nothing is important forever. Thighs go back under sheets. Balloons burst.

*   *   *

She waits till the nurse leaves the room and then lifts her leg, sticks out her foot, points her toes, and with a twist of her ankle makes one of those discrete ballet circles. She's not as limber as she wants to be, even after her daily practice walks to the window. Standing is exhilarating, but tiring. She's definitely making progress. When she started out she had to steady herself on the edge of the mattress and then the bed post and finally the wheelchair next to the window. It didn't roll. The brake was always set. Now she can even make it to the door as well as the window without holding on to anything. Maybe not tomorrow, but soon she will get out of here, not home, home is an ocean away, and not really home anymore.

Home is just a wayside along a journey to who knows where. With him or not, home will have to be wherever she is free, unencumbered, and responsible primarily to herself. And that will feel like that first morning on your first trip on an ocean liner. The sea is gently rolling. The afternoon sun is heating your deck chair. Your own thoughts are more interesting than the chatter of fellow passengers. You and the ship are all that matters. The sunset is too beautiful to put into words and so you seek no one to share the moment. All is well as you are rocked to sleep in your berth, until the rocking is less gentle, and the water slaps against your port hole. That's when you jump out of bed and run up the stairs to an open deck. You feel the spray, you rock with the waves. You hold on with only one hand. You let go. Fate is tempted. Fate doesn't expect you to come alone in the night while all its forces are mustered against you. Fate doesn't like being surprised. Fate wants to surprise you.

For Sidonie, that's when she feels most alive.

She makes her way back to the window. This time she only pulls back the edge of the shade. The nurse is right outside her door. Shadows are puddling under the trees across the street. The branches are twisting over and under each other into a thicket. There isn't room for anyone to hide. Besides, it would be a scratchy hiding place. She can feel the scratches on her forearms. She can see the skin pucker, turn red and then sting. But that doesn't happen to predators. Their skin is protected by thick, coarse, gray fur. Fur keeps them insulated in all kinds of weather and no one can guess their age unless they limp. She will not limp when she walks out of here. She spreads out her arms, closes her eyes, and wills back her sense of balance. She is teetering only the slightest little bit. No one watching from across the street could possibly tell.

She knows he's there. She lets him think she doesn't know. Everyone says he shot her by accident. They are certain he's no longer interested in her. She got in his way. She saw his angry black brows. No, that was the man who called the doctor. She mixes them up in her mind sometimes. She mixes them both with the dark man in those dreams she had so long ago. Anyway she spoiled the gunman's shot. But for some reason she knows he will not shoot her here. There's no sport in it.

And so she is willing to tempt fate. What else can you do with fate? It ignores you most of the time, disregards your wishes, and sends your life into a spin. She used to like to spin. She still has a twirl or two in her. It just seems a waste of all the other things she might do – like stand on her own two feet, look someone in the eye, and say enough, no more. I'm done.

She retraces her steps to the bed. She moves more quickly now. Strength is there building, she only needs to help it along. Tomorrow! She can't wait any longer. It has to be tomorrow. The more nimble and lithe her legs, the more closely they will all be watching.

163

Chapter 28

Of Pomegranates and Persimmons

The woman standing at the door of the hospital room is not wearing white. She's not a member of the staff. With the shades drawn and the only light coming from the door behind her there's no way to tell if her traveling suit and matching feathered hat are navy blue or jet black. And her features are lost in the shadows. But Sidonie knows exactly who she is. It's there in the way the creature holds her head, high enough to make her as tall as she possibly can be and level enough to balance a pomegranate.

Hardly anyone ever notices how small are these woman's shoulders or how tiny her feet. Men open doors for her, but stand aside once she enters the room. Presence. It's called presence and today it is most unwelcome. Mother has to know that. And still she crosses over the threshold, her taffeta skimming the dust.

Sidonie no longer expects the hot fury that would ignite every time she smelled roses and thought of white pavilions. She can feel herself become colder and colder and it seems like a good place to live. She could put it to work in a chilling "What brings you here? The Grand Tour?" But why bother. What she says is, "Clare, how nice of you to come." Her eyes don't avoid, neither do they challenge. Sidonie is simply looking at Clare on the level, woman to woman. This is surprisingly enough to send her mother into an apology, but for the wrong offense. They are in a public place after all.

"With a little encouragement I would have come sooner. You ignored my letters. You never answered my cables. But now that you are being discharged someone must pay your bills and set up a place for you to convalesce."

"I have my own resources." A blanket shields Sidonie's breasts. As she lifts her chin and straightens her back it drops to her waist.

Clare tidies the bed with a sweep of her hand, before sitting down on its edge. "By resources I supposed you mean that Amalendu person. Is he coming to pick you up himself? I would imagine he would delegate that to someone in his extensive entourage."

"Everything is taken care of, Clare." Sidonie starts to move to the other side of the bed. It's an out-dated reflex, a ritual that has lost its meaning. She stops short an inch from the edge.

Her mother opens her purse, plucks out a tiny silver compact and flips Amalendu into the obscurity where he belongs. Then with an even tinier powder puff she reaches for her daughter's cheek, her obvious intention to rouge back the color.

Sidonie makes it a full inch. Competition or no competition, her mother is still trying to pretty her up, still trying to protect her from unsuitable alliances. And if she doesn't watch herself Sidonie will start defending the latest. She settles on, " He is a man of peace."

"More's the pity." Clare flips the compact closed and resists another urge, this time to fluff Sidonie's hair with her fingers. "My daughter wouldn't be scarred for life if he had taken a few sensible precautions. I can hardly wait to meet him and tell him just what I think!"

Clare doesn't like either way – if he arms his men he is evil, if he relies on his God he is foolish. She dislikes him before she's even met him. If she ever met him she'd have to choose between being rude or being a flirt. "Mustn't be rude, Clare."

"I'm never rude. Manners, courtesy, etiquette, are the sign of a true civilization. They come even before religion. Women have always known that. No doubt it was Eve who first told Abel to wipe the persimmon juice off his chin."

"She should have told Cain it wasn't nice to hit."

"Well, well. You still know your Old Testament. That's reassuring. I thought by now you'd be quoting other texts."

"I'm only trying to widen my spiritual experiences."

"He's a man, Sidonie. Just a man. You haven't met Mohammed on a mountain."

"Close enough."

"And just how close is that, my darling?" Clare looks her daughter directly in the eyes.

Sidonie can't believe her mother is still trying to shame her. They both know that the usual veil between mothers and daughters, the veil between expectation and pretense, no longer applies. And who cares? There isn't a care left in Sidonie and, certainly, no sense of shame. Shame never came naturally to her. And now it seems quite pointless.

Clare itches to slip the top button of her daughter's bed jacket into its loop, but then she'd have to lean across the bed and admit the distance between them. "That jacket would be better on you in blue. The peach only makes your skin look pale. Still it's a nice contrast with your dark eyes."

Sidonie wants to sink back into the pillow. This conversation has to end before Clare sees how physically depleted she really is. Mother Hen will really take over then. Sidonie needs to convey that those days are over, not because Sidonie has been hurt so deeply, but because she has healed so completely.

Clare wants to put a protective arm around her too quiet daughter, impossible if she doesn't lean across. "It's just, it's just that, it makes me so angry. If I could I would have kept you inside a glass dome to keep you safe. As it was I have tried in every way I could to keep away the dirt of the world. But you had to run through every dust storm. Ordinary men I expected. I even knew you'd somehow survive the ones I couldn't sweep away. But a man who thinks he is a god - he was not a danger I foresaw. I thought my Sidonie was more earthbound, that the only assaults would be against her body, not her soul."

Sidonie lets her talk, waits for her trip up on her own hypocrisy. It will be fun to see Clare realize her faux pas and fall flat. In the end hypocrisy always trips you up. You set up standards or at least you agree to the ones society imposes. Than the standards get in your way and you realize that you of all people should be above them. Your happiness depends on it. You deserve it. And so you skip along until you fall on your face at the feet of the poor fools still toeing the mark. The trick is not to toe the mark. The trick is to fly above it all, on your own cloud, and not pay attention to anyone on the ground below. Yes, that's it. Sidonie looks out the window. She knows her cloud is on its way and she has her compass.

Clare can't stand the apparent lack of concern. She reaches over and gives her daughter's shoulders an urgent shake. Nothing, no response, let go. "You should be afraid. The assassin is still out there. He's looking for his chance to get it right this time. If you were smart you would take yourself out of the line of fire. If you must follow Amalendu 's theology do it at a distance. Buy his latest book."

The acid wit. Sidonie's almost going to miss that.

"Here you lie in a hospital bed, with a wound that still aches and will ache every time there is a chill in the air and you still think your way is the only way. What will it take to make you stop for a moment and think instead of feel your way? Watching your own daughter on the edge of a cliff deluding herself that she has wings? Every mother curses her child with that scenario. What you did to me your daughter or son will do to you. I hate to be that predictable and I don't want to wait that long to know you have learned your lesson."

There are a lot of lessons to learn. Being careful is pretty elementary and even emptier. Clare must know that by now or why would she be back in her lover's arms?

"You think you know it all, now, don't you, Sidonie? Your study of metaphysics has made you the superior one. Your new religion gives you permission to flaunt every lesson your less enlightened mother has taught you. Yes, that's the insidious allure of that man and his scriptures." Clare again snaps open her purse, takes out a handkerchief trimmed in lace, and dabs at her eyes.

If only it were that simple, but it's fruitless to try to explain. There is really nothing bigger to hold on to – be it a divine plan, a faithful lover, or your own dreams. All of them are crutches till you learn to stand on your own. Seems Clare is the one still hanging on. "Let it go, Clare."

Clare snaps her purse shut, an edge of the handkerchief pinched between the tortoise clasp. She gets up from the bed and stands by the window. "Look at me. Look at the lines on my face. Look at the dust on my hair. You will lose yourself soon enough. Your body disintegrates a little every day. Every day you are closer to dust from which you came. There is time enough to be swept into Krishna's dustbin. Maybe there is a glorified body waiting for you, maybe not. Till then you must live as a woman who knows exactly who she is and goes after what she wants, not what some man wants for her."

Clare's right about that.

"I know. I've done it all wrong. I've told you the rules but not the reasons behind them. Going against the rules signals the world to line up against you. Obeying the rules puts the world off guard. Then you are free to do and be what you want."

Sidonie smiles for the first time and Clare knows she just left herself open for the perfect retort. "Unless you're caught in the act!" But no words come, just the smile, the infuriating smile, almost a laugh now.

"Well, I don't choose to stay in this stuffy little room one minute longer. Goodbye, Sidonie. As my mother used to say to me, 'God bless you and the devil take you.' " Clare turns in the doorway, perhaps just a little sorry for what she just said, even worse, almost meant. She buries it in minutiae. "I've been away from my home too long. There are crocheted doilies to starch and silver teapots to polish. And I am thinking of buying a little dog to keep me company in my little prison. He will sit on my lap and stick out his little tongue whenever I want him to. I will feed him strawberries and clotted cream. He must be a pug. Don't you just love pugs? They're so homely they're cute."

Clare hates homely. Sidonie knows that. Still she lets her mother have the last word. And for once Clare doesn't really want it. She wants a rise out of her daughter, a flicker of an eye lid, a twitch of the mouth, a head thrown back in defiance. Anything but that damn knowing smile!

There's nothing to do but leave, her crisp taffeta swishing its way back across the threshold. She takes little notice of the dark man walking up the entrance stairs. She expects him to move aside and leave the railing to her and, of course, he does. She doesn't expect him to stop at the top of the stairs and watch her stop at the bottom. She doesn't know he is watching her look up at her daughter's window, and make the sign of the cross. She wouldn't want anyone to see her do that. It's a silly superstition. But whenever she does it she feels something release in her chest and fly away, something heavy, something burdensome, something that accumulates when she isn't paying attention. It's also a thank you sign of the cross. Sidonie didn't ask how Marc was these days. And Clare shouldn't know. The truly contrite are supposed to repent.

169

The man continues to watch her as she straightens her shoulders and pats in place an errant feather on her navy blue hat. He's thinking it would be foolish to kidnap two beautiful women, but exhilarating to double the damages. Not one, but two men would be screaming out in the night. Exhilaration. How can you miss what you have rarely before felt?

Chapter 29
School Boy Games

Of course, she can't stay inside, not with Paris waiting. Her first excursion won't be a boat ride on the Seine. But there are parks near by, parks she can walk to on her own. Hardy perennials bloom there, nurtured only by the sun and an occasional shower. Those past few weeks in the hospital she was treated like a hothouse flower with heat and moisture carefully monitored. But now in his suite of hotel rooms Amalendu may be considering pulling out some weeds. His little garden row may have some undesirable foreign vegetation. He is a dedicated gardener. Cultivation is one thing. Pruning is sometimes necessary. But she prefers to do her own transplanting.

One of his female followers is always in her hotel suite, tucking her hair under a *hijab*. To a point the head scarf has been an uneasy accommodation to her host. And then there are the doors. One of his personal guards opens and closes every one she passes through, every inner door, that is. Today her legs feel strong enough to walk out the lobby door and keep walking. But she owes him a proper thank you. Today will be a test run only.

His people are gathering this afternoon in the hotel ballroom to prepare for tomorrow's prayer meeting. One thousand people are expecting to be moved and The Master is not above rehearsing. It seems he lives by the old Christian adage, "God helps those who help themselves." It's not that there isn't often a mid-meeting inspirational moment of reverie. She has seen that happen, has seen those brown eyes turn black and then gold, heard the catch in his throat, and watched his lush lips say words she had never heard him say before.

Even from her detached viewpoint it has been difficult to miss what appeared to be gentle lightning strikes that seemed to give the air around him a shimmering opacity. Those moments were diverting, and she couldn't help but enjoy his gift of drama. It came as an amusement for her while she her body healed and gathered strength.

This afternoon she has been invited to come to the rehearsal. They have a chair set up for her in a balcony box. It was easy to feign a headache, especially in this condition they keep insisting is delicate. And her constant companion was delighted to tuck her in and go and admire her idol with no distractions. But she's wishing now she hadn't lied. Her relationship with the truth has always been quite comfortable. She is not afraid of the truth. But she's not above taking the easy way out, although it seldom feels right. She just doesn't want an argument when she chooses to go on her own.

The park is a block away from the hotel. Before an audience of peonies and lilacs she tears her scarf off and watches the wind carry it away. She and head scarves have made their final farewell. Then she spreads her skirt, lets the wind tickle her ankles and thinks of Central Park. She laughs at herself. Here she is in Paris dreaming New York. Those two little boys throwing a ball could be Americans. That little girl skipping a rope held by her two little friends could be Sidonie long, long ago. Sidonie just might jump in and skip with her. Strawberry shortcake, blue berry pie, what's the name of your best guy? A, b, c, d, e, f, g . . .

The indulgent reverie closes her eyes, until she feels someone's standing too close behind her. Before she can whip around, hands bind her arms to her sides. The force tells her it's a man. She is pinned so close to his chest that she can't turn her head, but she can feel him laughing into her hair. Does she know him? Is this a joke? It's a bad one. "Let me go!" Her wrists are bound in a vise behind her back. The more she twists, the more it hurts. It's time to scream or pull away. One of her arms is suddenly free. The cloth is as soft as his hand is rough. It smells like hospital. The children are standing still now, their faces filled with wonder. They're watching a puppet show in the park. Now she knows who he is. He's Punch and she's Judy.

"Mustn't bite, Sweetheart." Little girls giggle nervously. "It's all right I won't let her hurt you. She just needs to go back to the asylum. Bad Darling, I've been looking for you everywhere." She can't open her eyes any more, but she can hear the girls running away. Where are the boys? Are they fooled too? The smell hurts. Smells don't usually hurt. Maybe in hospitals. This smell is making the world around her turn into a swirl of watermarks. She bites down harder on the cloth and wishes it was skin.

"Struggling will only make it hurt. Wouldn't want to hurt.'

It already does and she knows the soothing voice doesn't care at all. He's lying to her as surely and sweetly as he lied to the children, but she also knows for now she has no choice. Her legs are going and her fingertips are numb. Pretty soon there'll be no conscious thought. Already her mind's thinking more slowly. "Stop!" She groans into the smothering threads of his coat. He's carrying her now. She's going to die in a park in Paris and she can't think how to yell for help in French. She knows the word. She knows lots of French words, but they're all drifting away. And she was so close to running free.

He can speak French well enough, something like *Make way, my wife is faint.* No one seems to be stopping him.

*   *   *

The first sense to come back is her hearing. But all she hears is the rain, and a faraway clap of thunder. She's still in this world. She'd thank God if she still believed in him. There's a rustle of paper. Another living human being is nearby. Someone's reading a newspaper to pass the time till she wakes up. She listens as the pages are turned, folded and creased to read one particularly interesting article. That someone is, for the moment, not paying close attention to her. She pays attention to herself. She's lying down. Feels like on a bed. A hard one. Nothing's broken. Nothing's bleeding. Her ankles ache. Her wrists hurt. She's bound, but not blindfolded, and the drug has worn off.

But when she opens her eyes that person will know for certain that she's awake. She hopes it's not the man with the cruel hands. His breathing sounds male. Her breathing has probably betrayed her. You breathe differently when you are asleep. Females aren't supposed to snore. It spoils the illusion that they are delicate, beautiful, and less earthbound than men are. Mums told her to quickly leave the room if she felt as if her body was about to do something that wasn't ladylike. Clare. It's Clare now. Not that it matters. Not that being feminine matters. Staying alive is the point. She can't be certain the man who grabbed her intends her to stay alive. What does he intend?

She had thought a hospital bed was confining. Being strapped in is worse. God bless you and the Devil take you. There's a scream welling up, very likely another useless scream. He mustn't know she's awake. He mustn't talk to her, laugh at her. It could still be a dream if she doesn't let him become real.

She wants water for her cracked lips. She knows they are cracked although she doesn't dare run her tongue over them to tell.

She almost groans with pleasure when she feels ice run across her mouth, ice that sends little droplets of water down her chin.

"Go ahead, my Bad Darling, suck. You know you want to. And I already know you are awake."

It's that same soothing, frightening, lying voice. She closes her mouth against it. She has no power over her ears.

The laugh again! She hears the ice fall back against the sides of a glass. "Your wish is my command, your Ladyship." He walks away, opens and then closes a door.

She knows he's still in the room. She won't turn her head. She won't open even one eye ever so slightly. She doesn't want to hear that laugh again.

And so, of course, he laughs again. "You're right. I'm still here. And you're still hopelessly fighting back. No matter, I can wait. Besides, there's a warm croissant and hot coffee waiting on my side of the door. I like a snack before bed, don't you? Night is falling fast. Pretty soon only the moon will light your room and it's a cloudy night. I'd open my eyes if I were you. You might be pleasantly surprised with my preparations, the soft rose-colored settee in the corner, the watercolor hanging over your bed, day lilies drenched in rain. On the nightstand I've left the ice that felt so good on your lips. The glass is lead crystal, like the ones on your mother's dining room table."

This time she believes the sound of a door shut. She knows he wants her to look around and see no rose-colored settee to cushion her back and legs. She knows there'll be no garden in any medium, yet alone a floating watercolor. She would prefer an oak with strong branches reaching over a fence, with enough burs to make a ladder.

She's sure the room will only contain the bed she's lying across, the chair he sat on, and possibly a nightstand. She knows there'll be no glass of ice, and on the other side of the door he'll be laughing.

She knows all this, not because she's so smart, but because she heard the ice move slowly away, the tiny tinkle, the ever so softly resettling. It would have been a very plain glass, maybe even a tin cup, with chips in the lacquer. But where did he get the ice? This is hardly a hotel. It doesn't smell like a hotel. He probably took some trouble to get the ice. He knew how to turn it into a torture.

She's remembering the ice wagon coming through the neighborhood. She used to watch the children run into the street to steal a chip when the iceman was making a delivery. One boy cried out in pain when an embedded splinter from the wooden slats

175

on the back of the ice wagon pierced the inside of his cheek. But the next delivery day she watched him take another chip. Brave little boy! And he was right. The cool moist suckle was worth taking a chance. She should have pulled the ice into her mouth. Her tongue would be cooler. She wouldn't be feeling the roof of her mouth. You don't even notice the roof of your mouth when you are not thirsty. He probably took his newspaper with him. He tucked it under the arm that held the glass. The other arm opened the door. Did she make the headlines?

What kind of obituary will Clare compose? Murder is not the cause of death for people in polite society. And death by misadventure would only prompt questions. Best keep it short, Mums. Date of birth - date of death – beloved daughter of - private interment - donations to the New York Public Library in lieu of flowers. And then Papa would book a nice long trip on the Orient Express - something they could talk about after the dust had settled, after the grass has taken root on my grave.

*   *   *

From the other side of the door he can imagine her disappointment, anticipate her regret, and savor what must be growing fear. She has no idea what is to become of her. And indeed he hasn't quite decided. Oh, of course, he'll have to kill her eventually. Inevitably, she'll open her eyes and he can't be bothered with a mask. And besides, she's seen him before, that day he cradled her bloodied body and called for a doctor. She's confused now, but she'll put it together. Then he may have to hurt her to make her docile. One thing he's not sensing is docile. Her body refuses to sink into the bed. Her lips are a straight line. And she's denying him her voice. He'd like to hear her voice. That will come. The scream was nice, cut off mid-shrill. Damn! He's having fun again. That can't be good.

Time and place will dictate her type of death. If he doesn't have to leave these accommodations, the Seine will wash away her drugged body. It's close enough for a short carry and tip. She's light enough to make it fast work. She'll float for a moment.

Then he'll see her sweet face sink into the water. Maybe she'll start to regain consciousness and her feet will do a pitiful little kick, her fingers will claw, but there'll be no strength behind any of it. Maybe she'll realize for a second or two that she's about to die and then she'll discover there is nothing. Jesus, he wishes he could be there. The biggest disappointment of all!

Everyone likes to believe there will be something. Maybe he would too if there was a reward waiting or one God damned soul he wanted to see again. But an afterlife means the witnesses to his crimes who will be only too happy to call him out. Many of them would have no trouble identifying him since he was the last person they saw on this earth. He's counting on nothingness.

He hits the iron bar and sends it sailing into place. She has to hear that. She has to open her eyes. The dusty lashes will fall back into the darkness beneath her brows. The darkness was real. He had run a moist fingertip across to be certain. The bloom in her cheek was real as well. And her lips are naturally pink and, until recently, very soft.

Sorry to miss the eye opening, he walks across the room and looks for a loose cigarette in the breast pocket of his touring jacket. Not in that pocket.

There's a knock at the door, that special knock, that silly schoolboy knock. The games these people like to play.

He opens the door and steps inside yet another room. Rooms with no hallways in between. He loves buildings like this. You must knock at each door, identify yourself at each door, till the person in the last room feels comfortable letting anyone in, no matter how they knock. This has got to be friend, not foe. There has been no hail of fire between doors. None of his guards have been killed in between - unless they were bribed which isn't a stretch of the imagination, but not likely. What the hell! He opens the door.

"Well?" He never wastes time on formalities and he knows this pair of strong arms well enough. He keeps his hand on the back of the door and his knee at the ready.

"The Organization wants to know if your hostage is worth a man's reputation. I'm here to make that determination." The big head poking through the crack of the door had fun with that last word. He'd let go slowly of one syllable after another. It's a direct quote from his orders and it sounds impressive. De-ter-min-a-tion.

Unimpressed, Sidonie's captor keeps his reply simple. "Not until I clean her up."

"Sounds like a nasty task."

"I take the risks, I reap the rewards."

"You take the money. You take the orders."

"Not from you. And all you do is take orders and from both directions."

"The Organization contracts us to deliver. Righteous Wrath will be very angry if we don't. You're the one in the cross fire."

"Come back tomorrow. And you won't have to disappoint anyone."

"I - "

"I know. You have a discerning eye. But tomorrow I will brush her hair, powder away a bruise or two and make her wish to do anything to please me, if only to have the use of a chamber pot. Go." He starts to push the door closed.

"Powder? You have face powder."

"I am a professional." Of course he isn't taken at his word.

A foot jams the door and a hand reaches into an inner pocket. Fortunately, the tough guy isn't as fast as he is strong. A quick grab to the throat, just close enough to the pulse point, helps him recall the usual fate of messengers bearing bad news. And, of course, someone else's gun is pressed into his ribs. Where did he come from?

"Tomorrow, but later in the day. She needs her beauty sleep. And so do I!"

His ear still close enough to the closed door, he enjoys the healthy round of curses. Big toe hadn't quite cleared the initial slam.

Chapter 30

The Eyes Have It

It's easy to lose yourself, your sense of self anyway, when you're bound to a bed that's not your own, in a room that holds none of your things, not even a mirror to see if you still look the same. All that's familiar is the taste of your own salt. From the inside feeling out, the tears on your cheeks feel like silk ribbons splashed by rain and dried into puckers. The puckers run from your eyes to your chin. One trail ends close enough to your mouth to taste the salt, but your tongue isn't long enough to lick it away. Any other woman in your place would be shaking when she wasn't pulling at her bonds.

I know better. Shaking's a waste of energy. And my wrists and ankles are already rubbed sore from the ropes binding me to the bed posts. Talking to myself helps. It's calming, maybe even useful – all that is left for me to do really. And there may be a clue, a hint of how I might escape. Maybe I can sort things out. I can still see and hear well enough.

There's the door. It has to open again. Every once in a while there are foot steps, but not often enough. He's not pacing, probably not worried. He's alone, most of the time anyway. He talked once. His voice was low. He didn't need volume to make a point. The other voice raised, sometimes agitated, sometimes annoyed, finally thwarted. There was petulant menace in that frustrated retort, "You're the one in the crossfire." It seems my captor is the one in command - of the situation and of everyone else. And maybe me. Of course, me.

O.K., O.K. But, my mind still belongs to me and I'm going to figure this out. I'll close my eyes and make the back of my lids two clear sheets of paper. There're so many questions bombarding my poor brain. Writing them down will help me deal with them one at a time.

First question: Is he alone or is there a pack?

He was the one who slammed the door. He had the last word. But there is, at least, one alpha male challenging his authority. Still, wolves eventually unite in the pursuit of their prey. They attack in packs. They shred in packs. Although by himself he could probably chew up one young woman quite nicely. Not helpful, not calming.

Question number two: Is he the one who missed and shot me?

Probably, but then why doesn't he just kill me, the ultimate get-even? Maybe he's into torture before the kill. Again, not soothing.

Question number three: How do I get him to untie me?

It's my only hope for escape, and besides my arms ache. Mustn't dwell on wrists and ankles that are of no use to me whatsoever. I can move my head. I can see the window. I can watch the door. I can listen through the door. A sad inventory. I could have added the ability to moisten my cracked lips with my tongue, but that would really be pathetic.

Question four and five already depress me. How do I get through a barred window and a locked door? How to I overcome a jailer who's having so much fun tormenting me?

For now, I'll just lie quietly. He may forget me for a little while. Quiet may put off the next torment, buy time for rescue, if not escape. A few flutters and twists never work when you're caught in a web.

O.K., O.K., quiet or not I'm still securely fastened. And bars outside the window look like wrought iron. Not really bars like at a jail, but strong enough to keep people in or out. What kind of web is this? Could be an insane asylum. The pretty grillwork may ease the guilt of families locking in loved ones forever and a day. An asylum would be a good place to hide someone. He told the children I needed to be returned to one. The screams of other inmates could be muffled by thick walls. Or perhaps they long ago gave up screaming.

I can't think that way. I can't give up. I can't scream. Suddenly I want to. All this rational thinking only makes it all seem more and more hopeless. Besides, screaming will frighten me more than anyone else. Screaming will only unnerve me. Back to thinking, back to observing, back to licking my lips. The walls don't seem to be padded. It's probably not an asylum after all. I'll look more closely in the morning. It's beginning to get dark.

I know one thing for certain. I've got to keep my eyes open the next time he enters the room. I need to see my wolf, look into his eyes, and see if it matters even a little to him whether I live or die. Silly fly! You mean nothing to him.

He will watch the light go out of my eyes with less interest than watching a candlewick go from a little red spark to that last puff of smoke. He might like rolling the hot wax in his fingers, rolling it into a ball, tossing it away when it starts to cool and harden. Then again maybe he won't linger that long, compelled to move on. Either way his will be the last face I'll see before becoming nothing. Nothing is more terrifying than whatever pain comes before. There is no way to think of nothing, to picture it, to settle on it. And sleep with no end is another horror. I want to live, to dance, to go on. I want to be Sidonie. I haven't had enough of being Sidonie.

There it is. Again I want to scream. I'd press my hands over my mouth if they were free. All I can do is fold my bottom lip over my top lip and close my eyes. No, closed eyes don't help. Phantoms are now menacing the back of my lids. I'll look at the window instead. Maybe there will be a full moon tonight.

O.K., I've still got to look at him. Maybe someday I'll be free. Someday I may be able to say, "Yes, that's the man." Maybe someday I'll be dead and have to settle on haunting him to his grave.

*   *   *

The moon turns out to be a pathetic thing and there's no street light near by. What light there is comes from behind him. A candle. It looks like a candle. More than one. Lucky him. And he's got melted wax to play with. If only I had warm wax to sooth my strangled fingertips. How my thumbs would love pressing the wax into a big, bright harvest moon!

Even in this light I can tell he's tall. Marry a tall man, Clare had counseled. You will always look feminine and petite beside him. His shoulders are level. No chips. His hand is still on the doorknob of the open door. He's not one to hurry. I half expect the scratch of claws on the bare wooden floor as he moves out of the light of the door and towards the darkness around me.

The moon remains feeble, but there's still enough shine to show me his shirt. It's white. It's unbuttoned at the neck. It's carefully pressed. Thank you, moon, any help is appreciated. Although, I'd rather not see the strength beneath the shirt – in his shoulders, his chest, his arms. Strength's not good for me, nor is speed. He's next to my bed before the moon reaches his face.

But the light from that open door is still willing to help. His lips are thin in their tight line. They're even thinner when stretched into an almost pleasant smile.

"We are wide awake now, aren't we?" His eyes move from mine down the whole length of my body. A slap feels in order.

"Yes, we are." *I snap back without thinking if snapping is such a good idea. It's certainly not quiet. It calls attention. And it makes me a mouse to his cat or lamb to his wolf. Animals are all over the room, scrambling, squeaking, crawling. When he runs his finger down my cheek I feel the spiders. If only I could slap one down.*

"You've been crying. I don't like crying."

"I don't either. I won't do it again." *It's the closest I can get to that slap. My bound hands revert to fists, powerless fists, pointless fists.*

A laugh catches at the back of his throat. I surprised him. I surprised myself. I really must think before I open my mouth. He turns away, a little too late to hide his amusement. I hate his amusement. He moves young. He moves like a dancer in the ballet, the kind that makes short, swift steps, from behind the curtain to the footlights and then surprises you with a sudden leap. He turns back. It's almost a twirl. Oh the days of the twirl!

His nose is too close. It's straight and long. His chin's too determined, square, with no dimple. His eyes are still in darkness, in the shadows of his own black brows. If he were in standing in front of me on the top of a hill with an eleven o'clock sun shining straight in his eyes, I would only see black.

My eyes are definitely not up to engaging his. My eyes have all they can do to try and read his. Clearly he will not offer an easy way out of this room, out of this world perhaps. Quiet, silence may still be the best tactic, but it seems I'm not too good at that.

I'm not going to win anyway. Might as well talk, but no back talk. I'll try playing the role he expects from a woman captive - abject, compliant, grateful for kindnesses. God, I may not be the best actress, but I know my craft. Pace the lines. Keep the gestures small, but important. Build suspense with less not more. Keep on the mask

184

of my character until the final curtain. No, let's make that the last act. Not much better. Anyway, I'll enjoy surprising him, even if it's the last thing I do.

Face it. He'll enjoy toying with me either way. Cats play with their prey before they kill. I hadn't realized wolves do that too. I need to convince him that it would be more sport for him if I were unbound. Then I could go to the window and check how secure the bars are. I could see how far the fall.

I lower my lashes and soften my voice. "It does seem silly to keep me bound up this way in a locked room. You're bigger than I am, and probably have a weapon on you." *In the darkness I can't see, but I feel a weapon.* "Please, would you think about it?"

"I'm always thinking. I was thinking of giving you a candle but then you might find a way to burn us all down."

"Why would I do that? I still have a small, slim hope I'll live through this." *Question six jumps from the back of my eyelids to my mouth. I shouldn't ask. I shouldn't make him think about it.* "Why haven't you killed me?"

"At the moment you're worth more alive than dead."

"I'm being ransomed? Just how much could I be worth?"

"A man's reputation."

"I don't understand."

"Think about it. You have nothing else to do."

"You are cruel." *I shouldn't have said that. I just baited a wolf. My fists are back. I have no coherent strategy.*

185

"I'm a professional." *His smile through half closed lips is white. Again the moon's dancing off him.* "I will untie your arms, but your legs must stay secured to the bedposts. That way you can sleep, your discomfort minimized, your mind satisfied that for now it can not think you out of this."

Of course, he knows I'm thinking escape, always thinking escape.

"Thank you!" *It's an insolent thank you. I was just baited. And I jumped at it.*

Still he unties my wrists and takes a moment to massage the blood into a natural flow. I almost enjoy the touch - strong, warm, prickly. "Bruises. I love bruises. They are never prettier than against alabaster skin." *He had to ruin it.*

Pulling away only makes him smile.

"Don't think you have a prayer of untying your legs. Those are fishermen's knots. They will hold in a gale. And you, at best, are a lovely spring rain. And there will only be more bruising."

Chapter 31
Use Both Hands

It's a strange dream. She's in a wheel chair and Terry's pushing it. Sidonie has this feeling they are on their way to somewhere she really wants to go until four men in top hats jump out of the shadows and bar their way. One of them pulls her chair out into the street and lets it roll. There are automobiles all around and horses with carriages. The automobiles are black. The horses are white. In all the drivers' seats there are clowns. Only they look more like actors wearing white and black Kabuki masks. And all the masks have scowling red lips. Terry is nowhere near, lost in the swirl of traffic. She reaches for her purse and searches for her makeup. Maybe if she turns herself into a clown, but no, it's more important to steer the chair out of traffic. How does she steer a wheelchair? Cars are backfiring, first one, then another, and still another, like echoes bumping and slamming into each other in a very small canyon. She can't find the brake. She mustn't bump. She mustn't bump. But her hand can't seem to reach down and find a way to stop the wheels.

The Kabuki cars are coming closer and closer to the ledge, the ledge that came out of nowhere. She holds on tight, her eyes closed against the darkness below. When she dares look down she sees a frayed blanket. She's back in her bed still tied to its foot, secure and safe enough except for the smoke coming under the door. It doesn't smell like exhaust. It smells like gunshot. She knows gunshot from that quail hunt with Daddy. These shots sounded close enough to have hit the bed. It's shaking that much. Or maybe it's her.

He bursts into the room. His lips are scowling red. "If you want to live, you must do exactly what I say." He's holding a gun. If she touches it she's sure it'll be hot. This is no longer a dream.

She nods not once, but twice.

"Excellent." His hands are on the move – tucking the gun into his belt - untying her ankles - sliding her across the bed. His first command, "Take a deep breath and stand." And she does, for one shaky moment, before he pulls her into a lean. "Full marks!"

Two bearded men lie on the floor of the next room. One has a clean bullet hole in the middle of his forehead. The chest of the other man is an open wound. He still has a gun in his hand. Their blood smells like hot beets, not just a pan-full, but lots more, like a full vat. Beets don't have a very strong smell, no matter how many of them are heated. It isn't a scent you associate with any extreme, be it good food or bad body odor. It's more like musk, not strong, but lingering, present just enough to make you want it to go away. Not many people like beets just as they are. They seldom heat them. What they do is soak their beets in vinegar to enhance the flavor. They add white onions to brighten the muddy color. In itself beet red is not pretty. You certainly wouldn't want to see the juice splattered on your walls or pooling on the floor at your feet. Blood red is cheerier, now that she looks at it more closely.

He pulls her in closer, surprised when she pulls away. She holds up her skirt and tiptoes through the blood, one bare foot at a time, that eager to leave the bodies behind.

He smiles and rewards her with a gun lying loose on the floor. "Shoot when I say shoot and we may get out of here alive. Shoot me and you're on your own."

"I don't, I really don't know how …." The gun weighs down her right hand. She catches the falling handle with her left.

He untangles the flailing fingers and puts the right ones in their proper places. "Look where you want to shoot. Point the gun in that direction. Hold it steady. And squeeze. Walk behind me while I lead the way out." His dark brows can also command. Another nod. She's beginning to feel like a toy dog with a spring connecting its head to its body. Bounce, bounce, bounce. She doesn't much like the feeling. Still she follows.

There're no corridors, just open doors leading from one room to another, not a building for living or healing, simply storage. Empty crates here and there, some wrappings in a corner, all dusty. At each door frame she waits, only inches behind. She could pull the trigger without even taking aim. Her gun's that close to his body. Only one jerk upward to the back of his head. His dark hair sweeps back around his ears, covers the top of his collar. It shines more than hers. Is it black or dark, dark brown?

"Full marks!" He already knows her decision, just as she knows he's not surprised to find two of his own men dead over a card table, one still clutching his royal flush.

At the door to the street he turns and searches her eyes. It is dark, both their eyes are dark. Still when he says, "Go!" he's satisfied. He knows she will break into a run behind him.

"There they are!" Someone shouts from the darkness to the right. He turns, aims and nods at her. "Use both hands. They're going to shoot at you as well as me."

The gun springs to life. She's thrown forward with the bullet. The recoil actually hurts her shoulder, a shoulder not used to such treatment. Sidonie has just learned something. Pain is not unlike an emotion. When it's really intense it sweeps you away. She likes being swept away.

"I said both hands."

She pulls again and again, easier every time. Her shoulder's quit complaining. Then it gets quiet. The firing stops. People just may be afraid she'll hit them.

"This way!" He's actually laughing as he pushes her across the street and into a automobile with its driver's door left open and the engine still running. "Scared the poor bastard out of his car." His gun salutes the thicket in the park. "Thanks for the keys, buddy."

"Your gun!" He's talking to her but concentrating on pulling out into the road. "Stick it out the window."

He wants her to shoot again. Her hand is still trembling from the first three times.

"You don't have to shoot. Just make them duck for cover." He takes a sharp right that sends her halfway out the window. The car teeters with her. A horse and carriage would've more cleanly made the turn "That's it. But look as if you mean it. Furrow your eyebrows. Grit your teeth."

He wants her to play a role. These are headlights, not footlights. If only she could slip back into a dream, a lovely dream this time, the sun warming her shoulder, a dandelion yellowing her nose, waves kissing her feet. But there's blood on the bottom of her feet and these are headlights, not footlights. And the night wind keeps biting her face into reality. The gun's growing colder and colder in her hand, but she can't let go. It's part of her now, not just a prop. It's helping her escape. It's moving this car forward into the night. It's keeping her alive, not lying on the ground, with blood in her hair as well as on her feet.

"Ah, there they come around the corner. They're going to hit those tables and chairs. Not used to sidewalk cafes, are you gentlemen?"

Sidonie can't believe their luck. Behind them the braking car's going into a skid. Now it's headed for a cafe window. Glass sprays across the car. Her eyes see it happen before her ears make sense of the ping, ping across steel. She recognizes wood cracking. The window frame has nothing more to hold, no reason to be. So it lets go. A head bloodies as it pitches through the opening gap. Will he get up and dust himself off? Will he pick up his gun and fire at them? Their car has slowed enough to be in range. Seems the man on the seat next to her is taking just a moment to enjoy the mayhem he's caused. "Yes!"

Another car is careening around the corner. And another.

"That should make a nice pileup and give me time to decide what to do next."

He doesn't know. My God, he doesn't know. My life depends on him and he doesn't know what to do next. And now he's laughing. I hate it when he laughs. He laughs too much. His teeth are too white. He's having too much fun. But then so am I. If he's mad then I'm halfway there. I just tiptoed through blood. I just fired at people I don't even know. And now I'm feeling this rush, this you-can't catch-me-rush. The car can't go too fast for me. My fingers can't let go of the gun. My eyes can't get enough of the road behind. I want another target. Part of me is even enjoying the bile burning and churning its way up into my throat. But for all I know these people could be out to rescue me. There it is, another car coming fast.

"Duck!" He yells as a bullet spins past my temple. My hair is still tossing. It was meant for me. The windshield is cracking circle by circle. I lean back out the window, a gush of air brings tears to my eyes, but I can still aim. I pull the trigger until that awful, empty click.

He's firing for both of us now. He makes a sudden left and sends me flying across the front seat and up against his thigh.

"Delicious!" He strokes my leg.

I should pull away. I will when the road straightens out, when there are no more cars behind us.

"Simply delicious!" He strokes me again.

Chapter 32
Out of Harm's Way

The man at the wheel doesn't have to push Sidonie to the floorboards. Ducking-and-covering's becoming as natural to her as sardonic laughter comes to him. She looks up from her crouch to see the crisp jawline of a head thrown back, way back. He's enjoying this too much, way too much. And he's holding on too lightly. There could be a curve ahead, another car careening towards them. That slow smile. She's beginning to expect it, even look for it. His dark eyebrows relax then. They go down towards the bridge of his nose, their arch no longer superior. He's intent on enjoying the moment, not intimidating whoever may be watching.

"Hold onto your bustle, Mademoiselle!" He fires another round at the headlights coming fast down the narrow back street behind them. "Now for a little misdirection." Before making a quick, sharp left he downs his lights. Sidonie can feel the wheels on her side of the car leave the cobblestones. She can hear her heart pick up speed. Is she smiling too? No, that would be crazy. She's not crazy. She's not like him.

With a nasal curse a Frenchman flattens himself against a brick wall. The angry bark of a dog sends a cat into a spat of hissing. So many innocent creatures in harm's way, all because of them. She reaches up for the steering wheel. His eyebrows slap her down. It's a dream. She'll close her eyes and pretend it's a dream.

The car's moving slower now. No more bullets are whistling by. And the moon's beginning to meet them at each intersection. She may not die tonight after all. She puts her head down on the seat and lets the tears come.

There's another little cat. This one has a kitten in its mouth. It's going to cross the road. This time she reaches the wheel, but the turn's too sharp. The brakes can't stop the skid. She feels the bumper hit the stone embankment and tip the car upward into an arc. They hit the water in a belly flop. Water starts filling the car. Cat eyes watch with interest from the darkness above. The car disappears into the black waves. The cat gently drops her squealing kitten and soothes its ear with a lick. The kitten purrs and bumps head. The dog catches up. He stops to sniff the ground for other dogs. A warm cognac makes the Frenchman forget he ever saw the I couldn't-care-less car and its driver with the maddening grin

No one will drag the Seine for her body. And he will swim free with his gun held high over his head.

It is impossible to scream under water, but she tries anyway.

"For God's sake, woman, wake up. With any luck the real nightmare is behind us, hopefully a good twenty miles." He gives her shoulder a shake rude enough to clatter her teeth and snap open her eyes.

"Where are we?" She looks for the moon. Black trees reach up in vain. The wind is teasing their lacy arms. She pulls herself back up onto the seat. Her arms are stiff and so are her legs.

"Let's just say we are not in Paris environs."

Her wrists aren't bound, but they feel that way. She massages out the kinks. Maybe she just wishes they were bound, wishes she'd been forced into doing what she just did. Maybe she didn't do any of it. The gun isn't in her hand, on the floor boards or on the seat. She stops kneading and really looks at her hands, especially the one that held the gun. It still looks soft. It even feels soft. In this light not one nail appears to be broken. On the horizon the tip of the sun glimmers, like the halo of a secondary saint. "Is it almost morning?"

"Just about. And just as well. I wouldn't want to wake Madame Lafarge. She's not pretty with sleep in her eyes."

Dickens. He reads Dickens. She has a feeling it wouldn't be wise to act surprised. But it does make him human enough to ask, with only a trace of impertinence, "So you do have a destination?"

"Let's just say I know where to get cafe au lait and a basket of croissants."

Making conversation could make her human to him. "You really like your croissants, don't you?"

"Warm with whipped butter."

"And will I get one?" She holds her breath. Does he like coquettes as well as croissants?

"One can hope. Keep behaving yourself and you just might."

Now he's smiling at the open road ahead of him and the empty road behind him. Pleased, he slows down while one cow languidly follows another. But the goose must be honked at, and honked at again when it jumps, flaps its wings, and stumbles on a stone. Move, please move, she silently urges. He just might decide its more fun nudging goosey gander along with the hard steel of his car or stopping it dead with the cruel crunch of his tires.

For more than an hour they ride through the dust of a dirt road, pushing aside sheep, cows, an occasional barefoot child, always that smile. Get out of the way. Please, get out of the way. He really wants to. He really does.

Trees are close enough to tickle the top of the car, but not friendly enough to entice him to stop the car and stretch his legs. Sidonie would welcome a nice long stroll, but there are no footpaths for Gretel, Goldilocks or Snow White to skip merrily down, no clearing for a gingerbread house, and no hot porridge on a table. There just may be a poisoned apple. She can't tell with the vines and underbrush. Still he finds a turnoff, without signs to say it's coming or sorry, too late, you've missed it. In fact, there is a log blocking the way. Now he has to get out of the car, so quick, so agile, no kinks. He pulls the log aside to navigate past. His legs are wide apart as he dusts his hands off on each other. Or is a bit of self-applause?

"Seems she's expecting me!" He chuckles as he puts the log back in place behind them. Chuckling is usually a warm, friendly sound.

"Madame Lafarge?"

"Ah, I see, you're paying attention. Actually, she's not French at all. She speaks it abominably, so don't go showing off your finishing school skills. That's part of the reason she stays way out here. She doesn't have to talk to the locals."

"How does she live? How does she get food?"

"Money talks for her when she needs it to. Friends bring her things. And she has the farm. She supplies her own needs, pretty much. And then, of course, she has this sideline."

"Sideline?"

"Being there when I need her."

"And what do you need her for?"

"Coffee and croissants."

I can't believe I'm talking breakfast menu with a mad man. Cream or sugar? Jam or jelly? I still have this feeling talking is good. "I like warm milk in my coffee. I like it when it froths."

"It's usually warm right out of the cow. But if I were you I wouldn't at this point ask for special treatment."

Yes, he's sounding almost human. Talking is the way. He's getting to know me. Maybe he'll even like me or at least want me. Most men do. But asking the questions whirling around in my head will only bring us back to the subject I want to avoid.

What are you really going to do with me?

Am I going to be ransomed or killed?

Why are you taking me here?

Is it a good place to keep me safe till you decide?

Or have you made a promise to Madame Lafarge to share all the really fun killings?

Is her hideout a nice secluded place to bury a body?

I certainly have the right to ask, "Just who were those men shooting at us?" After all, I've been shooting back. But, I've no reason to believe he'll tell me the truth. And I've every reason to want him to believe I'm an unthinking accomplice. I've been more than cooperative during our escape. He's got to think I'm frightened enough to follow him and without question.

And so I don't ask, who were these men, if they did not come to rescue me?

Is anyone still looking for me?

As the car puts Paris farther and farther behind them, Sidonie has to know the trail is becoming harder and harder to follow. They are farther from the wonderful buildings, the indifferent women, and from the constant talk of the war. The farther south they go the farther in the distance the war seems. The trees on either side of this back road are a dark tangle, rising sun or no rising sun. If there are farm houses they are behind the tangle. No one is around to question why their windshield is shattered. No one is close enough to see how the shards of broken glass turn Sidonie's face into a work of modern art. Pablo Picasso comes most readily to mind.

Chapter 33

Cross the Threshold

Once the log is repositioned, the dirt road is clear to drive down, not smooth, but clear. The bumps remind her of her empty stomach. If it were full she'd lose the contents. But it's not full and she's painfully aware of her bare feet, her cold feet, so aware that when he opens her car door and motions for her to jump out, she stops short. Thistles! He's inviting her to take her first step into what looks to her like an enchanted forest and it's through a patch of thistles.

The laugh again. He reaches in, one hand going under her knees, the other round her farthest shoulder.

She's not about to be yanked out. "No!" She holds on to underside of the seat.

"Walk or be carried. Your choice."

Maybe some of the dried blood will brush off if she walks through the crab grass and occasional wild flower. Then again with all those thistles she may just add her own blood to the mix.

"Too long." He makes up her mind for her. She's up, out of the car and in his arms before she can even think to scream. Crickets! She hears crickets. Of course, under these brooding branches they don't know its morning way up there where the sun is probably shining. She has never been carried before.

It is not at all like I'd imagined. His chest is hard. I imagined resting my head when I was carried over a threshold. His chest doesn't invite that. His body is stiff. This is a chore for him. He's exercising muscles, not feelings. I'm a package he's delivering, and not a particularly precious one. There is no tender glance downward. Why did he have to be the first one to carry me over a threshold? This will be my first memory. I can only hope there will be a second. Oh my God, he's dropping me. My arms are around his neck, the hair on the back of his head tickles, his neck is warm and I can feel as well as hear him laugh. It was a malicious little toss up. The last thing he wants me to feel is secure, especially in his arms. Little chance of that! I take my arms back and cross them over my breast. He laughs again, damn him!

His black boot knocks on the door. It isn't immediately answered. It looks like the entrance to an unhappy marriage between an English cottage and an American farmhouse. The cottage wants to sag and look picturesque. Rust brown thatches are comfortably inclining into November gray shingles. The farmhouse is still trying to look like it works. The drooping porch shelters a butter churn with no sign of dust.

Doors say a lot about the people who live behind them. This door says, "I dare you!" Its heavy oak might open to a battering ram. But only a primeval key will turn its primeval lock. And there is no way to look through the tiny casement window, even if it is set at eye level. Shuttered from the inside, admittance is carefully controlled by the person within. Madame Lafarge, Sidonie presumes. Suddenly the shutters rip open. Just as suddenly they slam shut. Seems the Madame isn't anxious for company. Still, there is the sound of something sliding across the back of the door, like a metal bar. And then there are those little clinks and clangs, as if the lady of the house is busy unfastening several chains.

"You fouled up." She speaks with economy, but that is the only thing about her that is cut to cost. Her hair is a big burning bush. Improbable red tangles drip down an overheated neck, if that is a neck. It's hard to tell where head ends and neck begins. The hand wiping her apron is big enough to punch out the brindle bulldog squatting by the fire. His short muzzle is surrounded by hang-dog skin. His lips droop over a particularly pointed underbite. His tail is tucked under his legs. He hasn't barked once. His head is bent low. Looks like he's had the bark and the wag knocked out of him at some time or the other or he is waiting for the snarl command. There's drool at the corners of his mouth. Somehow Sidonie knows the drool is warmer than most drool

200

and certainly murkier. His eyes are also clouded, as if he's looking through phlegm. What he's looking at and drooling about appears to be the pocket of his mistress' apron. Perhaps there's a bribe inside. That apron is straining around her middle. You aren't supposed to see the ties from the front, are you? Sidonie doesn't think so. Taken as a pair they make quite a presence.

"Do I smell soup? Or is that one of your evil potions?" He could have laughed. He does so annoyingly often. It would have made it a joke between them. It might have erased this tension that is making Sidonie more aware than ever that she is in the arms of the enemy, and perhaps in the middle of two adversaries. He could toss her across the floor just as easily as let her down gently. He could feed her to the lioness in the undersized apron. She can feel his fingers cup her outer thigh and then move down to that soft spot behind her knee. They are opening and closing as if they are considering the alternatives. Suddenly they loosen and feel restless. Just as soon they hold tight enough to hurt. The dog watches, one eye clouded more than the other. He seems to have lot of reasons to be mean.

The big woman laughs a big laugh. It comes from way down low, like the sound of a train on the far side of the tunnel. "Potions are for cowards. I'm more direct. Didn't you see the log?" The dog makes a move toward one big clog, but stops short of curling round. More often than not he's felt its kick.

"You and I both know that wasn't for me. Where shall I put this?" He gives Sidonie a little bounce. The hands feel careless now - another cavalier bounce already in them.

"You only come here when you foul up." She mutters as she pulls a stack of yellowed newspapers off a torn and stained wing-backed chair. The upholstery might have been cheery once, with all those little windmills dotting its faded blue. "Or would you be wanting the dungeon?" Her big foot grazes a black metal ring in the floor as she directs her gaze to Sidonie. Madame's eyes are bright brown, almost shiny, like the button eyes of a toy bear, but with less humanity. Sidonie hates herself for holding on tighter to the man who has just called her "this."

"Not much fight in her right now. The chair will do."

"Pretty feet, pretty dirty feet."

 He wrinkles his long nose short as he puts Sidonie down. "Yes, I'm offended too. Got any old socks?"

"And please, a wet cloth." It's probably futile asking these two for a favor, but Sidonie does want the blood off. It almost looks like mud. She's been pretending that it's mud. The dog takes a sniff of one foot to see what all the fuss is about. He pulls away, offended. How do you offend a drooling dog with one eye uglier than the other and a tail with no wag left in it?

"I forgot. She's a lady. What? You didn't think I'd know? Hermit though I am, I have my sources. A lot of bungling. Not like you, not like you at all." Madame Lafarge is shaking her head, more at Sidonie than at him. A toy bear has less shake. Its round face has no jowls to ripple. And it can't cross its fur arms over ominous breasts.

He's moving over to the stove where he rescues a green enamel ladle from a sink full of neglected pots and pans. He blows softly on the smoking broth. "Ox tail. Perfect! Just like Mother used to make."

She snorts. "I doubt that."

He closes his eyes and savors. "Truce? Sorry, Maggie Marie, I usually give you fair warning. "

"Truce. It's been boring around here. We do our work, throw some clay, and wait for news from the front. I could use the diversion. Let's wash her down, soup her up, and tie her to a bed, so you and I, Simon, can have a nice long talk."

He has a name. Somehow that's comforting. She never before knew the meaning of that phrase, small comfort.

"Best take what you can get, little one."

Did he really say that or did I just imagine it? He's in and out of my head. At least it seems that way. I'll have to guard my thoughts. Reveal only what I want to reveal. Yeah, like now. Look at me, damn you! Do you really know what I'm thinking? Wink! Grin! Give me some sign that I'm not turning fanciful. But no, there he goes, avoiding my eyes. He motions Lafarge out the front door. He says to her, not me, "First let's talk."

But there it is again, wink or no wink, grin or no grin, through the closing door, I feel him say, "Sit tight. Be good. This door is the only way out anyway."

And the dog is on her side of the door, watching, drooling, and being offended. She hasn't had a chance to see his teeth, but he probably has enough left, and a few sharp enough, to break skin.

Chapter 34

Her Honor to Protect

Sidonie eases up out of the chair. This may be one of the few times she will be free to walk around. The socks are ridiculous. They are gray knit with red toes and heels. Perhaps they were white once, but she's not going to think about that. They're warm and they make her feel less vulnerable.

She's seen paintings of peasants in the field looking quite noble as barefoot they work the fields. Some stop and listen to the noontime Angelus. Their work ennobles them. Women and men look strong and capable with their farm tools at their side. Being a captive is another matter. There are no heralding bells in the background, nothing heavy in your hand and if you get a chance to make a run for it you better be wearing a good pair of shoes. She should just be thankful she's no longer bound.

It's hard to be thankful when you're cold. I don't deserve to be this cold, even when it was my choice to wear this ridiculously thin sari. But then it's probably all part of his master plan. Keep her off center in every way. Chill her to the bone, chill her to soul. Damn him. Damn my own weakness. I'm even looking with longing at that faded green dress hanging on a hook over in the corner. Nice long sleeves, yards of soft warm wool. It's probably stained with grease from cooking and dog fleas are no doubt darting here and there in the folds. And I would be drowned in the excess wool. When sleeves touch your fingers, you are a little girl wearing her older sister's hand-me-downs. I don't want to feel like a little girl. The last thing I need right now is to be little.

Mother would say being small is a good thing. She'd call it "petite." Petite was feminine. Petite was dainty. Petite was pretty. And pretty was everything. I never thought to argue, but at this moment "petite" sounds more like "powerless." For God's sake why are women all so willing to make themselves as small as possible, to take up as little room on this planet as they possibly can? Men certainly encourage

them, court them, and feed them compliments as long as they maintain eighteen-inch
waists and size five shoes. The wool's probably scratchy anyway.

Even as she goes by, Sidonie will not touch Maggie's dress. She won't be tempted to
be little, petite, pretty, and powerless just to be warm. The last thing she needs is to be
little.

The fire crackles, throws off heat. Heat is good if you don't have to give up who you
are to get it. The bull dog grunts, not ready to move over enough to let Sidonie pass.
Tentatively she touches the top of his head. Here it comes, the deep, dark growl. His
tail is actually wagging but she has to suspect it's one of his few tricks and only
employed for a nefarious end. They all want to keep me off base, every one of them.
Pet me and you just may be sorry. She settles for "Nice doggie." That one eye in
particular suggests anything but. And instead puts her hands out flat to absorb the
warmth of the fieldstone fireplace. If they come in and see her standing by the fire
they might not suspect she is poking about for another exit, if not for now, for later.
Would he lie to her about there being no other exit? Probably. She knows so little
about him. One day he is shooting at her. Another day he is kidnapping her. And
then one night he hands her a gun and expects her to help save them both. She still
wonders why she so blindly followed him. The blood on her feet could have worked
either way. He had killed someone, hadn't he? But then there was his hand offering to
help her pass through safely, shades of the parting of the Red Sea. Unlike the bull
dog, Simon is not ugly which, of course, makes him doubly dangerous.

If she saw him in a box at the theatre, examining his program, she would have found
his dark brood more mysterious than menacing, just dangerous enough to be
intriguing. She was always drawn to a man with a hard jaw and a cruel mouth. More
of a challenge, she guessed. She'd have fancied linking her arm in his, leaning against
his deep chest, thinking what a dramatic pair they made walking down the marble
staircase, her delicacy framed against his power. She would be willing him to look up

so she could see his shadow eyes brighten as they took her in. She'd be in white, softly draping white, with no adornment except a camellia in her hair.

Then again, maybe not! Sidonie shakes her head and laughs. A blood red rose would be more appropriate! With thorns! No! She won't link arms and lean on her taller, bigger, stronger companion. She'll never think small again. Without being aware she stands on tiptoe and squares her shoulders. The bull dog growl deepens as he scuffles into a dark corner. He knows a threat when he sees one. Not his fault, she thinks as he shrinks back from an expected kick. She thinks of petting him to reassure, but why should she comfort him when no one is comforting or even warming her? The whole point seems to deny, to withhold, to confound. Simon, Simon, Simon! She looks to him for too much, even while she expects the worst. Crazy. She's giving him more thought than he deserves. The point is to find a way around him.

But the truth is there is something mesmerizing about Simon, besides his being her own personal kidnapper. Somehow through this whole surreal journey he is making her feel differently about herself. As he pulls her through gun fire a change is coming over her. Because of or despite him? She's not quite sure. The fact is with him she has walked through blood. With him she has returned fire. Blood and bullets are enough to change anyone. If with him she ever kills, something will die inside her. Perhaps it already has. Maybe that's not all bad. Sometimes something has to die for something else to grow. Or is this one convoluted exercise in rationalizing and she's already damned and just doesn't know it?

Sidonie sighs. She's virtually run with the devil. Deep down inside she is chilled, but it's a hot chill. He never intended to empower her, but it seems he has. He's making it possible for her to do things she never thought she could do. Maybe he's given her enough rope to hang him. Again she stands up straighter. Again she's less afraid. Pretty sure he wouldn't like that. Doggie certainly doesn't. Another growl from the corner. Another scowl from a face in perpetual frown. She threatens him with that kick he always expects. Did she just laugh? She heard herself laugh. Poor baby! Now he's whimpering. He'll survive and just maybe so shall she.

Like the recoil of a gun against a soft shoulder, from now on pain will always remind her that she's alive and making a stir, all on her own. Being cold is a kind of pain, isn't? Nothing she can't handle.

There must be another exit! But the hall is in darkness. Not even a window is visible at the far end. The corridor is long enough to open up to two bedrooms. She likes the word corridor better than hall, but it is probably too grand for the size of this cottage.

A ladder leans against the wall to the left of the hallway entrance. Looking up she sees a loft, where she assumes she'll probably be chained up for the night with the ladder removed. It doesn't look promising, unless she can build on the alliance she and Simon formed dodging bullets from what appeared to be a common enemy. The gunmen certainly weren't trying to miss her. She can still feel the cold breath of one or two those bullets whispering by the soft skin of her cheek. She remembers him pushing her roughly onto the floorboards. But there is no reason for the lady of the house to protect or trust her. Sidonie has certainly not received a warm welcome thus far. Warm. There's that word again.

Stop being a baby!

The cast iron pot on the stove is bubbling now, a slow bubble, but the Madame should turn it down before it cooks into glue. Sidonie picks up the spoon and takes a taste. It's good! Her stomach gives a little moan for more. She takes another spoonful. If only she could fill a bowl and sit back on her winged back chair and enjoy. And why not? What more can they do to her? One bowl in the cupboard looks clean. Lafarge must use it regularly. Sidonie takes her chances on a dusty one.

She's beginning to feel human again. Her stomach has something to play with. Her mouth is coming alive to the flavors running over her taste buds.

I just made three independent decisions: to get out of the chair; to taste the soup; and to eat it from the bowl of my choice. Four decisions actually. She'd rather be cold than small. Keep your damn dress, Maggie Marie.

*   *   *

When the door opens she is too asleep to notice if any one cares. Her feet are tucked under her. Her nose is nestled in the wing of the chair. Her cheek is resting against the back of her hand. Her mouth is ever so slightly open. And the soup bowl is about to tumble out of her lap.

"She didn't exactly sit tight, did she?" Simon laughs as he catches the bowl and spoon in mid-roll.

"Least she didn't eat out of my favorite piece of fine china." Madame makes her first little joke of the day.

"Looks like your soup was just right."

"Where are you going to put her?"

"In the loft. With no ladder."

"I wouldn't put it past that one to jump. I think there's more spit left in her than you think."

"Oh, I know there's more spit. But I'll be sleeping right below, on the spot where the ladder used to be. I'm tired enough to sleep anywhere. I feel like an ape pulled through a knothole. I've been driving all night."

"Suit yourself. I'll get you some pillows and a blanket. The chair is comfy enough if you want to pull it over. But I must warn you, Francois usually sleeps and drools in that particular chair. Me, I'm off to my own little bed. I could use a little mid-day nap myself."

"Something tucked under your pillow with a finely sharpened edge."

"Why should that change? I have my honor to protect." Her laugh is at the forefront of the tunnel now, reverberating and bursting out at one and the same time. She is anxious to end this conversation before he realizes she's been up all night too. Word gets around. She wouldn't want him to think she cared if he was dead or alive. "Sweet dreams." Francois' dirty nails tip, tap on the wooden floor as he follows his mistress to bed. It's been a strange day for him. He doesn't much like company.

*   *   *

The sleepers spend the rest of the day and part of the next night in companionable silence until something shrieks and is carried away in a flutter of wings. Simon opens his eyes. Sidonie keeps hers closed. She is praying for a nice solid thud, the sound of a mouse or a rabbit falling to the ground and making its escape. Something very little can sometimes slip away. Madame Lafarge doesn't even roll over. Her snores are the only sounds in the night. Sidonie knows he's awake. Simon knows she's awake. He might as well go up the ladder.

She doesn't have to see the top of his head to know he has arrived. But she is surprised to see the cowlick. The moon coming through her dormer window is making it clear enough. Cowlicks are for little boys. Cowlicks are beyond a little boy's ability to discipline if he ever even thought of doing such a thing. Simon should have beaten his cowlick into submission a long time ago. Careful, Sidonie, you're not only giving Simon human characteristics, you're thinking of him as little, young, almost appealing, nonthreatening.

"You should be getting your beauty sleep. In the clear morning light you are going to look like the scullery maid who stayed too long at the ball. The clock struck midnight, your coach turned back into a pumpkin and you had to walk through the forest all night long on one bare foot. In tatters and tears, you greet the morning after. Not a pretty sight, sad really." He throws her an extra blanket. She tries not to look grateful.

"Could be worse. I could be one of the ugly stepsisters who no amount of sleep will improve. Or the wicked step-mother who has an ugly soul. Or the stupid prince who lets his parents decide when it's time for him to seek a bride." Simon is minimizing her. He thinks because she is a woman she can be manipulated by fairy tales. The fairer you are the more happy your ever-after. He doesn't seem to realize that the last few days, no, the last month, have left her with no illusion that being pretty will keep her safe, that being warm will help her survive. Thinking carefully is the only thing that is going to save her. But he doesn't have to know she knows. "Still it's nice to know you care." She holds her breath, waiting to see what he makes of insolence frosted with flirtation.

At the top of the ladder he turns round and seats himself on the edge of the loft. His legs dangle over. His white shirt is open wide at the neck. If he had a straw in his mouth he'd look like a carefree farm boy. From the way he is moving his legs, he is probably in his stocking feet. There she goes again, making him benign, pastoral even. There's no way to minimize his supple mouth and all its possibilities for cruelty. And picturing him shoeless wouldn't slow him down if he were in pursuit He's like a snake, relaxed in a coil, but ever ready to spring out of it.

"I don't really care whether you care or not." Sidonie lifts her chin. "But you understand. I say what you expect me to say. You say what you think I expect of you. And we both end up confounding each other."

"It's a pleasant way to pass the time, sparing if you will."

"Pleasant! You think this is pleasant!" She'd stamp her foot if she was standing up and she had shoes on. She satisfies herself that at least she has contradicted him. A small smug smile is tugging the corners of her mouth.

"Actually, it is. Well, at least it's unusual. I like unusual. I rarely have conversations of any kind with people I meet, shall we say, on the job."

"Maybe the conversation would flow more naturally if they weren't chloroformed or bound to their beds." She could have added "or shot in the chest," but she doesn't want him to visualize her on the other end of his pistol, in his sights.

"You may have a point there. But then chatting takes time. I'm not always willing to waste time." He lifts his legs off the ladder and twisting around, goes down on all fours on the floor of the loft.

My, God, he's coming towards me in a slow crawl, like a cat pretending it's just wending its way, with nothing particular in mind, certainly not small prey. He has left his shoes behind, perhaps at the bottom of the ladder. Cats need no shoes. Shoes would only make them less graceful, less quiet, less able to sneak up. He's not sneaking up. He wants me to be fully aware of this moment and how it's playing out. He wants me to be a little afraid, maybe a lot. So, of course, I won't be.

He stops mid crawl, his eyes engaging mine, he pinches my toes. That was a surprise. "You have lovely arches when you recoil."

I've no answer for that, too angry with myself for recoiling.

He's next to me now. I won't look up at him looking down. How does his shirt stay so clean? Even the wrinkles look starched. He must have changed shirts. There might have been blood on the other one, at least sweat. Does he keep shirts here? Crisp cotton moves out of view as he quietly moves up the bed and flips over on the mattress next to me. His hands go up and behind his head. Shades of Marc. Marc lay next to me like that, with that same nonchalant pose. Marc has become a shade, a ghost. The cabbage roses in his wallpaper are fading in a mist of memories. I'm remembering bouncing out of his bed, appalled by something he said, something that hurt, words that broke me into little pieces, bits and pieces that reassembled, but not exactly as they were before. I can't remember word by cutting word, not under this musty roof, on this hard mattress, with this man lying so close, feeling so starched, so solid, so real. He makes my whole life before him a memory, a dull memory, a dull ache. All that matters at this moment is the hip warming mine. His quick intake of breath surprises me. The smell of a lit match makes me turn. A little red dot burns brighter as he inhales again. I close my eyes and remove him from at least one of my senses. It's then I feel moist paper on my lips and the soft tickle of his fingers moving away, ever so slowly across my face.

"Inhale. It will relax you."

He's right. I'm not relaxed. This is a game I've never played before. I've flirted with men for sport. I've kissed them for power. But I only gave myself to someone I loved and who loved me back, I'd hoped, forever and ever. This man simply wants to feel me, up, down and around, now, for this moment only. And I'm thinking of those hands, those lips, those eyes closing, only that, nothing more.

A puff might actually be a good idea.

Chapter 35
Cherchez La Femme

Marc can't believe he's standing next to Clare. She still smells as sweet as that spring garden where they first kissed.

Clare can't believe she's let Marc this close. He's sure to see strands of hair as tarnished as the silver ring in her jewelry box.

Terry has no trouble at all believing that at this moment these two people are aware of no one else. And he has little hope of snapping them out of it. When the wind isn't pushing them against the ship's railing, the ocean waves are crashing them together. Shoulders and hips are engaged. Eyes are carefully averted. They've been in tandem since he and Marc met her at the ship landing and told her they were all sailing on the same ship. The men had also booked passage back to France. Sidonie was nowhere to be found and somehow, some way they had to be the ones to find her.

Clare and Marc should be thinking about Sidonie. Most of the time they are - just not now. He wishes he were as easily distracted. The only time fear subsides is when longing takes its turn. Sharp pain alternates with dull ache. Sometimes they over lap like the lush petals of a peony. You don't know where one petal begins and the other ends. And when the petals start to turn brown. . . . He lets go of the struggling image. It's another dark place where he could be trapped. He'll leave Marc and Clare to this little piece of the railing. There's plenty more at the back of the ship.

He believes it's called the stern, though he's not sure why. It makes sense that the front of the ship be called the bow. You bow down from the front. A captain greets the water with the front of his ship. At the stern white froth leaves a long, lonesome path through the dark blue waves that end somewhere over the horizon. He's almost certain that's called a wake, another word to ponder at another time

The water looks very cold on this overcast day. The wind certainly is. He pulls his coat collar up, buries his hands in his pockets and wonders how he would paint cold into the sea. Chunks of ice would be a short cut, cheating really, since there are none to be seen and this day is brisk enough. Perhaps steam is the right approach. It comes as warm waves smash against a frigid wind. It comes as hot air recoils from a splash of an arctic current.

He hasn't thought of her for a full two minutes. What he really wants to paint is Sidonie, a smiling Sidonie, a laughing Sidonie, and even a Sidonie looking away from him at someone else. She would look lovely in this wind, dark hair tousled, excitement sparking her brown eyes, red lips parted in a half smile. If he were lucky she'd fall against him as they made their way along the promenade deck. The sea's drama would exhilarate her. Now, in some dark place where she can't escape, she must be sick to death of drama. She must be very afraid and maybe even cold. He hates himself for his wool vest. She must know they are looking for her, but afraid they will come too late. He hates the boat for going so slow. He hates the wind for beating it back. He remembers his toy boat and how it whirled toward the drain when he pulled out the plug.

The French authorities have told Clare nothing. Their telegrams promise more details as the matter unfolds. Until then no one in the family should return. Clare has already been helpful enough with the investigation. And Sidonie might not even be in France anymore.

She may not be anywhere, anymore.

Terry will start with Amalendu. Sidonie was under his care, but did he ever really care about her? A leader needs followers, takes pains to gain their loyalty, and then moves on to find some more. He must continue his journey, his holy pilgrimage unimpeded. Every so often he looks back, but not for long. He smiles benevolently. He raises his hand in a blessing.

He quotes something inscrutable and pretends it's just for her.

But thanks to the authorities Amalendu's forward momentum has stopped short. Their only link to Sidonie's disappearance must stay put. They've pulled his passport. They think he knows more than he is telling them. Terry thinks so too and has a feeling he would be less impressed than the authorities with those soulful eyes. He might ask the questions the police would consider irreverent for a man of God. Tell me, your holiness, do you pray before or after sex?

"Mr. Terrence!"

He pretends he can't hear a voice that is carrying over the wind and water as well as the shriek of that gull looking for a place to land. She calls him Mr. Terrence, not Paul, his given name, certainly not Terry the name Sidonie always calls him. Even now, buffeted by this gale, Clare is clothing herself in formality, as if etiquette is going to land them safely. Propriety is in its heaven, all's correct in the world.

"Yes, Madame Adair." He one ups her. French is even more formal, precise enough to be the language of diplomacy. He only wishes he'd said *oui*.

"Marc tells me he also wrote to the authorities and received no better answers than I did. What have you done?" Her eyes hold his, not a simple feat for a small woman trying to steady herself on a heaving ship. She grabs the rail just in time.

"I went to the public library and did some research."

"What?" Her voice cracks with disbelief. The gull is circling the ship's tall chimneys now. There has to be a perch to wind her talons around.

215

"It's a fairly big story in the French press. Not so much as the war, of course. The New York Public Library has newspapers from all sorts of places. And I do read French."

"You really think the French press knows more than the authorities.?"

"I thought the press might speculate. Damsel in distress, that sort of thing always makes for a good story. The police can't speculate in public. But that's how you begin to solve any mystery. You consider all the possibilities that make sense. Then you move on to those that only make sense to the insane. Sometimes that's exactly were the answer lies."

Clare moves hand over hand across the rocking railing to look up into his eyes. "So speculate." She is close enough now for him to feel a tremble, to see a furrow, maybe even spot a mother's tear. All he sees is a jaw hard as a man's. All he hears is a voice without a quiver. All he feels is her resolve. "I want to know everything you know or suspect."

For the first time Terry would like to know more about her. Clare is, in her own way, as baffling as Sidonie. Maybe understanding one would make it possible to understand the other. Sidonie came to life under Clare's heart. Her childhood was played out on the stage Clare created. Clare chose Sidonie's clothes, picked out her toys, and decided when her daughter would stop wearing pigtails. The time had to come when Sidonie would want to do and be the very opposite.

"Well, the reporters are less sure than the police that Sidonie was shot by accident. They wonder if she wasn't targeted by a rival for Amalendu 's affection."

Cherchez la femme. Of course, they would think that. They are French. What other theories?"

"Some suspect that Amalendu made her disappear when she wouldn't join his harem. It was an affront. He could tolerate no such an affront."

" Amalendu has no harem. And if I know my daughter she might have considered that a challenge. She'd have every confidence she would make all the other women superfluous. What else?"

"Well, there is the assassin. He may have resented her for getting in the way and he decided to have his revenge."

"An assassin is not going to waste his time killing someone no one has paid him to kill. Is that all?"

"Well, personally, I think Sidonie accidentally tripped onto the board of a chess game between Amalendu and his enemies. She was a pawn easily surrendered. Her hero values her less than he values himself. He has already forgotten why she was important to him. I mean to remind him."

"And how do you propose to do that? How do you propose to even get an audience? You must know he isn't about to say anything to someone who has no authority or influence over him."

"I hadn't thought that far." Confound these Adair women. This one's sucking the hope right out of him. Clare's got him ready to climb over the rail and jump in. And then as if she sees into the depth of his despair, she pours more bleak into it.

"And there's the awful war. They say the artillery fire sometimes actually reaches Paris. And desperate men hide in desperate places. Bullets go astray. And there's the chance to capture a rich American. God, I can't imagine all the possibilities."

Terry, undone, grips the railing and tips forward.

Now his arm is the one she is touching. It's a reassuring pat, almost motherly. "It's a beginning, Paul. It does make some sense. Let me take over the thinking from here." She stumbles away from him into the wind. When she turns back her hair flies back across her eyes and into her mouth. "One thing I know, I feel." Her voice rises again to sea gull level. "My daughter is still alive!"

"Of course. A mother knows these things." It's the thing to say, even if he only half believes a special tie exists between these two very different women.

She doesn't miss his mutter. "Don't patronize me, young man. From the moment she was born I have felt Sidonie chafing against me, questioning who I was as well as everything I said or did. She wasn't sure this nipple was something she wanted in her little mouth. Maybe she'd prefer the breast I hadn't offered. Little fists banged against my dressing gown, little fingers fidgeted with my buttons. I can still feel her fretting, fidgeting, banging at me. In Heaven she would be at peace in the arms of our Holy Mother and I would feel her disappointment finally dissipate."

A patch of fog covers Clare's back from any more patronizing and Terry looks down at the sea. There's no longer a horizon beyond the trail of rolling foam. The sea and the sky have lost themselves in each other.

The thought that Sidonie may be lost in nothingness is a horror his mind refuses to consider. He could accept that he came out of nowhere and would return there at the end of his borrowed days. But Sidonie no more? Impossible! He won't imagine a life without her eyes, her lips, her dancing feet. He needs to know her hand will once again rest on his heart.

A bank of fog is enveloping the ship. A nice touch, Terry thinks. It so beautifully reflects his state of mind. It also serves to send the last remaining passengers to the comfort of the public lounges. He knows he presents an interesting study in courageous resolve - his tall, solitary body, pressed against the wind, the collar of his coat swept up and over his chin, his soul striking a bargain with the dark clouds above. If he were to do a self-portrait he'd need the most delicate of bristles, the palest of oils to fill in the more telling details, like that little waver at the corner of his mouth and the moisture beginning to well in his eyes. A greater challenge would be the constriction in his throat and the fear turning his chest into one big knot. Maybe someday he'd be up to it.

Chapter 36

Lullaby and Good Night

Sidonie wakes up to the sounds and smells of an early morning kitchen. Her face is buried in her pillow but it's all coming through. A kettle settles on a grate. A well-fired log falls into the ashes. The coffee's strong. The bacon's burnt.

She's never before slept in the roof of a kitchen, but it feels nice, homey, like hot cinnamon rolls floating in white melted frosting. She doesn't smell any rolls. Pity. And if she opens her eyes she will only see how dirty this stale blanket really is. She knows there's no slip on the pillow. What she doesn't know is whether she's alone. She listens a little harder for breathing, afraid to shift her body and bump into him.

She hears his voice, but it's coming from below the loft, low, conspiratorial, and then, Madame Lafarge's chuckle. In this company all chuckles sound nasty. This one reminds Sidonie of the backed-up sink the butler once tried to unplug with the pressure of his usually white-gloved hand. The sink wasn't happy. The hand wasn't happy. But something deep down in the pipe erupted in a strange sort of glee.

Of course, they don't want her to hear what they are saying. She'll just have to listen even harder. Quietly she shifts onto her back and pulls her hair away from her ears. It's not much better. She edges down towards the foot of the mattress. Luckily, there are no springs to squeak.

"Well done! I like my bacon crisp. And if the eggs are brown and curl up on the edges I am in heaven. But the coffee could use some fresh cream from one of your bovine beauties."

"Then you go out and milk her. I'm down to one now."

"Jeanette or Isabella?"

"Why? Did you have a favorite?"

"I prefer three syllable names."

"Since when?"

"Since you asked me and I took a second to think about it."

"Then you're in luck."

"As if I would know the difference. Never could tell them apart when they were both alive. Big brown eyes, nice pink nipples, contented snorts. "

"And they thought you loved them for their minds! Better wake up her ladyship. I'm not making breakfast twice."

"In a minute. Let's talk about what you are going to do with her while I'm gone."

Sidonie creeps closer to the edge of the loft. A button from the bare mattress scratches her inner thigh. She's half-off and half-on the makeshift bed.

He's going away. Sidonie should be glad, one less person to watch her. But where is he going and to do what? And who will prove to be the less caring caretaker? Just what will two women do if the men with guns show up before his return?

"Are you sure you should go? Someone obviously knows who you are. You've lost your prized anonymity. They can spot you now. Just what did you do wrong that they traced you and the girl so quickly?"

"I'll think about that when I have more leisure. Now I have to find out who *they* are."

"And how are you going to learn that?"

"My old friend has never failed me."

"He got you this assignment didn't he? They're usually less complicated."

"I may have complicated this one myself."

"Yes, kidnapping the girl is a round-about way of killing her lover."

A coffee cup is being refilled. Two coffee cups.

"The point was to render him powerless, without influence, to ruin his reputation."

"Because he had a woman? His kind collects them and keeps them in a tent in the middle of the desert." Again the pot settles down on the grate.

"He's a little more complicated."

"That word again!"

Sidonie is looking over the edge of the loft now. Things are getting too interesting to be careful.

"Mustn't scold, Maggie Marie. It doesn't suit you. It makes you too human, maybe even caring." Simon's arm is around Maggie Marie's shoulder. There is a humph in the line of her shoulders, but she's not moving away.

"God forbid! Don't eat that one. It's a cinder." Maggie Marie plucks the bacon strip out of his hands and dips it into her egg yoke. The bacon breaks up on the plate. "Can't throw it away. I loved that sow!" She rescues the remaining splinters, kissing the last one before popping it into her mouth. "Rest in peace, Pegeen!"

Something is crawling up Sidonie's leg. A spider she could have handled. Not a cockroach! She stuffs one hand in her mouth and with the other tries to bat it away. It comes all the faster up her leg before sneaking under her petticoat. She can't help it. She has to jump up to jog it loose. Of course she bumps her head.

 The shriek and subsequent moan send him running for the ladder, gun pulled out and held above his shoulder. He's ready to confront anyone who may have come across the roof and through the little window quietly enough not to be heard over the din of kitchen dishes. The climb up the ladder is swift enough, but probably feels to him like the slowdown of a bad dream when your legs are disobedient blocks of lead. But there she is, all in one piece, dancing on one foot, to avoid a cockroach, a nice, fat juicy one in shiny maroon. The handle of the gun turns out to be his weapon of choice. He makes a nice dive across the mattress and neatly cracks its shell.

Sidonie is taking refuge behind one of the "unshod" pillows. It's over her face and in her mouth. What wants to be another shriek is turning into a gulping sob.

"Hey! Watch the mattress!" Maggie Marie bellows from below. "It's a family heirloom. My grandmother and three generations of bed bugs have slept on it." Again she does the nasty chuckle. "As long as mademoiselle is up, why don't you ask her how she likes her eggs? Pond-scum runny or mouse-dropping dry?"

Sidonie listens for his response, wondering if it's safe to come out from behind the feathers. Does he think she's a fool for being afraid of something smaller than a mouse? Is he tempted to use the butt of the gun on her?

223

"Look what you made me do?"

She can't help herself. She looks. He's doing the glower. Black brows are meeting in one angry clash. Brown eyes are opaque slashes above his nicely carved cheek bones. In this light, his skin is olive, soft and creamy, especially at the neck, against his damn white shirt. But now a smile is teasing the corners of his full mouth. The lower lip is the fullest. His mouth opens. He is about to talk the smile away. Good thing. For a moment there he was almost handsome.

"You've made me kill one of Mags' little friends. Are you going to tell her or should I?" His eyes come alive. They are suddenly engaged in reading Sidonie's. He's wondering what it will take to push her over the edge. It seems to her as if she is surrounded by a variety of edges to topple over. Simon chooses for her. Hysteria. He flicks the dying cockroach into a roll across the mattress, to the edge closest to her foot. Then with one swift snatch, he palms it.

Next thing he'll do is pop it into his half-smiling mouth. Or worse, he'll throw it down her cleavage. And that wouldn't be hard, seeing the state of her buttons. She can't quite remember how they came undone. He's certainly taking his time getting up from the mattress. On one knee, he is pausing long enough to look up at her, every inch of her that the pillow isn't covering. Best move the pillow farther down, Sid.

"You must agree," now he is in full smile. "The very least we can do is give Mr. Roach a proper burial." He opens his hand and pets the split with his pointer finger. "He's a handsome rogue, don't you think?"

She isn't fast enough to retort "Handsome is as handsome does." Man and bug are down the ladder that fast. In the kitchen he must be preening, smirking, maybe even winking to his friend Mags, what ever a man does when he thinks he has checkmate.

Sidonie chooses to sit down on the middle of the mattress, where she can watch for more intruders. There is a dark stain where the first one met the heel of Simon's gun. She will not cry. He won't make her cry. It's only a bug.

"Simon! Not in the soup! That's going to be our dinner! You are a nasty, nasty man! No manners at all! Throw it in the chamber pot. You think all I've got to do all day is cook?"

"I dare say Miss Nibs is at the moment off her food. And I believe a leg iron will be sufficient until I return. Should be back by midnight. If I'm not, you have my permission to carve her up."

"Sounds good. I'll bury her next to Jeanette. Any words you'd like me to say?"

"She had lovely eyes and gave sweet milk."

The door closes behind him.

I've never sat Indian style before, but somehow in the middle of this hard mattress, after what seems like a long siege, tucking each foot under the other knee feels right. Sucking my thumb doesn't. The pillow, still in my hand, is at fault. Without it I would have never remembered sucking my thumb with one hand, while holding the pillow to the side of my head with the other. I'd toss the damn thing into that spider-webbed corner, but I have to sleep on it tonight. Still, what's a spider or two or even three? Last night I slept next to a man with a gun and shared his cigarette. And for a moment there I almost thought he was handsome. But then even a cockroach has shine to his shell.

A shiver reminds her of her buttons and the need to re-fasten them. Instead her hand reaches in and strokes her own breast. She is quietly going insane and it doesn't feel all that strange. You must get used to it, like dirty blankets and mildewed pillows.

225

Gradually you feel the warmth and savor the softness. Eventually you close your eyes and fall asleep. Waking up is not as easy to get used to. It's like closing your eyes on a roller coaster. You hope when you open them the worst will be over, only to discover you are coming to the top of what you have a feeling is going to be another deep fall. As you clear the top, your heart is back in your throat, the wind is forcing your eyelids back into your head and you can't stop screaming.

At first the gun felt strange in my hand. Soon enough I was holding on for dear life. I can't remember letting go. He took it back, of course, probably when I fell asleep. I could get used to having a gun. I could press it to my breast and feel the cool power.

Chapter 37
Simon, May I?

"May I come down now?" Sidonie asks before Maggie Marie can go out the door and leave her alone in the loft. The lady of the house has a pail in her hand and a coarse knit cape over her shoulders. The cape looks like it was once light green. She must have liked that color when she bought things new.

Mags puts down the pail with an exaggerated sigh and a barely distinguishable mutter. "More trouble than she's worth." She pauses before turning around, one hand reluctant to let go of the knob. "The loft works just fine for me. If I let you come down I have to shackle you. And you wouldn't really like shackles. I've never treated my hardware all that gently. There are gouges and sharp edges on the metal. And the rust loves to lodge in fresh wounds." She stoops down and makes a show of picking up the ladder and then putting it back down. "Awful lot of trouble! How 'bout I just throw you up a crust of bread and a newspaper. There might even be something about you in it. "Heiress disappears. Police are dragging the Seine."

Sidonie is tempted, but she doubts that Mags has that recent a paper. How could she? It only just happened, although it all seems like a hundred years ago. "No, I'd rather come down. Maybe I could even help. There are a lot of potatoes on the table. I could peel them."

"As if I'd give you something with a sharp edge!"

"I could wash them then."

"Ever milk a cow?"

"You know I haven't, just as I've never used a knife against another human being."

"Simon tells me you never used a gun before your grand escape and you learned fairly fast."

"I was just making noise, trying to look fierce." And, Sidonie is thinking, this wasn't the first time she was a shot at. Sometimes, like now, it still hurts.

"Fierce would be a bit of a stretch. I'll let you down when I'm done milking. And don't even think of jumping. You wouldn't get far with a broken leg."

The big wooden door slams decisively behind her.

Sidonie's sigh is deep with frustration. Even if she managed to get on the other side of that door, she wouldn't get far without any shoes. She's never thought so much about feet before in her life, bare feet, bloodied feet, feet with stockings, feet without shoes, feet touching someone else's leg. She does have pretty arches. You can see them even through these ugly old socks.

There are some wooden clogs next to the fireplace. She can see them from here, something to think about if she ever gets the chance to make a break for it. But where would she run? Maybe the men shooting at them were with the police. In the darkness she couldn't really be sure who they were. Police would wonder why she shot at them. They might shoot first when they see her next. She still can't believe she so readily followed Simon's lead.

Simon says aim the gun. Simon says shoot the gun. Sidonie says, Simon, may I?

The window under the eaves is dirty. She makes a circle with the edge of her hand in the middle of the glass. There must be someone looking for her out there, someone who means no harm, then again, maybe not. Her mother is back in the States. She may have told Mark and Terry about this. And what would they do if they did know? Her father might be using his influence at the American Embassy. But none of them would expect to find her in a cottage in the middle of the woods sucking her thumb in a loft.

Somehow she must find her own way out of this and get back to Paris. might still be there. He had a lot of speaking engagements. If she found her way back to him she would be safe inside of his entourage.

Entourage is a lovely word. It takes so long to clear its way across your tongue - three lovely syllables with a long lingering "g" to hide inside.

She's getting fanciful again, even as reality is creeping under her petticoats. And she can smell the cow. It smells better than the chamber pot. She has her very own, white with a red circle around the brim. The chips are rusting like the shackles they keep threatening her with.

She'd like to think Mags was a crusty old madame with a marshmallow heart. But marshmallows don't get soft and gooey unless they are put close to the fire. Sidonie lies back down on the mattress and looks at her fingernails. Not one of the nails is broken. All of this ordeal and her hands still look like a lady's, but not her hair. She can feel the tangles.

Once, long ago, her mother brushed her hair one hundred strokes before bed. Sometimes Sidonie's scalp bristled as she burrowed into the pillow and tried to fall asleep. But she always knew why. A skip through a puddle, a stolen piece of candy from the lead crystal dish kept for company, turning down the edge of a page in her mother's favorite book of poems, a stolen glance at the yellow-haired lad who led her pony through the park. It was usually worth it.

She closes her eyes and remembers her mother's hairbrush. It was mother of pearl with a matching mirror. The mirror was fluted on the back like a seashell. There was a little crack on the face of mirror, the right side, bottom. Her mother never threw it away as she so often did to things that weren't perfect. Sidonie never asked why not, afraid her mother would notice and throw it away right then and there. She wonders if her mother still has the set. There was a little round bowl that went with the set. It had a perfectly round little hole in its cover. Clare put hair in there from her brush and comb. Her hair and her mother's have lived together in that little bowl until it got too full. She wonders if any of her hair is still in there now. Probably not.

Sidonie doesn't hear the ladder hit the wall. What jars her eyes open is that familiar cackle. "Have a nice nap? Must be lovely to be a lady of leisure!" There's Mags' disembodied head grinning like a Halloween pumpkin. And just like the Jack O'Lantern, she's missing teeth.

Sidonie considers giving the head a push.

"Don't even think it, my girl. My hands are firm on the ladder. And I have a paring knife in my apron pocket. I'd be doing Simon a favor. One less body for him to worry about."

"I wouldn't do anything of the sort." Sidonie lowers her lashes.

"What you need is something to occupy you, in a place where I can keep an eye on you and still attend to all my chores."

Sidonie tries to imagine what those chores might be. The place looks like it hasn't been dusted or swept for weeks. And the cooking amounts to dropping in the broth a fresh half of an onion, a clove of garlic or handful of sliced carrots every hour or two or three. The ever- simmering pot depends on the fire to keep it clean, to boil off one layer of burnt food and make way for another. Still, it smells good.

Should I ask for some? No. Mags would so enjoy saying no. No is a word with power. Yes gives it away. Yes, I'll give you what you want. No, I'll disappoint you. Not yet. I prefer to make you wait. Never! There's no hope for you. Might as well give up. NO! NO is my word now. No, I won't ask for some soup. No, I won't ask for an extra blanket. No, I'll ever trust any good to come from either of you. No, I'll never give up. I'll just bide my time. And then one day I'll veto all your plans for me. I'll make that run for it. I'll reclaim my life. Somehow. I'm not sure how. But YES, I'll find a way. Simply biding my time.

A plotting Sidonie enjoys looking down her nose at her tittering jailer. The ladder is not all that secure. The impudence only makes Maggie smile. God knows the girl will need all the defenses she can muster in the days ahead.

"Coming down or aren't you? Wait till I get down the ladder. It won't hold both of us."

Sidonie scrambles across the mattress with thoughts of escape temporarily on hold. For the moment she is looking forward to standing upright and moving one foot in front of the other. She only hopes Mags has forgotten about the shackles. Sidonie doesn't see any such contraptions lying in a corner or on a shelf or attached to a wall. They are usually attached to something, most often in a dungeon. There was mention of a dungeon, under the floor.

"I'll make a deal with you, *Mademoiselle*. Behave yourself and I won't cut you. Make one false move and you lose the stockings."

Sidonie nods. At the moment it's an easy promise to make. She still hasn't figured out where to run and to whom. Maybe if she could get to those clogs. She tries not to look at them, heels together, waiting for someone to jump in and take them for a ride.

"All right, all right, put on the damn things. You'll need them to walk through the manure. Just remember to leave them outside. Believe me, they are not good for running unless you have years of practice and by then you are too old to run very far." With the pork chop flat of her hand Mags pushes Sidonie out the door. "*Vite, vite, depechez vous*! See the barn? That's where we're headed. *Marchons*!" Sidonie is not surprised that Mags has a weapon in her apron. Her facility with French is another matter.

Mags accent is just fine, just one more of the many lies Simon has told her. He probably lies just to lie. No, more likely, to confuse. She would guess him to be a calculating liar rather than a habitual one. And Mags is just as calculating. Sidonie has to wonder just what is going to happen in the dark recesses of that barn. Maybe that's where the shackles are, or worse, a cow. The last thing Sidonie needs is a lesson in milking. Her hands want to search for pockets in which to hide, but she needs them out in the open to help her balance through the rutted yard.

One bad-tempered goose glares at Sidonie from its perch on a pile of fireplace wood. A rooster stands his ground over a fresh layer of seeds. His ladies scatter just far enough to avoid the wooden clogs and rubber boots. There is a small door next to the big barn doors. Mags motions Sidonie to enter and then barks the reminder, "Off with the clogs!" Sidonie is only too happy to stumble out of them. As predicted, they have accumulated their share of the barnyard.

Through the open doors of the hayloft the morning sun shines on a freshly swept floor. Although there are no farm animals in the stalls, their earthy smell lingers. The dust of a leftover bale of hay also tickles her nose. Sidonie wants to run her hands over the surface of the wooden table in the center of the barn. Nicks and bruises are the very best kind of patina. There are no benches or chairs around the table. Serious stand-up work is done here.

She recognizes the tools of the trade. Brushes muddy a jelly glass. Paint mixed with turpentine is perfume to an artist. She's often thought of dotting it on the backs of her ears and behind her knees. That way she would carry her work with her all through the day and fall asleep to its musty fumes. There's still a crust of clay on the carving knives.

And, of course, that oven in the corner cooks pottery, not food. A potter in a hurry, not a mason with a master plan, threw together all those unmatched bricks. On the back wall rough-edged shelves display the products of all this creativity. There are bowls with lips for pouring and vases with graceful necks and a smattering of cunning little animals. A stolid cow stands patiently, a frisky rooster prances, a swift hare outruns an arrow, and a piglet holds his head high, as if he were listening for the footsteps of the farmer's wife with a pail of leftovers meant just for him.

She can't help herself. She rushes over and runs her fingers up and down the rabbit's swept back ears.

"You would be most interested in the worthless pieces. I just do the figures to keep my fingers agile. Helps when you are making pinch pots. Pinch pots take the least time if you have the knack and so you can make and sell more at a better profit. Here. Sit down at the table where I can tie your leg to its frame." She's holding a rope, a thick rope, but, thankfully, no shackles. Sidonie is used to rope. "This morning I got a fresh pail of clay from the banks of my pond. Little streams are constantly feeding it with fresh bits of dirt, dirt malleable enough to be rolled or bent to my bidding. You can make yourself useful by pulling out the small pebbles and pieces of sticks."

Sidonie runs over and offers her ankle. She can hardly wait to get her hands in the clay. She has always wondered what it would be like to work in the earth, water and fire.

"Today I'm going to make some soup bowls. Since you might be here awhile we'll need more dishes, some for the cupboard and some to soak in the sink. I don't always get to the dishes. It's best to have a stockpile. Besides, a sink is happiest when there is something in it. And I also have some orders to fill."

Mags has customers waiting. I'd be surprised if I hadn't noticed the glaze on that pot. A pot only needs to be round and sturdy to be useful, but isn't it nice that this one could catch a ray of kitchen sunlight if placed on a shelf by the window. Mags' glaze betrays her. She's an artist after all. If that little rooster was just for practice there would be no real need to smudge its comb with a gentle coat of yellow. Give me a brush and I'll be an artist too. I'll splash pink on the nose of the bunny. And the cow's bell must be blue, cornflower blue. Or maybe sea green. Green would be more surprising. I like surprising.

Chapter 38

The Devil You Know

It's midnight and she's lying on a bare mattress with no idea what's going to happen next. Somewhere deep in the house, probably at the end of the hall Sidonie has yet to walk down, an old clock slowly strikes twelve times. She finds herself resenting the clock's leisurely pace. It's completely indifferent to the beat of her heart. It beats one to her three. She tries calming herself with words, today's new words. She'll let them drizzle over her - throwing a pot - pinching a vase -firing the kiln - glazing and re-glazing. Someday she will form a little golden fish so delicate, so graceful and so illusive before the last coat it will swim away. Swim away, swim away, swim away.

It's maddening! Midst all of Sidonie's inner turmoil, Mags goes quietly about her life, day after day, hour after hour, minute by minute. Her life moves as slowly as Francois settling on the hearth, first curling this way and then the other, until he is one with the stone. In the softness of the moment, Sidonie calls the dog by his given name. Everyone deserves a given name. Every pot deserves a glaze. Today, after two days of showing how, she let Sidonie lay her hands on an unfinished vessel. Vessel is another nice word. Mags showed her how to knead the bubbles out of the clay and then cut out and roll a strip long enough to encircle the top of the bowl, and then another a little longer, and then another still longer. Then all she had to do was coil them onto the rim, joining each securely, one on top of the other. Mags said the Woodland Indians of North America made their pottery that way. Tomorrow, if Sidonie behaved, she could add designs to the hardened pot. Indian women used scalloped shells, the teeth of combs and even their fingernails. Mags has more modern tools, but Sidonie likes the idea of using her own fingernails, putting something of herself in the vessel, letting her own spirit melt into the clay. She's never felt this way about a canvas, never wanted to crawl inside the pretty picture she was painting. She certainly never thought of putting her blood into the paint. A brush was always between her and the world she was trying to bring to life. She now knows the need to be closer.

The clay knew before she did. It clings to her skin, imbeds itself in her pores. It crawls under her finger nails. It responds to her touch like a cat being stroked, from the top of its head, to the tip of its tail and then under its chin. The clay doesn't purr, but somewhere deep inside Sidonie feels a rippling of pleasure.

The clock does that tinkling shutter as it settles back to just keeping time. Simon said he'd be back by now. Damn clock. It unsettles her even when its chimes stop. Sidonie doesn't actually believe Mags will get up and out of bed to kill her at this very instant. The snores are rumbling along quite nicely. And there is no good reason for Sidonie to want her captor to return. Still she finds herself listening for his footfall and the turn of the lock. When he's around his presence fills the room, like a wood fire brings a kitchen to life in the early morning just before the sun comes through the curtains. Kidnapper cozy. She's losing her way again. What were those calming words? Throwing, pinching, glazing, vessel, swimming away, and now, kidnapper cozy. Hardly that! He's the one who has put her at risk, not once, but twice. Still he's a buffer for what ever else is out there in the night watching and waiting. He's the devil she knows.

She tries to revisit her coiled vessel, to imagine the design she will make tomorrow. She pictures an Indian maiden, squatting on the ground, using a hole in the dirt to steady her creation. The girl would probably draw a small bird or a butterfly or maybe the deer she hopes to eat for supper. Sidonie's thinking she might try a ballet slipper and notes from a page of music.

She's almost there – from three beats down to two – from composed to almost calm – when a sudden knock breaks the rhythm. Someone is at the door, someone who doesn't have a key and is playing at the lock. She wants to believe that someone is Simon. But Simon would call out, "Maggie Marie! Open up I'm back from Paris." This someone isn't announcing his arrival. This someone doesn't know there is a bar across the inside of the door. There are more little scrapings at the lock and then the click of a gun being cocked, such soft little noises, as soft as a dog's nails crossing the kitchen floor or a cricket beginning it's evening's ritual. But these soft little noises do not offer the comfort of the familiar. Francois doesn't like them either. From the back bedroom the big bad dog is softly whimpering as if asking permission to bark. A muffled thud sounds like it just prodded him into silence. The knock is now a pounding, an insistent pounding, a demanding pounding. Her hands are forming fists with no idea what or who they should be pounding. Swim away, swim away, swim away!

Sidonie pulls the mattress as far back from the edge of the loft as possible and mentally measures her hips against the small window behind her. She never considered escaping through it. She figured it was too small. Now she has to hope she was wrong. She can feel the crash of an angry fist against the door. Her shoulders start to hunch over, her arms crisscross her chest. If only she were a ball and could roll unnoticed into a corner.

"Open up. Company's come to call."

Slap, slap, slap. Ping, ping, ping. Maggie Marie's slippers are moving fast, so are bulldog's nails, little sounds that could be homespun if they weren't coming so quickly and didn't sound so agitated, like a humming bird's wings when it's too far between branches.

"Coming, coming, coming!" Maggie turns the words into a bird song, loud enough to be heard, lilting enough to disarm or so she pretends, perhaps for Sidonie's benefit, perhaps for her own. The person attacking the door couldn't really be fooled. There's another crash, a tree trunk size crash. "Sidonie! Duck down in a corner! Now!" Mags stage whispers over the noisy door.

Sidonie's already at the little window. She's pulling her skirt over her hips and squirming through. There's a flat little ridge just before the roof meets the outside walls. She lies down, flattens herself and holds onto the edge. She should have closed the window behind her, but not falling off the roof takes precedence. Just as well. Eavesdropping works better with a window open to the eaves. She has no trouble hearing the third crash and Mags' less lilting, "I said I was coming!" She has more trouble believing this is really happening. She's on a roof, in her stocking feet, holding on to a surface that is inviting her to roll off.

Maggie has opened the door and is making her regrets. "Sorry, gentlemen, I'm out of the egg and cheese business. Down to one cow and the chickens are slowing down." Sounds like she's having a hard time re-closing the door. There are creaks and scrapes before the heavy wood pounds against the inner wall. Sounds like a break in the plaster.

"Check her pockets. Her kind is liable to have something in her pockets or under her skirts."

There's a scuffle and a curse. Maggie doesn't give up her weapon easily.

"So unfriendly! But then in your line of work. I suppose you must protect yourself. Egg poachers and all. Still, I wouldn't be threatening you in the middle of the night if you didn't have another interesting sideline - hiding people I'm out to find."

"I'm all alone."

"Forgive me if I don't give that story too much credence. Be a good fellow and check the bedrooms."

Sidonie sticks her face into the roofing. This isn't really happening! Close your eyes and forget there are two of them and at least one of them is armed.

238

"You're wasting your time. "I'm just a lonely wid-" Her voice strangles off. Sidonie can almost feel the gun that must be at Maggie's throat. Or it could be her own paring knife.

"Lady MacGirth, you would do better not playing games with me."

Furniture is being overturned. Drawers are being pulled open. A voice calls from the back of the house. "She's got a shotgun in the wardrobe."

"Pack it up! Wouldn't want the Madame to shoot at our backs."

"Then we're not going to kill her?"

"Let's give her hope. Maybe then she will make a deal."

"I have no idea what you are talking about. I'm the only one here."

"Me thinks you protest too much. Your gentleman friend may be out killing, but I'll bet the girl is still here. His kind likes to travel light. Save us some time and some of your furniture."

"You've seen the whole house, except of course the wine cellar. Only, please don't go there. It is important to maintain the temperature. The wine is all I have left of my beloved Henri. He had such a way with the grapes."

"What a marvelous idea. We'll drink to your health and, if you're cooperative, long life."

There's a complaint of rusty hinges. The wine cellar entrance must be close by. Of course, they had called it the dungeon. She remembers that iron ring in the middle of

239

kitchen floor. She stubbed her toe on it. How smart of Maggie to admit to the cellar since the ring was at their feet and the thought of wine will keep them from looking up. They've yet to discover the loft. And Mags thinks Sidonie is still up there. Could she be forgotten during this madness? It's getting harder to hold on. It would be easy to roll down. The ground might be soft. She could run for it. Then Sidonie would at least be taking control, not waiting for someone to decide her fate. How dangerous could they be? Mags doesn't sound all that worried.

"Ladies first." Mags' howls roll down the stairs after her. Bulldog's barking now until a sharp cry tells Sidonie he's been kicked down the stairs after his mistress. "Ouch! Damn dog broke my skin!" Well, at least Francois put up a little fight.

"What are you doing? Don't we want to go down and look?" Intruder number two doesn't quite understand.

"Once we went down our gracious hostess would have lowered the lid and covered it with a heavy chair or whatever else she could find. There's no one down there. On the other hand, I am quite certain there's someone in the loft."

Too late to roll down. They'd notice the thud.

The ladder falls against the wall. He must have seen a corner of the mattress. She couldn't pull it any farther back. With Maggie locked in the cellar this is her chance to reveal herself and be rescued. And she would if these men didn't seem to be just another version of Simon. Men with guns are out to capture, not free her, may be even kill her. What else are guns for? Somehow, some way, dead or alive, she furthers their schemes - nefarious, mysterious, and it would seem, at cross-purposes. For reasons she has yet to figure out, she is important to them, almost key, but not quite. A key is something to keep and use again. She has a feeling she is less than that. More like a piece of wood used to prop up a window with a broken sash. Once the sash is replaced the wood is tossed aside. Tossed aside, tossed aside, tossed aside.

If only she had closed the window all the way. They'll quite naturally look through. Sidonie lets go of the edge of the roof long enough to pull her skirt down over her knees. It's silly to be modest at a time like this, but maybe that's when dignity, decorum, all those things her mother treasured so much, suddenly become meaningful, even for Sidonie. She mustn't look graceless when she dies.

There's a low, wicked laugh. It's crawling up her spine and down the outside of her arms. "Looking for a breath of fresh air?" He's pointing the gun at her through the window that had once been her ally. "It is a lovely day, Mademoiselle Adair, is it not?" A full beard obscures his face, but not the cheerful malice in his eyes. All these killers do seem to enjoy their work.

"Found her, did you?" Even this voice is cheerful, like one sportsman congratulating another.

"Yes, seems she likes scaling roofs. Agile little monkey!"

"Don't expect me to go out and get her." Another face sticks out the window. She's reminded of a bowl of oatmeal, spongy, with an uneven grain.

"Not necessary. She looks like she's pretty much settled in. I'll just latch this little window and we'll reconvene in the yard."

Sidonie pulls at her skirt again. It's all that's left for her to do. Standing or crawling she would only make a bigger target.

"Moonlight becomes you, Miss Adair." They're in the yard now with their guns aimed directly at her. One man stands tall. They are aiming from two vantage points. She buries her chest into the roofing. The old wound is starting to throb.

"Come on, make it a little more fun for us. Try to scramble away."

Bullets are just missing her, not because the gunmen can't shoot straight, but because they can. A piece of thatch flies up and hits her in the face. She's sliding down and doesn't know whether it's worth holding on. They're going to kill her anyway. A broken neck might be cleaner. Hold on, hold on, hold on!

"Gentlemen. How nice of you to call." Simon's voice is followed by a gunshot. She opens eyes she can't remember closing. He's standing in front of a tree, his legs spread apart, both hands on the gun, the gun smoking like midnight mist. He steps over a body - giving Oatmeal a poke with his polished boot. When there's no response, Simon corrects himself, "Only one gentleman now."

"One gentleman and a swine!" The remaining gentleman hasn't put down his gun. It's still aimed at Sidonie.

"Shall we see who's the better shot?" Simon throws out a dare.

The bearded man laughs. "Oh, I'm absolutely certain I can hit her from here."

"Fire away. You'll kill her, of course, but I'll kill you. Is she really worth that to you?"

"Her life must be worth something to you or she'd be dead already. You're not known to take prisoners."

"In Plan A she lives. But I always have a Plan B. In either one my safety comes first. I'm betting yours does too. If you want to live you must shoot me before I shoot you. It's that simple."

Sidonie closes her eyes again. This is the time to pray. Then she thinks better of it. She has a pivotal role in a stage play with a limited engagement and the curtain is about to fall. Flatten out, become smaller and smaller, disappear, but watch.

The bullet comes straight for her heart. She feels the vibration in the air and in the roof beneath her. But she can't feel the penetration. Must be like a clock when its pendulum moves back and forth, back and forth and then stops. It doesn't hurt. It just happens. Someone's moaning and it isn't her.

Simon's darting across the yard. With the barrel of his pistol he opens the man's still gasping mouth. "Any last words? Take a moment. Think about it. Too late." He pushes the barrel farther in and fires.

Sidonie keeps watching. Blood, flesh and bone fly across the moon-lit crab grass and with them all traces of humanity, except for the twitching feet, still trying to run away. The shoes are quite nice patent leathers with cream cloth uppers.

"If you're all right, stay put." He calls up to her. "If you're not all right, hang on even tighter."

She's not about to move. She's quite fond of her roof. It almost feels safe, like a tree in a lightning storm. You know you shouldn't stand beneath it, but it is dry under the branches, and they do seem to be folding over and protecting you. And if she moves she might see her own blood.

He's inside, up the ladder to the loft and at the open window before Sidonie can work up the courage to feel her breast. His hand's reaching out the window. "You're fine. The roof took the bullet."

But she isn't fine. Her legs are shaking and her hands won't let go of the edge. She has no reason to believe in him, to trust him. He's just another hunter and she's a

243

game bird with a clipped wing. That old wound has another throb in it. The man with the gun wants the wounded bird to come out of the thicket where he can finish it off. And then, of course, there's the fall.

"Don't look down. Just crawl over here. You can do it. You'll be safe inside." He's offering her both his hands. She's never before looked that closely at his hands. They're slim, tapering, with a masculine tan, but no sign of manual labor. It seems murder doesn't callus the fingers. But it can leave a spattering of blood. He laughs as she pulls her hand back. "Just be glad it's his blood, not yours." And as if it were all a jolly lark, he sticks his arms out farther and waves his fingers. "Come on. I dare you!"

She can't make herself reach out and take hold. The devil she knows, but still the devil.

"Like it out there?" Simon laughs. Seems he always finds her amusing. "I grant you there is a nice breeze and the moon is full and bright. But the temperature is dropping, a wind is whipping up and you are about to be blown away. Come inside and be safe." He says safe softly, quietly. It almost soothes. How ready was he to shift to Plan B? But the wind's beginning to whip as he predicted and she's cold and it's silly to stay on this roof. If only she didn't have to touch his bloodied hand.

"I'm coming in feet first." She lies as flat as she can on the sloping roof and braces her feet on the window frame. He'll be looking up her petticoats but it'll be better than her face. She doesn't want him to see her face. Emotions are flying across it. Relief and fear are taking the most turns. But there's also a flush, the deepening flush of a girl who knows her cheeks are turning a betraying shade of pink. And it's not about modesty defiled. It's about touching his bloodied hands. She won't be bound to him in another man's blood.

He's cradling the back of my legs. He's massaging my hips through. He's touching my breasts, but just barely, at the outer rim, so briefly I can't be sure he really did or I

244

only wished he had. His hands linger longer on my shoulders. I'm in his arms now. His face is close. His lips are moving closer. But his eyes are wide open.

Like a clock chiming midnight her heart's going to do that little shudder when the chiming is through. She hates him and fears him, and here she is, handing herself over to him.

If I keep my eyes open it doesn't count.

Chapter 39

A Gift Horse

"Try them on. I'm certain they'll fit." Simon pulls a lady's boot out of one coat pocket and than the other. He holds them up for Sidonie's admiration, but just a little out of reach.

They are really quite nice. Shiny black leather circles the toe and heel. Gray kid carries the rest of the boot up past the ankle. The row of hook and eye buttons to Sidonie look like a string of black pearls straight from the bottom of the sea. And they are reflecting firelight as he gives them a twist and a twirl. She only wishes they didn't remind her of last night and the two-toned shoes on the twitching feet of a freshly dead man.

Mags makes humph sounds. She's shifting from one big foot to another and circling around like an elephant not sure there is enough room to sit. And there is that annoying girl, perched in her favorite chair. Bull dog is also making humph sounds, curled up in the corner behind a dust bin. It seems Francois has had enough excitement, but feels he has to make his presence known, if just for the sake of form. He licks his paw as if just remembering a recent hard knock.

When Simon finally places the shoes on the table in front of Sidonie she wants to press them to her breasts. She settles for running her fingers down the buttons. Pretty things are such a comfort, like a new doll at Christmas. A head of bouncing curls and a dress with fresh starch makes a little girl's world brand new. There it is – that little sliver of joy. There is still a little girl deep inside Sidonie.

"I know, I know, Maggie Marie. They're not as practical as the clogs you have so generously shared with Sidonie. And I certainly wouldn't suggest she wear fashion footwear around the barn yard, but she will have to fit in with the other stylish Parisian ladies when we move into a new hiding place."

Mags doesn't argue the wisdom of a move, just the location. "Aren't you jumping back into the frying pan?"

"That's what everyone would think. That's why it will be perfectly safe." He leans back on the door, arms crossed, just a little bit pleased with himself.

"When are you planning on making the move?" Mags decides to give up sitting down. The soup needs a sampling and an extra stir.

"I figure we have a day's grace, maybe two. Those fellows won't be expected back right away. No one would think I could have been found that easily."

"Yes, that *is* strange. Either you are losing your touch or someone who knows you is a traitor." Mags makes a face as she puts the ladle back in the brew. It's not her best effort. "The question is who? These fellows looked like the kind who would hire out to anyone as long as the price was right."

"You can't be betrayed if you have no friends."

"I thought you had at least one." Mags hands are on her hips.

"I thought so too." He doesn't miss another humph. "Of course, I can always count on you, Maggie, my darling." He blows her a kiss. "That reminds me. I've got some more surprises. I dropped them behind a tree last night. Hope the night creatures didn't drag them into their cubbyholes. I'll be back straight away." He smiles at Sidonie over his shoulder, a sunny smile, with no malice, no irony. Very, very dangerous. Think twitching feet.

She hopes the boots fit. The buttons open and hook easily enough. Once she takes off the Maggie's socks they just might be a perfect fit. How could he know?

247

"You'd think you never had shoes before. Maybe I should have taught you how to milk. You certainly look the part, a barefoot milkmaid waiting for her prince to kneel down and slip on her magic slipper."

Sidonie feels that flush again, as much anger as embarrassment. Why should she be grateful for the fulfillment of such a basic need? "The socks are way too thick."

"Mademoiselle requires silk stockings, no doubt." Mags pulls some dried herb leaves off the ceiling, crushes them into the palm of her hand and drops them into the pot. "Whatever it takes to get you out of my hair, I will heartily approve."

Simon's back and smiling sweetly, at Mags this time. "Guess which hand." There's a leaf in his hair. The green is tinged with yellow.

Mags is the one blushing now. "You didn't forget." She wipes her hands on her apron.

"No, I didn't." He produces what looks to Sidonie like a museum catalog. "Read it and be inspired."

Mags sits down hard on a kitchen chair for a contented browse.

These two people keep surprising her. They make her think of the clay waiting in the pottery barn. God made his children out of clay. He kneaded, folded, shaped and pinched. But he never fired them. He never glazed them. He let life do that. It seems these two added a few coils of their own, wrapped round and round and round, so thick that the clay never quite dried on the inside. The outside is certainly hard enough. But until now, only Simon and Mags knew about their soft inner layers.

"Here!" He throws a big shopping bag at Sidonie. "Some clean sweet smelling clothes." He could have stopped there and distanced himself from last night's exploding head and his casual quip, "Any last words? Too late." She might have talked herself into believing he would only kill the bad guys and that he liked her and was capable of being kind. But he just has to add insult to injury. "Let's just say your perfume is no longer equal to the task."

She lets the bag slide across the table and fall to the floor. There's blood all over it, as real as it is invisible.

"Pick it up." Without looking up from her catalog. Mags manages to make it worse.

Sidonie bends over and picks it up, glad to escape into the shadow between the table and the floor. She needs time to clear the hurt off her face and the horror in her heart. And the anger. It keeps welling up. First you feel relieved to be alive. Then you think about the cost. You try not to think about the cruelty and his ease in dispensing it. And while you try to tell yourself the cruelty saved your life, he lets you know that someday you may be the target.

He will kill me. He will kill me not. *Expect the worse. Remember. You are a big girl now.*

He's watching her, waiting to see if she is as unbalanced as he wants her to be. One eyebrow has become a question mark. He wants to believe he has knocked the stuffings out of her. She should let him think that. But she can't help herself. She's not quite ready to be vanquished. "Forgive me, but at this moment I'm not particularly concerned about perfumes and whether my particular bouquet pleases or displeases you."

"Whatever are we going to do with you, Miss Adair." Simon is standing above her as she rights herself. He reaches for her elbow as if she were too fragile to settle back in her chair all by herself. With the back of his hand he strokes the side of her face downward towards her chin before rudely tipping it up. He's searching her eyes for those telltale signs. She must not look away, but her eyes must tell him nothing. He must think fear still keeps her in his power. Not sure she is pulling it off, she carefully chooses her words. "Thank you for the clothes. I will, of course, freshen up before I wear them."

Simon doesn't laugh. He doesn't even smile. He just keeps on looking.
Maggie may be missing the delicate negotiations going on between them or she just doesn't care. "She can use the water from rain barrel like the rest of us. Should I guard her or would you like to do the honors?"

"I'm thinking the water trough. If she tries to run away I'll simply push her head under."

Sidonie puts the shoes in the bag and starts climbing the ladder to the loft. "If you don't mind I think I'll take a nap first."

Simon's hand is around her ankle. She's glad she left the socks on. He pulls down the cotton and lets his fingers curl around.

She looks down expecting a leer.

There's no leer, just eyes focused only on her. "You're going to sleep away what promises to be a lovely day?"

She can't imagine how that could possibly be, but she's not about to ask. Her "If you don't mind" came out sassier than she intended.

"Off with you then!" His hand threatens the sanctity of her bottom. "You do look the worse for wear."

She goes up the ladder as fast as she can, too fast. The bag drops from her hand and scatters its contents all over the floor. There are two dresses, one a buttercup yellow, the other posy pink. Only the cloak is a sensible black. There's lingerie with eyelet trim, a sheer white night gown, a soft cloud of stockings, and, of course, the shoes.

He picks them all up, shoves them in the bag and sets it back on the table. "Of course these can keep till after you've had your beauty sleep."

Of course she can't sleep. Of course she can no longer ignore her need for warm water and soft suds. And yet, she has never felt more fresh and alive. Here in this wretched little cottage with its perpetual smell of garlic and onion, under the constant threat of death, she feels like a girl about to become a woman, a tinker in the arts about to become an artisan. She only hopes they are here long enough for her to leave her mark on her little coiled pot. Someday someone may find it, take it home and put it on a shelf where it will bring pleasure every time the light falls across it. Maybe someone will even put some flowers in it or crush some walnuts with the rough little bottom. She really wants to fingernail in her initials, maybe just a nice swirling S. Maybe it's because she can no longer think of life as a long and wide path in front of her with a fresh horizon behind each new hill. She has to enjoy the small stretch of earth visible to her.

The door closes. Simon and Mags have stepped outside. They are not speaking loud enough to be overheard. Of course he's telling his Maggie Marie what he learned in Paris and why he's Sidonie's best hope. They are outside planning and plotting. She is inside dreaming, pretending, and fooling herself. He must have some idea who sent yesterday's visitors. They didn't seem the type of people with whom Amalendu would traffic. And he would be sending someone to rescue her. Wouldn't he?

If she hadn't let herself be so caught up in shoes and stockings and pottery she might have learned more from Simon. He might have let something slip if she'd asked the right questions. Then again he may have only been dangling a carrot, pulling a rabbit out of a hat to distract her. Pretty shoes were, in her case, the best conjuring trick of all.

They are magicians, the two of them, very good at slight of hand. They are pulling her attention away from what is happening in the real world and she has made it so very easy for them. All they have to do is keep the smoke coming and the mirrors flashing. Sidonie has already locked herself in her own box just waiting to be sawed in half. She is shut up inside with her longings, her desire to conquer the next handsome man, her need to make beautiful things as well as be beautiful. Who will be next? Just how great will be her achievements?

Only she's never really conquered anyone. She's just been passed from hand to hand. And the last pair is definitely bloodied. As for her own hands, to look at them no one would know they have wielded a paintbrush or brandished a prop. Yet now she dares to believe she can use them to sculpt a new Sidonie. She can see scuffed nails. She can imagine dry and roughened skin. She can feel strength in fingers bending, forming and molding something into being. She doesn't understand. She doesn't know.

I just have this feeling. It's like the first time ice skating. It's so much fun turning those steps into a glide. You just know you'll be able to manage a turn when you need one and eventually a twirl. You don't even think about pulling up to a stop. When that time came I usually tumbled over, but that was fun, too. I won't be good at first, but I'll learn. I'll master the technique and then I'll add Sidonie, Sidonie's special curves, Sidonie's way with color. I'll look at my little vase or my little fish and I'll be proud. No, better than proud. I'll be delighted with what I'm looking at, holding on to, giving back. Finally I'll have found my way to reflect the beauty of this world.

When this happens, Sidonie's beginning to realize, she won't really matter, but she will really count.

She straightens her body out of the fetal position to which she had quite naturally reverted. She stretches out her arms and her legs. She pushes her back into the mattress. She makes herself as open as she cannot afford to be when the two of them are watching, always watching. The little window is open again. Sunshine falls across her face. She is coming out from behind the lace curtains of her life, the gossamer dresses, the flirtations that screened her real feelings. She's been a mystery to herself for too long, maybe not quite a mystery. Maybe more like an actress trying to find the right role for her debut. Should she play an artist struggling for survival in a garret? Should she do a play within a play and be an understudy about to have her big break? Should she be the heroine in a star-crossed love affair? Seems life has cast her in a real life murder mystery and the question is will she survive the reviews. Seems her kidnappers have typecast her as a dupe. She is their way out of what looks to her like an unsuccessful assassination attempt. To them she is completely transparent, easy to manipulate, fun to play with.

Simon knows that a little stroke to her vanity is as effective as a gun pressed into the small of her back. And there is no need for shackles when an unfinished pot turns Sidonie into a child in a sandbox. And when they want to shake her up, they show how they really feel about her. To Simon she is a pleasant diversion, but he will be just as pleased when it's time to kill her and he does it well, with a dramatic flourish and a ready quip.

God, I'm being such a baby! I'm still playing at life while Simon's playing a game of Kill or Kiss. Who pays most? He's asking himself. Is this embrace strategic or just a pleasant diversion that won't slow me up all that much? I could die at this man's hand no matter how he rules. I can't let that happen. I've just found beauty in a lump of clay. There's still too much of life to live. Grow up fast! Sidonie tells herself. *Grow*

253

up or die way too young. Just what does growing up mean? Taking care of yourself, not waiting for someone to save you? Mother, with a broader view, would add taking care of others. Sidonie's never had reason to do much of that. She could start with being aware of others and not just how they fit into her plans or she fits into theirs. Right now she should be aware of everything that is happening around her. Right now she should be worried less about who she is and how she is changing, fascinating as that might be. Right now she should be eavesdropping, quite literally. Two people may be deciding her fate without her right here and now.

She opens the window onto the roof and sticks her head out to listen. First of all, she has to find out what they know that she doesn't. Simon enjoys pulling colored scarves out of his sleeves, giving her glimpses of the truth, but way too fast and gone in a twinkling. Somehow she has to convince him that she is willing to follow his lead to protect herself from mutual enemies. She'll ask him to teach her how to shoot – straight and right through the heart. Then maybe, just maybe, he'll take her seriously.

And that just might be his first mistake.

Chapter 40
A Lovely Web

They are standing behind the barn where Maggie and no one else could possibly see them.

The sun is behind them, halfway up in the morning sky. Shadows fall in front of them but not far enough to obscure the target. It's big enough, one of Mags' wide-brimmed straw hats. If there ever was a ribbon, it's long gone and it looks as if some small creature has taken a bite or two.

"It's big enough. Guess you have very little confidence in my aim." Sidonie licks her lips.

"Yes, well, you have yet to prove you can even hit the tree." He's still in possession of the gun. His thumb lingers on the trigger. His fingers move slowly down the barrel. He's in no hurry to hand it over. "Of course you will be firing blanks."

She laughs at his reluctance as well as what is probably a lie. "Already afraid my aim may be too good?"

"I'm afraid for Maggie's cow. She only has one left."

Sidonie plants her legs far apart and deep into the earth. It's easy to do since she is still in Maggie's clogs. The lovely new boots must be saved for strolls down Parisian boulevards. "I'm ready as I'll ever be." She holds out her hand.

"First you must have your lesson."

"You already told me to hold on with two hands. I can see for my self I must look at the target and then pull. After that I must practice till I get it right. What else is there to know?"

"Nothing at all." He hands it over, barrel first, his eyes, as always, trying to find hers.

She turns the barrel away from her breast. For just a moment the weapon wants to fall free.

"Heavier than you remember? Of course the last time your arm was resting on the ridge of the car window. Now only you are holding it."

"I can manage, thank you." She looks anywhere but at his knowing gloat.

"Both hands. Remember?"

"Is this really the same gun she shot before? It feels familiar and yet . . . .

"Okay, fire away."

The hat remains secure, although the breeze of the bullet knocks a few leaves from the upper branches of the tree. If this is the same gun it has no allegiance, at least not to her.

"Try again."

A rotted fence post railing falls to the ground.

"Again."

The bullet goes out of sight, so far Sidonie can't even hear a thunk against a tree.

Her two hands and the gun she still grips fall below her waist. She bites her lip.

"Ready to listen?"

"Yes." She drags her eyes up to meet his. Yes, he's gloating. It's at the corners of his mouth. It's in the arch of his eyebrow.

"The trick is in the breathing. Take a deep breath. Breathe half way out. Hold it. And then look where you want the bullet to go."

In, half way out, hold. He's looking again. Seems her ascending and descending bodice has his attention as much as her hold on the gun.

This time she hits one tree over. Next time she hits the tree. The third time it's the poor fence post again.

"I've got better things to do." He takes the revolver and reloads it then turns to be on his way. A lifted arm dismisses her, her poor aim as well as her bosom. "Keep practicing. I'll be back. And don't even think of running. Mags wasn't lying about the wildlife. And you can't be sure there aren't some other assassins out there waiting."

"You never told me who they were, what you learned in Paris. Two sets of people shooting at us. Just how many sets of enemies do we have?" She's raising her voice to his no-longer-interested back.

"When you've proved you can shoot straight, you will become an official member of my band of merry men. Then I will tell you what you need to know." The disappointing news is tossed over his shoulder.

"Isn't that a little backwards? Once you tell me why you are my best hope my loyalty will be assured. Isn't that more important than how well I can shoot?"

"What you need to know - " She's been straining her voice but he's letting distance do what distance does.

"Yes?" She cups a hand to her ear.

"The secret is - "

"I can barely hear you!"

His laugh's loud enough as he turns and mimics her cupped hand. The message coming through his little megaphone is both slow and deliberate. The intended recipient is not only hard of hearing, but not very bright.

"Pretend you are trying to hit someone you really want to hit, like one of last night's visitors. You know they would have killed you if I hadn't come along. By this time today they'd be thinking lunch. Not very nice of them. Wouldn't it be nicer if they were dead?"

After a few more errant bullets, Sidonie makes the slightest of turns, just enough to be sure he's gone. She takes aim. In, out, hold. Pretend. Someone you really want to hit before he hits you.

She hits so close to the nail hole that it widens. The hat dances in a circle before settling back down.

The way Sidonie blows the smoke away from the barrel, one might well think it's a lover's kiss.

She's thinking, "That one was for you, Simon."

Behind the rain barrel Simon might well have reached up and caught that kiss.

He's shaking his head. "Sidonie, Sidonie, Sidonie! What a lovely web you weave."

Chapter 41

Conundrum

It felt like leaving home. Maggie Marie stood at the door waving like a mother might. She didn't throw a kiss. That would have been too uncharacteristic. But she did wave. She did smile. And her last words were, "Be careful." Although Sidonie would guess they were meant for Simon rather than her.

The long drive into the city was a silent one, but not what you'd call a companionable silence. To Sidonie it felt like they were each in their own snow globe, being pelted by their own storm. It felt as if she was somewhere between nowhere and nowhere safe. At least Simon knew where he was going, could make an experienced guess at what he could expect. He must have gone into hiding before. He must have slipped in and out of many lives, pretending he was one person or another. Maybe he is no one. Maybe he is a blank slate and just pencils in what is required. But his persona is always white on black or black on white. There are no colors, not even gray.

When she shoots him red will enter the picture. Surely she has to shoot him and to do that she has to remind herself what he looked like when he put that gun into the mouth of the man lying at his feet. She must try to remember. She was looking more intently at the man about to die. But she must have seen it all. Her eyes must have taken in the whole scene. She tries to remember, but all she can see now is the man driving into the rising sun. She's never seen him in profile. His face has either been turned away or full-on looking at her, intimidating or manipulating, pushing her away or, worse yet, drawing her in.

The difference is now Sidonie knows not only what Simon's doing, but why he's doing it. At the moment it's manipulation. He's got her on the run, from who knows who, on a road to who knows where, not sure if he's taking her to safety or to an out of the way grave. He wants her unsure. This is fun for him, an amusement midst the

260

serious business of murder and mayhem. He's so good he has the leisure to play games. Women are also good at games. They've had to play hard, even dirty, in the power struggle that began in the Garden of Eden. Men, fortunately enough, forget this simple reality generation after generation. Most likely Simon is just another man with a short memory.

Well, maybe not an ordinary man. His looks are too romance-language for that. With his thick black hair and his tawny skin and the already, this early in the day, dramatically darkening beard; he could be Spanish, Italian or maybe even Greek. But he speaks English as fluently as if it were his first language, educated English. She's not sure if he was educated in England or America. There are so few nuances of place – no Oxford English, no Harvard English. It's as if he learned it in a bolted and windowless room away from anyone or anything that would color in an accent. His teacher must have been a book. But how do you hear a book? How do you recognize a long *o*? He's more a mystery man, but mysteries are simply puzzles waiting to be pieced together, yet another game.

She'd like to run her finger down his long, slim nose. He would pull away, of course. He's the sort who wants to control the touching. He'd whip his head away and send her hand flying. His eyes would lock with hers, daring her to try that little bit of impudence one more time. But if she were quick, if she tweaked instead of touched, his nose would probably turn red like any other nose. And she'd turn him from complacent, to surprised, to angry. And that would be one up for her side!

"Cat got your tongue?" He turns to her and smiles. It seems like such a mundane question. She has been sitting here thinking him into some kind of superior being, complex anyway. And here he is expressing himself in a cliché. Again he's looking at her too long and too hard. Is he simply puzzled or actively calculating? More likely he's plotting his next move.

An innocent smile is as good a bluff as any. "I'm just letting you concentrate on your driving. And I imagine you are watching out for unexpected company."

"Sidonie, I haven't known you long, but I already know that nothing stops you from talking when you have something you want to say. I don't like your silence. It tells me you are thinking. And, I suspect, a thinking Sidonie can be dangerous."
He really should be more attentive to the road, but his hands look as if they could do the steering all on their own, long fingers, with strength at the knuckles.

"I can't imagine how I could be a danger to you."

"That's exactly what you are imagining. So let me make it easy for you. I will never hand you a loaded gun unless you are faced with someone you should fear more than you fear me. I'm counting on you being smart enough not to waste your bullets on the one person who can get you out of the line of fire."

She considers this for a moment. True or false? Nothing is ever easy with him. Either way, though, she might as well play along. "I do want to go home. You can't expect me not to want to escape. Living in the woods, wearing clothes someone else chooses for me." She is careful not to add, watching you look a man straight in his eyes as you end his life. The man looked so frightened. And Simon looked, yes, now she remembers, urbane. Just like now.

He turns the steering wheel towards the side of the road. He parks. He turns off the engine.

"Sidonie, Sidonie, Sidonie. How much should I tell you? How much can you handle? What good will it do me? What's in it for me?" He lifts her chin again. He seems to like her chin and the angle of her eyes when he tilts it up.

262

"How much can I believe you? Why should you tell me anything that even resembles the truth?" She doesn't pull away. She hopes her eyes do their usual magic. In his eyes she sees nothing to hold onto, nothing to keep her from slipping, falling, going under. She remembers brown, but she's seeing black, obliterating black. He turns away from her, tilts his head back, and closes those lids. Around the steering wheel his hands open and close. She wasn't the first to look away. Just what did he see in her eyes? She doesn't smile. He needn't know she knows that the match has officially begun and she's one down.

"That is the conundrum."

Simon slides across the front seat and kisses her, too quickly to change his mind, too deeply for her to protest, with enough passion to ignite hers. She finds herself holding on so tightly to his taut back that she slides with him out the door as if they were one body. Then they do a slow roll in the brush - sharp blades of grass, tiny stones only adding exquisite little bursts of pain. It's wrong, it's dangerous, it's evil, and it overwhelms. She feels herself aching and opening and moistening. She feels as if something has been unleashed inside her, something that demands to devour something else. She's not thinking, just feeling, doesn't care, must have. And he's just as hungry, ravenous, and unwilling to wait.

"Sidonie, Sidonie, Sidonie," he whispers as his lips leave hers long enough to pull off the last pieces of clothing getting in the way. "Sidonie, Sidonie, Sidonie." Her name and his saying it over and over, sounds like the rush of water over a waterfall. There's no where to go but down, nothing to feel but the splashes against the rocks below. Exuberant splashes, sparkling splashes! Everything is falling away, especially any of those last traces of fear, not that she wants it all to go away. Fear heightens every feeling it touches, like pain it makes you feel more alive, just when you are most vulnerable.

*　　　　　*　　　　　*

He carries her back into the car before the thought of leaving this place, this time, this moment, this man has even occurred to her. He lays her tenderly across the back seat, pulling down her wrinkled and soiled yellow dress. He'll get the buttons later. His coat will keep her modest till then. She's still chaste, still untouched. Something in her is beyond any harm he could do, like a flower that won't wilt or a sunset that refuses to disappear behind a hill. She is perpetual spring. And he is a complete fool.

Her eyes open with no loss of innocence. They don't darken with remorse. Her smile is languid, her eyelashes too heavy to stay open.

"Sleep now. I will wake you at the Hotel. Tonight you will lie on silk sheets."

*   *   *

He wakes to find her side of the silk sheets cool and empty. He reaches for the gun under his pillow as his eyes adjust to the dim light. There she is looking at herself in the white pedestal looking glass. She's probably looking for change, looking to see how she could have done what she did, may be even having second thoughts. That will not do. She's back in her nightgown. He grabs his robe. A man naked in bed is one thing. A naked man coming across the room is something else. He mustn't frighten her. He must keep her in the dream, as much for himself as for her. He can't remember living in anything but cold reality, not since he was a boy and hid under his covers. The world was nicer there. A boy could sail a ship to China or race through the grass with a yellow dog. Or just close his eyes and feel the black velvet of the night.

Gently he turns her away from the looking glass and into his arms. The mirror is at his service now, letting his eyes follow the curve of her back while his chest feels the billow of her breast. Her shoulders and back are bare, her nightgown little more than a few waves of white chiffon. Her face is pressed into the niche between his lapel and

264

his square jaw, her long hair falling between them. His black robe frames her ivory body. It's as if his darkness, his clothing, his complexion, his mood define her. The moonlight flowing down her temple, over her shoulder and to her arm keeps her from disappearing into him – only the moonlight and the single pearl at her ear. He's glad he bought her the earrings, glad and a little sorry. He would like her to disappear into him.

His hand holds her elbow. Strong fingers open and close over delicate bones. So delightfully opposite, so male, so female, they should be immersed in each other. But his eyes are already looking beyond her, into the depths of the mirror, into the backward and twisted world he has made for them. He is not surprised to see his mouth turned down, not enough to be a frown, but no where close to being a smile. He can understand why breath is coming fast and flaring his nostrils. He's a racehorse at the starting gate. What he doesn't know is why he's in this race and what he will find at the finish line.

She moves in his arms, not away, but closer in. He enjoys feeling her there, smelling her there, a scent as light and pervasive as a drop of vanilla. But if he needs to break away he can do it in a quick step or a furtive twist. He knows there may come a moment when he will leave her alone at a bedroom window or in the middle of a dance floor. He is prepared to push her aside or throw her to the ground; which-ever move takes her, them or only him out of harm's way. It would be nicer if he could save her, more pleasant if he could keep her by his side. Her breath warms his neck. Her hair caresses his cheek. He only wishes her lips would move in a little closer. Gently, he pulls her in.

The need to cut and run may be a minute, an hour or a day away, but right now, in this moment, it feels good, not safe, but good. But then safe has played no part in his past, just as she will play no part in his future. In his life she has only a cameo role. In her life he is a walk-on. All the more reason to incline his head and let his mouth skim her shoulder. He feels her tremble. His has given her no words, but she thinks she has heard them. He will only say her name. She loves hearing him say her name and he doesn't mind saying it. It's a small price to pay for a sliver of her moonlight. But he will have to pay more. He will have to make some sense of this when she awakens from this reverie. What story will he tell her? What story will best serve? Whatever is he going to do with her now? Why does he think he still has a choice?

I like his silence. I like knowing his mind is tumbling, scrambling like mine. I know he's confused. I can tell by his touch, bold before, tentative now, wondering whether, not sure what comes next. We both know there's more, more to feel, more to risk. There it is. His finger is following the shape of my ear, memorizing it, the way I'm committing to memory this lovely crevice in his shoulder, where I fit so perfectly. I pull my hand from his chest, slowly, one reluctant finger at a time. It feels so good, the return, one eager finger at a time. He was warm before. He's warmer now. And so am I. Everywhere. And so it begins again. It's an interesting circle, but circling can make you dizzy. You can lose your footing. And yet I've never felt more on the level. This really is my game. I've felt before. I've loved before. I've gone on to love again. I wonder, I really wonder about Simon. The competition may have reached a new level, a new depth, and he may be the one lacking experience. Of course I could be fooling myself. But do I have an advantage. Emotion doesn't frighten me. Emotion is where I live.

Chapter 42

The Rescuers

"How did you get in here?" Amalendu doesn't ask who she is. He can see the resemblance. And he doesn't ask her why she's here. He knows she's come on a rescue mission. What confounds him is her ability to climb over a six-foot fence and walk through a maze of closed doors.

She isn't a young woman, but then she is the woman who gave birth to Sidonie. There's an American saying. Something about fruit not falling far from the tree. Apple? Pear? More like a blood orange. In the case of Adair women the fruit must be more exotic. And it appears Madame Adair won't be that easily shaken loose.

A half hour ago two men were stopped at the gate of the *Chateau Du Printemps,* most likely her companions. His host guaranteed the security of his ancestral home as well as inaccessibility. Tucked into the countryside, with no formal gardens, it looks from the road more like a monastery or a retreat house. No frills. No compelling architecture. No reason to visit. But here she is, so many questions in her eyes, her hands coiled, seemingly ready to strike if she doesn't like the answers.

"If I tell you, I may never make my way in again. Let's just call it subterfuge." She's smiling now. Benign? Not likely.

He moves towards the white French doors. He's never before felt threatened by a woman. Subterfuge he can understand. Women have depended on guile for centuries. She probably posed as one of his rich benefactors. She has the air. There is money in the teal blue plumes of her hat as well as in her voice. It sounds like it is accustomed to being heard, even when, like now, she is speaking as low as the whispers of turtledoves or the hiss of a snake.

In his world a woman doesn't hiss. And she never stands her ground or speaks her mind, no matter what the volume, unless she is invited to. And she seldom gets that invitation. "No doubt you have a mastery of deception. But in this encounter you are wasting your ruses, artifice, ploys, whatever you obviously take such pride in. I don't know where your daughter is. If I did, I'm not certain I should deliver her to you. At this stage in her life she needs to come out from under her mother's wing."

"And perhaps out from under your wing as well. As I understand your philosophy women's wings are more likely to be clipped. I would have imagined that by now you would have discovered she isn't harem material or philosophically gifted. She isn't right for your world."

"My mission is to awaken perceptions and arouse expectations, to broaden rather than shrink the worlds of others."

"And because of you my daughter's world may have already come to an end."

"You think that? Then why have you come to me?"

She moves in closer. She is touching the sleeve of his white tunic to get his full-face attention. He can feel her fingers through the silk. No one touches him. He turns on her the full weight of his authority, the strength of his convictions, the aura of his holiness – it's all there in his eyes, the way he holds his head and the delicate recoil of his arm. He is a holy vessel.

She doesn't move away from his holiness. There is no fear of God. "I've come because I dare to hope you too may want her safe. You have never met anyone like her." She looks up through lashes, not as long as Sidonie's, but more artfully darkened. For her it requires a little work, but she's still pretty, with delicate features, smooth skin, small waist, and breasts still riding high. "You know you haven't." Now it's a purr.

They stand facing each other down. He decides to be merciful. She is, after all, only a mother in search of her child. Mercy will feel like that gentle rain from heaven. Maybe it will even make that proud head bend low, those lashes close down. He gives her the smile he saves for moments like this, when the person before him can only be reached through the senses, not the mind. He takes her small hand in his big one. It's just as well manicured as hers. He lets her smell his cologne. It's more pungent than her perfume. Gardenia is no match for musk. He looks into her eyes and speaks in his intimate voice, the kind you use after putting your finger to your lips and looking around to see if anyone is watching. "Trust me. My disciples are searching as well as praying for her."

"Your disciples? Searching? That doesn't sound like something they are trained to do." There is a trace of insolence, but she is holding on to his certainty, perhaps a little too tightly.

He disengages his hand and his eyes and steps back. "I have disciples in many disciplines and walks of life."

"What does that mean?" She moves back into his aura, this time uninvited. It's a trespass.

He moves still farther back. "It means I have the resources to find your daughter - for her good, not for mine, nor for yours."

"And they have found something, these clever, well-meaning disciples?"

"They are close."

"And they will keep searching?"

"O course." He opens the French doors and looks out at the balcony.

"One more question."

Of course there would be. He welcomes the breeze cooling his cheek, and sees significance in a woodpecker pounding a fence post instead of one of the many trees around him.

He doesn't sigh as he says, "And what question would that be? Why haven't they found her yet?"

"My question is 'Who?' Who are you all looking for? A follower or a belonging? A person or an object."

"You've already decided for yourself that she isn't up to following my philosophy. Now you insult me by suggesting I consider her a possession. She is a human being with an eternal soul. And she came to me for a little guidance as she walks her own path. I was happy to pour in as much wisdom as she could contain."

"I'm wondering if there isn't more to it. Perhaps you want her back because she is a threat."

"A threat? We are talking about the same Sidonie? Your daughter?"

"A threat to you in the hands of someone else."

"Madame, what a fertile imagination you have. Sidonie is a lovely young woman. She is a joy at any gathering. She asks relatively thought-provoking questions. She must have got that from her mother. She was just in the wrong place at the right time."

"Twice? Once I could believe. But there must be a reason she was taken. Has there been a ransom or a blackmail note?"

"Blackmail! A man must have something to hide to be blackmailed."

"There we are in agreement."

A rock comes through the air and falls hard enough on the floor of the balcony to chip the marble. Amalendu pushes the woman clear of the doors and against an inside wall. She's surprised by his gallantry, but pulls loose and runs out on the balcony to the rock. She had seen a note attached to it. It might be that ransom or blackmail note.

She's reading it aloud before he can snatch it away. "Release Clare Adair at once or we will call the police." She laughs and leans over the railing. He thinks she's gone mad, but is too fascinated to return to the safety of inside.

"I'm just fine, gentlemen!" Clare yells at the brambles below. "I've just been having a nice chat with his Eminence here. I'll meet you at the gate. That is, if he doesn't send out the dogs." Then she twirls round to Amalendu. "Promise you won't send out the dogs."

The smile reminds him of Sidonie, the smile and the pretty please. He's used to *please* from a woman, an expected part of the natural order of things.

"I wouldn't think of it as long as you get your cohorts out of here once and for all." But as he tosses the rock out he aims for the brambles. "Nothing, it's nothing." He shouts to whoever is pounding at the gilded outer door. "Stay at your posts." He takes her hand again. "I understand your concern, Madame. Here's another promise. I'll send word to you as soon as I know something. At what hotel are you staying?"

She fishes a card out of her purse. "Oh, you know something, more than you trust me to tell. But I don't really care about your palace intrigues. I just want my daughter back. As do my rock-throwing Galahads. If you have anything to hide, you better find her soon, before they lob more than rocks. When you skip stones across a still pond you make many, many ripples."

Back to threatening, is she? As she slithers out the door, the guards step aside, not a little confused. Should they detain her or not? They look to their leader. He waves a silent dismissal. He has to think.

Chapter 43
Dark Deeds

While Clare has left Amalendu with much to think about, and her daughter equally bedevils Simon. Two men, each hiding in a personal darkness; two women creating sparks in those dark places. Events will be both confounded and illuminated.

For three days and two nights Simon has successfully hidden Sidonie in a luxury suite of a Paris hotel. It would be easy for him to lose himself in the moment, to believe they are on an island in the middle of the sea or on the top of a lighthouse or at the base of giant redwood. But that would be getting fanciful and fanciful is not good for him. He can feel her getting comfortable, feeling safer and safer in his embrace. And comfortable is dangerous for her. But it's a different comfortable than he might have expected. It's not that she's so sure of him. It's that she seems surer of herself. Maybe that's just the way women are. Being held by strong arms makes them feel strong. They confuse holding on to a man with holding him. They see eternity in an instant.

He has left their rooms to get some perspective before they spend another night together. The hotel has a formal garden, too formal for his taste. The topiary bear is particularly repellent, frozen forever in one pathetic gesture of defiance. The bear is made of leaves after all and his arm will never crush down on anyone.

Simon hates topiary gardens. The animals are too still, too perfect, as they are caught between life and death. No one is perfect at the moment. Faces contort in fear. Eyes roll back. He feels like he's surrounded by the ghosts of the dead who haven't admitted the possibility. Somehow that makes an assassin feel cheated. Victims must fear death first, gradually accept it, almost give in. That brave collie has acquiesced. It's lying down, chin on the ground, eyes closed, not fighting for the moonlight, ready for the growing darkness. Good boy!

He lights a cigarette. The flame brightens his hand and his trigger finger. He still has power to act, to disentangle. And he still has his wits. He knows reality when he sees it. Sidonie is young enough to still prefer the illusion. Then again how long has he really known her, how permanently-molded can a young girl really be? Certainly Sidonie will not be the same after him. Has the change already begun? Of course, it has.

There's that smile. Does it mean she sees a happy ending coming or doesn't it matter to her anymore? He can see her stop mid-spin, perhaps not at all sure what a happy ending is, and then throwing out her arms, bending one knee and spinning just for the spin. All he knows is that he wanted her the moment she hit the target and imagined it was he.

She was standing in the sun. She was holding a gun and squinting one eye. Her tongue caressed her upper lip. She hit the mark. Her feet did that waltz step. Her arms sent her into that spin. The loaded gun hung carelessly in her outstretched hand with sunlight glistening off the barrel. It was not unlike a solar blessing bestowed on a freshwater stream or the feathers of a raven in flight.

*   *   *

The pillow's soft. There's no reason it shouldn't cushion her into sleep. Being in hiding is tiring. Looking over your shoulder, second-guessing your complicity, wondering why you don't feel more fear or more guilt, longing for him to come back. It's when he's here next to her that she can stop watching and wondering and fall asleep. When he's here beside her, she isn't trying to figure him out. His mystery engulfs her. She's enjoying the waves too much to want to swim for shore. She loves the spray on her face. And her head is still above water. If Simon needs a good woman to save him, she is not the one. He wouldn't want her if she were. And he does want her, almost as much as he wants to be the architect of his own ruin.

Sidonie likes to imagine his past. He was no doubt a perverse little boy. His parents gifted him with intelligence, education, impeccable manners and good looks. Very likely there was a fine library in their country home and a shelf of classics in his bedroom. They couldn't know he would read their books backwards. If the last page ended in the death of a dream he would go back and read the first. They would have enrolled him in the best schools, bragged to their friends about his *Summa Cum Laudes*, and never met again with any professor who dared to suggest their son's last test paper was too perfect to be true. His father forced him to play soccer. His mother refused to cut his curls. And they always liked his sister best.

Sidonie rolls over on her back and stares at the ceiling and the moon light bouncing off.

Now I'm turning him into a cliché – a bad little rich boy cliché. A cliché is the way we try to box a mystery. I don't really want to contain him. I love his mystery. Something in me wants to be folded into that mystery. But then I would be the one contained and that, I have a feeling, would be foolish, very foolish indeed. Perhaps just as foolish for him. I could complicate his mystery. There's a reason two spiders never spin a web together and it's more than fighting over the same food. Could be they are safe in their own silken strands, but not nearly as sure-footed in the other's?

Sidonie snuggles her face back into the pillow. She wants him to find her asleep, not worried about when he'll return.

He'll be here soon. Won't he?

*   *   *

He feels her eyes on him. He looks over his shoulder and up at the hotel behind him. There she is at the window, just behind the sheer panels of their second floor bedroom suite. She's wearing that sheer white nightgown he bought her this afternoon. There's

275

a pink satin rose mid yoke. It will have settled down at the spot where her breasts begin. It's time for bed.

By the time he bursts into the room, she's lying down, her head turned away, her body gently rising and falling. She's Sleeping Beauty. He knows the ploy and is happy to play his part. Chestnut hair covers half of the pillow. He reaches over and winds a dark tangle around his finger. He considers pulling it, tugging it hard and hearing her small cry of indignation. They will both know it is pretend indignation. Her hair will flip in his face as she frees herself and rolls his way. Laughter will be teasing the corners of her still-closed eyes. Her mouth will be half- open, waiting, wanting, anticipating.

He'd wager most of her life she has expected each day to be brighter than the last, at least until he snatched her so rudely out of that languorous world. And in one lovely tumble, with no words, just the gratification of a natural urge, he made her feel safe sleeping next to him, only one thin sheet covering them both.

She thinks he will only do her good. She thinks she has broken through his feigned indifference and let loose the passion that is giving her so much pleasure, giving him so much pleasure. She thinks she has made him as vulnerable as she is. At least she hopes so. He knows she always watches where he puts his gun.

He bites her shoulder and waits to see how that plays out.

The yoke of the nightgown offers the only resistance. So much for the pretty pink rose.

*   *   *

"Tell me about what you were like as a little boy." This time she wakes him and with a kiss - now two, now three – all warm, all moist. "Did you parents love you best? Or did you have a prettier little sister or a brother who was better at games?"

276

"My parents were no fun to torment. You have to care to be tormented. Teachers were more fun. Suspecting a student is smarter than you are can be quite unnerving. You can't quite look him in the eye. And there's nothing sweeter than seeing the playground empty because the meanest boy in school has possession of the bat."

"You're making that up. No little boy is that mean." She pulls the sheet over her head as if he's talking foolishness. She knows he's not. She's seen that grim smile before.

He laughs. "They all knew about Robert Hawley."

"Did you hit him with a bat?"

"I broke all my crayons in half and left scraps of the broken wrappers in Robert Hawley's desk. I cried very convincingly in those days. Still all the boys knew it was me. No one told, no one wanted to be the target of my next dark deed."

"What did Robert Hawley do to you?"

"I don't remember. Does it matter?"

And, of course, it doesn't. If the past mattered to her, she wouldn't be here. She is staying under her little tent so he won't see how much it doesn't matter. When he pulls the sheet away from her naked body her hands cover only her smile. She should be frowning for poor Robert Hawley. She's ashamed of nothing else.

"Do you have any pleasant memories of school?" She persists, as if she cared, as if she wasn't aware that he was more lost in her than in memories. His hand is on her shoulder and working down.

"There was this little girl who sat in the desk in front of me." He kisses one nipple. "She thought I liked her best because I never pulled her braids like the other boys." He kisses the other nipple. "Her braids were twisted into a convoluted pattern she proudly called French. Her mother's hands must have labored over those overwrought braids for at least an hour before every school day." He buries his face in her belly. "If I pulled them I would be touching her mother, bonding more than I cared to a woman with awful taste in braid design. Some of her sweat and her cheap perfume would be transformed from her hand to mine." He kisses her belly button.

Sidonie almost wants to roll away. It's not a pretty bedtime story.

"You smell sweet. You always smell sweet. I lied when I said you didn't. It's your hair," he works his way up, "your skin, and your breath on my cheek, my neck, my chest. It smells like a vanilla as it's rolled into whipped cream."

She stays put. She even ventures another question as if she cares about anything but this moment when his eyes are looking into hers. "So you never pulled her braids."

"Nor stuck them in an ink well. That was much too unimaginative. Instead I ignored her. It drove her crazy."

"I feel a little crazy too." Sidonie confesses as she places her lips over his and ends story time once and for all.

*   *   *

He usually plans things quite well. He usually gets the desired outcomes. No. Desire is the wrong word. Expected would be better. He never lets himself really desire something. That implies hope. He has no real hope. He does things carefully. He plans with precision. Things work out. There's no desire about it. He will satisfy a basic need when it demands satisfaction. It comes. He satisfies. He expects the

278

satisfaction to last long enough, if a wall is at his back, his gun is loaded and the windows and doors are secured. But he doesn't think about it, anticipate it, eagerly await it - until now. And now she's on the other side of the room and he wants her back. He didn't feel her leave their bed. These nights he's sleeping deeper than he's slept before.

Sidonie's standing in front of the open window in her torn nightgown. A breeze billows the chiffon. The torn yolk keeps falling off her shoulder. It looks quite charming to him, but apparently not so to her. She pulls the damaged garment over her head and tosses it onto the floor. There is nothing on her skin but the wind.

She couldn't be more vulnerable. Yet her back is straight and her shoulders are squared. She's looking at the first light of day. She's thinking.

Things are not going to work out. She's got to know. And he couldn't want her more.

Chapter 44
Waiting for the Tremble

Doors to a balcony have to be open. Especially, French doors, with windows that tell you what you're missing. Think about how hard it is to resist opening them to a summer breeze or the free fall of moonlight across a Persian rug. Open doors are entrée to a man who can easily climb a wrought iron trellis and land quietly on worn marble tiles.

"Call off your men." Simon whispers, his gun behind Amalendu's right ear as he bends over his desk in silent meditation.

His head jerks backward into the barrel and then recoils. The steel is cold. The gun is loaded. He doesn't want to bump into it again. While his head locks into a straight line with his body, his eyes focus on the night outside his casement window. He lets his book of prayers fall shut. It's as if he is waiting for air to fill his lungs again, for his heart to restart, for his soul to return to his body. Only the index finger of his left hand moves on its own. It has one mission, to smooth the wrinkle in the green desk blotter.

Simon doesn't miss the tremble at the end of the holy man's finger. He always looks for the tremble. He's waiting for the lips to tremble. But no words are coming. "I said call off your men. And don't waste my time pretending you know nothing about it."

Amalendu brings his hands together, taps the fingertips against their counterparts, and then presses the little steeple against his lips. "It's complicated."

Simon cocks his pistol. "Does this simplify things?"

"If you kill me, my men will have the best motivation of all - vengeance."

"The gun is just to get your attention." Simon swivels the chair around so they are now face to face. "And now that I've got it we can talk." The gun is down at his side.

Amalendu leans back in his chair and tries not to sigh. "I do have one rather obvious question. You were hired to shoot me. You missed. Just now you had your second chance. Why am I still alive?"

"Let's just say I'm inscrutable."

"We all like to think that. But men like you respond to the more basic urges."

"Your men are in my way. I want them out."

"That's too simple."

"You're right. The truth is I have seen the Light. I want to protect instead of kill. And I have good reason to believe that you are a man in desperate need of protection. My employer is losing patience with me. No doubt my replacement has already been hired. And he is probably younger and hungrier."

"You intend to recover your losses by extortion. What makes you think I have enough money to hire your gun?"

"I think you have quite a lot of money - do -gooder money, little-old-lady money, young-girls-with-bright-ideas money."

"Wouldn't it have been simpler just sending me a ransom note for Sidonie?"

"Let's just say I've rethought Sidonie's role in our little drama."

"You decided to keep her for yourself?" The Holy Man's holy eyes are boring into his. He actually thinks he can read minds.

Simon confounds him by not looking away and then ups the ante by laughing. "Intriguing idea, but no. Ransoming didn't seem to be such a good idea after your men shot at her and at me with equal enthusiasm. You liked her well enough to stand by her during her hospital stay. What changed your mind? And don't say it's complicated. Was she becoming an embarrassment to you? I could see that coming. I just didn't think you'd see it this soon and act so quickly and dispassionately."

"You think I'd be shamed by being attached to a woman who is not my race, religion or intellectual equal? You think I'd have Sidonie killed to avoid such an embarrassment? "

"Something like that. Christ wouldn't have as many followers today if he did more to Mary Magdalene then forgive her sins. Call off your men and one way or another your Sidonie concerns will disappear."

"You will return her to her former life?"

"Yes."

"And our dear little Sidonie will go quietly?"

"Let's say by that time she will be less passionate about following your lead."

"And you will become my faithful protector." The little steeple is back at Amalendu 's lips.

"Let's just say if I were your protector you wouldn't be having this conversation with an intruder in the middle of your inner sanctum."

"You've fallen under Sidonie's spell and you want her out of the line of fire. That's what this is all about."

"That would be the simple explanation."

"Ah, my friend, admit it. It's not simple at all. Sidonie has complicated both of our lives."

"Let's just say you may not be the only one gunning for me right now. I need cover while I find out what other parties may be, shall we say, interested in me. Protecting you will give me something to do in the meantime. I like to have something to do."

"After you eliminate your threat you will cut, run and leave me defenseless."

"I have a feeling we share the same enemy. What's for my good may also be for yours. What have you got to lose? If you don't agree I go ahead with the original plan and kill you now."

There's the tremble, in Amalendu's right knee, just before his hand whips under his skirt for the dagger strapped to his leg. Simon brings down the handle of his gun hard enough to crack open a skull. Things become instantly very quiet. All he hears is the mantel clock - white porcelain with a gilded face. Very handsomely it ticked off the moment of death and now it ticks on, just as self-absorbed.

He listens for footsteps on the corridor and hears none. There's not even the normal hum of a country house. No doubt this floor has been reserved for its special guest, and the guard at the door is either asleep or out for a smoke.

Simon slips out the French doors to a balcony that should have been more secure.

"Amateurs!" He starts his climb down the trellis.

You can't trust amateurs. They are too impatient, too rash. If only this fellow had hired him or just talked a little longer he could have found out which set of guns were his or if they both were. Did Simon have one set of enemies or two? Neither set seemed worried about killing Sidonie.

That's the trouble. After meeting and killing Amalendu he was less inclined than ever to think the man really wanted Sidonie dead. There was a tone in his voice when he spoke her name. Simon recognized the tone. The man would more likely have sent out his men to recapture her. After all, he did come back with the car to rescue her after that first bungled assassination attempt. Amalendu had said she had complicated both their lives. Simon already knew that. But he would love to know exactly how much. But nothing was complicated about the knife. You don't pull a knife unless you are ready to kill. But then again, it could have been a simple reflex as one man recognized the same longing and desire in another. Simon paused for just the briefest of moments and looked quickly over his shoulder, as if to question the events that had just transpired.

Simon hears doors opening and shouting. With no more time for introspection, he drops to the ground and runs through the wet grass. The water smears but does not penetrate the highly-polished leather of his black boots.

Chapter 45
Truly, Deeply Wicked

Marc and Terry are in the hotel garden as Simon makes his way back to Sidonie through the back entrance to the hotel. He doesn't know them and has no desire to be formally introduced. Too much has changed. Caution has become even more important than usual. Still, news doesn't spread that fast. He slips behind a topiary to consider why these men are here at midnight. Unfortunately, the sculptured bush is not a bear, but a deer with very slim haunches. His hand runs over the leaves in unconscious tribute to the artist. The muscles look that real. He should know better. He has long witnessed life's illusions. Tonight he had deluded himself. He actually thought he could make an unholy deal with a holy man.

"Why do you think she's in this hotel?" Simon already dislikes Marc for the pearl-handled walking stick and the way it is twirling and pointing to a second floor window. "And why are you so sure she is in that room?"

It's not their window, but it's close enough.

"I told you. I got this note. It was under my door." Terry's long legs start to pace. Long fingers smooth lank hair back into place. Simon would give him a haircut, otherwise he's inoffensive enough, and too unsettled to be much of a threat. "We have no other leads. Why shouldn't we follow this one?"

"Seems rather grand accommodations for a kidnapper. And rather public." Marc's walking stick comes to rest on the ground, gently, not to dent the tip.

"There has been no ransom note." Terry stops pacing and confronts his colleague with a raised chin. "Why are you being so argumentative? Are you afraid for your own safety?"

"Of course, I am. And you should be too. The man who has Sidonie is not that stable. First he shoots her. Then he kidnaps her. Then he asks for no ransom. Either he is crazed or he is more than one person and they are working at cross-purposes. Let's face it. We have no idea what is going on, what we are up against, and how our actions might endanger Sidonie."

"That's all true. But we just can't stand by and do nothing." Long legs are again on the move.

"We can think before we act." Marc sits down on a stone bench, his cane across his knees. "Who would send this note? What would be the purpose? If they were really concerned about Sidonie why wouldn't they go directly to the police? Why do they want to get us involved?"

"All I know is that if Sidonie is in that room I have to get her out." Terry raises his arm towards the room he thinks is hers. Simon almost has to muffle a chuckle as Terry's chest expands just as a canine would raise his tail to appear larger and more intimidating. God help me, he thinks, more amateurs.

"We must get her out. Of course, I'm with you on this, but we must be cautious. If she hasn't been killed by now we probably have time to be tactical."

"Killed? You can use that word and tactical together? You can use that word and keep breathing?"

"Swooning is for women, overly impressionable, weak women. Sidonie is not a swooner and neither shall we be."

The two stalwarts look at each other for a long moment, and Simon raises both palms and shakes his head. Finally Terry says, "What do you propose we do then?"

"Watch awhile. Since you are in such a distracted state I'll watch till morning. I'll see if someone comes to the window, see what happens when the lights go on. In the morning you can watch the lobby, follow room service carts. They have to eat." Marc's chin lifts. He's being the rational one.

"I'm not leaving." Terry plants his feet wide in defiance.

"Okay then." Marc stands up and wipes imaginary dirt off the tip of his cane. "You take the night shift. But to be most effective neither of us must act until we are together. There is strength in numbers."

"What about the police?"

"They haven't been much help so far. I have to wonder if they are somehow involved in all this. I have this feeling they are thinking about what they consider larger issues than our Sidonie."

"You may be right about that. Get some sleep. You need it more than I do." He dodges the swing of the cane. "Just kidding! I promise. I'll watch and watch only. If I see anything conclusive I will send for you."

Simon notes how the older, but not that much older, man pats the younger man on the arm. They are less different in age than in confidence and impetuosity and the older man is not above pointing that out. "We are going to find her. We are going to bring her home safe to Clare."

Simon rather doubts the two could overpower a topiary mongoose. But amateurs always have a way of complicating things. And someone is sending them notes. Just exactly how many players are out there? He waits till Marc's foot steps fade on the path. Right now the smartest way to Sidonie is the direct approach. He takes time to light a cigarette, with the more silent scratch of a match. Then he pulls up his collar, pulls down his hat and walks right past Terry to the lobby. "Nice evening, isn't it?"

Terry, too surprised to reply, watches the dark figure disappear into the entrance of the hotel. Now you see him, now you don't. The man moved too fast to see one single feature, only broad shoulders that tilted sideways through the half-opened door. Could it be? No, that would be too easy. Still, he smells ominous in the lingering smoke rings. Damn! It's these Frenchified garden animals! They are unnerving him. And they will be hovering over him all night, watching, waiting, ready to come out of their crouches and attack. What's wrong with rose bushes or the spill of flowers in an English garden? He wishes he were home safe with Sidonie next to him. They'd be painting on twin easels. He sits down on a stone bench, cold, rigid, like the cold hands of a girl in her coffin. A sculptor can bring warmth to stone, a face behind a veil can look soft enough to caress. Not death, death doesn't free illusions or grant wishes. Death simply doesn't care.

*   *   *

The lock slides back into place, but Simon doesn't immediately turn around. He wants to savor the moment. He heard her quick intake of breath when he entered the room. He can smell her perfume. It's that moment when he knows he's won but he's still the first to know. She feels his excitement when they come close and mistakes it for love. Women think love is all. How limiting for them! And how disillusioning for her when she discovers he has just come from killing a man she reveres, how frightening for her when she realizes he has thrown fresh meat at the hounds licking their heels. And now there are those two gallants waiting to rescue her with, but lacking anything resembling know how. Civilians!

"Sidonie." He lets himself linger over her name, knowing she will make too much of it. "Sidonie, Sidonie, Sidonie." Saying it three times doesn't take off the edge. "Why are you still awake? Nighttime is best spent sleeping. Always question the motives of those awake at this hour." She is sitting at a chair by a window. She must have been looking up at the stars and not down to the overcrowded garden, but clearly she hadn't seen the exchange.

"You've been gone a long time, I assume things have happened." With a lilt in her voice she tries to make light of it. She walks to him through the darkness, hoping nearness will bring calm. She's ready for calm. "You are going to tell me you've killed someone." She waits for him to contradict her. He's just standing there, his arms at his side. She reaches for his hand and kisses it. His hand is cold. She needs him to hold her or at least laugh. "Unless it's my mother or father why should I care? I'm like you now. I'm not wicked, not truly deeply wicked, but I feel lost. And alone. Like you." She waits again, this time for him to laugh away the seriousness on his face. She likes seriousness on his face, even anger. It's the blankness that really frightens her. She has yet to dispel it completely. It comes back at off moments, when he's not talking to her, when he's looking at the distance or just his hands. Somehow she feels she'll be safer when it's entirely gone.

"I had no choice -" His voice is calm, but he's saying it too evenly.

"You killed my mother?" She pulls farther away, setting him off balance as he reaches for her and only captures the air.

Now he laughs. "Of course not. Maybe if I knew her better."

"Then let's not talk about it. You did what ever you did to ward off your enemies." Her face is back in his neck. She wants to distract him. She wants to distract herself.

"Your enemies too, it would seem." He pulls away, but keeps hold of her hand as he walks over to the window and pulls the heavy drapes over the panels.

She resists the impulse to pull the drapes back open and open the windows. She'd like to hear crickets. They could be allies in her pretense. They would be saying everything is fine out here. This is a lovely night for a rendezvous. The darkness and the danger make her feel so alive. And always there is his presence. "We could disappear. We could go to Algiers. We could become new people. I could pot and you could, well, we'll think of something. Of course, you would have to stop killing." He lets go of her hand. She shouldn't have said that. He's got that look again. "Tell me, Simon, do women wear veils in Algiers? Is Algiers the Middle East? Or is it Africa? No matter. No one would know me in either place."

"The Middle East might not be a good idea. But getting away is. We must go separately. I'll put you on one train and I'll go on another. We will meet somewhere no one will expect to find us. And then we will hop a boat – "He pulls her into his chest, his arms tighten around her. He looks up and then one eyebrow arches before finally both eyes widen as if accepting something.

"Or a camel. I've always wanted to ride a camel across the desert."

"Sidonie, Sidonie, Sidonie!" He tips her chin up, and smiles. "The truth is we have to leave now with no suitcases. Put on two sets of underwear, a couple pair of stockings, and a layer of dresses."

"And you, you will be allowed to remain slim and stylish?"

"I always travel light."

"Now?" His urgency frightens her. The pretending may be coming to an end, camel or no camel.

"Now would be wise."

"We could wait for the moon to go behind a cloud." One more try for let's pretend.

"That might be wiser still." He's looking at her lips.

She moistens them. "We could spend the time thinking about what dresses I should wear."

"Thinking is good."

"We could lie down while we are thinking." It isn't difficult leading him to the bed.

"Let's see. I'll wear black trousers over brown."

"Black stays cleaner longer."

"And you mustn't leave behind this lovely torn nightgown." He fingers the rose. "Wear it under your petticoat."

"I'll wear it instead of a petticoat."

"Sounds wicked to me."

"I told you. I am a wicked, wicked girl!"

"Truly, deeply wicked!"

A night bird calls a little too loudly from the garden.

"We'll be wicked together, but later." He jumps up and out of the bed. "We must leave. You'll have to dress in the dark."

She reaches out to lure him back. "The dark is for undressing."

He's not listening any more. He's checking his pistol for bullets, metallic clicks and rolls, a strange kind of music. She can hear the music too, but instead of soothing, it makes her wonder.

Who did he kill? It should matter to me. A few days ago it would have. I feel like a leaf torn from a tree. The tearing doesn't matter once the leaf is caught on a breeze. It's so lovely floating through the air. It would be lovely to float forever. Just when the ground is coming closer, a ground filled with other leaves that look safe and intact, another breeze comes along, and heads for the sea. A sea landing is even softer. But the waves are churning and no leaves are left floating on the surface. Different trains? He sees them on different trains? He trusts me that much or he wants to be rid of me.

She fingers the rose and remembers the tear. Reckless disregard. She packs the thought in the back of her mind.

Chapter 46
Till We Meet Again

Sidonie stops at the entrance to the dining car. It's just opening for lunch. Standing on tiptoe she looks through the small round window at the top of the door. She sighs, shrugs her shoulders, and turns to leave, but a couple is coming up behind her. With a slight bow and the flourish of his hand the man invites her to precede them. And so she does. There's air beneath her steps. Maybe it's being on a train. The cars are floating over the track and so are you. Or she hasn't come down to earth yet. She's been expecting him since he left her. It makes no sense, but there it is. She and Simon are on different trains, but the tracks will eventually cross. There will be a rendezvous somewhere down the line. And who knows, it could be sooner. He's so good at surprise.

The steward offers a table immediately to her right. One chair is open. A man and two small children occupy the other three. She shakes her head and points to an open table at the back of the car. He leads the way down the rows of starched white tablecloths and vases, each with a single rose and a sprig of baby's breath.

She picks up the menu and just as quickly puts it down. The door of the dining room car is opening again. She looks up as two young men in college blazers enter. One playfully punches the other in the shoulder. She opens the menu. Her fingers drum the shiny cardboard cover. Her tip-tapping and the sway of the train car conspire to make the white sheet inside slip out of its black satin ribbon. She puts back the sheet and stops the drumming. She takes a moment to look at her fingernails. It's not the best manicure. She had to do it with Simon's little cardboard nail file. He says it's something new. It's called an emery board. Imagine a man having his own manicure tools. Not so hard, really. He is quite fastidious about all the tools of his trade. Appearing to be a perfect gentleman is probably one of his disguises. Always on the run he has learned to travel with the essentials. He even had some buffing powder.

Strange man, strange mysterious man! But she loves mysteries as much as surprises. And he loaned her his emery board. It's a promise of sorts.

Three older women in hats with matching broad brims hesitate in the doorway. Each one points to a different table. Sidonie takes off her jacket and hangs it over the chair next to her. She picks up her bag from under the table and places it on the seat of the same chair. The women choose the table across the aisle.

The waiter approaches with a steaming coffeepot. She turns her cup right side up, half smiles, watches him pour and waits for him to leave. She takes three lumps of sugar, one dollop of cream, tastes, makes a face and then pushes them all away. Instead she toys with the vase. Her fingers caress its cut-crystal pedestal. She leans into the rose. The baby's breath goes off center. She puts it right.

More people come in. She looks up each time, but gives no one a welcoming smile, no one a "You're welcome to join me." And she doesn't move her jacket but from her purse she takes out a book and sets it next to her plate. The book is covered with one of those cloth covers people give their friends at Christmas to preserve their favorite classic novel or to hide the romance they don't want anyone to see. It's a paisley print in shades of burgundy and puce. Her fingers run over the rippling velvet.

The waiter once again approaches. She holds up one finger. He nods but points his white-gloved finger to his watch.

She watches as the waiter reaches over and lights the gas jet of the lamp over her table. It seems they are heading for a tunnel. She and the other passengers look out the window as they approach the darkness. Her nose is close to the glass. Her hand is shading her eyes, until the dining room door opens yet again. The man looks over his shoulder, smiles and takes the hand of the woman emerging from the shadows behind him. He leads her down the aisle, his arm outstretched behind his back, still holding onto hers. He pulls out a window chair for her, leans over and whispers something in her ear.

When the man reaches across the table and puts the rose in his companion's hair, Sidonie stops watching. Instead she places more than adequate currency under her saucer, hurries down the aisle and out the dining car. Her eyes are looking down. She is carrying her jacket and purse, but has left her book.

Of course he will come. Of course they will meet again. But Sidonie has to wonder if he will ever place a rose in her hair where everyone can see, if he will ever be with her in a public place without looking behind her or over his shoulder. She's not going to think that way. She's stopped looking to the future for happiness, stopped expecting a man to fulfill all her needs or tell her who she is. It's strange to feel this way. To an outsider looking in she's this man's captive. Her life or death may depend on him and how he really feels about her. But somehow allying herself with him has set her free. She has left everything behind that once mattered and misses none of it. She has this odd feeling that she could leave him behind and go on with Sidonie still in tact. She'd rather not. But she could.

The train tosses her about its little corridor. She doesn't mind being tossed. Trains make her feel safe even when they jostle. It's a contained little world, full of life's niceties as well as necessities while outside the world of adventure is rushing by, new places to see, a growing sense of wonder, becoming someone new as you go. She is feeling all of these things when she sees the familiar number marking her door. Number eleven. Eleven is like ten with something extra, a good round, superlative number. And there is the newspaper part way under her door, another one of those niceties on a train ride to someone, whether it's to a man of mystery or the mystery of your own ever-changing self.

She plans on reading The Times in a little bit, but first she must indulge in some romantic daydreaming, looking out the window, thinking of him. Missing him is even delicious. You don't need that bonbon. You'd be better off without that bonbon. But for that moment it fills your mouth, the pleasure is all-consuming. It's hard to remember the exact sensation of pain. But pleasure is easily recalled. It takes the merest whiff of chocolate to make you lick your lips in anticipation.

She drops the paper on the floor next to the seat where she is about to indulge in one of those sense memories, but it flops over tempting her with its headlines. She refuses to read them, but she can't help responding to the photo just above the crease. It's Amalendu . He must be back leading his seminars. He's forgotten her already or is trying to. They have shared some bad moments, so he must feel some responsibility. He's probably praying for her. Maybe that's why things are working out so well. But then maybe he would not see it exactly that way. She sighs and picks the paper off the floor. Perhaps he mentions her, expresses worry about her.

*   *   *

Amalendu is dead. But the photo looks so alive. Some photographer snatched it when he wasn't looking, when he was leaving a hotel or a train station. He hadn't had time to put on serene. Perhaps he was wondering if his luggage was lost. Perhaps he was wondering if he'd ever see her again. She can't believe she will never again see his eyes, see the sureness in them, hear the certainty of his words - even though she seldom had any idea what they meant, even when she suspected he was making it all up, so cleverly, so inventively. Such a lovely, improbable, incomprehensive world he promised.

She can see him so clearly, looking out his own window, praying into his hands, walking up a hill to its clouded peak, always a little out of reach. But that he would disappear so soon, that he would become one with those elements he so passionately described, that she had not expected to see, at least not this soon. The print is blurring but she forces her eyes to focus and read the who- what- where- when paragraph again.

Amalendu, noted exponent of Middle Eastern spiritualism, was found dead Wednesday night in a chateau outside Paris. Police are not revealing the details but, a murder investigation is underway. The religious leader was 33 years old and a rising star in his field. This was the second attempt on his life.

She doesn't have to read on about the first attempt. She knows about it all too well. Has Simon finally fulfilled his contract? He came back late that one night. And made love to her. Was it Wednesday? The paper slides out of her hands on to the floor. She watches the countryside slip by. She can feel herself slipping through. One farmhouse appears at the front of the window and disappears at the back. One horse starts to chase another and she will never know what they did when they united. Maybe they nuzzled. Maybe they raced some more. Maybe they galloped away from each other. Maybe, somehow she was party to Amalendu's death. She may even have given his murderer comfort afterwards, as if he needed comforting.

She rests her head on the glass and closes her eyes. She can feel the train's sway lessening, the clack of the tracks softening. They are coming to the next station. She looks up to be sure it's not the one where she is supposed to get off. She's still thinking about getting off at the appointed place. She shouldn't, but she is.

Two men are running along side the platform. One is way ahead of the other. Longer legs, but not long enough to keep up with the train. She ducks into her bathroom, closes the door with only a little crack to watch them reappear. They will catch up when the train stops. They will start looking in the windows. Marc and Terry are here to save her. If they've tracked her this far, they may even know her compartment number. If she gets off the train before they find her she will miss her connection. This train is her way to him. She will not ask him about Amalendu till Simon has held and kissed her, till she has felt the safety of his arms, till he knows that's where she wants to be. Then she will ask him in a way that will let him know she does not believe for a moment that he has killed again.

But that *is* what he does.

She bolts out of her compartment door, not sure which way to run. She should run to the exit and throw herself into the arms of her friends. With them there will be no questions. They will simply want to bring her home.

People jostle past her, heading left for what must be the main exit point. She goes against the flow. It will put all those people between her and her rescuers. It will give her time to think. But all she can really do is feel. She loves to feel. She's alive when she feels. Simon feels just as deeply but with less joy. Her joy erupts. Each time one desire is fulfilled another demands its own explosion. Her world has been leveled explosion by explosion, house by house. But she is not in the flattened bricks and mortar. She is in the cloud of smoke rising to the sky. Simon is in the mist and he can walk away, untouched, if he so chooses. She can too, float away, far above him, but not just yet.

She steadies herself between the close walls. The train is not moving and yet she feels unsteady and unsure. The wobbles, the cranks, and the whistle disappearing behind the moving train have been taking her somewhere she wanted to go. The cars are getting emptier and emptier the farther back she goes. The people remaining are dozing, reading the paper or quietly talking. In the very last car she will get off. This is yet another chance she will have to take, but surely Simon will find her. Staying on would tangle her up with the past she's left so comfortably behind. With luck no one will be in that car or at least not looking up when she makes her silent exit. She tries not to run although she is sure the next car brings escape. As she reaches the connecting door, a hand circles her wrist and pulls her into a stumble. She falls into Simon's face. He is sitting in the first row, the last seat on the aisle.

His grip is tight, but it's his face that brings her down. It's the blank face - the eyes with no light, the lips with no curves, the eyebrows in an indifferent line. He gets up, lifts her by her elbow, and steers her to the back of the car, down the iron steps and into the tall brush on the side of the train away from the station.

"I don't understand -" She has to ask how long he has been on the same train, if he's been watching her all along, if this was a test.

He puts his fingers to his lips and pulls her deeper into the field. She's reminded of the lovers on the train, the way he held her hand behind his back as he led her down the aisle.

She opens her mouth again to speak, and once more he silences her. He arches her arm over her head and sends her into a spin. He makes her face the tracks and her defenselessness. Porters are running up and down the aisles. New passengers are being asked for tickets. At her back, so very close, he whispers, "Be still." His lips stay at her ear. His hands go around her waist. He eases her into him. Her eyes shouldn't close but they do, her ears should be listening but all they hear is his breathing. His hands move down her hips and across her belly and she feels that treacherous weakening, pulsing. The world gets light and he seems to be the only thing holding her up. She can feel herself turn around and bury her face in his chest, but his hands have locked her into place. Seems he likes her just so. Against her neck she can feel his mouth smile. He felt the tremble. She resents the smile. She regrets the tremble. And she knows the kisses behind her ear are meant to make her dizzy. She is a butterfly being pinned to a velvet board, but in the hands of a collector a dead butterfly no longer feels pleasure. Sidonie is very much alive.

She hears the train whistle but it has no meaning, until he gently pulls out the pins. One hand moves to support her elbow. "Mustn't fall!" The other is pushing the small of her back. "Must run!" The iron steps are moving so very fast. Now both hands cup her. She's up and on and rising in the sparks of the steel wheels.

I seem to have made my choice. I'm running with him when I should be running from him. I haven't had enough of his face, his hands, his dark will. When I have, I'll run. I'll have the strength to run, but not just yet. He's laughing as he jumps up and joins me on the platform of the runaway train. He pushes my hair back in place. There are still wet wisps on my neck. "You need a mirror!" he yells over grinding wheels. But we both know I may never look more beautiful and be more damned.

Chapter 47

Starry, Starry Night

Sidonie smiles as the derby and picture hats turn on their reentry from the back of the train. She lowers her eyes and feigns embarrassment. Already flushed, she's halfway there. She's finally found some use for her foray into acting. They are meant to think two lovers have been sharing a stolen embrace, as indeed they have. The acting part may be the love, who's loving, who's using, and which is which?

Simon's arm looks protective enough. No one can see the red mark she can feel forming on her inner arm. He doesn't need to smile. He's perfect for the role. Tall, dark, broad-shouldered, a man with the lips for which a playwright writes declarations of love. Lips don't have to be lush to tantalize. They just have to know what to do - when to suggest a smile about to form or a kiss waiting to be fulfilled. A younger Sidonie dreamed of someone just like him standing next to her on a starry, starry night. Star light, star bright, first star I see tonight. I wish, I wish, I wish I might, have this wish I wish tonight. A very young girl who had yet to be disappointed and learn she can get past it. That's what's hard about being young, those first bad experiences that you don't know you can live through, don't realize you will come out on the other side, not only whole but unafraid to try again. Or better yet, ready to take another risk, for its own sake, for its own set of possibilities.

Sidonie still wishes on an occasional star, but she expects, even looks forward to, the stardust that so often transforms that wish into something else. Sometimes a wish needs a little shaking and is better for being pulled inside out. At least it turns out to be a surprise. At best it's a desire that was, until now, secret even to you.

He adds dialog to their role-play. "You must be tired, my dear. I'll have the porter open the bed."

She can hear a woman sigh and a man snicker. The playwright has written her no lines. Instead she just looks up at Simon and then away as if shy revealing her feelings in front of strangers. Without a word of complicity they are writing another act in their play. She has to wonder just where they are in the arc of this little melodrama.

His compartment number is 17. He was that far away from her and that close. She should have felt him go still and watch from his half-closed door. Now he is pushing her inside. He takes off his coat, brushes off the brambles and then hangs it on the hook on the bathroom door. His hands are very clean. She can see all the little half moons on his nails, so white next to his skin. He doesn't crush her to him. Instead he sits down and looks out the window, eyes hidden by those black brows and lost in the always calculating thoughts. She does her own brushing but keeps on the light cloak she grabbed when she first ran out of her compartment. "May I go back to my compartment and get my things?"

"They won't be there."

"You think Marc and Terry have taken them?"

"So the names are Marc and Terry." He laughs. "Even their names seem amateur. In any event, I think the railroad crew will soon be clearing out your cabin, making it ready for the next occupant. When your friends couldn't find you on the train or in a compartment I'm sure they didn't waste any time getting off and searching the train station."

"But my ticket is still good. Why wouldn't the crew be concerned?"

"People come and go. You are a mystery they don't have the leisure to solve." He doesn't look up. It's as if she has already disappeared, even for him. She's gone and forgotten, in a train compartment assigned to him. Once again he has done his best to wipe her off the face of the earth. People come. People go. She goes into the bathroom to check the mirror. Yes, she is still there, with only a few curls out of place. The only visible wound is the small frown line between her brows.

"Did you kill Amalendu?" It's coming out all wrong. She'd plan to be watching his eyes, not looking in the mirror watching her mouth move. But this is better. This way she's not dependent on his warmth, his strength to make the answer more acceptable. But there's still flush on her cheeks from his hands. She isn't completely on her own facing his truth.

"That *was* my assignment."

She turns from the mirror and steps out of the bathroom. Now it's his expression she wants to see. He's looking straight at her. There's no frown line. "You knew that. You always knew that." He should be looking out the window, afraid to meet her eyes. Or he should be smiling and telling a lovely lie. But he doesn't seem to feel the need to play the hero. He knows she already made her choice and doesn't need to faint across a couch or into a berth. Just as well, this compartment is too small for a couch and the berth is tucked away. Her own words are the only support she really needs. "I see." And God help her, she does.

He gets up and maneuvers her into the small chair. "My job is done. And so is yours. I no longer need you to discredit your lover. I've destroyed him in the intended way." He raises both eyebrows almost as if there might be a question forming. Their eyes hold each other for a long moment, another moment of understanding and perhaps acceptance.

"Then why didn't you let me get off the train and go with my friends?"

"As I recall you were running toward the back of the train. *You tell me* why you didn't let them be your rescuers?"

"Why were you on the train?" If she had a fan this would be the time to hide behind it, not because she is afraid, but because he doesn't have to know everything, better for her if he doesn't find something to read in her face. "We were supposed to meet farther down the line."

"I suppose I could have let you run around the continent all alone. Not sure why I didn't, except perhaps to deprive Amalendu 's people of the fun of wringing your pretty neck once they caught up with you wandering about, confused and broken-hearted."

She registers "broken-hearted" but chooses to ignore it, not sure whose loss he thinks would be breaking her heart. He's probably not thinking Amalendu 's, although well he might. "I don't understand. I never would have hurt him. You were the death threat, never me. Why should they want to hurt me?"

"Those fellows aren't into subtleties. Perhaps the smart ones saw you as a threat to their leader's reputation before they knew I was on the job."

"I was his student, his student and nothing more."

"You do have a lot to learn." He starts to pace. There isn't enough room.

"Then where do we go from here?" There goes a field of daisies. Daisies look their best in the sunshine. Like little suns their faces reflect the warmth shining down on them.

"There is no *we*. The sooner you realize that the better for you."

The train is passing a patch of rhubarb, not pretty unless a cook turns them into pastry. "You don't think I haven't always known that?" She looks up at him with the eyes

304

that so rarely let her down. They failed her with Marc. That was a heart-break, as she remembers, barely remembers. It feels like the curtain has gone down on *Act Two*, but the curtain is sheer. She can see through it, make out the images, hear the emoting, but the emotion is being filtered, tempered and is losing its edge.

"Quiet. I have to think." He doesn't really. He just needs an excuse to turn his back and savor another Sidonie moment. She's always known and was willing to do it all anyway, thrilled to do it all anyway. There's a twisted beauty in that, a crazy loyalty he has never before inspired. No, it's not loyalty. It's lust. She just hasn't figured it out yet. Lust will do. It's strong enough to confuse her. Next she will ask him for a gun. And maybe he'll give it to her. It would be amusing seeing how she uses it. He's remembering target practice in Maggie's barnyard and the look on Sidonie's face when she hit her target. He thinks of that a lot.

Sidonie looks back through the window but there are no more daisies. She won't cry for herself or for Amalendu . Poor Amalendu who saw so much but never saw his own end. The train is moving fast, bringing her and Simon closer and closer to who knows what. Crying will only cloud her eyes and put her mind in overcast. She doesn't know why it even occurred to her to cry. It must be the tear ducts. They haven't caught up. She is finding it easier and easier to be as unemotional, as analytical as Simon. "I could be of help to you." She pauses and waits for him to ask how.

*   *   *

He thinks it's wise to get off the train at the very next stop. If her friends found her compartment with her discarded layer of clothes still in it they would have known they were on the right track. If they are smart they will have already gone to the police for reinforcement. The longer Simon and Sidonie stay on the train the more time for the authorities to figure things out and muster their troops. Simon and Sidonie. S & S. Has she thought of how nicely their names link? She would like the serpentine *s* sounds. She might think the syllables flow together like a stream and a brook meeting and breaking over rocks. There are splashes and swirls. Women think that way. The question is what is she thinking this very minute, what is spinning through her mind and making her heart beat fast? Her breasts are going up and down so very nicely. He shakes his head, and once again has to find the will to focus. Focus is everything, he knows that, but knowing and doing are becoming harder to coordinate. Why is this becoming so difficult?

"We have to get off this train very soon," he tells her as the whistle prompts him to get back on plan. "No, you can't have the gun, not just yet. You're liable to shoot yourself as you fall. And I've put enough holes in you as it is. I hate to repeat ourselves, but I think it's best we depart from the last car. Fewer people to see us. Most people are moving forward, eager to disembark at the coming station. Most people, not us. We're not waiting for the next stop."

"Jump from a moving train?"

"You're young. You can do it. I've seen you twirl alongside your hospital bed." And twist and roll and spread in mine, he knows better than to add. Better not to remind her how completely they have come together. He has no regrets, but this can't change, this, whatever this is. It can't become more, but the distraction of it all will get them killed. And killed is undoubtedly worse than regret.

"Couldn't we at least wait till the train starts to slow for the next station? Otherwise, we will be in the middle of nowhere, no cabs to hail, no cars to steal. We can hardly ask someone for a ride."

"You've done this before. I can tell." He laughs and she's half laughing too. It's a small laugh, little more than a smile. The full laugh is brewing in her racing heart.

I can't quite believe it, but I'm excited again. Despite his callous disregard for my safety or perhaps because of it, I'm feeling less and less the captive and more and more the cohort. He doesn't really need me to further his plans. Yet here we are. Whatever his reasons, he stayed on the train, held me in the bramble bushes and promised me a gun.

The gun will give me back the power to choose, although it may be a terrible choice. It's the difference between being the leaf blown off the tree and the wind shaking the branches.

An absurd distinction, but it pleases her nonetheless.

"The next stop is a half hour away. We'll jump just short of the station, within walking distance for Mademoiselle. Spend the time preparing for your leap. Find some way to tuck up your skirts so they won't trip you up. Yes, use your sash. Be sure your shoes are buttoned to the top so they won't fall off. Button your cloak. Too bad you don't have your ladylike gloves. They would minimize the scrapes, stop the stones from imbedding in the heels of your hands." He waits for her to look up and react. But her eyes are busy assessing the length of her sash. "And tuck my clothes brush in your pocket. We'll need to make ourselves presentable once we hail a cab, probably not till our train leaves, but before the next train rolls in." Then with a pause for effect, "Guess we'll just have to hide in the brambles again."

This time he gets his look. Too bad there's not time to explore it.

Chapter 48

Smoke Rings

There's a pebble in her stocking. It tore a hole at the knee and then worked its way down to her ankle. She has to sit down on the side of the road to roll it back up to the hole, not a very lady-like position to be in when a car makes its approach. She's staring into the wheel well of the front tire. As she struggles to get up, his hand is under her elbow.

"Speak of the Devil!" He's smiling at the driver as he puts himself between him and her. Sidonie knows the language of Simon's body, enough to understand he wants her to stay that way, close and covered.

The hand dangling out the car window is holding a cigarette. It has only recently been lit. "Speak no evil, hear no evil, see no evil." He's got it backwards, but Sidonie has a feeling this isn't a figure who would take well to correction. His face reminds her of hardened clay. There are no laugh lines, not even a furrow between his brows. The smooth unlined contours look as though they were sculpted in a way that had nothing to do with feeling or conscience. His presence seemed to disrupt the air around him. It seemed to take on a texture of waves, and she finally had to look away.

"I hadn't expected to see you here. As I recall we were supposed to meet at another station down the line." Simon takes the cigarette and draws it down a quarter inch.

"And I might ask why you disembarked here instead of there."

"Situations change. One must be flexible."

The man looks beyond Simon. "Good morning, Miss Adair." He tips his fingers to his fedora. "Lovely day for a walk."

She resists the urge to wipe the road off the back of her dress. "Perfectly lovely, but I wouldn't mind a ride." Her ankle is starting to smart and although it seems to be a chilly reunion, the men are not exchanging gunfire. Sidonie steps out from behind Simon. With a small shrug he gives up playing the shield.

"The young lady is as practical as she is pretty." Now the man is doffing his hat. "I can see why you have prolonged the acquaintance."

"The young lady has nothing more to do with our arrangement. My work is done, the contract is fulfilled."

"No reason not to give both of you a ride." The man reaches back over the front seat and opens the back door.

Simon nods her in. Going around to the front seat passenger side, he lets her shut the door for herself. Sidonie can feel it. Something has shifted between them since the car pulled up, it's like the way the sound of the sea changes as a fog horn sounds. The horn is at a distance, the fog hasn't reached the shore, but you know trouble is out there. You're just beginning to feel it, smell it, taste it coming to you on the wind and you've just been warned. You may be on your own.

"Just like old times." The man laughs. "I'm driving the get-away-car, you're riding shotgun."

"Then, Wendell, you will know enough to drive the back roads."

The car makes a full circle, going away from the station, and kicking up enough dirt to make Sidonie roll up the window she had only just opened. The leather seats cushion her bruises but the inside of the car isn't as cool as she had anticipated. She wants to fall asleep, to stop watching and wondering, and she might as well. The two men have exchanged nothing but cigarettes in the last half-mile. She closes her eyes to the sound of a map being unfolded. It's like a lullaby. Hush, little baby don't you cry. Daddy's taking you home by and by. By the back-roads, with the sun warming your arm, with your head resting on the closed window, while the car bump, bump, bumps along. But she keeps listening. This does not seem to be the end of things.

*   *   *

Somewhere, sometime while she flirts with sleep the car pulls to a stop. Both men get out of their doors and walk a few feet ahead of the car. Sidonie can't make out their words and opening the window again would only signal them that she is not asleep. So she stays still and hopes their voices will rise, the wind will change or her ears will wake up and do their job. Men do get careless. Maybe one of them will become impatient with the other or angry and they will talk louder than they mean to. But it seems both men have been controlled for too long. Peeking under her lashes she doesn't see their hands leave their sides in even the smallest of gestures. Their lips stay in straight lines as they speak, as if they are both too stingy to waste any words. She will have to wait till they return to the car and maybe, just maybe, continue their conversation. People do that. They think they can speak in code based on what secrets they have just exchanged.

"She certainly is a sound sleeper." As if to prove it Wendell slams his door after he gets back behind the wheel.

"It's the sleep of the just." Simon knows better. She's not that deep a sleeper. He wants her to keep faking it. Otherwise he'd turn around and poke her in the ribs. It's one of the ways he keeps her off base. She's never to get more sleep than he gets. Now he wants her awake and aware.

*   *   *

Watching through the rearview mirror Simon doesn't miss a flicker of those eyelashes and the overstated stillness that follows. For a moment he allows himself the luxury of thinking about her as an intuitive being, adjusting, adapting, knowing just what to do. A smile comes to the corner of his mouth. He rolls down the window and watches a fragment of cottonwood or a fluff of dandelion skip across the wild flowers. He raises his right hand and lets the thumb and forefinger cup his chin, counterfeiting thought. It's a gesture designed to rattle his old cohort. The Organization never liked nor encouraged original thinking.

"It's too late to change anything. There are too many people ready to be of service. We take the back roads for now, but the final rendezvous point is all arranged."

"Since when have we depended on others?"

"Since I can't count on you. Since you don't get off at the right stations. Since it takes you two tries to make a kill. Since you choose your own travel companions. Since you have called the dogs out on yourself not once but twice. Isn't it amusing that the second set were hired guns just like you? Not as competent, I grant you, and definitely not as smooth. If I had contracted the hit, you would be dead by now. Amateurs! They should stick to their worry beads."

"I say drive us to the next town, find yourself a nice room, and let us take the car. Then you won't have to count on me anymore."

"That's what you want?"

"Yes."

"I *could* hire another car and say I missed you. Let others deal with you. That *would* simplify my life. "

"Simplify. That would be a novel concept for both of us."

"But you know I can't do that."

"I know."

"There are too many questions being asked, excuses we must coordinate. We both have a lot to answer for."

"And a lot of money owed."

"That may need to be renegotiated."

"They want to give me more? How generous!" Simon makes no attempt to hide the trace of sarcasm where his smile goes sideways.

Wendell's laugh is dry like the wine that leaves Simon least satisfied. He prefers a taste that is true one way or another, even if it's too sweet. Anything is better than hedging your bets.

"Turn here." At the fork Simon points to the left.

"I've already driven these roads. I know where I'm going."

"Exactly. I'd rather we were both lost."

Wendell's shrug is an innocent shrug, except for the change in the air when his eyebrows go up. Simon wants Sidonie to recognize the change. If her eyes weren't closed she would see, and certainly understand. The difference. "After all this time, Simon, you don't trust me anymore?"

"After all this time we both know trust is making sure you know all the details."

"Tell me exactly how you dispatched our late friend."

"Which one?"

"How many friends do you think we have? And just how many have you dispatched?"

"Don't tell me you haven't kept a head count. I've felt your eyes on me all along." Simon moves his head as little as possible as he looks to the back seat. Sidonie's a little too still. He must give her a lesson in proper breathing while pretending to be asleep. She is intuitive, but there's still so much craft to learn.

"I heard you used the butt of your gun. That's not your signature kill. Weren't you afraid you wouldn't get credit?"

"Turn here. See the sign? There's a little village up ahead. I think we could all use something cool."

"Is that such a smart idea?"

"It is unless you are in a hurry to be somewhere at an appointed time. Are you in a hurry? I'm still less than clear about how you found us so fast."

"Just lucky, I guess."

"Perhaps. You could have been the one of many loyal associates dispatched to meet me at any one of many stations. You just happened to be at the right one."

"You're right. There were several welcoming committees along the line. But not only your associates are anxious to find you. People communicate."

"They even send notes." Simon watches Wendell's face. "You knew I'd find you when I wanted final payment. I suggest you tell management that you missed us. We in turn will disappear to some nicely distant country and never be heard from again. You wouldn't even have to give me the money you surely have with you. Not having handed the money over to me would insure your credibility with all concerned."

"About the money -"

"Or you could say you killed us." Sidonie's eyes open with the click of Simon's pistol. It's at Wendell's temple. "That is the back up plan, isn't it? Plan A was to leak enough information to my enemies or the authorities so they would do it for you. You never like to dirty your hands, if you can help it."

She's pitched forward against the front seat. The driver stopped quickly enough to send Simon against the windshield. The gun has pitched out of his hand and is on the floor at her feet.

The man with a cigarette is now the man with a gun. And it's pointing at Simon. "Get out of the car. And you too, Sleeping Beauty. I don't mind dirtying my hands. What I do mind is blood on my upholstery."

"Concern noted." Simon's hands are up to emphasize their emptiness, but there is no tremble. "But if you're concerned about a mess, just don't contract me again. The easiest way to neutralize an assassin is to put him out of business."

"And he will never kill again. I think not." Wendell waves his weapon, a flourish, a fanfare, to keep Simon aware of its threat.

"Why would I kill you? Why would I bite the hand that has fed me?"

"You are no longer eating out of my hand. For all your talk of money, you haven't once contacted me for get-away money. I have to ask myself 'Why?' And so, for that matter, does management. They don't trust a man who is still carting around a woman who has no reason to be alive. They think you have lost your dispassion. And if I spare you, I become compassionate. In our profession compassion is a liability."

Sidonie's right foot is cupping Simon's gun. It is closer to her than the men may have realized. Putting her toe in the ballet position she can hook the handle and position it for a quick grab. If she shoots while Wendell is still behind the steering wheel concentrating on Simon, she doesn't even have to aim, just put the gun behind his ear and pull the trigger. All she has to do is move lightning fast.

There's something to that expression, keep someone at arm's length. If she wasn't so close, blood wouldn't be spraying in her face. She wouldn't know how warm it feels. She wouldn't have the metallic taste of iron on her lips. It's like when you cut your finger and put it in your mouth to stop the flow, only in this case there were too many fingers. Suddenly she has to get out of the car. Now. Blood smells as well as tastes and feels. And it lingers. And it is everywhere. But her legs aren't quite ready to move.

Simon's in motion. He's already pulling the body out of the car and dragging it to the side of the road. A limp head smears blood across the top of the seat. He'll be gone long enough to bury it deep in the brush - brush, brambles and thistles so much a part of their story. Once he's back she will lose her chance to open the door and run. She wants to run from the man she has just killed. She wants to run from herself and this strange elation, this odd release, this quickening. Her cheeks are flushed, and the sensation is warm and languorous as it spreads across her chest. If she took a moment she could enhance the feeling. Her lips are asking to be licked. They want to glisten. Her legs are coming alive. Now they're ready to run.

There's no wind. She wishes there were a breeze to toss her hair, cool her body and air her dress. Droplets of sweat are moistening but not quite cooling her neck. How can she be so hot when she has just done something so cold? And where does she think she's running? Ahead of her the road is long, long and dusty. The little houses at the edge of the promised town are just barely visible. She could hide in the brush.

His arm hooks hers and pulls her into a trip. "It's okay, Sidonie. It's okay. You're safe now."

She looks in his eyes to verify his words and finds sudden confusion, then amazement, and finally what almost appears to be regret. He's seeing what she's feeling, what she doesn't want to feel - the way you feel when you run up a hill, reach the top before anyone else and then roll merrily back down, past the ones who will never make it. A nice little girl would feel sorry for them, the ones who will never make it, might even offer a word of encouragement. Simon isn't seeing that nice little girl anymore.

"Sidonie, Sidonie, Sidonie!" He's dropped her arm. He's smiling, but only half.

"We're alive, aren't we?" Her chin is already up.

There's no need for him to tip it up, if he is so inclined, which he doesn't seem to be. And my lashes are nowhere in play. We both know playtime is over. An amateur with worry beads hired the second set of assassins. The first could have been Amalendu's as well. He wanted me out of his life that much. And this man, this freshly dead man, what was his name? Oh, yes, Wendell, a nice ordinary name. Wendell also wanted me out of the way. Both came up disappointed. How nice. And what's this man thinking as he pins my arms to my sides? His eyes are flashing mine like the beam from a lighthouse searches back and forth across the horizon. Somewhere a ship is floundering, somewhere in the fog. But I'm right here in front of him and my feet are now quite firmly planted.

316

"What have we done to you?" He slowly shakes his head. "Come back to the car. It's a much quicker getaway. And it would seem time for you to learn about getaways."

It's natural to lean on him when he puts his arm around me that way. It's even a little cooler in his shade. And he hasn't tried to take the gun out of my hand. It's starting to feel heavy, like those beautiful rings you wear to a party. You don't even feel the opal, the pearl, the garnet until you enter your bedroom and see the little ring tree and you just have to free your fingers one by one.

Chapter 49

A Stone's Throw

Another station, another train, another set of missing passengers. Sidonie's travel plans are confounding Marc, Terry and Clare, not to mention the authorities and two men in dark coats who wait in the shadows. If there are any new notes, Marc and Terry haven't been back to their hotel to receive them.

Terry kicks a stone that had somehow landed on the wood platform. Maybe a train wheel threw it up. It might prefer being back with its fellows. He could have kicked it that far, but instead he toys with it, moves it around with his toe, controls its destiny.

Marc makes the decision for the stone. The point of his cane persuades it over the edge. It bounces twice before disappearing below into the rest of the rocks. Terry gives Marc a look. It's not exactly a glare. He wouldn't want to look all that committed to a little stone. And putting his disgust into words would make him look small. So he welcomes the distraction of Clare's hand on his arm and her smiling request, "Could we go sit in the shade for a while? There are benches inside. We can wait for the next train there."

Terry nods his yes as he pats her small, soft hand. He's come to wonder what Sidonie found so chafing about her mother. Or maybe he's come to enjoy being chafed. Not that he had any complaints about his own mother. She didn't chafe. She didn't hover. She only watched. She seemed to enjoy seeing him dig roads for his toy truck. She praised him when he won solitaire and without cheating. She didn't mind that much when he lost. And when he put color into the black and white illustrations of his favorite book, she bought him his first drawing pad.

"I have a better suggestion." Marc pokes his way into their *tete-a-tete*. "There's a bench down there under the trees. We can hear the train announcements clearly enough." He points to the neglected piece of grass right next to the station. "And while we're there, let's consider an alternate strategy."

Terry would love to argue with Marc. But he's probably right. Sidonie may no longer be riding trains. And then there's this little voice inside him that every once in an unguarded moment says Sidonie may no longer be. Amalendu is no longer with us. Men with eyes that mirror ancient philosophies can end with one sharp blow. Why couldn't fate work in just that way for a young emerging woman?

Terry never bought that metaphysical mumbo jumbo. All those self-important words and convoluted phrases! He likes his truth simple, like the way his paintings are going these days, simple and down to earth. More and more he finds himself wanting to draw ordinary things, like a milk pitcher with chips around its lid or the discarded and crumbled stockings of a woman in a hurry to go to bed. He has even considered a chamber pot. He might still do a chamber pot.

Of course, his favorite subject is always Sidonie. He longed to see her first thing in the morning, with tangled hair, sleep in her eyes, and maybe even a little drop of moisture at the corner of her mouth. She would look beautiful even against a wet stain on her down pillow. Sidonie would be like a night-blooming flower with life spilling out of her like early morning dew on the grass or the petals of a rose. Like that bottom step of the porch, the last to dry after a spring rain. Sidonie is water to him, playful water that wends its way across the rocks. Lucky rocks.

Terry's pleased with the portrait coming to life in his head. He aches to move it to his fingertips and onto his paintbrush. He can hardly wait to get back to his easel and mess her hair and crease her nightgown. Most men wouldn't go into raptures over the wet stain on their beloved's pillow, but he sees beauty in Sidonie's reality. He longs to paint her in the glare of this afternoon's sun. He loves thinking of Sidonie unkempt. Unkempt she is even more his. And he truly believes that when you think of someone you love, they are thinking of you.

Sometimes this may be so, just not today. Today Sidonie has other concerns and more than her hair is messed. If Terry were to paint her now, the moisture at her mouth could be a splattered red. He would have to smudge charcoal under her eyes. But there would be no need to stroke lush black curves into her lashes. If he could see her eyes now he would be reminded of the shades of a window rolled up so tight that all that is visible is the glass below. At this moment Sidonie's eyes are wide open to reality unveiled. There is no lace, no dotted swiss, not even dust from the road to add charm or mystery to the pane she is looking through.

Marc puts his hand under Clare's arm as she sets one slippered foot down on the platform stairs. He dares because he saw her touch Terry and it would be ungracious for her to pull away from him. He loves the tiny recoil. Indifference, now that would really hurt.

On the ship for a few moments here and there he felt the connection again, the closeness she would deny. It was like reuniting with someone at a wedding or a funeral, feeling their hand on your shoulder or their arm around your back, feeling that spot grow warm again, familiar warmth that you didn't even know you missed. And now it feels so right.

The steps are too long to take one foot at a time. But Clare is determined to do it. If she sets down both feet, Marc would be helping an aging woman he fears might fall. If she sets down one foot Marc is simply being gallant to an ageless woman who still inspires gallantry. To keep that illusion she must first believe it herself. But what she's feeling these days is tired, tired and pointless. She is a woman of passion with no place to put it. She's a mother of a child who has even more passion and dispenses it without thought or calculation. Sidonie is a milkweed with endless supply of little silk pinwheels blowing into and against the wind. Everyone wants to catch one.

But perhaps the supply has come to an end. Maybe Sidonie is spending these last few days being plucked and stamped upon. Clare doesn't feel that. Maybe she is deluding herself. But she was there when Sidonie came into the world. Clare felt it, heard it and screamed her own herald. She must know when her daughter has ceased to exist. Something inside a mother dies. The stem of a flower becomes useless when the bloom is pulled off. It browns and fades. But why would she think that, she who never before felt her worth depended on being anything other than Clare? She would welcome Sidonie's forgiveness, at least her understanding. Her daughter also fell for Marc's charm. No, it was impossible. That kind of understanding isn't helped by sharing.

The men in the shadows are starting to move, not all at once, but every time someone else in the crowd crosses the platform. If Clare, Marc or Terry had been paying attention, they would have noticed the small contingent of dark hats heading for the back of the station. If Marc or Terry had got up and followed, he would see the men huddle for just a moment before heading for their cars. But when one of the cars backfires, Clare's hand goes to her heart, she gives a tiny scream and Terry heads for the road.

He comes running back. "I'm going to follow them. Marc, you wait here with Clare."

Marc starts to get up and then sits back down. "It's only a backfire."

"That's why I am the only one going. I'll be back as soon as I prove you are right." Terry doesn't even wave goodbye to Clare. First things first.

The cars all turn left. They are moving too fast and are a bit too far ahead to concern themselves with Terry. He follows at a safe distance as they approach the fork in the road and exchange hand signals. There are enough cars to cover each road choice. His dilemma is which one to follow. Straight ahead is a town. He decides to go with that.

There is a lovely inn at the beginning of that town. Simon had driven past it. He had stopped at a small house midtown with a "Room and Board" sign that he threw behind the fence as he steered Sidonie to the shade of the porch.

With his best Parisian French he explained that the lady was with child and had overtaxed herself. Could they have accommodations for a few days while she recovered? Of course, of course, the landlord, replied, and she'll need a some ice for that head and a glass of lemonade to refresh. Would she like to sit on the porch? There was always a cool breeze. No, no, she needed to lie down. The landlord understood. He had a lovely room at the back, overlooking the garden. No, a room at the front would be better, so she could watch the cars go by. She loves to watch the cars go by. Sorry, that was all there was.

Sidonie let Simon do the talking, let him hold her tenderly around the waist, let him make these decisions. She was busy concealing herself under his coat. The landlord could well wonder why on such a hot day she should be covered with a man's coat, but he would wonder even more if he saw the condition of her clothing, her chest, and her neck, her hair. She wished she'd thought to cover her hair. Her hand wants to reach up and cover but she can't risk letting the coat fall open.

Simon's hand was gentle. Difficult to know if it was an act, or sincere. But no matter for now, it was forestalling the horror riding just below the surface of her skin. The farther down the road they had traveled, the more dust the tires kicked up behind them, the more emphatically the tremble wanted out. Her bullet had stopped all thought processes in a man she had just met. He was here, thinking and plotting. And then he was blank, nothing, no more.

Killing was not something she was equipped to do for a living. She wouldn't even know how much to ask. Did the scale depend on the number of people or the importance of the individual? Were women less expensive than men?

Her eyes wandered to somewhere in the distance. The questions became irrelevant. She was trying to answer the wrong questions. She knew what she had to know, and the knowledge brought focus to her eyes. If she had to kill she could. If she needed to save herself she would.

*   *   *

Once in the room Simon steers her to the wash basin and hands her his stained handkerchief. He had used it earlier on her face and mouth and the car upholstery. And now it wouldn't do to bloody the towels or splash the forget-me-not wallpaper. The handkerchief can eventually be carried away and tossed into the bushes on the side of the road. There would be no evidence they had been here.

It's reached the point where Simon doesn't have to explain to me why he does things. Maybe our minds meet somewhere above our heads and talk things over. No, it's more like we're facing the same obstacles and work out similar strategies. Pretty simple strategies when you think about it. Your enemy has a gun and intends to use it. Another gun falls conveniently at your feet. You pick it up and try to shoot first. Maybe it's because we are both pretty simple ourselves, Simon and I. When a choice is to be made, we come first. And thanks to Simon I had plenty of practice defending myself behind Maggie's barn.

When I was a little girl, I was good at jump rope, but only when I was the one doing the twirling. But when two other girls were holding the handles, it was tricky knowing just when to jump in. It was easy to trip and lose your turn if you hadn't practiced jumping that way. Miss, Miss, little Miss, Miss, when she misses she misses like this!

There was no way I could have missed hitting Wendell. I was so close I could see evidence of a fresh hair cut on his shirt collar. His gun was at Simon's temple. I had no choice but to pull the trigger. The thought of Simon's head exploding all over me was one bit of madness I was not going to endure. I once saved a squirrel from the wheels of a motor car. He had been drenched in the gutter by a sudden rainstorm. He didn't know which way to run. I picked him up by his middle so he couldn't reach back and bite me with his sharp teeth. I ran with him to the safety of the side of the road. I didn't stop to think how foolish that was. I just couldn't stand seeing his furry little body crushed under those heavy wheels.

I was just as compelled to stop Wendell from shooting Simon. I still ended up with blood and brains on my face, in my hair and across my breast. But not Simon's, not his.

He's peeling off her dress and folding her under the covers. There is still color in her face. The color of a woman not at odds with events. She relaxes into the down of the pillow and he says "Sleep!" He tucks her in like the little girl she no longer is and tells her what she already knows. "You need to be strong. There is more ahead."

As Simon opens window to listen to the road noise, Sidonie pulls the covers over her head to shut it out. Both are asking themselves the same question. What do I do next? Sidonie has faced the fact that she will never slide back into her old life. She'll be lucky to have any life at all. Simon is thinking only as far ahead as the next automobile that may pass by a little too slowly. Where is the best place to take a shot?

"The gun, Simon. I need my gun." Sidonie lifts away the blankets.

"Of course, you do." He takes it from dressing table, where she had dropped it, right next to the silver brush with the initials of some other woman. He checks for bullets. "You'll be fine. There's only one missing. For now I'll put it under your pillow."

Sidonie's asleep when that first slow car passes by. The dotted swiss bed curtains are in a flutter around her head, cooling her mind as effectively as her cheeks. Simon's wide awake behind the lilac bushes that shield the house from the road. He's willing the car to keep on going. He's ready but not eager. He prefers targeting to being targeted. Still the straw gardening hat is an excellent camouflage. And the reed basket next to him is filled with enough purple and white sprigs to cover several weapons. The landlord actually suggested fresh flowers might help revive the little mother. An unwitting accomplice! Sometimes things break your way. Sometimes you make your own breaks. Sometimes all you do is wait and see. He looks down the road for a long moment, considers the distance, but his eyes come back to the window of the room at the front of the house. A confident smile forms. That first slow car is already down the road, but the second is coming to a stop, and a dark hat is turned Simon's way. His smile broadens.

Chapter 50

At the Fork

Sidonie wakens to the sound of gunfire. She does not confuse it with a backfire. She's been too close to a trigger to make that mistake. She's out of her bed, down the stairs, on the porch and trying to decide where to aim before she realizes she's in her petticoat. With an improbable straw hat on his head, Simon is holding his own. He's dug in between three lilac bushes, purple, white and deep maroon. Shots coming from the road have shaken the branches and sprayed his shoulders with the tiny buds.

Two automobiles seemed to have locked bumpers after the driver of the first car was hit between the eyes. The driver of the second car looks equally surprised. Their passengers have jumped out and are shooting from behind their stalled vehicles, over hoods and roofs, through open windows. They don't see Sidonie as she moves from apple tree to apple tree. Behind a hefty oak she raises her gun, shoots, and sends them all into a collective duck.

Simon waves her back without taking his eyes off the heads about to reappear. She remembers to support her gun with both hands and waits with him. One bobbing head is fast enough to take the bark off her tree. Simon's return shot is accurate as well as swift. The survivors cut their losses. One dead driver is pushed onto the dusty road, the other onto the floorboards, and they drive off.

Another car pulls up just as the others speed away. It *is* easier when the target is in the driver's seat and has both hands on the steering wheel. Her arms are steady. Her finger is ready. She has the driver in her sights. Her arms go to her sides. It's Terry.

Terry's face has turned to wax, melting wax. Her name is on his lips. She can't hear him speak. The gunshot din seems to have left her temporarily deaf. But she can see the letters drag his jaw into a horrified slack. "Sid!"

"Simon!" She screams as he turns toward the new car. His gun is aimed, he is focused, and it will be over in a moment. "Don't shoot. Don't shoot. I know him." She has no time to explain he's a friend, and this is apparently some sort of misguided rescue mission. Just as well, that would hardly endear Terry to Simon.

Simon's already walking towards Terry's car, certain he no longer has any more to fear from the other cars, equally sure he is confronting an unarmed man. Otherwise, white knuckles would not be frozen on the steering wheel and Sidonie would not be out from behind the oak and shouting so protectively. Simon waves her a come here.

Of course she knows what he's thinking - fresh getaway car, right there in the middle of the road, ready to go before more reinforcements arrive, just have to get rid of the occupant. She wants to run and throw herself in front of Terry, but something tells her this would not be a good move. Instead she lowers the gun to her side and negotiates the tree roots. Turning her face to Simon, she wipes away what he might consider a telltale tear. It's just smoke, but men often see women sentimentally. They hold each other's eyes and she wonders what exactly it is he does see. Is it even important? Or does he see anything beyond the lashes and the hair and the curve where cloth tends to cling? Men miss so much because they don't understand transitions. They miss the growing up part. In their eyes you go from ingénue to old woman. One interests them, the other appalls. Nothing in between exists. That's how they make women disappear. That's why a mother, a mother-in-law, a wife raises her voice and becomes a shrew. Hear me, see me. I really am here.

At the car she and Simon stand together watching Terry. "It would appear introductions are in order. I've seen this character in a topiary garden, but we've never been introduced."

Terry's looking at her, really looking at her, and the horror has not left his face. In fact it went up a notch with the intimacies just exchanged. And she must look a fright. The bodice of her petticoat betrays the under layer of blood spatters, muted, but just as real. A smile and battering of lashes is not going to make it all better, even if she could manage them, even if she wanted to. She swings the gun behind her back but not soon enough for Terry who is pulling himself deeper into the car.

"It's me, Terry. Look at me. It's Sidonie." She steps closer to the car. "You recognize me, don't you, Terry?"

"Of course, he does. He just doesn't like what he sees." Simon reaches in and pulls out the keys before Terry recovers enough to stop him. "And he has a pretty good idea what is going to happen next. I'm out of bullets, Sweetheart. It's up to you to shoot him."

Sidonie puts the gun farther behind her back. "He's someone I know, no danger to you at all."

" Of course he's not. But I know clowns like this. And he's just seen you wage war on my side. He's never going to forget this picture. He's going to tell the world how revolted he is with this Sidonie. He's going to tell the police and, even worse, your Mums. No way you're ever going back to your old life if this disillusioned fellow has anything to say about it."

Sidonie's already figured out there is no going back, whatever happens today on this road. There is sunlight on her hair. There are lilacs on his shoulder. But Terry's limp hand hangs out a window. And more cars could be coming around the bend. The best she can do under the circumstances is convince Simon to let Terry go.

Simon's leaning back on the car hood as if he has no care in the world. *Nonchalance!* The French have a word for everything. He's not even looking down the road to see if anyone in that little French village has called for reinforcements. But if there are police they are remaining inside, in the shade and out of the line of fire. He looks cool, always cool and always efficient. Except for the lilacs, he is not even ruffled.

I can picture him leaning against a white marble pillar with a glistening glass of champagne. His eyes will start with my hair, the artful fall across my forehead, the curls released just above my ears. He will approve the release. He may want to release more. His eyes will move to my lips and linger just a heartbeat before challenging and holding my eyes. If he reaches for my hand, I will follow him to the dance floor. Like now, I will not be able to look away.

It's not my first cotillion. I know the other men standing at other pillars waiting to sign my dance book. I have but a single slot left. One prospective partner I know very well indeed. He's smiling. He's already thought of a bit of delicious gossip he wants to whisper in my ear. And there will be a compliment or two or three. He would lead me in a lovely, long flowing waltz.

The lips of the man with his hand at my back are in a straight line. His dark eyes are what offer the promise. He knows me, really knows me and wants me anyway. Our bodies have already met in a tango.

Simon watches her think, sees her feel, and knows exactly how horrific this decision is for her. She can't kill the man who followed her this far, a man who has been searching for her, hoping to save her. Given time, Simon just might have finessed even that. Passion can burn out the core. But she hasn't been with him long enough.

Yet with the right provocation she could kill Simon and free him from what is beginning to feel like a pointless existence. Better her than some others he could think of. And that would go to her core. In his arms she had felt more than she ever felt before. In a strange way, in a way she would deny, this betrayal would make her belong to him forever. He had taught her to kill. He had taught her so well she could even kill him.

Her arm's moving. The gun's coming out from behind her back. The other arm's reaching over to help with the grip. She's learned that lesson well enough. Her hold is still too low for her friend, too far to the left for her lover. It would be easy to pluck it out of her hands and end her dilemma. Instead he slaps her hard, hard enough to send her to the ground with her weapon skittering across the lawn. "She who hesitates - " he laughs as he pulls Terry out of the car. Simon's counting on Sidonie remembering he can kill as easily with a butt as a barrel. The time it takes her to retrieve the gun will be just enough for Simon to set the stage.

The scenario goes as quickly as Simon's thought process. But for Sidonie it's as if she is under water. Every movement requires a kick, a stroke frustrated by currents and waves. Still she gets off a shot when Simon turns his full attention to Terry and presents his own back to her. She watches his shirt bloody. He always wears a crisp white shirt. He wore a crisp white shirt the first time she saw him. He still has enough life in him to land a back-handed blow that sends Terry to the ground and rolling towards her. His roll into her hip speeds up her world and Simon's escape. The car's suddenly coming to life, belching out smoke, and kicking up dirt and stones. She's up, running, and once again shooting. Her bullets ping against the steel body moving so quickly away. As he drives around the stalled cars, she runs to the center of the road. She hits his trunk dead center. "Damn!" She was aiming for the back window.

Terry watches the sun shining though her petticoat. She's standing tall. Her legs are wide apart. He didn't know her legs were that long. He never saw her back so straight. He can't see her eyes, but her head's held high, her neck ever so long and white, with those damp chestnut strands of hair curling down to her back. She's been shooting in the right direction, but he's not sure why. He has this feeling she could just as quickly turn and start shooting at him. He doesn't know this woman, but this woman certainly knows her gun. There is no hesitation between shots, no recoil, no hysterical choking cries. She hasn't for one moment taken her eyes off the car. She's giving Terry no thought whatsoever.

The car's getting smaller and smaller. She should've aimed at the tires. But what she really wanted to do was slap him across the face as hard as he'd slapped her, toss him to the ground, and leave him without even looking back. The car is stopping at another fork. Just before he turns left he pauses and does look back. He gives her that much. She has to wonder how far he will be able to get with that wound. She has to wonder how far she will go with hers. She can feel it beginning to ache, a reminder of the time she was within his sights. She fires one last time although she knows it's futile even before the gun signals empty. It's all about anger. It needs to be spent. During all they'd been through together he never once hit her. He never knocked her to the ground. He never left her in the dust. And just now it came so easy.

She can't even see his dust anymore. How is he going to make it with an empty gun? He said he had no bullets left. Of course, he could have been lying. Of course, he was lying. It was a test and she failed it. And there may have been more than one reason he didn't waste the last of his ammunition on Terry. There are no doubt more enemies in pursuit. On command she had aimed at whoever was at his heels, but not at Terry. He's still on the ground.

"Are you all right, Terry? Did he hurt you?"

It's the right thing to ask your rescuer. And you have a reason to look at him instead of the dirt road behind you. For a moment you can let go of all those questions that may never be answered.

She wipes both sides of the gun barrel on her petticoat. She is feeling like a soldier who has survived his first combat. He knows he will need this weapon again and again if he is going to stay alive. He must keep it clean and secure. She holds hers to her breast as she walks from the road to the grass where Terry sits, hugging his knees. His mouth is open, but words have yet to form on his lips. Just as well. There are enough questions in his eyes. There was a time she could have kissed his eyes shut and it would have been enough for him. Now she will simply have to lie.

Chapter 51

A Backwater Town

Lying is easy when you tell people what they want to believe. They even help with the story. They see sorrow as shock. They see regret as confusion. They see anger as terror. They see determination as growing strength. Determination does bring strength and, sometimes, even guile. And if you cry they pat your hand, pull the drapes and leave the room. That's when you channel that determination. You think. You plan. You plot.

I know now what I'm going to do once they've finished their tender ministrations. Well, all right, not exactly. But what I do know is I will get away. Where to may not even be important. Maybe somewhere, like a mountain village. It will have to be as isolated as an island. Best if it's almost forgotten like a backwater town or an abandoned monastery. I need to be alone - alone and unfettered. I need to be free of a mother who still hopes to make her daughter happy, free from lovers who disappoint or have yet to satisfy or who discard you when they're quite through. And someone, good God, someone I don't even know may even want me dead.

Then again maybe it's not really my hiding place I'm after. Maybe it's the one that's keeping him safe. Where would Simon go to heal his wounds, bury his reputation and be free of everyone, including me? And why should he be free while I'm still not free? And why do I care, why is he even important? I'm marked now. This scar from his bullet will always be there. I can't change that. But these other scars I don't have to live with. Those I can soothe.

It seems insane. Impossible, really. But Sidonie is already considering it. And, she's telling herself, it's not nearly as insane or impossible as fitting back into her old life. She's finding it hard enough playing the docile invalid to someone she truly adores, like Terry, or someone she might still want to bed, like Marc. And Mums is not so bad as remembered. How could she be? She's a woman smart enough to know when she's lost the war, pragmatic enough to settle for a truce, and crafty enough to aim at an alliance.

By now Simon could be any place in the world. The only place they ever talked about was Algiers, but that was her idea. There's really only one place to begin the search and that's not a place at all. It's a person. Maggie Marie was down to one cow the last time Sidonie saw her. She had to keep the milk and cheese to feed herself. Her delightfully primitive pottery was not easily accessible to a moneyed clientele. Simon had to be supporting her. She was his outpost, his hideaway and his confidante, at least she was until Sidonie came into his life and the farmhouse was invaded for what was probably the first time. Mags must know where he is or at least have a pretty good idea where he might be headed.

Her farm sits on the outskirts of Allouez, population seventy-five. Sidonie remembers seeing the sign on their way back to Paris. They passed four shops, a smattering of cottages, a small church and a granite horse trough. The farm fields looked well tilled, but during a good part of the year those seventy-five people would have plenty of time to watch. They would be as interested in the comings and goings of strangers as the eccentricities of their neighbors. They would know about a reclusive widow who threw pots and no longer sold eggs. They might talk to a young woman who happened to pique their curiosity. They could give directions or even drive her there on a donkey cart.

Sidonie gets up out of bed and walks to her mirror. She smiles at what she sees. These days she usually finds satisfaction in her reflection. She's still young. But today the mirror adds the effects of a very full year. And the results are not unpleasant, and maybe not even that important. The dark circles are light enough to be romantic. The jaw line looks more defined. And she didn't know she had such nice cheekbones. She can see in her own face the beginnings of her mother. That is the measure after all. We look at our mothers and see our destiny, ultimately ourselves at another age. But that's still at a comfortable distance for both of them and Clare's as beautiful as ever.

How nice for her! Sidonie brushes the tangles out of her hair, pinches her cheeks and licks her lips.

She does need to look rested and revived. A smile helps. It lifts the face. She tries a few variations. Just how wide should she open her mouth, how much teeth should she show? The more they look at her upturned mouth the less they will look into her eyes. A sparkle is harder to fake. If only she had a dimple.

She will have to convince whoever is watching that she's well enough for the first walk in the garden and a day or two later that ride to the museum. The bench of her vanity falls backwards as she demonstrates her spring. Perhaps that was a little too much for this stage of her recovery. They have diagnosed her with a nervous breakdown. Of course they have. What else would explain her behavior, this pact with an unrepentant gunman. She rights the bench and demurely sits back down. Well, at least now she's got the smile right.

Everyone will be pleased when she expresses interest in the Greek and Roman artifacts. She won't have to fake that sparkle. Isn't it nice, they will say, that she is out of herself! Isn't it natural she is drawn to the artwork! Pursuing this new interest in pottery could be restorative. Father will be happy to pay the tuition at that fine school outside of Athens. Mother would love to come along if it weren't in the middle of The Season. How much money does she think she will need to stay in a reputable boarding house this time through? That much! Better than repeating the mistakes of Montreal, Mums would think but keep to herself. And, of course, their daughter will need new clothes and art supplies. Well worth it, they will both agree, to once again see that sparkle in her eye and that spring in her step! And those questions over a punch bowl, they could be troubling. Best keep her out of the public eye. Poor child she needs no more trouble, no more trouble whatsoever. Sidonie feels a twirl coming on. It's been a long time.

Sidonie doesn't arrive in a donkey cart. It's actually the automobile of the village priest. Pere La Forte had insisted. It was no inconvenience whatsoever. He was making a sick call a little past the turn off. And he confides, as they clear the city limits, he's worried about Madame Margaret, living out there all on her own. Did Mademoiselle Adair know anything about the state of her health or how she sustained herself? He himself wouldn't dream of intruding on her privacy. Some people prefer living that way. But she was always in his prayers. Will Mademoiselle Adair be staying long? Mass is at 9 A.M, every Sunday. Confessions are on Saturday between 3 and 5 P.M. Did he know Madame Margaret's husband? There was one? He must have died before she moved here. That was about two years ago, maybe three. Isn't Adair a French name? It certainly sounds French. Funny, after all this time he doesn't know Madame Margaret's last name. Does she? Lafarge, you say. Yes, that does sound familiar. Oddly familiar.

Maggie Marie is not happy to see Sidonie coming up her overgrown path. She tosses a handful of grain on the head of a now squawking rooster. She's considering running inside the cottage and bolting the door shut. But she can't move as fast as Sidonie and she knows it, especially in her favorite clogs. And that stupid dog is blocking the doorway in his afternoon recline.

"You've obviously forgotten the dung." Mags kicks up a small clot with the round wooden toe and aims it at the dusty but pretty boots of her unwelcome visitor.

Sidonie skips out of the way. "I haven't forgotten a thing, Mags. That's why I'm here." She holds the woman's eyes until Mags finally looks down.

"Then you are a fool. Why walk back into the lion's den?"

"Then the lion is here?"

"Not likely, probably never will be again." Mags kicks another clot. "When Simon sheds one identity he sheds it completely."

"You've only known him through one identity? That seems hard to believe. You seemed so close."

"Well, let's just say I've known him through the European ones."

"And what is he now? Mediteranean? Maybe Greek?"

"You're seeing him wrong. " Mags searches Sidonie's face to see if she's struck blood. She gets a knowing smile.

"And you don't think he would like to see this again." Sidonie straightens her jacket. "Well, you could be right. But in any event I'm not so concerned with what he wants." Sidonie's smile close-mouthed and dismissive.

"You've got a score to settle? There's a line forming and the ones ahead of you know a little better how to make that happen."

"I'll do him no harm."

"That's not what I heard."

"Do you know if he's all right?"

Maggie Marie wipes the sweat from her brow, releases the skirt tucked up at the waist, and starts for the door and the relative cool inside. It takes two kicks to move, "Stupid dog!" She leaves the door open just enough for Sidonie to pass through. "He's not dead if that's what you're wondering. I would have heard."

"So what exactly have you heard?"

"Nothing that I'd share with you. You're bad luck."

Sidonie sinks into that old familiar winged back chair. "I am. That's probably what he thought when I shot him."

"I read about that in the papers. You were quite a little heroine there for a while. Hard to picture you out-shooting him."

"He turned his back on me. He must have counted on me being a poor shot."

"The Simon I know wouldn't leave that to chance."

"Well, one way or the other I shot him. I saw the blood."

"He must have been fit enough to make it out of the country. I'm not his only hiding place in France but we do talk among ourselves. No one in France has seen him since the shoot out."

"What country would he consider safe?"

Mags feels the conversation moving too quickly. "Have you rehearsed these questions? Whatever you're after, I have no reason to help you figure that out."

"I suppose you don't. But I do have money, and he may need that now that he has burned so many bridges."

"Give it to me and I'll get it to him." Mag's hand drops the ever-stirring soup ladle and reaches out.

"Of course you would. But as you say he's not in France."

Mags chuckles as she fills a bowl and sets it on her end of the table. She places a spoon next to it. The bowl is one of her creations. Little fish swim around the inside rim. Sidonie would give them more attention if she weren't so hungry. But there is only one place setting and her hostess is now sitting in front of it, closing her eyes in ecstasy over the first spoonful.

Sidonie walks to the cupboard and gets her own bowl and spoon. "He'd thank you for telling me. You know he would."

"But he left you behind."

"He had to. It was the only thing to do."

"Then why did you shoot him."

"I was play-acting too. My friend was watching, judging me."

"You're clever, my dear, but not that quick."

"So I was angry. At that moment it felt like a betrayal." Sidonie snaps back as she fills the bowl to the rim.

Maggie has a good chuckle. "And so now, safe, secure and recovered from your ordeal, you are considering giving him a chance to explain or at least apologize before you get even. He couldn't have left me behind because he was just plain done with me. He just couldn't! Wishful thinking! You don't believe that and neither do I. Just who are you trying to fool, me or you? Or is this some kind of a game bored society ladies play before they settle down by the hearth? "

Sidonie pushes away the bowl. "Mags, you're making this too complicated. And I'm not really interested in explanations. I have money, and I suspect he could use some. He might have some qualms about taking it from me, but he would not thank you for limiting his resources."

Maggie Marie gets up and looks out the window. Sidonie's surprised at how the glass pane is the only thing in the room that shines clear. But then Mags is an artist and the window does see out at the trees and the occasional wild flower. "I suppose you are going to go on looking and asking and making people think he might still be alive and worth hunting down. Someone has obviously put a price on his head. More than one someone as I understand."

"Yes, I'm going to go on looking and asking."

It's a flippant remark but Mags sees more in the focused eyes, the angle of the chin, and even the shine on the nose. If there was powder or paint, it's all worn off. And Sidonie's taking less care of her clothes. Gloves are unbuttoned. Hat has no chiffon to flirt or hide beneath.

"All right, but I'm going with you, just to be sure you don't mess up. And, after all, I do know the language."

"And what language might that be?"

Chapter 52
Dénouement

A carriage has stopped at the end of the winding road leading up to his cliff house. He can't see or hear the horses' hooves from the balustrade of his garden but he hears the whistle and has no trouble interpreting its variations. Mario, the yardman/watch dog, is always on the alert. Everyone in this household has a double duty, a second identity. Carmela, the housekeeper/body guard, routinely checks his bed for the spiders or snakes. Tina, the cook/taster never serves him food she hasn't prepared from scratch.

At Villa Adolpho he is the absent landlord who only appears once or twice a year to inspect his property. Sometimes he reserves rooms for a season. Sometimes he doesn't. He is a capricious landlord but then the residents of the little village below are not worried about eccentricities. They tend their grapevines, they age their cheese, they fish their shoreline and they smuggle American cigarettes. They know when to look the other way.

He gets out of his green wicker chair and walks to the stairs. It will take these visitors at least ten minutes to walk up the worn path. It narrows as it winds. Small rocks, dislodged by the foot traffic, fall away and plunge down the precipice and into the sea. White waves break against the rocks below. Visitors don't have to be told to take their time and be careful. There will be ample opportunity for the next whistle. And there it is – two short - one long and sustained. Two people, both women and there are no guests booked for this month.

He could go down and meet them. Instead he slips into the shadows of his pergola and waits. He doesn't realize the hand holding on to the arch is shaky till crimson bougainvillea flutter down on his shoulders and head. Damn wound. He's used to healing faster.

Sidonie's not even winded as she beats Maggie Marie to the top of his hillside, but her hair has come free during the climb and a spring breeze is still playing with it. Slowly she pirouettes. The heavy branches of the flowering trees form a pink valance above the circling balustrade. She's happily surrounded. So are the cupids in the fountain. She goes down on one knee to smell and touch the yellow tulips ringing the fountain pedestal. Her finger bounces back. The tulips are that firm and strong.

He watches and recognizes the feeling. As a boy he thought they were marzipans. He wondered if the white ones were vanilla flavored and the red cinnamon. She stops, stands and straightens. She knows he's there. He can see a delicious flush beginning to warm the back of her neck. He can feel his own heat.

"Sidonie." He sighs as he steps out and moves in behind her. She doesn't evade his hand as it goes to her shoulder, as his fingers play with the clasp of her seed pearls. "Didn't you read the script? You must know we were not meant to meet again."

She steps forward and turns to face him. "These days I write my own scripts."

"And what role have you written for me? And why am I not sure I'm going to like it?"

Her hand reaches up and tears off a tree branch. It's a jagged tear that sends pink petals scattering across both of them. This time he steps back. "Simon, since Act One you've been slipping in and out of more characters than I care to remember. I'm rewriting Act Three, *the denouement.* That's where the fate of all the characters is forever fixed."

"And you are prepared to promise me a forever? Sidonie, Sidonie, Sidonie." He pulls the branch out of her hand and throws it down the hill. He takes her hand in his. She's probably expecting he'll try to kiss each finger. Instead he moves her hand to his wound. He wants her to feel the bandage under his starched white shirt. "How long is your forever? Only the other day you made a fair attempt at shortening mine."

Her fingers lightly follow the bandage around to the back. She had shot him clear through. He can see in her eyes that this is the moment when it's becoming real for her. He would be disappointed if he saw sorrow or even guilt. The tiny twitch at the corners of her mouth tells him she has a new understanding of power, and it's more than just the power of life over death. But what is it? What is the new depth in her eyes? He feels like there's something he's not keeping up with.

To a man a gun is a tool. It gets him what he wants. It could get him someone else's money or someone else's life. It could protect his own life, his own money, maybe even his woman. Most women see guns as a last resort. If they had to kill to protect someone they love some women could actually do it, maybe even to protect themselves. But most women holding a gun for the first time find it too big and unwieldy. The power frightens them before they even pull the trigger. Then the boom makes it impossible for them to think. And actually hitting the mark can send them into hysteria. If a woman's still a threat that's when you end her, between shots, mid-regret.

He has yet to see Sidonie in regret, even now as she touches his wound ever so gently, ever so reverently. She may be feeling awe for what she has done, what she might have done, how easily she could have annihilated, how much she was exhilarated. He knows she loves that gun. Why else would she wipe it clean on her petticoat and cradle it to her breast. It has leveled the ground between male and female, between him and her. But that's a man's way of thinking, of getting even. Of maintaining control.

Sidonie's probably feeling something he has never felt before. How he'd love to crawl inside her brain when she pulls the trigger. How he would like to know how she felt when she had him in her sights. Or how she feels now when all he wants to do is drag her into the grass or the bushes or the brambles. She's come all this way. She's hunted him down. Does she even know why? He loves that, hunting him down, not knowing why.

"Just a few more inches up and over," she marvels. Her hand is again on the front of his shirt. It lingers on his heart, his heart is very much aware. But she's really interested in how many stitches.

"Are you going to tell me why you are here?" It's then he sees Maggie Marie lumbering up the stairs. "And how you talked Mags into betraying my confidence?"

Mags makes her way to the wicker chair. "She told me she had money. I figured you could use it. You never minded before where you got your advances. And she was drawing attention to you, asking questions, visiting your old haunts. I could have killed her but I know you like to make those determinations."

"Thank you, Mags. You're always most considerate. You remember Tina, don't you? She's inside. She'll have something to refresh you after your long trip. There's new brew cooling in the cellars. And there's a more comfortable chair, with a footstool. "

Sidonie's pretending to seek her own refreshment in the shade of the pergola. She's acting as if she never saw an arbor before, that there is something wondrous about the bougainvilleas growing overhead, in and out of a lattice. But they both know it's the shade, the darkness that compels. They are better together in the darkness. When he dreams of her, of her in his arms, she is black and white. The straps crossing her back are black velvet. Her bare shoulders are white satin. And in the shadow of each ear shines a tiny pearl. Somewhere along their winding way all the color has left her cheeks and her hair, her brows and her eyes have turned black. Even now, under the afternoon sun he sees her as the moon in the night sky and somehow he dares to believe he can reach out and gather her in. She would deny it but there is still this need, this need to touch one more time to see if it was real or only imagined, if it was real but finally over.

Perhaps it's his eyes that bring her back into the light. Careful.

She's opening her purse. "There's more in my suitcase. I left it behind a tree half way up the hill."

Now she looks winded, maybe from the climb. The lace running deep down the neckline of her white dress has a beguiling flutter. His hands come together and then move to his sides and then back together.

"In case you decide to cut and run?" He teases with his eyes as well as his words.

"Coming here wasn't the best idea. Even I know that." She snaps the purse shut and stills herself with feet planted firm in the warm earth.

"You want answers. You want to be clear."

"Nothing about you is clear. I wanted to know how badly I'd hurt you, if I was a murderess yet again." She stops her hand short of his chest.

He wants to help it go the rest of the way. He liked it there. "After the first kill most of us stop counting."

"This second one was different. We both know that." She moves back into the shade of the pergola where he can't see her eyes.

Of course, he follows. "It was your way out, your way to prove you were held against your will."

"I see. It was a favor to me, your parting gift."

"That would be a nice light to put it in."

"Beware Greeks bearing gifts."

"Not a bad axiom." A smile might have made light of their exchange, but he doesn't offer one. He is not ready to make light of this.

"You're not going to give me a straight answer, are you?" An earlier Sidonie would have stamped her foot. This one shakes her head and laughs.

"Straight answers are boring and rarely true, well, maybe a little true." He wants to run his finger down her throat and follow her skin down to the ruffles. Cool would be nice. Hot even better. Instead he waits for her rejoinder, not sure he has another one in him. There's a smile on her face. She's thought of something.

She moves in close, stands up on her toes, and lifts her face to his. He's never felt lips more delicately placed or more highly charged. Her hand's on the back of his head. His lips can't help but respond to the gentle push. And there are her lashes, so dark and so lush against her white skin. He wants them to stay closed. He closes his own. Now her hips are against his. He can't move away. He can't think why he should. The air seems to become liquid around them

Chapter 53

Purely Decorative

In the Garden of Eden an apple was the forbidden fruit. But to Sidonie a pomegranate looks more tempting. She's already picked one and is balancing it on her palm. It's more exotic than any apple she's ever seen or tasted. The red is brasher. So are the occasional yellow and green streaks. They are the vivid colors people wear under a bright sun. Like the pomegranate they will not be outshone.

She rolls the pomegranate between both palms and remembers the one Tina cut up to garnish breakfast. You don't eat the seeds of an apple, at least not on purpose. They may slip down during an impetuous bite. But you don't bite into a pomegranate. You've already armed yourself with a knife if you're going to eat its fruit. Your sin may be driven by passion, but it's definitely premediated. She remembers that premeditated kiss in the pergola.

I meant to kiss Simon. I came all this way to kiss Simon. It was meant to be the kind of kiss that sweeps a man away, makes his world disappear, makes you disappear with him. All that's left is feeling, a delirium of feelings, sometimes in a rush, sometimes languid and slow, and then a slip into dreamless sleep, as if no dream wants to suffer in comparison. This time I had been the wave pulling them under, pushing them forward, relentlessly, folding them into high tide.

His hip was against mine when I woke up this morning. Not the first time, by any means, but still brand new.

Simon is taking the pomegranate out of her hand and dropping it into the basket at her feet. "You better hurry up or Tina will take you off the kitchen crew." He doesn't kiss her. He doesn't wipe the sweat from her brow. He doesn't even pick another pomegranate to help her out. All he has to do is stand close or even at distance, for that matter, not able to look away and she knows.

"I'm not cut out for this type of work. I'm more the creative kind. I could dance for you or do a scene from Shakespeare. And were I to paint a tree you would feel the bark, smell the blossoms and taste the fruit."

"You're that good are you?"

"Of course not! But someday, someday I know I will be."

He plucks three more pomegranates from the surrounding branches. "I can juggle."

"So I see," she claps. "What I'd really like to learn is how to make pottery. Maggie Marie has already given me a lesson or two. Does she have a kiln here? She and I could keep ourselves happily employed. But what would you do? I don't imagine victims come to you. 'Here I am! Shoot me if you must. Just make fast work of it, if you would."

"You've only been here a day and you're already bored?" He pitches a fruit to her, then another. Here comes the third. She scoops them all into the folds of her skirt.

"I suspect you bore more easily than I do. You have already decided what you are going to do next and where you are going to do it. You might as well tell me. I don't see you leaving me behind, just yet."

"I don't really know, just yet." He doesn't smile. Not smiling makes it more than one of those sweet lies a man tells a woman when she's getting too close.

She's equally open. " You can't stay here much longer. You've lived here before. You've left traces. And with Amalendu 's followers it's a holy mission."

"I'll get you a globe. Point your finger and that's where I'll go."

"Please. You were doing so well." Past the pretty pout, the new Sidonie simply turns away.

"Honestly? I haven't decided. In my business you don't survive by making impetuous decisions. Besides, your guess could be as good as mine."

"You know you've put yourself out of that business."

Now he laughs. "You had something to do with that."

"What do you put in Maggie's pots?"

He doesn't look surprised at her change of subject. He knows it's not really a change. "Sometimes tea. Sometimes flowers. Some are purely decorative." And it's another chance to spar.

"You can't tell me you never thought of smuggling something in Maggie's pots."

"She considers pottery to be an art form. She'd prefer to sell one of her creations to someone who could appreciate it, cherish it, and use it carefully – certainly not crack it open for contraband."

"She's a practical woman. I can see her making pots for just such a purpose and saving her best effort for a more serious work."

"Or she could make a pot so carefully, so authentically it would look as if it had been made by hands a thousand years dead."

"Ingenious! I can learn to do that, perhaps even better than the Madame herself."

"Maybe. But first things first!" He cups his ear with his hand. "Listen. Three quick whistles and one blast. These fellows are not staying for dinner."

"So I was followed?"

He shakes his head in a never-mind and tosses her a gun. Once again her apron comes in handy. Always the weapons are at the ready. Hers just came from his very slim pants leg.

"Did I ever tell you I've been educated in the classical arts?" She snaps off the safety.

"That settles it. It's Rome or the Greek Islands."

"Greece!" She ducks behind a pillar and cocks her pistol.

He slides next to her, but only long enough to kiss her trigger finger. "For luck!" Then he's down the stairs and slipping from tree to tree.

"Who is after you today? Amalendu 's men? Your partners in crime?" She calls after him, as loudly as she dares.

"Does it matter?" He smiles at her over his shoulder. "They keep coming. We keep shooting."

She smiles to herself. *We! He said it first.*

Chapter 54
Gone Cold

Sidonie loves walking on the beach mid-morning, when the sand is warm but not burning. Of course she can't resist running in to meet the cool splash of the cascading waves. She doesn't mind the damp line creeping up the bottom of her skirt. It will dry soon enough. And wrinkles make pretty patterns. You can touch as well as see them like your grandmother's crochet work or the ripples on a stick of licorice.

It's been a productive morning. She's put in the kiln her first pot of the day, a purely decorative vase, a just-for-fun vase, meant to sit on a lady's dressing table and hold the last surviving lily from her birthday bouquet. Sidonie has a birthday of her own, coming up soon.

Birthdays! She hasn't thought of birthdays since she and Simon found this island, more than half a year ago now. Time doesn't seem to exist here, just sunrises, sunsets and the tides. Their island is remote enough for hiding out, although there's no real reason to hide any more, from friend or foe. Simon, always the better shot, has taken care of the last of the foes. That's what he tells her. That's what she chooses to believe. And she has calmed family and friends with notes that reassured long enough for trails to have gone cold.

She thinks of them all often. But the day-to-day of her life involves little second-guessing. Much has happened, but nothing rises to the level of regret. There is an uneasy feeling though that it doesn't stay that way.

Marc and Terry are certain their little Sid will climb over the convent wall and give up the contemplative life long before Christmas next. There will be no bright lights or presents in her tiny little cell. They know how much Sid loves having something beautiful to look forward to. Mums must be relieved that her daughter has taken a break from scandalizing polite society. No one has to know Sidonie is following a nomadic Indian tribe through the American Southwest learning how to make turquoise necklaces. How long can she live in a tepee? Each believes they are the only one to whom she has confided her true destination. And Father, who never expects explanations, will be certain she'll be back when the money runs out. None of them would dream of looking for her on an island in the Aegean Sea.

It's a life of good clay, good company and a perpetual ocean breeze. Simon was content to walk beside her in the sun and sand while new wounds healed. He hadn't escaped from his cliff house without some return fire. Today he has taken a boat onto the mainland to place their fourth round of "ancient" pottery for sale to the tourist trade. She and Maggie are not yet good enough to fool the experts. Simon has promised to "borrow" some books from the museum to give them a better idea of the patterns, the color and cracks of ancient clay. Sidonie suspects he is just jollying them along, keeping them busy till he comes up with a more practical game plan. She and Mags need more than examples. They need tools, secret potions and an expert willing to share the mysteries of counterfeit. Still, it might be possible. She'd like to give it a try.

A wave has just deposited another sea creature at her feet. She's been on the island long enough to pick them up without hesitation, even if she has no idea exactly what they are, especially this particularly exotic one. Its claws are wriggling, reaching eagerly out. It's trying its best to pinch her browning arms. Not to worry, little fighter. You aren't destined for Maggie's stew. Sidonie just wants to watch you move. It would be fun tracing that movement around the rim of a bowl. Or maybe she could shape a statue of it. She's already done a fish. They are easy. Clean round lines, with bumps for eyes, gills and scales. And she would really like to make a new glaze, one with luster, colors that gleam in and out of each other, and make claws so luminous they look like they are moving. She must ask Simon to steal a book on glazes. There might be one.

Stealing doesn't seem so bad when you have no other choice. Still she has every intention of returning the books, hopefully without too many stains and water spots. There are other artists and students of archeology besides her. It seems the more she feels comfortable in who she is, the easier it is to imagine someone else just as worthy of consideration. Maybe it's Maggie influence. Maybe it's Sister Rose. Somehow in her mind those two mentors have merged into Sister Maggie Rose, a wondrous teacher convinced that her protégé has enough beauty inside her to share with the world.

Here she is thinking of the world at the moment she is most cut off from it. But she is not caught off from life. A new life is growing inside her. She hasn't told Simon. It's too new, too chancy, and impossible to believe. She has never thought of herself as a mother. It isn't a name she would have applied to herself. It doesn't as yet fit. It's like a dress made for someone else. It falls too full over her body. The sleeves are over her wrists. She can only see the tops of her fingers. And her shoes have disappeared under a hem that drags across the floor. She has to wonder if Simon will find her among the cascading folds, especially since more and more these days his focus is on the horizon.

When he holds her in his arms his eyes are not always closed. Sometimes his hand stops running down her back and his chin lifts away from her hair and it feels as if he is moving away, even though she can still feel his breath and hear his heart. What will happen if there is a baby between them? What will happen when a child looks into her eyes in search of love, protection and guidance? She has just learned how to make her own way and it is without rules, without a plan, with only trust in her own strength. And now when she is beginning to feel her strongest, some little barnacle wants to latch on. She's not ready to think about barnacles. She puts down the sea creature and watches it burrow into the sand.

Right now Simon fills her senses, dominates her thoughts, and sparks her imagination. But her soul is still hers. She knows and so does he. He takes pleasure in bending her to his will and then watching her unfurl. She's his boomerang, thrust into the sky in one direction and returning in another. Returning, always returning. She shouldn't always return. Sometimes she should fall back to earth a little beyond his reach.

There is one place where she's beyond anyone's reach, where her heart lifts her up and away. It happens each morning when she walks into her little pottery shack. It's then she sees what her hands have wrought the day before. As her hands begin the task anew she can think of nothing else, she needs nothing else, except the chance to make it better, to carve a vine, to paint a petal. It must be like a poet finding exactly the right word, the perfect simile. Yes, that is exactly what he wants to say. Yes, this is just how she wants it to look, to feel, to shine.

Sidonie follows what's left of her footprints back to their little camp. The tides have erased those early steps and are eroding the most recent. She hadn't realized how she had stepped farther away from the encroaching sea as she walked, avoiding the invading waves, except when she could no longer resist running in, just as she will not be able to stop herself when Simon's ship comes into their bay. She will run through the sand, no matter how it may burn, so very eager to kiss his lips, salty like the sea.

*   *   *

It's the moment I like best – when I'm close enough to the shore to see her feet – when I can imagine the sand kissing her toes. That's when I know. She still takes care with her hair. She can't help but choose colors that compliment her skin and, every once in awhile, she checks the newspapers for the latest fashions. But when she first hiked up her skirts, tossed off her shoes, pulled off her silk stockings and ran through the waves to welcome my skiff I knew I was loving the artifice out of her. If there ever was any artifice. There are things I'm unlearning. Things I had to unlearn so I could know what was real. Still, I hope she'll never stop trying to win me over with those eyes, one minute filled with sun sparks, a second later as black as the bottom of the sea. And her lashes, you never know when they will descend and veil her thoughts, her feelings, her desires. Good. I would miss the game we play. She suspects I'm completely hers, but she's not completely sure. Just as well?

Christ, what choices are we making here? What incongruous choices? Absurd really. She's choosing to love a man who has banked his life on feeling nothing. I'm choosing to run with a woman who can only slow me down. And can we ever stop running? At this moment we are on an island where no one knows or really cares who we are. Most of the inhabitants are here to forget other places or other people or be forgotten. How long will we be safe here? How long will we be content here? How long can she love a man who has to learn how to comfort with steadfast love, who for now can only love her with a boiling passion. Water evaporates when it boils too long. Nothing lasts. That's been my experience. But then Sidonie's like no woman I have ever known.

One thing I know for sure. I'm about to get my pants' legs wet.